THOU SHALT NOT

KILL

BY THE SAME AUTHOR

FICTION

CRADLE OF SECRETS (As Emma Lorant)
LULLABY OF FEAR (As Emma Lorant)
BABY ROULETTE (As Emma Lorant)
SPELLBINDER
THE GIRL FROM THE LAND OF SMILES

THE DOHLEN INHERITANCE trilogy:
THE DOHLEN INHERITANCE
HOBGOBLIN GOLD
LADYBIRD FLY

NON-FICTION

A VOICE AT TWILIGHT (*ODD FELLOWS Social Concern Book Award 1989)*
THE GROCKLES' GUIDE (with Jeremy Warburg)
SNACK YOURSELF SLIM (with Richard J Warburg)

KNITTING BOOKS

THE BATSFORD BOOK OF HAND AND MACHINE KNITTING
THE BATSFORD BOOK OF HAND AND MACHINE KNITTED LACES
YARNS FOR TEXTILE CRAFTS
EARNING AND SAVING WITH A KNITTING MACHINE
CHOOSING AND BUYING A KNITTING MACHINE
YARNS FOR THE KNITTER
THE GOOD YARN GUIDE

THE HERITAGE OF KNITTING SERIES
TESSA LORANT'S COLLECTION OF KNITTED LACE EDGINGS
KNITTED QUILTS AND FLOUNCES
KNITTED LACE COLLARS
KNITTED SHAWLS AND WRAPS
THE SECRETS OF SUCCESSFUL IRISH CROCHET LACE
KNITTED LACE DOILIES

THOU SHALT NOT KILL

Tessa Lorant Warburg

The Thorn Press

DEDICATION

To my sister Diana, a true friend and a
wonderful companion.

ACKNOWLEDGMENTS

I would like to thank Gillian Geering, once again, for reading, commenting on and editing *Thou Shalt Not Kill*. Gillian has, as so often before, been a wonderful help. Her expertise, historical acumen and knowledge of several European languages have been invaluable. I would also like to thank Evelyn Harris for being the first to read through and comment on this novel. Her astute remarks were very pertinent.

The Blue Room Writing Group of 2011-2012 – Deanna Dewey, Evelyn Harris, Mike Hayward, Jenni Jacombs, Donna McGie, Mike Plumbley and Ann Roberts - have all listened patiently to large sections of this novel. Their comments have, as always, been really helpful, and I would like to express my appreciation.

Any remaining errors are, of course, my sole responsibility.

PROLOGUE

Guernsey, May 1941

The scream wakes him – he knows it's coming from outside, from the seashore below his bedroom window. He couldn't have heard it through the waves crashing against the rocks, but he knows it's real. He's frightened. Should he call Maman?

The house is perched on top of sheer cliffs surrounding the bay. He grabs his father's spyglass, climbs on to his windowsill and stares down at the beach. A full-moon night, cloud cover hiding the shoreline, then lifting to reflect light from wet sand.

He jabs the glass to his right eye, adjusts the focus, concentrates on the sand lapped by the ebbing tide. Dark shapes are moving by the water's edge. People, not animals. Who are they? Not Guernseymen – it's long past the new curfew decreed only yesterday. Maybe this is the commando raid they've all been praying for? He goes on staring until he makes out four men in uniform. Sweat trickles into his eyes. Four German officers, their highly polished boots and brass insignia reflecting moonbeams.

Clouds scurry across the moon and hide the figures. He waits, pulse pounding in his ears, until there's enough light to see again. Now the black figures are bunched round a kayak beached on the shore. He sees them drag two people out of it, cries out as he realises who they are: Maman and Papa. Two of the Germans are holding his father. He hears a shot. The other two... A merciful cloud covers the beach.

He flings the spyglass on the bed, opens his window, throws out the rope he keeps fastened to his window frame, grabs his

1

catapult and the ice-pick Maria smuggled out of the kitchen for him. He abseils down the wall merging into cliff face.

The screaming is unmistakable now, daggering into his mind, crowding out thought. He jumps the last ten feet, fingers the ice-pick and begins to run. He's going to charge in attack.

A single rifle shot ricochets between the rocks surrounding the little bay and roots him to the spot. Rays of moonlight reflect from something which glitters at him – a knife? A man – Henri – hurtles out of the shadows and wields something long and gleaming. A bayonet. The one his grandfather brought back from the Great War.

He dives forward, but the four Germans have already scattered, running towards the cliff path. He falls to his knees by the water, weeps. The Germans have gone, but not their legacy.

CHAPTER ONE

I saw him again in that dreary little room used for the monthly coffee mornings. Politely stooped, but still head and shoulders above the sprinkling of ageing family men and spotty altar boys. I watched an uneasy smile flittering on and off his face as he balanced a cup on its unmatched saucer - I could see the water sloshing. The good soul disbursing the kettle's contents had overtopped the instant coffee granules in her eagerness to be the one to serve him.

I went on staring, mouth open, mesmerised. His presence among that motley assembly of uninspired parishioners was totally unexpected, almost ridiculous. What was he doing here? My heart missed a beat as my eyes flicked over his features, my pulse began to race as I took in his every move. He turned towards Father Oncey.

'I'll do my best,' I heard that glorious bass purr across the room. 'I can always play the...'

The end of the sentence was drowned by an infant deciding to bawl for milk. In spite of that reminder of the consequences of carnal bliss I felt my body tingle in a way it hasn't done for years, producing physical reactions I was confident were dead, not merely dormant.

My ears strained to catch the phrases tossed between the two men across the room. Matthew looked dynamic beside the passive figure of the priest bowing his favours. Why was this man singing at St Olaf's when the Brompton Oratory, or any of the other well-known Catholic churches, would consider it a privilege if he were to join their choir? I'd wondered all through mass about that bass. I'd even twisted my head back, looked up at the singers blurred in the loft, to see whether I could find the source of that magnificent sound. But he was hidden in the shadows, his sublime tones overpowering the quavery sounds of desperately squeaking sopranos who swayed, music in hand, in front of nebulous male singers. In spite of that it was clear that the bass had held himself in check.

My staring must have got through to him. The dark head moved up, alert eyes looked in my direction, swept across the cramped space, paused. My knees felt weak. I saw his face light up. He was going to come over. A shiver through my whole body made it hard for me to keep my nonchalant look. I felt blood surge to my face, felt the rush of heat, longed for an Arctic blast to cool me down. I leaned back against the wall, the blood draining from my brain.

It's been years since a man has affected me. The last one to do so, after all, was Jonathan. There'd been no one else from the day I met him. I'd never felt any temptation to be unfaithful throughout our thirty-five years of marriage. And when he lay dying, slowly and tortuously throughout a whole long year, I'd felt completely empty, almost dead myself. All I'd been able to manage afterwards was to try to energise the little spark of life left to me. I thought all passion had died with Jon.

Now here I was, reacting like a young girl, feeling like one. I was past all that, I hissed at myself. My once good looks faded, my once trim figure a twelve where it had been an eight, my once sharp eyes no longer quick and, at last, in need of reading glasses even for the hymns. My mind, imprisoned in this unspectacular shell, did not see me as I could see myself reflected in others' eyes. A woman on her own, poor thing. Must remember to invite her to lunch. Not dinner – no man to partner her.

Tall, dark and handsome, we girls used to whisper to each other in the refectory, giggling and drinking our Nescafé between lectures. I slipped back into that past, felt my body young again, tossed my hair in a remembered gesture of invitation. My eyes softened, my lips parted. I imagined myself the way I'd felt in my youth, fingered my amber necklace, pushed back my shoulders to lift my breasts – and smiled. My physical allure was, after all, drawing this man to me.

I saw him put down the plate of biscuits he was handing round and side-step over to me, skilfully winding between clusters of children well below his vision and skirting a group of huddled matrons, their broad beams rounded petals guarding a central bloom of gossip.

'Hello there.' He was standing in front of me, eyes bright, even mischievous. The purring voice was even headier once he was next to me. 'Ruth Samuels, isn't it?'

I'd been kidding myself, of course. Matthew Frelé had come over to greet me because he and I had already met. Otherwise there wouldn't have been the faintest chance of his noticing me. The magic of sexual attraction, that magnet which used to charm so effortlessly every time I met a man I fancied, no longer worked. My face, though not particularly wrinkled, is lined. No one mistakes it for that of a young woman. Jon, as it happened, wasn't prejudiced against ageing. The harsh real world, after his death, was quite a shock to me.

Occasionally, I'd comforted myself, people thought I was in my thirties. Like the immigration officer, the last time I'd flown to Boston. In fact he'd terrified me, grinning up at me: 'There's a mistake here, surely.'

'Mistake?' I'd been puzzled and then immediately unnerved. How could there be? I'd used that passport for the past six years, I was British now, quite safe...

'The date of birth,' the passport officer had laughed. 'Twenty years out, I'd say.' A wide-toothed grin had loosened into a smile. Meant as a compliment, I realised later. But at the time he'd hurled me back to when I was a child of six confronted by jackboots.

Perhaps he hadn't noticed. Place of birth: Vienna. My passport didn't state my race. How could he have known? His Anglo-Saxon heritage was clear, and he couldn't have been born till after the war. That a legacy of Jewish genes could be lethal would sound like something out of ancient history to him, the Holocaust an episode in a film, a history book, perhaps a TV programme.

I dragged myself back to the coffee morning. Meandering in

5

the past again. Not something that I did when young. I used to be incisive, analytical. My first ambition was to be a detective. Now I was much more inclined to browse tangentially along my tumbling thoughts and feelings rather than to analyse. The time had come to stop kidding myself. The banal truth was that Matthew Frelé and I first met a couple of weeks ago, when I'd agreed to have dinner with his brother Mark. That's why Matthew walked over, that's why he was being friendly.

CHAPTER TWO

I'd been reluctant about Mark, in spite of his good looks. I'd met him on that trip to the States, when the immigration officer had tried to compliment me. Mark was in the seat next to me. I'd decided to fly Club for my annual visit to my grandsons in Boston. What was the point of all that money my writing now brought in if I didn't spend it? Memento Jon, I reminded myself, often – I won't be able to take it with me.

Mark Frelé had been on his way to a conference of psychiatrists studying macrobiotic teachings. The Kushi Institute was centred near Boston. The convening medicos were gathering to investigate the effects of mind over body. Their aim, Mark had explained to me at length, was to try to establish whether the macrobiotic approach to cancer could actually affect the patient's body. Through the mind, of course; he'd dismissed the diet as irrelevant.

Jonathan had followed the macrobiotic way, had stuck to it religiously. I'd found the seminal book – *The Cancer Prevention Diet* – when he was in hospital, having that useless operation. The dietary recommendations had been our main source of hope. Jon had been so brave, so determined, so keen to live. I'd thrown myself into the concept, learned the basics, even rung up the Kushi Institute in London to enlist their help. The diet toned down the pain, made Jonathan calmer, helped. But Jon insisted on going through with radiotherapy. There was no proof that the treatment led to the collapse of his spine, making him paraplegic before he needed to be, but I knew it did.

I never could stomach the medical profession. People doling out sanctimonious life prescriptions put me off. As Mark was a member of that fraternity I'd been prejudiced against him from the start. But I'd agreed with him that we had a lot in common. He was a widower and, though widowed when still in his twenties, he'd never remarried. One of those awful things – his wife died in childbirth, way back in the '50s. There'd been some question of saving the baby at the expense of the mother, a common attitude at the time towards patients in a Catholic hospital. And Mark had never forgiven himself for allowing that to happen.

He'd been fascinated by my account of the way Jon and I used the macrobiotic diet. The hours of flight sped by. He'd asked for my son's address in Boston, and kept in touch. He'd even come to visit me at Bobby's house, dandling my latest grandson on his knee in a reasonably expert fashion.

I was startled to see Bobby frown when Mark wrote Barnsham House, Barnsham, Somerset into his diary. My younger son, normally friendly, paced round his living room, crashing into inoffensive furniture.

'That's quite near Downside, isn't it?' Mark asked, monogrammed fountain pen poised.

'Half an hour's drive, I suppose.'

'My old school.' Mark's hand was clear and legible, almost script. My estimation of his personality was that it was just as transparent. That was unusual for a doctor, particularly a psychiatrist. A book I'd read on graphology maintained that illegibility provides a convenient disguise of character and should be interpreted accordingly.

That was in January. Mark was in touch again after my return in mid-February.

'What about dinner?'

I wasn't particularly keen. Mark was a nice enough man, intelligent, well-off, good-looking. What on earth else did I want? Well... I'd absolutely no idea. I go for creative men and Mark was a doctor.

'A concert first, perhaps. You like Vivaldi. There's a really good programme at the Barbican on the 20th...'

I do like Vivaldi – though my real love is jazz. Traditional blues, in a live interpretation if at all possible. However, I accepted the invitation, trying to sound more gracious than I felt.

'I'll book a table at the Connaught afterwards.'

'Well...' The assumption that he knew what was best, that my preferences, even if they existed, were neither here nor there, irritated me.

He swept my hesitation aside. 'You'll enjoy it, Ruth. You can stay with Deborah. You said she has a spare room.'

It seemed churlish not to play along. 'Thank you very much. I'm sure that will be lovely.' And Debs was happy to put me up, as always. I was lucky to have a daughter living in London; luckier still to get on so well with her.

That's how I first met Matthew. Mark hadn't mentioned that we'd be having dinner with his brothers and their wives until we were in his Bentley, on our way.

He had three siblings he informed me as he negotiated London traffic. Psychiatrists do seem to have a penchant for that word. Three brothers, no sisters. Jean-Jacques was a much sought-after barrister, married to a Frenchwoman called Jeanne, originally from Rouen. They had five daughters and a son. I didn't say anything, but it struck me right away that six children was overdoing it by modern standards. Then I remembered Mark had been to Downside. A Catholic family, no doubt. I guessed his brothers would have been at the same school, and Jean-Jacques's children conceived in the '50s and '60s. Practising Catholics didn't go in for birth control in those days.

'Luke is an obstetrician,' Mark went on. 'Married to Caroline. They have one son.'

Another doctor. Interesting. Surely Mark had said his wife had died in childbirth? Presumably even Luke hadn't been able to save her. Then I realised that he was unlikely to have been more than a houseman at the time.

'And then there's Matthew.' A pause which stretched into a lengthy break while I waited for the description Mark seemed reluctant to commit himself to. 'He isn't married.' The tight vowels made it clear that he considered Matthew fitted into a different category from his other brothers. I looked across to see if I could catch an expression, but it was too dark to distinguish anything.

'Also a widower?'

Another pause, pregnant with tantalising implications. 'A bachelor.' And that was it. No mention of what Matthew did, and no time to ask.

Mark parked, got out of the car and came round to the passenger side to hand me out. 'I hope you don't mind,' he said, his voice so low it was hard to make out the words as he steered my elbow towards the hotel entrance. 'I tried to let you know. I rang several times, but you were always out.'

But I do have an answering machine. He distracted me from bringing that up by trying to take my arm. I shrugged away from him. I prefer to walk on my own.

The family group was seated at a magnificent round table, having drinks. The three men stood. I was startled to notice an unusual similarity between all four of them – a familiar look I'd seen before but couldn't quite place. Not then, at any rate. Later I was to realise that's what had attracted me from the start.

One thing was very clear. One of Mark's brothers looked remarkably like him, virtually identical. Were they twins? Mark hadn't even hinted at that. Fascinating.

He began the introductions, starting with the man standing nearest to me, on my right. 'My brother Jean-Jacques.'

He was shorter than Mark by about two inches, but still around six foot. A smaller frame, slighter shoulders, his dark hair straighter than Mark's, and with greying sideburns. He narrowed his eyes at me, gave me a supercilious smile and a slight bow, but didn't offer to shake hands. I smiled at him as Mark looked beyond him at a round figure hunched into her chair. She seemed to be dressed in a large caftan which disguised her figure. 'And his wife Jeanne.'

Her dark eyes were small, and sunk behind round cheeks. ''Allo,' she greeted me, her voice surprisingly loud and confident.

'Hello, Jeanne.'

Mark stopped, stared at me and frowned. I was speaking out of turn. I waited dutifully as he turned back to the table.

'And that's Luke next to Jeanne, and his wife Caroline is on the other side.'

Luke was a little taller than Jean-Jacques, and a good deal heavier. He needed the Savile Row tailoring to disguise his heavy paunch. His wife Caroline was quite a contrast. Though seated, she gave the impression of being very tall, and certainly slender. Her hair was swept back from her forehead ballerina-style, her hands beautifully groomed, her Jean Muir dress an understated gem.

'And Matthew,' Mark finished up, his voice dropped to a flat monotone.

I was still standing, smiling, while Mark went through the litany. Matthew, Mark, Luke and Jean-Jacques – John. But the thing that really struck me was that Mark and Matthew looked so incredibly alike. Were they identical twins? They could be brothers who looked alike because they were the same height, had the same colour and texture of hair and expressive dark-brown eyes. Only their frames were different. Mark was a big man, but Matthew, though leaner, looked bigger, broader-shouldered, hard and muscular. He had exactly the sort of male body I most admire.

Matthew pulled out the chair next to him, and snapped his fingers at a waiter. He turned questioning eyes to me. 'What will you drink?'

'A glass of red wine would be lovely.'

'Don't you want...' Mark began but Matthew interrupted him. 'Of course. The wine list,' he instructed the waiter while Mark moved the chair under me.

I sat and noticed Jean-Jacques's eyes probing me. He took his time. I stared back in turn. He was good-looking in a smooth sort of way, dashing in an Armani suit. His eyes were deeper set than Mark's, alert and mocking. I could see Mark hadn't been exaggerating when he said Jean-Jacques was a highly successful QC. He looked the part.

'Live in London, do you?' His voice was syrupy, but I was sure the sharp nose had already sniffed out my hesitation about Mark.

'Somerset, actually.'

Still-black eyebrows arched in what looked like genuine

surprise. Obviously Mark hadn't mentioned meeting me. 'Which part?'

'On the Levels. Barnsham isn't that far from Downside. I gather you know the area.'

He grinned. 'Mark's told you we went to school there. My son Jean-Pierre followed the family tradition, so I've been back in living memory.' He looked at me again, as though that would tell him more about me. 'Thatched cottage in a village?'

'Nothing as romantic as that. My late husband and I bought a mid-Victorian country house. Wonderful for bringing up a family, but a bit on the large side for only one. I'm trying to wean myself off it.'

A patronising smile, a glance at Mark. I concentrated on talking about Jonathan. That ensured that Jean-Jacques got bored. His questions petered out, but Luke took over.

'When did your husband die?'

Caroline put her hand on his arm. 'Luke...'

He shook her off. 'She must be used to it by now. She's not wearing black, so I take it she's not in mourning.'

Did he think wearing black was the same as mourning? Or that having dinner with Mark was being disloyal to my dead husband? I almost felt he did. 'Five years in June,' I said.

'And you're still in the same house?' His eyelids had completely covered his eyes.

'It's on the market. In fact it's under offer now. I hope to move in March.'

Luke was by far the heaviest of the brothers, and his hair had greyed more than theirs. His face was florid, with eyes sunk behind pronounced bags and under heavy lids. 'Found somewhere else, have you?'

He thinks I'm trying to collar Mark before buying a new house. 'Not really. I'm going to try living in different parts of the country. I thought I'd rent for a year at a time to find out where would suit me best.' Something stopped me from mentioning that I'd already opted for a house on Guernsey.

'What a good idea,' a deep voice rumbled beside me on my left.

12

Matthew's hair was still completely black, his eyes challenged me, probed. He wore an old faded velvet coat. Impeccably tailored, but in a '60s style.

I turned to him with relief. 'Mark's told me that Jean-Jacques is a barrister, and Luke an obstetrician. What do you do?' An artist of some sort, I was quite sure. His fingers were long and muscular. A musician, maybe. Perhaps a pianist.

'I paint.' Obvious, now that he'd said it. The threadbare trousers, the soft cravat. But I'd held back on a positive reaction for a few seconds too long. His eyes glinted what I took to be exasperation at my slow wits. 'Pictures, not walls.'

The dig brought out my competitive nature. 'Decorating is excellent training for painting I've heard. De Kooning started that way. He maintains it teaches you to handle paint and hold a brush.'

'Really? I'd call that a somewhat brutal approach.' Matthew's even teeth gleamed at me. 'But better than art school, perhaps.'

Why hadn't Mark told me Matthew was a painter? Because he didn't think of it as a proper job? 'Which galleries carry your work?' I asked, delighted to meet someone who dared to be creative.

'None.' The smile faded, the dark eyes blanked.

Jean-Jacques chipped in right away. 'He could have had any number of exhibitions, no problem. It's just that he simply will not take the time or trouble to sell himself...'

'My business.' Matthew turned away from both of us. 'Dance, Caroline?'

As she got up I could see that Caroline was, indeed, tall and graceful, slim and elegant. Gleaming black hair caught the light.

'Well, now. Just to put you in the picture.' Luke breathed heavily, leaning over the table. 'My wife used to be a ballet dancer,' he went on, his eyes following her. 'Of course she's very good at ballroom dancing, too. And B...' He half-closed his eyes, cleared his throat and went on. 'Matthew has some sort of flair for it.'

The couple warmed up gradually, dancing decorously to the stereotype orchestra playing their unenthusiastic rendering of a slow foxtrot. A change of tempo to Alexander's Ragtime Band, and suddenly they came alive. Nimble eager steps adapted to each

13

other perfectly. They spun twinkle-toed across the floor, the other dancers giving way in admiration, until at last they were the only couple left. The orchestra, enlivened by the display, forgot its pomposity enough to quicken. The twisting sinuous pair gyrated as though one being. I became aware of Luke as he rose to his feet. I felt Mark and Jean-Jacques tense.

A last fast whirl as the number came to an end. A ripple of applause accompanied the dancers as they returned to our table, flushed and triumphant. Caroline's eyes were aflame, Matthew's hooded as he led her to her chair beside her husband.

'And you're a lady of leisure, I take it?' Jean-Jacques now focused sharp eyes on me.

'I'm a writer.'

'That a fact?' He sounded startled. 'In that case you'll know how to ferret out people's secrets.' He raised his eyebrows at me. 'Can you put us in order of age?' There was a sort of cross between a grin and a sneer on his face. The broken capillaries round his nose made him look flushed.

How loaded can you get? Matthew looked by far the youngest, but actually I thought he was the eldest. He had that first-born attitude. Even so, there'd have to be a hierarchy for the other three. Guessing at their chronology would certainly put my sleuthing skills to the test. I decided to forget about logic. Knowing the order of the Gospels might be a better clue.

'I'd say Matthew is the eldest, then Mark, then Luke. And you're the youngest,' I announced, making it sound as though that were some sort of defect.

'Bully for you remembering correctly. Mark told you, of course.'

I'd got it right!

'No,' Mark said reflectively, looking carefully at me. 'Matter of fact I didn't even mention I had brothers until tonight.'

Three pairs of eyes seemed to zoom in on him. Were they offended? They looked surprised rather than annoyed. Naturally they weren't to know that this was the first time Mark and I had gone out together, but they must have guessed we didn't know each other very well.

14

Mark stared coolly back at them, then turned to me. 'So how much is there between us, would you say?'

He wasn't going to let me off the hook, then. 'That's rather tougher.' I examined each of them carefully. 'You can hardly expect me to get that absolutely right...'

'Well, roughly,' he pressed me, his face inexpressive, only his eyes intense.

'You're trying to play a trick on me. I know perfectly well it's a trap.' I compared Matthew and Mark again. 'I happen to think you and Matthew are the same age.'

No one said anything.

'I think you're twins,' I said, wondering whether I was making an idiot of myself. 'Your features are very similar, and you're much the same height.' The silence was positively deafening. 'I'd guess Luke's a year younger than you two, and Jean-Jacques is a year or so younger than that.'

'Mark must have told you,' Jean-Jacques repeated, shrugging his shoulders.

'No,' we both said together.

'So that's your secret. You're an investigative reporter, a lady journalist,' Luke positively condescended down his nose.

I shook my head. 'Not a journalist, no. I write books. About gardening.'

That smug small smile as though that were an easy option. 'And is that lucrative?' The familiar look of boredom about such a worthy subject crossed Luke's bloated face.

'Not necessarily.' I sounded sharp, even to myself. 'It's a very competitive business.' I didn't like the look of that man. Odd how the same genetic background can produce such different individuals.

'Is it, indeed?' Jean-Jacques put in, looking pensive. I preferred him, though I don't go for womanisers.

'She's an expert in her field,' Mark's loud voice surprised me. 'She writes under the name of Elizabeth Pilton.'

'Good, good,' Jean-Jacques's smile faded a little as he looked at me again.

'Elizabeth Pilton?' His wife Jeanne came alive for the first time. *The Self-sufficient Garden?*'

'That was my first book, yes.'

'My gardening bible,' she gushed.

I smiled at the recognition. 'How lovely of you to say so.'

'We're never allowed to buy plants, like ordinary people,' Jean-Jacques rushed to complain. 'The bloody things have to be able to take care of themselves, or even work for their living.' He moved his claret glass balefully.

So the plump little woman did hold her own at times. Now that I thought about it I could see she was very much in charge.

'But I thought your name is Ruth,' Jeanne suddenly said, looking at me as though she'd found me out in some terrible lie. 'Mark introduced you as Ruth Samuels. Why don't you write under your own name?'

'Elizabeth is my second name,' I explained. 'And Pilton is an anglicised version of my maiden name. I didn't think Pötzlinger would go down too well.'

Four pairs of eyes flickered, darkened. 'So you're from Germany?' Luke asked.

'Austria, originally. My family were refugees from Hitler. I came to England as a child.'

Jean-Jacques nodded, then grinned. 'We haven't finished the test yet,' he changed the subject back again, beckoning to the waiter to bring another bottle of Médoc. 'So how old would you say we are?'

That, of course, was a relatively easy one. I did have four bodies to base my estimates on. 'I'd say late fifties.'

'How late is late?' Mark's tone held that hint of condescension which was quite enough to turn my irritation into aggression.

It flashed into my mind that the reason they were all having dinner together – that it had all been arranged – was because today was special. Could it be that it was his – and consequently Matthew's – birthday? I guessed Mark had invited me in order to bring a partner. And, perhaps, to involve me further, whether I wanted that or not. I kept my eyes off Matthew in case I gave away

16

how attractive I found him.

'I'd say Luke is fifty-eight, Jean-Jacques fifty-seven.' I paused. Why would they all meet even if it were somebody's birthday? Unlikely. Then I remembered Mark had been really insistent on meeting today: February 20th, 1991. What was so special about that? The answer was obvious – because it was the twins' sixtieth birthday! 'And I think Matthew and Mark are sixty today,' I gambled. 'And Matthew is an hour older than Mark.'

'You've only made one small mistake,' Matthew said, and laughed. 'Ten minutes older. Counts just the same.'

'Elizabeth Pilton my foot,' Jean-Jacques dismissed that. 'She's obviously Miss Marple.'

CHAPTER THREE

Matthew took the plate of biscuits from the lady dispensing coffee and offered me one. He probably remembered meeting me at the Connaught dinner because he'd been quite amused by my guessing his and his brothers' ages.

'I didn't realise you're a Catholic,' he said, smiling amiably. He was wearing the same faded velvet coat he'd worn at the dinner, teamed with an equally faded silk shirt whose open neck was neatly filled in with a soft cashmere scarf. All spotless. I noticed neat darns where the cuffs had frayed.

'Convert.' I straightened up, my feeling of faintness about meeting him again forgotten, and spluttered over the cracked cup in my haste. There was a sense in which mentioning that was showing off. The sin of pride. All it needed was a simple agreement, a nod. I blamed the coffee. It wasn't merely weak; tepid, too. Because, I noticed now, the room was freezing. All that hot blood had ebbed away as my excitement changed to nervousness.

'I'm a cradle Catholic.' The customary apologetic shrug.

'There's no such thing.' I was off on the well-worn tracks of my hobby-horse before I could stop myself. It's always exasperated me that converts are treated as a race apart. 'Each person is received into the Church through baptism.' But the real irritation was with myself for being such an idiot. I'd put Matthew on the defensive.

The dark eyes flickered. 'It's a matter of polite expression. We cradlers are also taught the Catechism. Some of it even sticks.'

He hadn't taken offence, or fright. Why didn't I just shut up? 'I know. At Downside.' Showing off that I'd remembered his background.

His grin told me I'd neither impressed nor daunted him. 'Far too late to do any good. I was taught by the Abbé Saint Jude. Quite a severe catechist, as it happens. He'd have pointed out, for example, that converts from other Christian denominations are assumed to have been baptised already.' He took a sip of coffee, wrinkled his nose. 'Or at any rate that their christening was sacramental. So they'd be received into the Church by a welcoming ceremony, not baptism.'

Impressive. 'The Abbé was the French master at your prep school?'

His eyes took on that evasive look I'd already learned to recognise. 'Our parish priest. Well, he was a curé when I was a boy. He was our confessor.'

Was there a French connection? The feeling of recognition I hadn't been able to place when I first met Mark's brothers clicked in. They had the kind of Gallic look I'd noticed on my recent visit to the Channel Islands. It would explain why Mark had talked glowingly about Guernsey the very first time I'd met him. Foolish of me to imagine that the only thing he'd held back was his family tree. And curious that I hadn't thought about the implications of a French surname before. It would also account for the Christian name Jean-Jacques, and why he'd married a Frenchwoman. 'Are you from Guernsey, by any chance?'

'Mark didn't tell you we were born there?'

'He said he'd lived there at some time, and what a beautiful place it was.' Mark was clearly a master of lies of omission. What he did mention was that they – well he, since at that time he hadn't mentioned his brothers, either – were orphaned when he was ten. His parents had drowned; some sort of accident at sea. He told me he'd been brought up by his paternal grandmother. I'd assumed she'd died, in the natural course of things, and that he had no other relatives. In retrospect I found it interesting that, apart from that single reference, he never mentioned any family except his late wife and, of course, his daughter Sylvia. I'd wondered why. Hailing from Guernsey somehow made more sense of it.

No happy ties, then. I took it that none of them had been

back to the island for quite some time. They might well have been evacuated ahead of the German Occupation of the Channel Islands. The events of World War II still held a spell over me, still pushed me to delve into its history. I knew that almost all the children on Guernsey had been sent off to England, just before the Germans invaded in 1940. Perhaps the Frelés left before the Germans took over, then lost touch with anyone related who'd stayed behind. That's not such an unusual state of affairs for orphans to find themselves in.

'Do any of your family still live there?'

'No.'

Friendly banter had changed to a single abrupt syllable. I wasn't expecting such a strong reaction. I kept quiet, hoping my silence would draw him out, even though it didn't seem likely. I clattered the cup, pretending to drink.

'The only surviving family member to actually live there for the last forty years or so died yesterday, at the age of ninety-six.' It was hard to distinguish tones in the noisy crowded room, but the relaxation of the shoulders was unmistakable.

'You're a long-lived family, then.'

Returned tension showed in the stiffened neck, the forward thrust of the head. 'Not all of us. My grandfather died when he was only thirty-five. Killed at the end of the Great War.'

I pretended to drink again. Why was he talking about his grandfather rather than his parents? It struck me as peculiar.

'My father was only six at the time. He had to take over the male role early.'

I bristled a little at that, quite unreasonably. After all, he was talking about 1918. That period of history had affected my family, too, though in a different way. I completely missed out on my grandparents. The Treaty of Saint-Germain-en-Laye broke up the old Austro-Hungarian Empire, and many of my near relatives were scattered across different parts of the newly created territories of Austria, Hungary and Yugoslavia.

I wondered whether his being orphaned had anything to do with the German occupation of the Channel Islands. Were his parents saboteurs, by any chance? 'What happened to the rest of your family?'

'Mark and I were only ten when we lost our parents.'

Matthew sounded edgy where Mark had been matter-of-fact. Surely it wasn't tactless of me to bring up such long-ago events? I, too, lost relatives: apart from never knowing any of my grandparents I'd lost all the aunts, uncles and cousins I'd known as a young child. Not a single one of my extended family survived World War II. 'You mean they died at the same time?' Mark had told me there'd been some sort of accident at sea. A misadventure, presumably.

Matthew turned away and I couldn't see his face. 'Something of the sort.' A mutter which made it clear he wasn't agreeing or disagreeing, or intending to go into details.

'That must have been appalling for you.' My losses were nothing compared to the trauma of being deprived of both parents at the same time, and at such a young age. And, though I toyed with asking about the Frelé brothers' maternal side, I didn't want to put him off by being too nosy. 'So you'll be going over for the funeral?'

'I'm joining my brothers in St Peter Port tomorrow.' He examined the water dripping from the cup he was holding above the saucer. Drip-slosh, drip-slosh... 'My first time back for over thirty years.'

'I'm sorry.'

He brought out a handkerchief and soaked up the liquid. 'No need. Gran'mère and I weren't close.'

'Oh, right.' I paused. Should I tell him about my plans? Well, why not? The coincidence was unusual, though just coincidence, presumably. Actually I didn't believe that. Synchronicity – I knew that Jonathan was batting for me, somewhere. He'd said he would. I'd asked him to help me make a complete break with the old life. To help me find a new place to live, to meet new people. 'Oddly enough, I'm moving to St Peter Port next month.'

He blinked. 'You are?' He didn't sound altogether delighted.

'I've just heard that contracts have finally been exchanged on my place in Somerset. It's high time I left the past behind and made a new start. I fancy Guernsey. I don't know why, I've only visited the island once.'

'We shall be practically neighbours, then. The town's so small.' A short silence. 'I'm the eldest male in the Frelé line.' He stopped and stared at me. 'I dare say you've already figured that out,' he went on, voice dry. 'I'm moving back to the island. The estate passes to me.'

'Now that your grandmother is dead, you mean?' She was a woman. If being a male mattered so much, why hadn't he claimed his inheritance before?

'Not exactly. Lascervelle's been mine since my parents died. But my grandmother wanted to live there.'

I'd been busy searching through rental property details and opted for a house in St Peter Port for a year, to give myself the chance to decide whether my instincts about Guernsey were right. I'd gone for a place in the centre of the town. That's when I'd noticed Lascervelle. An imposing house, one of the finest in St Peter Port. It had to be worth a fortune, yet Matthew was clearly short of funds. I knew that Guernsey inheritance laws were different from those in Britain, and nearer those in France. Were surviving widows entitled to stay on in the family home until they died? Did that mean Matthew had decided against living with his grandmother, even in such a large house? Did not being close, not even visiting, imply a rift? I longed to know. 'On Candie Road?' I checked instead.

'Overlooking the gardens, yes.' The dark eyes searched my enquiring ones. 'You know it?'

'Indeed. I'm moving into Riande, next door.'

We both raised our coffee cups at the same time and clinked them, laughing out loud.

'That is incredible!' His smile was warm. 'And calls for a minor celebration, don't you think? I can offer you rather trendy transport on the back of an old motor-bike. We could be really daring and cross Albert Bridge.'

That took me right back to my freshman days. No spotty school-leavers among my admirers. A number of the students had been ex-servicemen, their education paid for by a grateful country. Many of them could afford their own transport. Wind in my hair, I remembered. A feeling of freedom, of flying. I rode pillion, hugged my first college boyfriend's – Geoff's – waist, encouraged him to speed.

I kicked my left shin with my right foot even though I now bruise easily. You're not a college girl now, I scolded myself. Have a modicum of sense. 'A little advanced for me,' I said, smiling encouragement. 'How about taking an elderly yellow Volvo instead?'

CHAPTER FOUR

'D'you like pasta?' Matthew asked me. 'I know a really good place near the river, in Cheyne Row. They make their own.'

'That sounds terrific.' And I meant it. No holding back as I had with Mark. Was I being foolish, allowing myself to get involved?

'And there's an exhibition I was going to this afternoon.'

'Paintings?'

'Some of Frank Bowers' latest sculptures. They're being shown in a studio in Chelsea Harbour.'

So we had similar tastes in art. 'Wonderful. I really like his work.'

'Good. We can go together.'

The Volvo was wedged in tight between two vans. My face must have shown dismay. I unlocked the passenger door and Matthew opened it wide for me, taking the key. 'I'll get her out for you,' he said. 'These old tanks don't have power steering.'

I should have changed to something smaller, lighter, years ago. I just haven't been able to get myself to do it. The car always brought a little of Jonathan back every time I drove it. I watched this other man at the steering wheel, a lump growing in my throat. Eventually it subsided.

Matthew didn't have the slightest difficulty extricating my trusty workhorse out of the parking space. Once in the driving seat he carried on, moving the old car fast and well, almost as though he were some sort of professional.

'D'you enjoy driving?'

'I'm good at it.' He accelerated sure-footedly out of a corner. 'It's what I used to do to earn my daily bread.'

'A chauffeur, you mean?'

'Lorry driver.' He grinned at me. 'I took on long hauls during the night. That gave me the chance to paint during the day. And in different locations.' A sidelong look. 'Lorry driving strengthens the arm muscles for holding a loaded paintbrush.'

So he had a sense of humour. I liked that. 'You use de Kooning brushes?'

'I handle large canvases heavy with pigment.' He kept his face straight.

'But you don't try to sell your paintings?'

The corners of his mouth turned down. 'Not any more.'

Intriguing, tantalising. Why not? Because he'd lost heart, lost his nerve? Not from what I'd seen of him. What, then? Because no one would even look, presumably. And why would that be? Was his work erotic? I embarrassed myself by the thought. Perhaps I thought along those lines because the man oozed sex appeal. 'Why's that?'

'Constant rejection doesn't progress the cause of art.' It didn't sound bitter, just matter of fact. 'Now I play the piano in a jazz band. It's night work, and it pays quite well.'

'Really?' I said. 'Modern or trad?'

'Just jazz. Mostly blues.'

'I'd rather see your paintings than the Bowers sculptures.' It came out, just like that. Well, why not? That's what I wanted, wasn't it? I preferred to make up my own mind, and to voice it. Age had to have some advantages I'd told myself after turning fifty. And lived accordingly.

He laughed, a sort of rolling, rumbling noise which, first of all, I thought was the car engine. But then he went on laughing, his thin face split from side to side, teeth showing white. And long, I realised, interested that the signs of age were there.

'I live in Brixton. Can you cope with that?'

'Is that a problem?'

He glanced across at me. 'It's a rough area.'

'Presumably you know how to survive.'

'And a '76 Volvo won't raise any eyebrows,' he agreed with me.

He turned left, then left again into a network of minor roads.

We'd both, I noticed, forgotten about lunch.

'I live right at the top,' he said. 'A sort of loft-studio. I like it for the light. North facing.'

I wrapped my voluminous coat around me, glad that I had my silk thermals on and was wearing the new angora sweater over the flared skirt which flattered my figure. At home I pampered myself with central heating turned up high enough to do without jumpers. Debs's flat was always on the cold side as far as I was concerned, so I'd come prepared.

Matthew led the way from the car to his building. I was glad not be walking on my own. The streets reminded me of the time Jonathan and I first visited Chicago. We wanted to stay a few days, explore Al Capone's home town, excited by stories we'd read about gangsters – and live jazz bands. Both of us had this terrible sense of direction. We turned the wrong way from the train 'depot' and found ourselves in skid row. We thought that was how Chicago was.

Brixton was very similar. Houses pockmarked by neglect, streets littered with plastic bags, spilt fluids, unmentionables. Newspapers riding the wind everywhere, cardboard boxes with people sleeping inside. I kept close to Matthew, trying to stop my heels from clacking, wondering just how I'd got myself into such a precarious situation. I hardly knew this man, and he exuded an air of recklessness, of danger.

'Well, this is it.' He used a key to open a front door, then pointed up some flights of stairs. The hall was tatty, though not unclean. The stairs were uncarpeted, noisy, steep.

'I'll go ahead.' He climbed the staircase in front of me, vaulted up to the second, the third, and finally some steep steps leading to the fourth floor. I was glad my gardening had kept me fairly fit. Though slightly out of breath I was able to keep up with him. The treads on the last staircase were narrower than the rest, and definitely precipitous. There was no handrail. I tiptoed on, holding the steps ahead to steady myself, and stopped. I watched as Matthew unlocked a single door facing us at the top. He opened it wide.

The other side was a revelation. A large, sparsely furnished, airy room. Willow cane chairs with gaily coloured cushions, home-made rugs scattered on a highly-polished deal floor, sumptuous velvet curtains – faded from claret to almost-rose – on either side of a picture window facing south. A wan winter sun streamed through clean glass.

Matthew slipped some coins into a meter and lit a gas fire. I began to look at the pictures on the walls. Enormous brooding oils primarily in reds and earth colours. Abstracts: flowing sinuous vibrating abstracts which had a strength and force which took my breath away. I stared, my mind at once entwined with the twisting curves which snaked in and out of forms which seemed to shimmer and move as I looked at them. Strong pictures, strong man. I knew then that I wanted to know him better. Much better.

'Yours?'

'Yes.'

'They are – incredible,' I finally brought out. The colours were not as based on red as I first thought. There was a lot of green, and gold, glinting and glistening in small patches, watching me, like eyes... The paintings were brooding, intense, with a hint of menace which should have put me off but only attracted me more. Just like the man.

'At least you didn't call them interesting.' He laughed. 'And don't worry about being polite. It's not obligatory to like them.'

'I don't think 'like' is at all the right word. They produce a much stronger reaction. I find them fascinating, almost mesmerising. They're...'

'Too dark, I'm told.' His voice sounded higher than normal.

Too powerful, maybe. 'You mean, if only you painted in light colours, they'd be acceptable?'

He shrugged. 'I no longer care.'

'Got any more?'

'Hundreds,' he said. 'I mean that literally. I may not be all that prolific, but I have been at it for over fifty years.'

'You started young.' I wanted to gorge myself on more, a greed to see as many as I could. I didn't allow myself to work through what that implied. Not then.

'As soon as I could hold a brush.'

'Sold much?' Surrounding myself with his paintings would be the next best thing to being with him.

'Not really. There is one fan.' He laughed. 'One major fan. I don't know what he does with them all. I'm told he, maybe she, has a private gallery.'

'American?' What really worried me was that she might be female, could become part of his life.

His head jerked up, as though I'd touched a raw nerve. 'Why would you think that?'

Now what? The rough voice told me to find a good reason – and fast. 'Americans can often be more open to new ideas. They're not so inclined to be hamstrung by establishment. At least some of them.'

'That so.' He straightened a straight painting. 'Well, he or she may be, for all I know. I have no inkling who it is. He or she insists on remaining anonymous.'

'So how does this person come across your stuff?'

He went on fiddling, his back to me. 'This old chap I know. He's an agent, or used to be. He comes round every now and again to see what I've been up to. He always picks up a half dozen canvases at a time, then brings back two or three. He has this uncanny knack of choosing the best ones. I mean to say, the ones I like.'

'May I see some of the others?'

He hesitated. 'I think of them as old hat. I always hang the latest ones – the ones I don't sell to the unknown fan.'

Greed can lead to courage – or foolhardiness. 'If you have no objections?'

'As long as you're sure.' I nodded my assurance. 'OK. The studio's through there.' He slid away what had looked like panelling along sliders to the wall.

The whole room opened up to the other side of the house, the north side. I saw why living here was right for him. The light was marvellous. His attic floor was higher than the other houses on the street, open to the skies. A magnificent skylight flooded the room with light – and cold. I put my coat on again.

'I've got used to it.' He smiled. 'Sit on this chair and I'll position a few paintings on the easel for you.'

I sat, entranced, as one spectacular picture after another was placed on the easel, then replaced with another. Huge – he must stretch the canvases himself to transport them up and down those stairs. Did the agent take them off the frames, then restretch them for showing? The unknown buyer had to be very keen. Not that it surprised me. There were at least a dozen paintings I'd have been happy – even eager – to buy. I persuaded Matthew to put them to one side.

'Enough?'

'For the time being,' I lied, because it seemed politic. 'I think you have a quite remarkable talent.'

'Thank you.'

'It does seem a pity that you don't exhibit...'

'Well, you know, I'm not really that interested in selling.' Irritability showed in the way he restacked paintings. Hard and fast. 'Of course, if you would like to enjoy some of these at leisure, you could have them on loan.' He stared at me. 'You'll be living next door, so I don't expect you to abscond with them.' A small darting smile.

'That would be a great honour.' His offer was just a promise I didn't know he'd keep. I wanted something certain. 'Perhaps I might also be allowed to buy some?'

He stopped moving paintings, turned away from me. 'Don't know about that. I wouldn't know what to ask for them.'

Was he turning me down, or was there some other reason? 'I could make you an offer for each one,' I tried, and instantly regretted it. Was I embarrassing him by talking about money? 'Would you prefer me to discuss it with your agent?'

He shrugged, picked up a folded piece of calico, flipped it open and draped it over several canvases. 'He's just an old man, a go-between. I'm sure he wouldn't know.'

I couldn't help my sigh. 'You have such an unusual talent–'

In the far corner of the room, almost hidden by a melange of frames, I spotted a small portrait. It was more representational than the rest of Matthew's work. The head of a young woman: a delicate face, large eyes, the sweetest Mona Lisa smile. She reminded me of someone... I walked over and touched the frame. 'Who's that?'

He moved across to me, lithe, fast. His arm shot forward, beyond me, to the painting. He turned it to the wall, saw me staring at its back and dragged some of the larger canvases to cover that. 'Someone I knew. A long time ago.' He went back to stacking canvases, mixing the ones I'd asked him to put aside together with the others.

Was she the love of his life? Someone he'd never got over, that's why he was a bachelor? 'You're saying you don't want to sell your paintings to me.' I felt let down, almost deprived. 'I don't really know anything about the art world, but I'm quite sure that even the most idiotic dealer, if he had any sort of eye, would be proud to exhibit you.'

'I don't want that!' The earlier friendly look turned opaque, shutting me out. He came up to me, towered over me, eyes roaming. 'You'll be warmer in the other room.'

I'd blown the whole thing, crowded him. 'You want me to leave.'

'I'll drive you wherever you want to go. Perhaps back to St Olaf's; you know the way from there. I've got to pick my bike up in any case.'

'Of course.' My disappointment turned my limbs to lead, but I forced my legs to move. He motioned the way to his living room and began to pull the partition closed again.

This man appealed to me on every level I could think of. Artistic, mental, physical – and sexual. Even in the cold of the studio I felt my blood warm, and my bladder press. 'May I use your bathroom?'

At first I thought he was going to say no. His hand snapped up, he pointed to another door I hadn't noticed, set right at the far end of his living room. I walked through, found myself in a small antiseptic kitchen, opened another door and found a sort of box room with a single bed. Beyond it was a tiny bathroom: shower, basin and loo. All immaculate.

When I returned Matthew was standing by his window, looking out.

'I didn't mean to be ungracious,' he said. 'It entirely slipped my mind. We have this understanding, you see.'

'Your agent would think I was poaching?' His shifting eyes told me he wasn't talking about that. What, then?

He blinked to hide the lie. 'He might think I was treading on his toes.'

How could he, as I'd suggesting buying through him? Such a lame excuse. But why? 'Well, if he'd like to get in touch...' I offered him my card.

He didn't take it. 'Don't think he'd want to know.' He was already holding his front door open.

'I see.' I stepped through, wondering how I was going to get down.

'Go backwards. Sorry it's so difficult.'

Physical difficulties weren't the problem. I backed to the third floor, then clattered down the rest of the stairs as fast as I dared. As we emerged from the front door I was about to become ultra dignified. I intended to thank him and walk away, pride in every step.

I changed my mind. Four large youths approached from the opposite direction. Four pairs of eyes took in my coat, my bag, my shoes – so out of place. I could see there might be trouble.

Within seconds Matthew was in front of me. The first youth's lips widened, showing perfect white teeth, very strong. Something glinted in the watery sun.

Before I could take another breath the youth was sprawled on the pavement, the knife now in Matthew's hand. The second youth, taller, sturdier, moved quickly towards me. I used my bag as a weapon. There was the sound of rending leather, then flesh on flesh. The youth dropped down.

The two others didn't stay to see if they could best Matthew. I saw him turn, kick the first boy in the groin. Then he grabbed hold

31

of my arm and hustled me to the Volvo parked only yards away.

'Let's go,' he said, sheathing the youth's knife and putting it into the inside pocket of the velvet coat. 'It isn't healthy to stay around.'

It wasn't healthy for me to yearn for a man like Matthew. Talented, capricious, powerful. But that wasn't going to stop me. For the second time in my life I'd come across a man I knew I could love. I sat beside him in the Volvo and thought I heard Jonathan encouraging me.

CHAPTER FIVE

It was the weirdest feeling. I sat in the tiny jet which flies between Heathrow and Guernsey and looked down at the little island which was to be my home for the next year. The plane circled the neat little airport. I craned my neck to get a better look. A glorious early April day. A turquoise ribbon of water surrounded dozens of bays jutting out from a jagged coastline. One inlet looked particularly inviting. It had a tiny tongue of beach with protective rocks set around it in a welcoming horseshoe shape.

Was I really starting a new life? Could I finally tear myself away from the past? I crossed my fingers and went on staring. A curious compulsion drew me towards finding that little bay as though I were coming home, as though I already knew it well – and loved it.

I started rationalising. What appealed to me about Guernsey was its reputation for natural beauty, its temperate climate – semi-tropical, the more effusive of the guide books called it. A gardener's paradise was another recurring phrase. What could possibly suit me better? And there was also the pull of continental Europe – a move nearer my origins, yet staying on British soil.

It didn't take long to deplane, to collect my luggage, to pick up my new Saab. The cloudless sky was how I excused my reluctance to drive straight to my new house. Neither Matthew nor Mark had been in touch since my visit to Matthew's flat. Would he notice I'd moved in, come over to say hello?

I turned right on to Petit Bôt Road. Navigation is not one of my outstanding talents – anti-talent would be nearer the mark – but I steered as though I knew that route, negotiating a narrow lane which made a mockery of Guernsey's speed limit of thirty-five. It was hedged high on both sides, with more S-bends than a snake trail. There was no warning of the sharp acute-angled turning to the right, but the car seemed to know it was there. I relaxed and followed my nose. And came to a full stop. A little clearing, a cul-de-sac. I laughed out loud. So much for my brilliant intuition.

I got out and looked around. Vague memories of the tourist guide I'd read suggested I was in one of Guernsey's renowned green lanes. And, though the track narrowed to a footpath, I knew it would connect with other lanes in an intricate network of venerable byways.

I ambled on to a cliff path. The view was staggering. A panorama of a jewelled placid sea with sunbeams sparkling into diamonds. A small enclosed bay below me, its empty beach inviting me down. The horseshoe outline was as clear from where I now stood as it had been from the air.

A narrow path twisted towards what I was sure would be the shore. Though very steep it wasn't difficult to negotiate. Broad steps had been cut out of the cliffs with a variety of rock plants between the boulders. This path was tended, planted like an Alpine garden in a natural setting. I almost clapped at masses of Livingstone daisies, leaf umbels still tight over buds which would open to flowers in vivid colours when the sun was high. The trail became a water lane trickling down to the sea.

Then I was on the beach. An intimate area of clean light-coloured sand with large round pebbles at the upper edges. Rocks jutted out from a stark cliff side giving good shelter from the wind.

I sank down exhausted, yet filled with a sort of joy. A gentle sun warmed my face and my spirits. This island had to be what I was looking for: an idyllic enchanted place with traditions from continental Europe and the British Isles – the best of both my worlds.

Gulls aren't my favourite seabirds, but their harsh wails were tuned softer by the screening crags. I closed my eyes, allowed the murmuring of the sea, the soft breeze, the heat, even the continuous mewling of the birds, to lull me into a doze.

Waking, I felt a chilly sensation as a brush of cold air dissipated warmth. I assumed the sun had clouded over. Instead, a large shape was blocking it from me. I focused, took in a man standing a couple of yards from me, his body black against the light, his features indistinguishable.

'I did not wish to frighten you, dear lady.' A modulated cultivated voice. Not English – was that a Guernsey accent? It sounded too staccato for the local patois, Teutonic rather than Gallic. Was this a private beach? Was I trespassing? I started up.

'Please do not be alarmed.'

The sun had gathered strength, outlining deep shadows around the tall cliffs beyond the man, dimming the sand. Unnerved, I watched the dark shape move towards me, crowding me. My eyes, now adjusted to the shade, made the man out more clearly.

He had the ramrod posture of a military man, his walking stick furled under one arm. I made out white hair trimmed to a crew-cut, pale blue eyes, a square-cut jaw. The straight back, the measured steps, looked quite springy. A veteran, possibly. He had that bearing. Standing, I realised that the facial skin and lines showed him to be over seventy. Had he been on active service in World War II?

He'd come far too close for my peace of mind, even though he bowed in old-fashioned courtesy. The white hair blended well with the very fair skin, the pale eyes had a keen penetrating look. North German...Prussian, I guessed – because he bowed from the waist down, like a toy soldier.

'Greetings, dear lady.' The genial voice had the guttural clipped tones of a native German speaker. He clicked his heels and something from the past stirred in my mind. He was wearing a black jacket, black plus fours and highly-polished black leather boots. Jackboots! It all came flooding back, and with it fears I thought I'd buried for ever.

Buried, perhaps – but not decayed. I was a child again, in Vienna in 1938, just after Hitler marched into Austria – storm troopers pounding the streets, waving from thundering tanks. I shuddered.

The man's years disappeared as I took in the arrogant posture, the piercing blue eyes, the fair complexion. I froze, unable to greet him back.

He went on smiling, unaware. 'The best time of the day is always before noon.' He squinted at the sky. 'Before the sun becomes too white and makes all the colours harsh.'

The voice was meant to be persuasive, even charming. I found it menacing and backed away. 'Yes,' I managed to whisper. I frowned. What the hell was wrong with me? This was Guernsey, it was over fifty years since Nazi troops crossed the border into Austria, the man was elderly, he wasn't in uniform – he was merely wearing black civilian clothes. Unusual for walking on a beach, maybe, but hardly threatening. Perhaps he was in mourning. I forced volume into my voice. 'Of course.'

'Please, do not disturb yourself.' The English was perfect, too perfect. And I was right. These were the phonemes of my mother tongue, though harsher than Viennese intonations. I'm not keen on the German they speak in Berlin and the North. Half-swallowed snarling syllables which don't have the lilt of the softer, more southern tones.

I pulled myself together. 'I'm so sorry. Am I trespassing?'

A discreet laugh. 'Well, yes. This is private property. But it doesn't belong to me. It used to belong to a very dear friend of mine, as a matter of fact. She passed away a few weeks ago. I've come to pay my last respects.'

So the black did signify mourning. He was courteous, even winsome. Why was I so uneasy? I moved back, picked up the anorak I'd been sitting on. 'Oh, dear. I hadn't realised there were private beaches here...'

I'd turned my profile to him. When I looked back he'd screwed his eyes into slits as he looked at my nose, then at me, in a different way. Something about the thin tight lips reminded me of street scenes in Vienna after the Hitler's triumphant annexation of Austria. Men in black uniforms forcing helpless people to scrub the streets for no better reason than that they were Jews; lorries screeching to a halt outside our apartment house in the dead of night, dragging off the Scheiderbauers living on the same floor;

my mother packing essentials and rushing us to the Paris train.

'You most certainly are an early visitor.' He looked at me intently. 'Not a native, I can tell. I know Guernsey well because I spent one of the war years here. I wish I could have stayed for all of it. It is a most beautiful island.'

My dry mouth made me choke. Had he been with the Wehrmacht Occupying Forces – perhaps one of the German officers in charge of the island at that time? 'You mean in the '40s?'

He nodded, the pale blue eyes searching my face. 'For nearly a year. I was transferred to the Eastern front in 1941. How time flies. That will be fifty years ago this summer.'

All feelings of contentment fled. My dismay must have been obvious. Then I stood proud, profile thrust out, knowing he'd made the judgement that had killed millions in the Holocaust. The Nazis had been defeated. Allowing this man to dent my self-esteem would give them retrospective victory.

He turned on his heel and looked at the sea. Two people were paddling towards us in a two-seater kayak. The waves were stronger now, the tide rolling in. The canoe was gliding on to the beach. I hated myself for being a coward, but relief rushed over me at the sight of the couple about to disembark.

The young man got out first, then helped out a young woman heavy with child. Her face gleamed radiant as she looked up at him. She stood, hair streaming out behind her, the yellow-white light of the noonday sun turning it into flame. The wind billowed her smock around her bulge, emphasising it.

The screaming took me by surprise. Gulls again, I presumed, swivelling round. And then I took in the face of the man I'd just been talking to. Distorted features had turned it into a gargoyle of horror as he goggled, not at me, but beyond me at the young people. It wasn't the noise of gulls I'd heard. At first I couldn't work out what he said, but after a while the constantly repeated phrases made sense to me.

'Dass ist doch nicht möglich, dass kann doch nicht sein!' he was howling, his voice pitched high above the roar of waves – 'It's just not possible, it can't be happening!' I pulled my anorak protectively around me. He really was German, and he did have the clipped tight accents typical of the north. 'Wo kommst du denn her, du verfluchtes Ekel, du verdammtes Weibstück?' he sobbed, a despairing wail in his voice – 'Where have you come from, you repulsive horror, you damned bloody bitch?' He stumbled, staggered towards the rocks, then swayed and slumped slowly to the sand.

The couple were staring at us. They couldn't have made out what he'd howled, even if they understood German, but of course they'd grasped something peculiar was going on. The young man strode towards us, frowning at the German, then at me. 'Is this man bothering you?'

I shook my head. 'Not me,' I said. 'It sounded as though he was swearing at your wife. Is he someone you know?'

He walked over to the huddled figure. 'Certainly not. Never seen him before in my life.'

Whoever the man was, whatever connection he had with the Third Reich, he didn't know me. Personally, that is. He knew me racially.

He didn't know the young man, either. So why was he yelling at the young woman, calling her names? There was nothing obviously Semitic about her, and he only saw her from a distance.

'Just before you arrived he told me he'd been stationed here during the war,' I said. 'For a year. But that was at least twenty-five years before either of you were born. Yet he's got some idea that he knows your wife.' I shrugged my shoulders at the young woman coming up behind the young man.

'You mean he was shouting at me?' she asked.

'In German, yes. And he was being abusive.'

She nodded, as though it made some sort of sense to her. 'Exactly what did he say?' she wanted to know.

I could only remember the gist of it. Words of long ago were still ringing in my ears. 'He called you the equivalent of an abomination, a bloody whore.'

'Charming.' The young man's features had taken on a furious look. 'You mean all that garbage was in German?'

38

'Yes. Very peculiar...' What was this man doing here? It wasn't just his black clothes, or my prejudiced guess at his politics, which had unnerved me. He didn't belong here, but he certainly qualified for some of my memories of Nazis strutting Viennese streets.

He was leaning back against the rocks, his mouth dropped open, his eyes bulging out. 'Du kannst doch nicht am Leben sein!' he spluttered, arms wide, the stick raised and pointed at the young woman.

She turned questioning eyes to me. 'He says you can't possibly be alive,' I translated for her.

Her partner had gone back to the kayak and was grappling with it, dragging it up the beach behind him, then lifting it over his head, so he couldn't see the loathing in the German's eyes, or the black arms raised, giving the man a vulture look.

The German was standing again, the stick held up. He was about to strike a pregnant woman! Feelings of fury I'd subdued as a child overcame prudence. I pushed ahead of her, threw myself at the man's hands, twisted the stick out of them and flung it away.

He crumpled back on to the sand. 'Wo kommst du her?' he moaned, cupping his head in his hands, as though afraid it would fall off.

I grabbed the girl's arm and tried to pull her to the cliff path. She shook me off. 'What's he saying now?'

'He wants to know where you've come from. I take it he thinks you're a ghost from the past.' I was still trying to pull her away. 'He must be mixing you up with someone else – he said he was visiting an old friend. Whoever he is, you don't want to stay around.'

He'd stopped making any sound, but spittle was drooling out of his mouth, showing a mixture of rage and fear.

The girl and I had reached the safety of the cliff path. 'What else did you say he shouted out?'

'Apparently you have no right to be alive. He's got some notion that it isn't possible,' I repeated a rough translation for her.

The young man had reached the man in black and was standing near him, the kayak poised like an enormous sombrero.

The girl was still puzzled rather than frightened. 'There's

something really wrong. I think he's having a kind of fit.' Her forehead creased into frown lines and her face showed concern. 'I'm a nurse, you see. I think he needs help.' She began to move back towards him.

It wasn't my business, but I couldn't stop myself. There was an evil aura about that man, and she was a young woman shortly to give birth. 'I don't think...' I began, and put out a restraining hand.

'We must do something!'

'You shouldn't even try.' Rational thought was flooding back. 'It could bring on your labour.'

She ignored me and started towards him. He gave a shout, his jaw dropped open, his hands pushed out to hold her off. 'Nicht weiter – no further' he croaked, clearly terrified she'd come right up to him. Then his voice disappeared into a sort of gulp which turned into a choke. He clutched his chest, doubled over.

'It looks as though he's having a heart attack.' She sounded calm, used to it.

Her partner had put the kayak down and was staring at the man. 'We're going to need help. I can't manage him up that steep climb by myself, and the tide'll be coming in at a fair lick. The most useful thing you two can do is raise the alarm. I'll stay and see he doesn't drown.'

'But...'

'I want you to go, Dominique. Now!' He steered her round and pushed her up to the path.

'I'll make sure your wife's all right,' I promised. The young woman and I began to clamber up to the cliff top. 'My car's not far.' The man had looked as though he'd lapsed into unconsciousness. In spite of my loathing for what I took him to be, I knew I had to try to help.

'That's all right,' the young woman said. 'We're camping at the house.' I took it she was referring to the house which went with the private beach. 'I'm Dominique Mansell, by the way. And that was my husband Sebastian.'

'Ruth Samuels,' I introduced myself. 'I gather I've been trespassing. I'm terribly sorry.'

She laughed. 'Don't think we'll worry about that just now. The whole place is in a very run-down state, though it was lovely once. It used to be the Seigneurie.'

'Are you–'

'Look, that's the gardener's cottage, just off to the right.'

I noticed another small track leading to a building I hadn't taken in when I'd climbed down. So that was why the path was so beautifully kept. There was a resident gardener. Seigneur was the French word for lord. The whole thing must be part of an estate of some sort.

'He's lived here all his life and knows this place like the back of his hand. You carry on, don't worry about all this. He'll make sure that everything's seen to properly.' Dazzlingly white teeth smiled at me as she began to walk towards the cottage.

The door opened and a man walked out. A wiry older man who stared at me without any indication of a smile.

I stopped and waited, unsure what to do. I heard her urging the man towards the beach in what sounded partly like the French I'd learned at school, and partly like the patois I knew some of the older natives used. Dominique hurried towards the cottage and went in. To phone for help, I assumed. She turned inside the door and waved goodbye, then firmly shut me out.

The gardener watched her go, glanced at me but jogged past without a word. There didn't seem to be much to do but leave.

I found the Saab, drove to my new home, unloaded, and then parked the car in the car park up the road. I walked back and into the little courtyard at the back of Riande House, looked at the windows of Lascervelle next door, but saw no sign of anyone living there. Had Matthew changed his mind? Put the place up for sale? The following day a man crashed out of Lascervelle and bumped into me. Younger than the Frelé brothers – late forties, perhaps. Shorter, thickset, dressed in jeans and a dirty T-shirt. He didn't apologise, just turned and walked rapidly away. Perhaps Matthew had already sold the house. I felt an absurd and disproportionate sense of loss. Ridiculous to miss someone I'd only met twice.

Curious about the incident on the little beach I made a number of enquiries. But I couldn't trace a young couple called Mansell. No one recognised my description of the pretty bay, nor could I find it again.

I didn't have any luck tracking down a heart-attack victim at the island's hospital, either. All the staff could tell me was that a patient had been transferred to Southampton General by helicopter the day of my arrival. But I couldn't find out his name, or his nationality.

I don't like unsolved mysteries, but I was busy settling in. And I wasn't keen on the memories the incident had stirred up. I decided to call it quits.

CHAPTER SIX

Old-fashioned Gardening was to be a lavishly illustrated guide to tending a garden in the style of the more leisurely days before World War II. I concentrated on working up the text, and then found I needed further illustrations. No doubt the Channel Islands could supply me with the right garden to photograph. Life on Guernsey was caught in a beguiling time warp of sixty years ago, during the relative peace of the 1930s. I decided to explore the less populated parts of the island, hoping to find something exceptional.

I walked up to the car park and loaded the car for a day trip one glorious late May morning. My new Minolta Dynax 7000i hung reasonably lightly across my shoulders. I'd been reluctant about it, but had abandoned my reliable Canon A1. It had done sterling work, but the Dynax sported automatic focus. I was finding it difficult to adjust my trusty Vivitar lens to the correct focal lengths, so I'd bought the Dynax dedicated Sigma 28–70 zoom for the new camera. It was light, had a reasonably short focus, and was of excellent quality. And I needed my tripod to hold the camera steady, to produce professional shots. Even the auto focus system wouldn't be able to overcome camera shake.

The car park was crowded. I passed a white Maserati cabriolet, and found myself irritated that I hadn't bought the equivalent in the Saab. A man opening the boot looked, somehow, familiar. He stared past me, but I realised I'd seen him before. He'd come out of Lascervelle the day after I'd arrived. And disappointed me by not being one of the Frelé brothers or their wives. Was he one of the sons, perhaps? I didn't think so. He didn't look the type to own a car like that. So could the car belong to Matthew Frelé, and this man was a caretaker looking after it – and the house – until Matthew moved in?

The sun rose high and brilliant in the sky. I'd have to wait for softer light for my photography, so I decided to fill in time by having another try at finding Horseshoe Bay. All roads seemed to point toward Petit Bôt, as I'd often been told. It did seem quite similar.

I parked the Saab and searched for the water lane trickling down. These enchanting lanes were important up to the middle of the nineteenth century, and have a stream trickling down the centre or side of the lane. The one I found wasn't the same – I'd have recognised the plants – but it was pretty. The sun was gathering force, fingers of shadow glancing off the tall cliffs, painting the sand with jagged shapes. Startled, I saw a dark outline move. Another visitor. Another man on his own. I felt a sort of panic rising up in me.

'Never forget a face,' the man's voice said. Not friendly, but not unfriendly either. Non-committal, I suppose. 'Thought it best to let you know. Worked out all right.'

He walked right up to me, nodded, then turned and walked off again with that slow measured tread that comes from tending gardens. It took me a little while to work out who he was. By the time I did he'd already reached a rowing boat beached on the shore, and tossed a pitchfork loaded with seaweed into it. I finally realised he was the gardener, the man Dominique Mansell had gone to fetch to help her husband rescue the heart-attack victim.

So I'd been right. That German was a survivor. 'Wait a minute!' I shouted as I ran after him. He didn't turn round. He pushed the boat out to sea and began to row away, not looking back. There wasn't anything for me to do except return to the car.

The familiar drive out to Forest didn't yield any interesting gardens. I veered off the main road, then took the turning leading to **Sausmarez Manor**. The public is allowed access on certain days, and today was one of them. I thought it might be useful to stroll through the gardens if there weren't too many holidaymakers there. I took it easy, parked, wandered out on to the cliff road, and paced myself to avoid exhaustion before the hard work of taking pictures. I wondered again whether I should try to find a small cart to put my gear in; a golf cart, for instance. Even light modern photographic equipment can feel heavy after a surprisingly short time.

The mesembryanthemums were in full bloom, opening their daisy petals to the sun, their mix of gaudy colours enlivening the native greens. Some of the balmiest weather in the British Isles, I reminded myself, feeling smug. Hardly ever any frosts...

'Is photography a hobby of yours, or part of your work?'

I'd arrived at one of those marvellous views at the top of a cliff. And there was Matthew, easel set up, dabbing the canvas. Except it wasn't a canvas – he was using a piece of hardboard. Cheaper, and available from any builder's merchant. So he'd arrived, and I hadn't even noticed he'd moved in. How could I have missed that? He was standing in the lee of a tall outcrop, sheltering in the shade.

'Work.' I wasn't keen on lengthy discussions about it. Photography has never been anything but a chore for me. 'Oils or acrylics?'

'Always acrylics for the sketches. I like to catch the mood fast.' He took the hardboard off the easel, stacked it on the ground against the rock face, and then carefully turned it away so that I couldn't see what he'd done. Secretive as ever. 'Which work d'you use that lens for? The detective agency or the gardening?'

'Neither,' I said. 'I'm one of the nosiest paparazzi, intent on the Lieutenant-Governor.'

He leaned against the rock, feet crossed, grinning at me. 'Your research is lousy. His country house is on the north side of the island.'

I shrugged. 'The truth is very boring. I need more pictures for my new book. I was hoping to find a garden kept in the old-fashioned way.'

He laughed.

'That strikes you as funny?'

'If you'll settle for someone less illustrious than the Lieutenant-Governor, I can introduce you to a Guernseyman who gardens in just that way.' The smile abruptly left his face. 'If you like, that is.

45

If you don't think I'm interfering.'

'So you still know some of the locals?'

'A few escape to England occasionally. And visit me. One or two have brought their gardens back to pre-war glories.' He looked at my equipment and then at me. 'They're rich enough to indulge their hobby.'

'I'd love the chance to see a garden like that,' I said eagerly. 'I'm looking for one started in Victorian times and kept in roughly the same way ever since.'

'That could be true of Charles's, though the Occupation is bound to have had an effect. We all had to grow what vegetables we could, you know.' He'd pronounced the Christian name the French way. 'I'm staying with Charles Grichard. He lives quite close by.'

'You haven't moved into Lascervelle House?' Another oddity, but it did explain why I hadn't come across him.

'Not yet. The others are going to be staying there.' He hunched powerful shoulders, as though that precluded him.

'Others?'

'My brothers.' Throwaway voice. 'All three have been over for a couple of weekends. This time they're bringing wives and families.'

'For the Bank Holiday, I suppose.'

'You've got it all worked out, as usual.' A long look. 'You'll have noticed someone else going in and out. One of my cousins is staying there for the time being.'

Surely that rather unattractive character I'd seen wasn't a cousin? Though, now that I'd thought about it, the white Maserati wasn't Matthew's style. 'There must be plenty of room for all of you. It's a big house.' Why should he be the one to be excluded?

'Not really. You've forgotten Jake – Jean-Jacques – has a large family.' His voice sounded firm, but he dropped one of his paintbrushes.

A rift? More likely he was staying away because he was a loner, unused to the pandemonium of family life. Or perhaps he preferred not to be involved. 'I thought you didn't have any other relatives.'

'What?' The frown turned into a grin. 'You're slipping, Ruth.

That's not what I told you. I said I didn't have any relatives living on the island. Actually I have two cousins.'

So he'd remembered precisely what he'd said. 'The one at Lascervelle doesn't live on Guernsey?'

'He roams around. France mostly. He's been at the house since my grandmother was taken ill. He was her favourite grandson.'

So that unprepossessing man was definitely one of the cousins. Matthew busied himself packing his gear. Had he finished painting already? And how much fiddling about does it take to put a couple of paint brushes and a palette away? There was something odd here. Perhaps Miss Marple had not been altogether a misnomer. I quite fancy myself as an amateur sleuth. Indeed, I have a certain talent for digging up family secrets. This situation smelt ripe for unearthing. And I wasn't averse to knowing more about Matthew.

'I've changed the yellow Volvo for something more suitable. An anaemic-blue three-door Saab 900.' I picked up my tripod. 'They were out of yellow. But there's plenty of room for the paintbrushes.'

He hoisted his gear easily over his shoulders. 'I'll take the tripod,' he announced rather than offered, and swung it just as casually as the rest of the equipment across his back.

I wondered how to break down the barricades that had been set up. Ambivalence showed in his carrying the equipment but keeping his distance as we walked towards the car. But he was the one to make his presence known; that had to be significant. We walked in silent unease while I tried to work out whether I really wanted to be involved with this strange, but very appealing, man. No contest, really. Sexy, intriguing, artistic. Nothing was going to stop me.

'I haven't come across any of your brothers,' I started tentatively. 'Is Mark here?'

'I said all three.' An impatient turning of the head. 'The clan's arriving later today. Once they do you won't be able to miss them.' The voice grew fainter as he stalked ahead. 'The cousin's name is Todd, by the way. He's the elder of two brothers. No doubt you'll want to know the pedigree: Todd and Milton. They're sons of my grandmother's younger son Michel.' He slowed and waited for me to catch up.

'Your paternal grandmother?'

He stopped short, leaving me to stride ahead. I turned back to see an expression of loss, almost desperation, on the handsome face. 'I never knew my maternal one.'

He'd said Michel was his grandmother's younger son, and he was precise. So the paternal grandmother had had two sons. Even if she'd had daughters they couldn't have had children because I'd just been told that Todd was one of two cousins, both sons of the younger son. The thing which struck me as noteworthy was that the Christian names sounded distinctly unGuernseyan, and very American. Had Michel Frelé married an American heiress because, as the younger son, he wouldn't inherit on Guernsey?

'I don't want to pry, but I still don't see why you're not staying in your own house.' Bad strategy, but I couldn't resist it. This time I'd turned and was waiting for him.

He stopped abruptly. He looked as though he was about to speak, then seemed to change his mind.

Had I offended him again, ruined the chance of a relationship yet again? My temper made me think I didn't care. I seethed as we marched on silently. I opened the car's boot and Matthew began to load the gear. I noticed he had a good eye for using space, so he wasn't a ham-fisted artistic type. I thought again how I'd known as soon as I met Mark that I was looking for someone like him, but not him. I knew well enough that it was Matthew. If he and I clicked I was determined we should really get to know each other. I liked his paintings, I told myself. But of course I knew very well that that wasn't the only thing, or even the most important thing, I liked about him. 'So now your brothers have taken over Lascervelle, even though you own it?'

'It suits me to stay with Charles, Ruth. All those young people scrabbling about put me off painting.' He grimaced, then shrugged. 'Let's go and get Charles to show you his garden.'

'I can hardly wait.'

He held his hand out for my keys. 'Shall I drive? Otherwise I have to direct you through rather tricky territory. Charles's place is well off the beaten track and a bit tortuous by car.'

I'd already decided he might as well. Why work when you don't have to? And the Saab was a bit on the heavy side for manoeuvring along Guernsey's narrow country lanes, let alone negotiating any tracks that getting to Charles Grichard's place might involve. Besides, the car was hemmed in by an MG which was now parked within inches of me.

'If you like.'

'Right.'

Matthew clambered in from the passenger side, and I followed. I sat and envied the way he turned the 900 in the small space available.

He drove back in the direction of Forest, then headed up a steep lane followed by a left turn into a hairpin bend within a few hundred yards. I held my breath. The passenger side made it round the embankment with half an inch to spare. Matthew revved on, undaunted. What would he do if we met another car? The possibility didn't seem to trouble him.

I'd lost track of where we were going. The twisting lanes, bordered much of the time by high hedges, wound past. Even someone with an outstanding sense of direction would find it taxing to keep their bearings. At last Matthew turned off the lane and bore right up a small narrow track which led to a stone house set on top of a cliff. It was neatly fronted by a large circular drive. I could see the sea view beyond as he parked the car. It was as spectacular as any I'd seen on the island, and oddly familiar.

'Isn't that Petit Bôt Bay down there?' As I said it I realised it was too small for that. Was I looking at what I'd christened Horseshoe Bay, or was that wishful thinking? We were standing to one side, and the shape wasn't entirely clear.

'Confusing, isn't it? Actually, it's Bôtnoir, another little bay by Petit Bôt. It's very similar. Bôtnoir Manor is next door to Charles as the crow flies, but five miles as the car drives.'

'You mean one could walk across?'

He turned off the ignition. 'Using the green lanes, yes. Twenty minutes at the outside. There's a bit of scrambling involved, with a water lane leading down to the bay, but it's quite beautiful. I'll show you sometime.'

49

CHAPTER SEVEN

Grichard House, set apart from a small enclave of old cottages hugging the hill a little further down, was unexpectedly dominating. Built in stone, with a tiled roof, it was remarkable for the two rounded turrets at either end. A miniature fortress, rather like a small chateau with a hint of Normandy in the stark lines. The turrets flanked two rows of windows, five at the top and four set below, with the space under the fifth taken up by a studded oak door. As we walked up to it I saw the sun ahead of us, winking reflections from the sea. So the front faced north. It was closely covered in climbing roses interspersed with honeysuckle.

Mermaid was evident at once. The shiny foliage glistened invitingly, and several of the exquisite single yellow blooms had already opened to the day. The balmy climate of the Channel Isles was perfect for this, my favourite climber. I tore my eyes away, swept them over the front garden laid out with shrubs, anticipating the garden proper with pleasure.

'You've noticed the climbers. They're not at their best yet.'

'Indeed. A wonderful choice. Mermaid's my favourite, but I love Zéphirine Drouhin as well.'

'How can you tell it's Zéphirine? It isn't in flower yet.'

I glowed inside. Perhaps I'd impressed him. 'I'd be in trouble if I couldn't. Rather like you not being able to tell an oil from an acrylic. The red stems, the lack of thorns, the delicate way it grows, the leaf.' I went up closer to examine the other plants. 'And this one's Etoile de Hollande, I'm pretty sure,' I said, moving towards the dark red flowers and sniffing. 'The scent is unmistakable. And there's that old favourite, Madame Alfred Carrière. That's so good on a north wall.' The pale pink buds were already there, but hadn't yet turned to white. Matthew was standing politely, waiting for me to finish. I stopped burbling on. 'I can hardly wait to see the actual garden. D'you think your friend will mind?'

'Not if there's something in it for him. Are you planning to name his garden in your book, or just take pictures?'

'I always offer a photo credit. Whatever your friend prefers.'

Matthew tugged at the bell-pull twice in quick succession, then let go. He slipped an enormous cast iron key, the sort one sees for sale at antique fairs, into the lock, turned it, pushed the door wide and stood aside. We went through to an entrance hall: neat, small, leading off to several rooms.

This was the second time I'd put myself into a precarious position with this man. How did I know there was someone else living here? Was I being naïve? Then I relaxed. One of the doors facing us opened, inquisitive small eyes busied themselves round it, and a figure minced through. The movements were slow but delicate, as though used to managing in a small space. Somewhat effeminate, in fact, and it occurred to me that 'Charl' could be short for Charlotte. I felt relieved.

That was short-lived. Matthew had referred to 'he' and 'him', and I could see 'Charl' was definitely a man. Apart from the male garb, which no longer proves anything, there was dark stubble on the chin. Five o'clock shadow, though it wasn't quite noon. Late riser, I guessed – retired, or without a job. Unmarried, perhaps widowed, and he hadn't bothered to shave as yet.

'Phone call-' he began. He saw me, squinted the small eyes under bushy eyebrows almost shut, then smiled. One side of his mouth twisted upwards, turning the smile into a sardonic leer. 'Ah. C-company, I see.'

'Charles Grichard, Ruth Samuels. Excuse me for a moment, Ruth. I'll go and answer that.'

Charles's eyebrows had settled down, but his eyes were almost closed. I noted the stocky Guernsey body, vestiges of dark hair now pepper and salt and receding into a widower's peak. Sixty-something, a contemporary of Matthew's. He was wearing old-fashioned flannels with an ancient tweed jacket. He removed a small object from the right-hand pocket and put a pipe-stem into the corner of his mouth. I wondered whether it was the effect of years of holding the stem that had made his smile crooked. Maybe it came like that.

The narrowed eyes opened and scanned my face. 'Have you come to l-lunch? There isn't m-much, I'm afraid. Just the remains of yesterday's j-joint.'

I didn't like this man. Not because of the slight stutter, but he made it clear he'd categorised me as one of that ubiquitous species, a devoted follower of Matthew's. 'Not lunch, actually.' Embarrassment at having to explain what I was doing here without Matthew's support made me hesitate. 'I was hoping to...'

'For goodness sake, Charles.' Matthew was back, his voice severe. 'Ruth hasn't come to eat you out of hearth and home. She's here to see your garden, if you have no objections.' He walked up to Charles, forcing him to move on. 'And she's not after any of your produce, either. She writes on gardening, and she's looking for a place like yours. To photograph, that is, not to beg plants - or even cuttings.'

I gathered Charles Grichard was a typical Guernseyman, complete with their reputation for thrift. That often goes with the amassing of fortunes, I remembered.

The house was well looked after, and he certainly wasn't poor. The furniture was period, the furnishings opulent. By now we'd progressed through to the living room. Victorian settles and chairs, a fine vitrine, two bookcases. An Erskine Nicol in pride of place above the mantelpiece, depicting the gloom and doom of a Scottish seascape. And at the far end huge French windows led out to a magnificent octagonal conservatory with a quarry-tiled floor and cane furniture.

'You mean to say it's a b-business p-proposition, what?'

I could see Matthew's nostrils distend.

'I'm afraid publishers can't afford to pay for permissions to photograph,' I put in quickly, 'or even for professional photography. That's why they prefer authors who can take their own pictures.'

The stooped shoulders stooped a little more.

'But I would be very happy to mention you in the acknowledgments. And Grichard House, if that is what you'd like.' I smiled. Maybe this man would be more trouble than the photos were worth.

The small eyes closed again. 'That s-sounds quite interesting, don't you know.' His lids flicked up, beady eyes examined me from hat to boots. 'I planted a vineyard a f-few years ago – only twenty-five vergées, but that should do for what I have in mind. I'm about to p-produce my first bottles this autumn. All p-publicity helps, don't you know.' I was treated to an intense stare.

I spotted a fellow gardening enthusiast and felt the usual thrill. 'You planted vines? How exciting. Which grape varieties?'

His eyes glowed enthusiasm. 'Mostly Seyval. That works on Jersey, so I thought it should do well enough here. Also some Reichensteiner and a small amount of Pinot Meunier. A few vergées are planted with fruit trees. Apples and pears.' The stutter had disappeared as his enthusiasm increased.

'Wonderful. I'll be delighted to do anything I can.' I couldn't remember the number of vergées to the acre. 'How many acres altogether?'

'About ten planted with vines, and a couple of orchard.'

'Quite manageable,' I smiled. I couldn't believe my luck. A vineyard could easily be a useful sideline for an amateur, exactly the sort of material I was looking for to add to my book. 'Can you really make that work on a commercial basis?'

'I expect to produce about ten thousand bottles of wine a year eventually.' His eyes disappeared again. 'For a gourmet market, needless to say. A little hobby for my retirement.'

'Before that Charles was one of our more celebrated Conseillers,' Matthew put in.

'Really?' That didn't sound like anything to do with gardening, but I was clearly expected to show interest. 'What is a Conseiller?'

'An officer elected by the States of Election for a six-year term of office. Charles is still serving a year. He's very well qualified, of course. He is – well, was, until he retired – one of our most distinguished lawyers. We call them advocates.'

'She's only interested in my gardening skills, Beau.' Charles stared at me, examining my shirt tucked into my jeans, lingering on my boots. He made me feel clumsy, a cow in a china shop. 'Where's your camera?'

'All my stuff's in the car.'

He looked at the grandfather clock in the corner. The tick was loud, reverberating the time. As though on cue it struck twelve. 'Maybe you'd like a drink?' I saw Matthew's head swivel in surprise, then his eyes met mine and he blinked. 'I make cider and perry as well as wine,' Charles went on. 'And I make a damned good p-perry brandy – Bonbeurré Grichard I call it. I'm trying my hand at a cider one, as well. Toying with calling it Pommegriche.'

'Is that a kind of Calvados?'

His hands were folded together as though in prayer. 'In a way. Did some research in Normandy, don't you know. Plus f-ferreted around in a couple of Irish whisky distilleries. Then tootled off to Madeira, looking at oak barrels for maturing the spirit. What about t-trying some?'

'I'd love to. What cider apples d'you grow?'

A glint as he notched me one rung up his ladder. 'A couple of the old Normans – bittersweets are the thing.'

'Do you now.' I tried to keep my voice from betraying my excitement. So far I hadn't even thought of adding a cider or perry orchard to my mythical garden. That would give it a seriously romantic touch. 'Which ones?'

'You r-really want to know the details?'

'You don't know what you've started, Ruth!'

I waved Matthew's warning aside. 'I certainly do. Especially where you buy your trees. I'm sure many readers would love to make their own cider, but it's hard to find the old cider-apple varieties.'

'What a lark! There's a nursery in Normandy which still has some s-stock. They're prepared to graft for me.' His face looked almost beatific. 'I've planted Strawberry Norman and Upright French. And a few bittersharps: Foxwhelp, Skyrme's Kernel,

Joeby Crab.' He opened a cupboard and brought out a bottle. 'I like the sweets to mix in with the others, don't you know. My favourite's Cider Lady's Finger and Eggleton Styre, but I use a f-few modern varieties as well. The thing is, people prefer smooth cider nowadays. So I grow Chisel Jersey, Dabinett, Yarlington Mill.' He took three glasses from his vitrine and poured from the bottle. 'Try it. Pommegriche is my first stab at cider brandy.' His voice was very plummy now – as though he'd been to an English public school. Possibly Downside, I realised.

I rolled the brandy round my tongue. Innocent at first, then the smooth liquid turned fiery, threatening my throat. I waited for several seconds. 'Perfection,' I said at last, genuinely admiring. 'Why bother with apple if you can produce pear? Surely that's more unusual, and would have scarcity value?'

'Thing is, one has to make the damned market,' he explained. 'Tough enough as it is.'

'Absolutely. But the Somerset Cider Brandy Company didn't start distilling till 1987, and they've done very well.' I took another sip of the brandy. 'This is sensational. Will you produce the brandy commercially, or just the cider?'

Matthew sipped the spirit, lifted his eyebrows, then put his glass down. 'Bit on the sweet side for my taste.'

I almost laughed. Sweet certainly wasn't for his temperament.

Charles pursed his lips at the criticism. 'Why don't you f-finish that pais au fou you were raving about, Beau? Then Ruth can stay to a p-proper lunch.'

Matthew shrugged. 'Not that much more to do. Already put it in the slow oven of the Aga this morning.'

'What's pais au fou?'

'A bean casserole. Very popular on the islands. The Guernsey variety is made with haricot beans, soaked overnight and then casseroled with beef or pork, carrots and seasoning. I've evolved my own recipe. A whole ox tongue, with any vegetables I can find to add to the beans, and whatever herbs happen to be in season.' He picked up his glass of Pommegriche. 'I could add a bit of this for an extra fillip.'

'R-right you are. We'll leave you to it, Beau.' Charles moved towards the French windows, opened them. 'There's some nier beurre in the freezer, old man. You could make an egg custard to go with that.' He looked at me and motioned his head away from the living room. I followed through the conservatory and on into the garden.

'Nier beurre?'

'A thick type of apple sauce made with cider. I always use Grenadier.'

'You grow Grenadier? That's marvellous! It's the best saucing apple there is, in my opinion. Frothy and thick, with a soft feel.'

'I'll be d-darned! You've grown it?' His smile had warmed as he nodded. 'Obviously you've used it.'

'I had an orchard when I lived in Somerset.'

We walked along a carefully tended gravel path, the grass trimmed neatly on either side. Charles walked slowly, gingerly picking his way among the rock fragments. He wasn't limping, exactly, but he walked as though he felt each pebble. It struck me as overly sensitive, irritated me. Was he gay? Was Matthew? Did that explain his brothers' dismissive attitude?

That was certainly a disturbing thought. I tried to put it to the back of my mind, to think it through later. Meanwhile I looked around and couldn't believe my luck. I'd stayed on, in spite of Charles's idiosyncrasies, because his place was precisely what I'd been looking for. A central lawn, long herbaceous borders backed by espalier fruit trees, shrubs fashionable from Victorian times growing strongly in a shrubbery beyond. The grass was virtually weed-free. It had been cut with a roller cutter to show the stripes.

'I suppose your family have lived here for generations?'

He nodded. 'Matter of fact they have.'

'And your children? Will they take over from you?'

'Haven't got any.' He looked at the liquid in his glass, put his pipe back into his pocket, and drank. 'Never married, d'you see. An only ch-child.' His shoe moved delicately between the pebbles. 'Last of my line, matter of fact.'

I looked at him again. Did that prove he was gay? The dainty steps, the tasteful furnishings, the emphasis on creativity. Not that I cared at all what his sexual inclinations were. But I did wonder about two bachelors being together when both of them owned substantial houses. Of course I was particularly interested in Matthew's orientation.

I pushed my thoughts back to my book. 'So would you mind if I took some pictures? I'd be very happy to add a small piece about any unusual vegetables or dessert fruit you've planted. D'you grow any?'

'Sounds tickety-boo. Actually, I do grow s-several eating grapes. Précose de Malingre, Pirovano, Chasselas Doré. In the walled garden beyond that wrought-iron gate.'

'The Chasselas. That's Royal Muscadine, isn't it?'

'That a fact? I've no idea.'

'I believe so. And the climate is mild enough for you to grow them outside?'

'Absolutely. They do quite well m-most years.'

'Terrific. I'll list the varieties of grape you grow, and the cider apples.'

Was I imagining it, or did he worry unduly where he placed his feet? I saw his shoes were exceptionally small. He placed them cautiously, evidently avoiding the gravel when he could, often choosing to walk on grass instead. Suddenly his eyes darted at me. 'M-matter of fact I don't think I've come across your work, and I read quite a f-few books on gardening. Can you mention a c-couple of titles?'

'*The Self-sufficient Garden* is the best seller so far. But I've done several others. *Blooms for the Winter* did very well, and you may have come across *The Scented Rock Garden*. My own favourite is *Roses through the Ages*.'

His eyes danced delight. 'Capital! That explains it. I g-gather you write under a pseudonym.' He stopped, turned towards me, bowed with mock elaboration. 'Elizabeth Pilton, I presume.'

'You've read some of my work.'

'M-matter of fact I read everything remotely original published on gardening. And, yes, I have enjoyed several of your books.'

57

'So may I fetch my camera?'

'What? P-perhaps after lunch.' He moved towards me, his eyes intense, his mouth taking that crooked turn. 'There is one thing while we're on our own.'

The small feet, though treading delicately, looked threatening. I stood my ground. I dislike the invasion of my private space, but I dislike bullying even more.

'Have you known Matthieu – Matthew long?'

My antagonism became a physical reaction. I stepped back slightly, then controlled myself and stopped. 'About three months.' Bared teeth made an attempt at a smile but I felt my eyes staying fixed.

'D-damned sorry, don't you know, but I really must warn you about him.'

That startled me. 'Warn me? Isn't he a friend of yours?'

'A great friend, and an old friend. But he wows all the g-girls. He's got any n-number of lady friends, you know. A real roué.'

He was standing so close to me now that my balance was in jeopardy. My right foot shifted and caught on his shoe. He winced, retreated, eyes focused on my boots.

'How kind of you to put me in the picture. I gather that worries you?'

The laugh was quite unpleasing. 'Not me, my dear lady. I'm talking about you.'

'How very good of you.' This time my grin was genuine. 'No need to worry on my account. We're just neighbours. I've rented Riande House for a year.'

'Riande? That a fact?' He took in the amount of rent per annum. 'So that's the way of it. You thought it would be nice and c-cosy, living next door to him.' The patronising smile of a wise uncle.

It infuriated me, but I managed to laugh it away. 'Not at all. Riande was pure chance. I'd no idea the Frelés came from Guernsey, let alone that they owned Lascervelle.'

'You mean to say you already know his brothers?' The surprise was genuine.

'Actually, I met Mark first. I happened to sit next to him on a flight to the States. One of my sons lives in Boston.'

'So you're married.'

I didn't answer right away. I don't like wearing any kind of jewellery when I'm working, but I keep my wedding ring on, even though it often catches in tendrils or, worse, thorns. 'I live alone,' I volunteered at last, rejecting the word widow.

He looked knowing. 'Meaning your husband left you, I dare say?'

I squeezed my nails against my palms. That didn't stop the red reaching my cheeks. 'In a sort of way.' An innocent dandelion seedling was nestling between two paeony officinalis plants. 'JC Wegulin?' I pointed to the single garnet flowers. 'That's one of the best.' I bent down and pulled the dandelion out.

'Well, he's either l-living with you or he isn't, I s-suppose.' The tone was getting testy.

Having had time to recover, I stood to face him. 'I told you. I live alone.'

'That does m-make you very vulnerable, you know.' His eyes swept over me. 'But if you met Mark first, how c-come you're with Matthew?'

'I'm not with him,' I said. 'He was sketching and I happened to come across him while I was looking for a garden to photograph.'

This time it was a full-blown belly laugh. 'P-pull the other one,' he gasped. 'You may not know it, but he p-planned that.'

There was a limit to what I considered amusing. 'I can't imagine what gives you such a preposterous idea. No one knew I was going out this morning. It was an impulse, on a lovely day. I didn't know where I was heading, so how could Matthew?'

He shrugged. 'It's a small island.'

'For goodness sake! He was there, his painting more or less sketched out, when I arrived.'

'D-did he spot you, or you him?' The laugh was even more irritating than the crooked mouth. 'It's really quite simple, don't you know. He f-followed you, realised where you were heading, brought his gear and showed you something he'd sketched before.'

'This is absurd! He couldn't have followed me. I took the car.'

He smirked. 'Exactly my p-point. He borrowed mine and brought you here in yours. I noticed your Saab from the hall window. My MG was m-missing.'

I had noticed an MG parked next to the Saab. And Matthew had given the impression that he'd walked, or at least I'd got that impression. I covered my unease by bending down to examine the other peonies. Were they Rosea Plena or Rubra Plena? I decided they were too crimson for the Rosea. And they were outstanding plants which must have been there for years. 'It really isn't necessary to make such elaborate arrangements to meet me,' I said. 'A simple telephone call is quite acceptable.'

'Matthew m-might not have wanted you to know of his interest.' Charles tried to put an avuncular arm around my shoulders. It was too much. I ducked and moved out of range. I saw him shrug. 'It's the usual p-pattern repeating itself. He's snared you with that d-damned charm of his. I think you're a t-terrific woman, you know. Talented, good-looking, highly intelligent...'

'You're too kind.'

'The thing is, he won't marry you.'

Did I tell myself Guernsey was fifty years behind the times? Feudal was nearer the mark. 'Nobody's asked him.'

'That's where you're quite wrong. His score must be in the high teens. He's never married, but he's had all the chances any man could wish for.'

I dismissed the gay theory. Sexual jealousy was more like it. 'I've no idea what this is all about, but perhaps I ought to mention that I'm not interested in marrying again.'

'Once bitten, eh?'

'My husband died. We were happily married for thirty-five years.'

His eyes dropped. 'I am s-so sorry; d-devastated. How damed s-stupid of me. Of course I should have guessed. You d-don't like t-talking about it.' Steady eyes looked me full in the face for the first time. 'Look here; I'm very fond of Matthew. He's a marvellous friend, and he's loyal, fascinating, exciting. But he leaves this trail of devastated females of all ages. I just d-didn't want you to be unaware. Many of his ladies know what to expect, and they carry on regardless. My instinct is that you have no idea.'

'Telling her not to have anything to do with me?' Matthew had come up to us, carrying three sherry glasses and a bottle on a tray. 'Here we go, lunch is almost ready. I thought a Madeira would be better than a sherry.' The bottle said Blandy Sercial, my favourite aperitif.

'Right you are. I'm just f-filling her in on your nefarious past.' Charles's tone was assured, untroubled. But his eyes were hardly visible.

'You'd better watch it, Charles. She looks innocent enough, but she'll have noted down everything you said and taken it in evidence.' He handed me a glass of the Blandy. 'She pretends to write on gardening, you know, but actually she's a feisty female bloodhound. Incognito, of course. We can only guess at her real name.'

Charles looked at me with the respect I never get for writing on gardening. 'That a fact? You write detective stories? Another pseudonym, I suppose.'

'That's just a fantasy of Matthew's,' I said, lifting my glass. But I did wonder whether I should start taking notes.

CHAPTER EIGHT

I didn't find it hard to push aside Charles's warnings about Matthew's lady-killer activities. From what I'd seen of him he certainly attracted women of all ages, and in droves. Not, I thought, because he tried to. It just happened – as it had with me, after all. His borrowing the MG rather than walking across to the Petit Bôt cliffs to paint could be explained by not wanting to lug equipment. I wondered why I hadn't thought of that at the time. But his offering to drive me to Grichard House rather than suggesting I follow him in the Saab was – unsettling. Possibly explained by the tortuous journey to the house. I had to find out more about this man. Maybe I should ring the Frelés now staying next door and say hello.

There was no listing of a Frelé at Lascervelle House. There was no listing of a Frelé at all, so the number must be ex-directory. A faint image of old Madame Frelé took shape in my mind. I saw her as tall, upright, severe, a redoubtable figure dominating her family. I envisioned her with four lively boys to look after. I could almost see them as they must have been in the early '40s: intelligent, demanding, brimming with testosterone. A grandmother bringing them up on her own must have found them daunting.

No one had, so far, explained why the parents put themselves at risk of drowning when they had four young sons. What were they doing, anyway? I didn't think I'd quite dare ask. But I wanted to know how the boys had reacted after being orphaned, and how the German Occupation had affected them. Above all, I was curious about the – clearly – strained relationship Matthew had had with his grandmother. I sensed it as the key to his behaviour. Perhaps I could invite Jeanne, or Caroline, over for a coffee.

Suddenly my mind conjured up the Frelé boys, in the living room of a large rambling house I'd never been in, sitting with their eyes round, not speaking, white. Four boys under eleven, told of their parents' death. Their faces masks, their bodies rigid. Except for Matthew. I saw him scowl at his grandmother, scrunching fists tight. I instinctively knew he blamed her, was plotting revenge. I'd seen him go for the four hefty youths in Brixton without a qualm, knew he was capable of violence beyond the norm. What had she done to him or he to her? And why did I picture all this so clearly? What had it to do with me?

I told myself that if I wanted to imagine fictions I should write novels rather than make up stories about people I hardly knew. Better still, I should go out and do the weekend shopping.

I toured Les Roches indifferently, placing an instant coffee jar and a small sack of potatoes into my supermarket trolley. It clanked to a stop as I realised I'd bumped into someone else's. I looked up and straight into Frelé eyes. Slim but not thin, well dressed. Mark.

'Good heavens. Ruth.'

He didn't just look surprised. He looked abashed. More than that. He looked guilty. As well he might. After all his protestations of interest he hadn't been in touch after that dinner party, hadn't bothered to find out when I was moving, or where. And, though I hadn't sent him my Guernsey phone number or address, phone calls and mail were being re-routed.

'Hello, Mark. How are you?'

'Fine, fine.' His eyes blinked rapidly as though that would blot me out. 'How come you're here?' His forehead wrinkled into a concertina. 'Are you on holiday?'

'Matthew didn't tell you?'

'Matthew?' He was too practised in social skills for his jaw to drop, but he sounded astonished.

So his brother hadn't mentioned meeting me, or my living here. I felt irritated – positively slighted. 'We ran into each other.' I tried a winsome smile, but his eyes were cold and unresponsive. 'I've rented a house in St Peter Port for a year. Whilst I'm finishing my book. I haven't decided where to settle yet.'

'You came to Guernsey because of Matthew?' He pushed his trolley against a stack of tins, crashing several down. He made no move to pick them up. 'I would have thought you'd have more sense.'

At your age, was the unspoken rebuke. I started to explain what had really happened, but he wasn't listening. He seemed oddly nervous and preoccupied, as though there was something he wanted to say but couldn't quite bring himself to. Surely he wasn't about to start a Charles Grichard type tirade?

'You'll think I'm interfering, that it's none of my business, but I'd steer clear of my brother, Ruth. I know you're attracted to him, and I'm responsible for introducing you. Take my advice and keep away from him. You'll only get hurt if you don't.'

'I'm an admirer of your brother's work,' I said, trying to retain my dignity. 'I'm trying to persuade him to show his paintings. With a view to selling them.'

'Arrange an exhibition?' More tins came crashing down as he hurled the trolley along the aisle. 'That's utterly absurd.' His nostrils flared, he stood tall, left the loaded trolley where it had landed and strode out of the place without looking back.

I gazed after him. Why was taking an interest in Matthew's paintings unacceptable? Did Mark think Matthew's paintings were rubbish? That wasn't possible. Perhaps he was jealous of his brother's talent. Whatever the reason, I simply couldn't let it go at that. Presumably Matthew was still staying with Charles Grichard. I'd give him a ring there.

'Ruth Samuels? Of course; the lady g-gardener.' Charles's voice on the phone was high and breathless.

I was too outraged to want to bandy small talk, so I didn't raise the small distinction that writing on gardening does not necessarily qualify one for the term gardener. 'Is Matthew there?'

'The headstrong lady g-gardener, not keen t-to take advice.'

'This is ridiculous,' I insisted to Matthew when eventually he mumbled an unenthusiastic hello. 'I came across Mark in the supermarket, quite by chance. He stormed out on me because I said I wanted to persuade you to exhibit your work.'

'Mmm.'

'What's it to do with him?' There was no answer. 'Well? Does it make sense to you?'

The answer took a long time coming. 'Sort of,' he said.

Evasive as usual. 'Could you perhaps enlighten me?'

'Err; well - he's never been a fan.' An uneasy laugh.

Strange. I remembered Jean-Jacques had been keen to encourage Matthew. A rift with Mark as well as the grandmother? 'So what? It's none of his business.' There was no further response, even though I waited a long time. 'Matthew?'

'I can't really say.'

Can't as in it would be indiscreet, or can't because he doesn't know? 'It was extraordinarily uncivil. You must have some idea.'

'Possibly he thinks it unladylike.'

'What?' I'd considered a number of possibilities, though none of them made sense: was Mark the anonymous collector and I was queering his pitch, did he think I'd use the paintings to further my own career, was I buying Matthew? I'd never have worked out 'unladylike'. A euphemism for 'trade', I took it. 'That's preposterous,' I spluttered. 'I know Guernsey's fifty years behind the times, but you're both living in London now. Have done, I gather, for over thirty years.'

'We did live in London. They're – he's – arranging to retire to Guernsey.'

Another surprise. Why, all of a sudden? 'You mean your brothers are going to live next door to me? All of them?'

The voice at the other end was reluctant to the point of being hard to hear. 'Off and on. Just while they look round for suitable homes.' He sounded strained. 'There's a place in the country as well, but that's in a pretty poor state. Jean-Jacques and his wife will take it over. But they'll stay at Lascervelle while Bôtnoir is being done up. At least in part.'

'Bôtnoir?' The way he said the name alerted me to something interesting. 'Didn't you say there was a Bôtnoir Bay?'

He sounded friendlier. 'You certainly remember detail well. The house is set on the cliff above the bay.'

A house above a private bay, and the one near Charles Grichard had the horseshoe shape. Was it really the one I'd been searching for? 'Bôtnoir's the name of your country house?'

Another long pause made me wonder whether he was still there. 'A sort of manor,' he said at last.

'It used to be the Seigneurie,' I heard Dominique's voice. Was she related to Matthew? One of Jean-Jacques's many daughters, perhaps? I tried to picture her, to see if I could spot any resemblance. I could have asked Matthew straight out, but I decided I'd risked his annoyance enough for that day.

Whether it was Horseshoe Bay or not, I thought I'd got it now. Guernsey originally consisted of fiefs – parcels of land administered by a 'suitor' to the crown – a 'seigneur'. 'So your father was a seigneur?'

'I'm not quite sure how you jumped to that conclusion.'

My turn to keep things to myself. 'You said a manor. I took that to be a translation of fief.'

'You've been boning up on local history. And, as ever, you've guessed almost right. My father inherited a fief.'

'Now you're the seigneur, and Bôtnoir is yours as well as Lascervelle?'

'As a matter of fact.' He was emphatic now. And animated in a way I'd never heard before. 'I claimed le droit de Préciput just in time. It was abolished in 1954.'

That sounded captivating, like a fairy tale. I instantly cast Matthew in the role of Prince Charming. 'What does that involve, exactly?'

'The Préciput? It was a legal safeguard so that the fiefs weren't split into too many tiny holdings. The eldest son was able to claim the house and enclos.'

'That's the land?'

'The estate, yes.' A pause. 'That's all history now. Anyway, Jean-Jacques wants to live there. He's having the place restored. Jean-Pierre – that's his son – is the next male heir in line. So, unless one of the rest of us produces a son before I die, he will inherit. Jake will want to get Bôtnoir into good shape for him.'

'Jean-Pierre's the rightful heir?'

'What in the world d'you mean by that?'

This time he sounded furious, quite unlike the supercilious, public schoolboy drawl he'd rebuffed me with before. Why snarl at me for such an innocent remark? Surely Luke was older, so his son must be the next in line. Had Matthew passed him over and created discord within the family? 'I was just wondering about Luke's son. Isn't Luke older than Jean-Jacques?'

'Ah, yes.' Matthew's tone was back to guarded, moderate. 'He doesn't count, I'm afraid.'

'What d'you mean, he doesn't count?' My mind flicked through the possibilities. Mental illness, illegitimacy...

'He's adopted.' A crackle down the line as he moved the receiver. 'So he's not Luke's biological issue. Not that it's supposed to matter a damn nowadays, but the estate is in my gift. I promised my father the fief would stay in the family.'

'The blood line. Of course.'

'Exactly.' The voice sounded far away. 'And I haven't chosen Jean-Pierre rather than one of his sisters for any chauvinistic reason. Males carry on the name.'

He'd stopped, and I was wondering whether he was still there. 'Well...'

Suddenly his voice was strong on the line. 'Anyway, I personally prefer to live in St Peter Port.'

'And your brothers?'

'The Lukes will want to be near the Jakes, the way they were in Chalfont St Giles. They'll find a house near Bôtnoir.'

'And Mark?'

'We've thought about sharing Lascervelle...'

'But now that I've shown an interest in your paintings...'

'What?' he almost shouted. 'My paintings have nothing to do with it.' Then silence. I wondered whether he'd put the receiver down. 'Why on earth would you think they do?' he asked, his voice curiously edgy.

There had to have been a problem between the brothers about the paintings. 'Well...' I'd no idea what to say, but I was sure Mark had something to do with Matthew's reluctance to show or sell his work. I knew he had reservations about Matthew. Jealous of his sex-appeal, his creativity? There was no way I could guess the real reason. I'd have to bide my time to find out.

'You're not even close, Ruth. Mark's recently met someone he's really taken with. He's looking for a place of his own.'

So that was why Mark had lost interest in me, and it explained his initial reaction when coming across me. But why had he turned on his heel like that? Guilt at not letting me know? 'Someone on the island, you mean? An old flame?'

'He met her in London. Not all that long ago.'

'A Londoner prepared to move to Guernsey? She must be keen.' There was no further comment at the other end of the line, and I knew I'd learn nothing more about Mark. Not that I was all that interested. But perhaps I could find out something about their island past. 'Why did you all leave in the first place, if you're so anxious to live here now? I want to know what it's all about,' I continued aggressively.

He laughed again. A lighter easier laugh than the one he'd doled out so tightly earlier. 'Burlington Outlook for dinner? Tomorrow, say? Around eight?'

'Perfect,' I said hastily, and put down the receiver in case he changed his mind.

CHAPTER NINE

Matthew offered to bring round my Saab to drive us, though we could just as easily have walked. I accepted. I was wearing very high heels for the first time in years. I'd bought them in one of these marvellous shops which act as tourist traps on the High Street of St Peter Port, so I was teetering about in a ridiculous fashion. Why not? I still had good legs. I wanted to make use of every advantage I had.

It wasn't that the staff hadn't been pleasant when I'd been to the Burlington before. But this time the head waiter treated Beau – that's what Charles had called him, and I thought it apt enough – like his most prized customer. We didn't have to ask for a window table. There was just one, and it was provided without question. Matthew only had to raise that reverberating voice of his for the waiter to come running.

'Let's start with sparkle,' he suggested smoothly. 'If you want to be told a sparkling story.'

'Lovely,' I agreed, happily enough. Then it crossed my mind that perhaps the bill would come to me. He was, after all, an impecunious painter and jazz musician, even if he was also a landowner with at least two prestigious properties to his name. For all I knew there were more. But if he'd had capital he wouldn't have been living in such obviously strained financial circumstances in the first place.

I thought that through while Matthew was studying the wine list. Perhaps he'd inherited some money now. His grandmother might have had capital of her own, or there might have been money held in trust. I dismissed my thoughts as unworthy. Why shouldn't

I pay for dinner if I could afford it and he could not?

'Pol Roger,' he instructed the waiter. 'Blanc de Chardonnay 1975.' He looked the menu over rapidly. No reading glasses, I thought enviously. 'Moules to start with?'

'Melon, I think.'

'How about lobster à l'anise for the entrée?'

'I haven't tried that.'

'It's like lobster Newburg but flavoured with mushrooms and tarragon, and the alcoholic content is pastis or Pernod rather than the more usual brandy or whisky.'

'That will be terrific.' So he knew about expensive food as well as pais au fou. I wondered how, considering his lean body and my guesstimate of his finances.

His eyes narrowed. 'Now what's worrying you?'

He was beginning to read my expressions far too well. 'You know a lot about food. I didn't think you spent your time in fancy restaurants.' Perhaps he'd been a waiter at the Ritz.

'Didn't think I could afford it, you mean.' How embarrassingly accurate. Could he actually read my thoughts? 'I like to cook.' The grin was so boyish I wondered about his age. 'For myself and friends, not as a job.'

'You've convinced me apart from one tiny point. Even ingredients can be expensive.' Lobster was certainly not on my everyday menu.

'If you insist on crossing 't's and dotting 'i's: I play gigs, often at fancy places. They feed us. OK?'

'For now,' I agreed. 'Without prejudice.'

'You working for the CIA?'

'Not at the moment.' I raised my glass to his. 'But I'm beginning to think it might be fun.' Perhaps I was putting him off. I smiled, but there was something so – unaccountable – about Matthew. And all that sex appeal was beginning to make me nervous.

'Well, are you sitting comfortably?' He had a tease in his voice, and the skin around his eyes creased. But the dark irises showed no emotion at all. 'Then I'll begin the story proper.'

But he didn't. He sipped some wine, stared across the table.

70

'Actually, it's not all that fascinating.' His face wore a fleeting apologetic smile which he blinked away, as though such long-ago memories were still horribly painful. 'Just the story of four boys left orphaned.'

I'd seen that look before. The bewildered helpless look of a child caught up in the adult world. Franz Scheiderbauer's parents were in the apartment across the corridor from us, in Vienna before the Anschluss. The annexation on March 13th was burned into my memory.

Franz and his family were herded out by the Gestapo a few days later. I'd seen his tight face as he waved to me. 'Servus, Ruthi. See you soon.' We both knew we'd never see each other again.

Had Matthew's parents been threatened with deportation to Germany? Because they'd been harbouring fugitives or acted as spies? 'Were your parents killed in the war?'

'What makes you think they were killed?' His voice sounded harsh.

'Mark mentioned an accident. You said they died when you were ten, so it must have been during the war.'

A flicker of fury, but his voice was even. 'They weren't killed in action, or by a bomb. But we lost them because of the war, yes. There was a boating accident; they went out to sea and never returned. Presumed dead.'

In some peculiar way I couldn't analyse Matthew's explanation sounded – unconvincing. And yet when Mark had said there'd been an accident at sea I'd had no problem believing him. Then it struck me that if the Frelé boys were orphaned when the twins were ten – in 1941 – their parents would have been caught up in the Occupation. Were they saboteurs? Did they have to flee for their lives, and it all went horribly wrong? 'Your father was in the Navy, I suppose. Home on leave when the Germans took over?'

'He wanted to be. Guernseymen did offer to join the British forces during both world wars, though constitutionally they weren't obliged to. But my father – his name, like mine, was Mathieu – had a gammy leg. Well, one leg slightly shorter than the other. A climbing accident when he was a boy. So they turned him down. That's why he was here, on the island, when the Germans occupied us.'

'June 30th, 1940.'

His head jerked up from studying the menu. 'Quite right. How come you know that so precisely?'

'It's one of those dates I can never forget. Like March 12th, 1938,' I said. 'The night Hitler invaded Austria. The day before the Anschluss. I was in Vienna at the time.'

His eyes searched mine. 'I see. You know what it's like, then. Jackboots in the streets.'

'And tanks, Heil Hitler yelled out whenever you went near a uniform, that arrogant Sieg Heil when they high-stepped in their revolting parades. And there were lots of those.'

'Clicked heels. That absurd hero-worship of a man's portrait.' The smile had left his face. Not just that. The handsome features had contorted into a snarl. Dark eyes brooded black, sunk back. Something deep and foreboding told me that this reaction was more than a child's memory of the Nazi occupation. I remembered Matthew was born in 1931; so he'd have been nine in 1940. He'd have known exactly what was going on. I did, even though I was only six in 1938. But, unlike me, he was thinking back to living under the Nazis. For almost five long years. I'd had better luck. My family and I lived in Surrey – bomb alley, maybe, but free from jackboots.

'Attitudes changed overnight. My governess sent me out to fetch milk the morning the Nazis marched into Austria. Usually the servants did that, but Hitler taking over made them think they could bully us.'

'Really?' He looked quizzical. 'I thought 98 per cent of Austrians voted for Hitler. Did they think your family was different?'

Surely he must have guessed by now that we were Jews. Then I remembered there'd been very few Jews on the Channel Islands, and that they hadn't been persecuted in the way they had in every other country Hitler invaded. But Matthew must have heard of the Holocaust, even as a child. 'I come from a Jewish background, Matthew. Many Viennese were openly anti-Semitic long before the

Nazis took over. So, though my family didn't practise Judaism, our racial heritage was known.'

I remembered myself as a six-year-old girl on her way to school, resenting the men in black uniform, unable to do anything but hate them in silence. One of them picked me up, swung me around, then set me down again. The others laughed, about to join in the sport. I owe it to a passing tram that nothing worse happened. I heard the driver ding his bell, scuttled towards the rails set in the cobbled streets and jumped across in front of him. It was safe enough, a game I'd often practised on my way to school. I heard the driver swear as the tram cut off the SS men. I'd rather have pushed one of them under it.

'Of course. Stupid of me. What did your people do to get you out?'

'My mother knew right away the danger we were in. She bundled me and my sister out of Vienna within the week. My father was in London, on business. He arranged a visa for us all. We lived in Surrey during the war.'

'How very fortunate. There was talk of our family leaving Guernsey, just before the Germans came. People who wanted to leave registered. In the end sixteen thousand islanders went, including most of the children. My family decided to stay.'

'Nowhere to go?'

'It wasn't that. My uncle Michel had emigrated to the States. He bought a ranch there, in Arkansas, so it wouldn't have been a problem to join him. However, my father and Gran'mère took the line that we'd been on the island for generations, and we weren't going to run just because some Germans turned up. The island history is full of occupations.'

'So what happened?'

'Within months the Germans decided to deport anyone who wasn't born on the island. To prison camps in Germany, we heard. My mother was born in France.' An air of bleakness, a sombre look, was followed by strong fingers twisting his napkin into a tight knot. Then the eyelids covered the expressive eyes and Matthew pretended to smile. 'Once we were occupied there were a few difficulties about getting out of Guernsey.' The features were almost back to normal, though the nose was pinched. 'You and your family were able to escape because the war hadn't started.'

'They rounded up lots of Jews right from the start. We were lucky not just to get out, but to have somewhere to go to.'

'Ah, yes. You said your father was in England. Well, we didn't have that option, we were very carefully guarded. Fortifications all over the place, beaches out of bounds, curfews. Even the tiniest fishing boats were only allowed out with a German guard.'

'They considered the islands a strategic military hold.'

He drummed his fingers on the table, looked restlessly around the room and beckoned to the waiter. 'Where's that wine?'

'It was important for their planned invasion of England,' I emphasised. 'I remember it all very well. We refugees followed every move with bated breath.'

His hand patted mine. 'It must have been uncomfortable.' He sounded polite, but not particularly interested.

'Not for me. I liked England, right from the start. And I always thought the British would hold out against the Germans.'

He looked at me reflectively. 'You said your family were Jewish. How come you're a Catholic?'

All roads lead to Damascus if you want them to. The leafy lanes of the Home Counties were no exception. 'My parents weren't at all religious. They became friendly with another refugee, a Catholic priest. He persuaded them to send us girls to a convent school because they couldn't afford any other private school fees. The nuns charged very little – and they converted me.'

He laughed. 'How very quaint to be converted to Catholicism in England.'

'It's you who're supposed to be telling the story here,' I reminded him.

'I keep my word.'

Why did that sound like a threat? I widened my lips, pretending to smile, but his forehead creased just the way Mark's had done. Tight parallel lines appeared between his eyebrows. 'You were saying the Germans were deporting anyone not born on Guernsey.

Both your parents were with you at that time?'

'Indeed. We were in our place in St Martin.'

'Bôtnoir, you mean?'

'The house, the cliffs it stands on, the little bay it fronts. They're all part of the enclos.'

I was becoming more and more convinced that Horseshoe Bay was Bôtnoir Bay. That would have to wait. I took in Matthew's fiercely protective look while he was talking about his inheritance. What was he doing, giving it up? 'How d'you spell that name?'

'B o circumflex t n o i r.'

'That's why Charles called you 'Bôt'. I thought he was saying B e a u.'

The dark eyes smouldered. 'I'd hardly tolerate that.'

'The whole family lived there?'

'We did then. Before the Occupation my grandmother lived at Lascervelle. She joined us when the Germans took it over. There were a number of servants before the Germans came. We were left with old Annie, the cook, Henri Dinard who was a sort of handyman, Maria Rochet and her son Nicol.'

'Maria was a governess?'

'A cross between a nanny and a maid, I suppose. We were all very fond of her.'

'What happened then?'

'Nothing much, at first.'

Was he going to tell the story, or not? Always that holding back. 'I mean, when it did.'

'My mother was very good-looking.'

I hardly needed telling. All four brothers were handsome, in a way the cousin I'd glimpsed was not. The man I took to be Todd Frelé, the one I'd seen skulking in and out of Lascervelle, was also dark and well-built, but his body tended towards the squat, his skin was ruddy, and his eyes were just too small to make his face as well proportioned as his cousins'. It's difficult to pin down the reasons why one person is better looking than another. Matthew was by far the most handsome of the brothers. Why? The challenge in his eyes, perhaps. The assumption that he was, I dare say. His macho attitude.

75

'The most senior German officers were constantly at our house. Not just Nazis. A couple of them were professional army types.'

"I only know because I spent one of the war years here," I remembered the man in black saying. He could easily have been a career officer in the German Army. And if Horseshoe Bay was actually Bôtnoir Bay – he'd have known the Frelés!

Matthew straightened his cutlery setting, arranging it meticulously. 'It seemed they just came to pay court, in a very proper sort of way. Not only to my mother, but to my grandmother as well.'

"It used to belong to a very dear friend of mine," I heard the German's precise tones. "She passed away a short time ago, so I've come to pay my last respects." Old Madame Frelé's death fitted in with that. I turned to Matthew. 'And your father felt threatened?'

'I don't know what he felt. It must have been hard for him to react in any way at all. The Germans brought all kinds of food, and drink, even some curtain material, I remember. I know my brothers and I...'

He didn't really have to spell it out. For some reason I could see him fiercely protective of his mother. He wouldn't have taken to the way those German officers would have looked at her.

'...just didn't like their attitude. So we made trouble whenever we could.' He grinned as he thought back. 'All kinds of tricks.'

'Like what?'

'Sawed chair legs so that when they sat down the chair would collapse, poured vinegar into the wine, punctured their car tyres, put sugar into their petrol tanks – usual schoolboy stuff.'

'Bit dangerous, wasn't it?'

'Sort of. They could never pin it down to one of us. We were sent to bed early, locked in our rooms. They even had a guard in the hall to make sure we didn't get out.'

'But you did?'

'The house has three floors, plus a marvellous glassed-in look-out attic perched on top. We were on the third floor, four small rooms in a row, facing the sea. Old Annie told us how my father used to abseil down the sheer cliff to the bay. From his bedroom window, when he was a boy. That's how he had his accident.'

'So you copied the idea.'

'Not that difficult. There are some good footholds between the clefts. We dressed to blend with the stone, making it hard for anyone to spot us, even from the sea. The coastline round there is pretty hazardous. German shipping didn't come close. So one of us would abseil down, scoot back via the caves that led into the garden from the bay, and do whatever we could to make life difficult. Then we'd come back the way we came.'

'And you got away with that? Didn't your parents know?'

He picked up his wineglass, raised it. 'The German were pretty drunk by that time of night. Maria saw to that. She made sure she kept their glasses filled.'

'Maria? Didn't they expect to be looked after by your parents and your grandmother?'

The animation left his face. 'Gran'mère entertained the top brass in the living room. They sent the lesser ranks down to the kitchen, and to deal with our little antics.'

'What about your parents?'

'They escaped to the glass attic – they called it their Captain's Cabin. My mother's hobby was bobbin lace making and my father maintained he was painting a portrait of her.'

'I see.' An almost instant sense of antagonism towards the unknown grandmother lodged itself in my mind. He'd said nothing about her directly, and yet I seethed with outrage. She was a woman who entertained Nazi elite during the Occupation. 'What happened about your parents?' I said, as softly as I could. 'What made them risk trying to escape?'

He opened the menu again and began to read it, as though it could tell the story. Finally he looked up. 'The deportations of non-islanders were going ahead.' His eyes went blank. 'At first we thought my mother would be safe. They'd hidden all documents showing her origins and told the German officials some cock-and-bull story about her people dying, that she'd been brought up in an orphanage on Guernsey, and that the papers had been lost.'

'Surely they checked that out? Germans are always so thorough.'

His face was hidden behind the menu. 'One of the high-up officers told Gran'mère he'd make sure no one investigated the matter further. It wasn't too difficult to carry the rest of it off. Because Maman sounded French the German officials assumed she spoke in patois. Then Gran'mère said that regulations were going to be tightened up.'

'Ahh.'

'My father couldn't face the thought of Maman being deported. He decided to get her out of Guernsey, to England. They used the tiny boat we'd hidden before the Germans even came.'

'How d'you hide a boat?'

'It used to be quite usual to haul fishing boats up for the winter. We still knew how to use the old rails, and the windlass. My father happened to be a keen sea canoeist, and he'd made a kayak, himself, out of canvas and lathe. No one even knew it existed. It was the ideal escape craft.'

A kayak. That's what I'd remembered. The man in black had gone berserk when he spotted the young couple beaching their double kayak. The same one, by any chance? Had that German been the one to find it, to report a couple had tried to escape? 'Really? How very farsighted of him.'

'It was quite small. A double-seat sea kayak, actually. They're not even particularly heavy. People manage to carry them all by themselves.'

The young man – Sebastian – had carried the kayak up from the beach. 'But surely canoeing is a difficult skill? How was your mother going to manage it?'

'They'd used the craft together many times. They were what are called sea tourers, and were skilled at paddling from Guernsey to the French and British mainland. It's what brought them together in the first place.'

'Wouldn't it take quite a long time to kayak from Guernsey to England?'

'They knew how to do it, made the usual plan, under cover of darkness and all that. They were determined, and it shouldn't have been difficult at all.'

'Leaving their four sons?'

His stare was cold. 'It was a two-seater kayak, Ruth. And we were born on Guernsey, and very young. We were safe enough.'

'Obviously they didn't make it.'

He poured more wine and drank it. 'They left as scheduled. There was a moon with cloud cover. Conditions were perfect.'

'So what went wrong?'

He said nothing at first, and there was no expression on his face at all. Just a blank stare out into the harbour. The waiter arrived with the first course. A steaming bowl of moules was set in front of him. He used the menu to fan himself, stared at the shellfish but didn't attempt to eat any. 'All we were told was that they'd disappeared, and that the kayak had been found, washed up. It was assumed they'd tried to leave one misty night. And that was it.'

'You never saw them again? Not even their bodies?'

'We never...heard from our parents again.'

I took in the hesitation. What did it mean? He was telling the truth, no question about that. But not the whole of it. Was I imagining it, or had he side-stepped the issue of 'seeing'? The dark eyes were looking away from me, examining his moules: he was picking them from their shells, eating without relish.

'Neither of them? You said they found the kayak. Their bodies weren't washed up, or anything like that?'

'Washed up? No.'

'And the Germans said nothing about the escape?'

'Not to us. Not a single word.'

'But they knew.'

'Naturally. Our parents had vanished, the kayak was on the beach. The German officers asked questions and were told the truth about the attempted escape. But not, of course, the motive for it.'

'Why would that have mattered?'

'Maria was born in Italy. We hoped they wouldn't discover that.'

'But they did?'

'Yes. And they made sure she knew.' His voice sounded hollow. 'She committed suicide before they could deport her.'

79

'How utterly appalling!' The waiter cleared my melon shell and hovered over the almost untouched moules. Matthew waved him away.

'What did you think had happened to your parents?'

He took a piece of roll and twisted it between his fingers. 'I thought they'd been betrayed and murdered,' he said, his voice a hiss. 'A lot of murdering was going on.' His eyes had hardened, his hands tensed, he gripped a knife and stabbed it into the roll.

There was no way someone like Matthew would have let it go at that, whatever his age. 'Did you do anything about it all?'

He buttered his mutilated roll, not looking at me. 'What could a boy of ten do?'

'That's what I'm asking you,' I said.

He shrugged, scattering crumbs. 'There was a daily news-sheet, giving the BBC nine o'clock news bulletin. G.U.N.S: Guernsey Underground News Service. We helped deliver that.' He drank some of the moule sauce. 'We went on playing tricks. Gran'mère tried to stop us, to starve us into submission.' He pushed a few empty shells around the plate.

'Starve you?' The islands had suffered from grotesque food shortages at the end of the war. Churchill had been petitioned to send supplies even though the Germans were still there.

'She'd been given all this food. She hoarded it, the old miser. But she wouldn't let us have anything at all. Towards the end she tried to bribe the neighbours with it, to pretend she'd always been against the Nazis.' He laughed. 'Without much success.'

It was becoming clearer why Matthew – and his brothers, for that matter – had left, and not been back to Guernsey for around thirty years. There must have been a serious break with the grandmother.

'We were always so damn hungry. We stole whenever there was a chance. Without old Annie we might really have come to grief.'

The waiter brought the lobster and removed the rest of the moules. Two huge red shells were placed in front of us, the contents grilled to perfection, the smell of aniseed pervasive. It would be a pity to ruin the main course with old tragedies. Perhaps it was time to change to happier topics.

'This is really delicious. I think I shall enjoy living on Guernsey. The food's wonderful, the people are remarkably friendly, and there's everything I need. But I do miss the countryside. I've decided to look for a country house once my year's rental is up.'

He stopped tearing his roll to shreds. The hardness left his eyes as he focused them on me. 'Which part of the island d'you fancy?'

'I suppose it depends on what's available. Now if Charles Grichard were to sell...'

'No chance of that. You liked his place, or just the garden?'

'I liked the whole set-up. What's so interesting about Guernsey is that you have a really splendid stock of outstanding houses. For such a small island, I mean.'

'The feudal heritage, I suppose. Each seigneur would expect to build a house to reflect his status. Even the farmhouses are quite impressive.'

'And what about you? Are you going to stay permanently, or will you go back to London?'

The pleated frown was back again, his look aggressive. 'Of course I'm staying. This is where I belong.'

Refusing to live here until the grandmother died was certainly extreme. 'Will you look for a young wife to try for an heir?'

He paused, a piece of lobster returned to the plate. 'Don't pull your punches, do you? I told you. I've decided to settle for Jean-Pierre. As far as the fief is concerned, he'll do.'

'I would have thought that that line of thinking was rather negative for you.' I gulped some of the Pol Roger to give myself courage. 'All this turning the other cheek doesn't strike me as the real you. Why are you doing it?'

I thought perhaps he might do a Mark on me – get up and leave without another word. Looking at the expressions ravaging his face I could see that he was tempted. But he did not.

'That's what you think, is it?'

'It's your inheritance. You're the eldest son.'

'There's only ten minutes between Mark and me.'

I looked at him. 'If Jean-Pierre were Mark's son I'd see the force of that. You're identical twins so he'd be your son as well.'

'How on earth d'you figure that one out?'

'You have the same DNA, so genetically speaking you're the fathers of each other's children. But even then I'd say that's not relevant. You chose to be the first. I don't believe in accidents of that kind.'

'You're saying I pushed my brother out of the way to be born first?'

'When you get down to it: yes, I am.'

'So you reckon I should find a woman young enough to bear a child, and go into heir production.'

'That's one of the things you might like to do. At least keep an eye out. But to marry someone just for breeding isn't good enough either. You want me to tell you what I really think?'

'Can I stop you?'

'Certainly you can. It's none of my business.'

'Carry on.'

'Right. You're a terrific painter—'

'Are you going to maintain that if I paint myself a son he will become flesh and blood?'

He was writing me off as a nut case. 'Not quite as literally as that. But, as I was saying, you're a terrific painter and you've done b... nothing to sell your work. You could live on in your work, if not in your genes. I'd quote the parable of the talents, but I'm sure I only have to remind you of it.'

He stabbed the fork into a last piece of lobster. 'You know, I hadn't thought of that sort of inheritance.' His grin was not unfriendly.

'You don't need flesh and blood heirs. Your paintings are your children, your immortality.' Dare I go on? I giggled, the alcohol now getting to me. 'But art only exists through the people it is meant to reach. For paintings that means viewers. I'm prepared to do the legwork, arrange an exhibition. Then you'll not only live on forever in your paintings, they'll be known about. Deal?'

He looked at me for several minutes without saying anything at all. My suggestion would, after all, change the attitude of a lifetime.

Then 'OK. Deal,' he said. The smile, when it came, was actually warm. 'Where the hell have you been all my life?'

'Married to a great writer,' I said. 'That's how I know about your talent. I understand about creative men. What's more, I'm giving you fair warning. I also very much take to them.'

'So the woman could come with the exhibition?' He beckoned to the waiter for the bill.

I lost my nerve. 'You never know,' I said. 'You might meet just the right one there.'

CHAPTER TEN

Every time I come to the end of writing a book I find it hard to say goodbye to an old familiar friend. There are always improvements that could be made. But what really holds me there is fear of the unknown, of the new. How can I be sure I'll ever write again?

I switched on my computer, copied the text to a couple of floppies and printed it out. The familiar feeling of parting, of deprivation. It was time to concentrate on the colour photography. I turned the computer off, and went down to the dark-room to view the transparencies.

Magnolia grandiflora was heavily featured in my text. Not just for its spectacular blooms. The bold and glossy foliage, a velvety rust-red below when young, adds stature to any garden at all seasons. The picture on my screen did not do it justice. It was in season now. I should be able to sniff out the pungent lemon scent of the creamy-white flowers which emerge in summer. There had to be good specimens somewhere on Guernsey. Not, unfortunately, in Charles Grichard's garden. I determined to look for one.

The doorbell rang through my thoughts, irritating me. I decided to ignore it. I consider my mornings sacred and don't encourage visitors. The bell rang again as the projector's heat blurred the slide out of focus. I knew it wasn't good enough and had to be replaced. I turned off the power, scooped up my camera and lens, and charged upstairs.

Jeanne Frelé was standing on the doorstep. Far too much of her short rotund body was displayed in a sleeveless summer dress patterned with huge flowers. Round cheeks were drawn up tight into a smile, almost hiding the small bright eyes.

'I have only just heard about it. Mark, he told me you are now living next door to us.'

'As you can see.' The frosty tone I always use to discourage people when I'm working.

The cheek muscles dropped half a centimetre, then rose again. But the eyes had lost their eagerness. 'I am so sorry if I have come at a bad time. But I am very excited. You are just the person I have been looking for.'

She sounded so genuine, so enthusiastic, I felt ashamed.

'Perhaps you have heard: Jean-Jacques and I are taking over the family manoir, Bôtnoir.'

'Ye...es,' I said uncertainly. Surely she wasn't going to start in on Matthew?

'It is three hectares of neglected gardens. I want to make that into something really magnificent.' Her eyes glowed with the zeal of a born-again gardener. 'I am giving myself fifteen years. After that it is for the heir to Bôtnoir to do as he wishes.'

I couldn't just let her stand on the doorstep. 'Do come in, won't you?' I led her to my living room, motioned her to a chair. And remembered at last that talking to Jeanne was what I'd been trying to arrange.

'So you're doing this for Jean-Pierre?'

She sighed. 'I hope so. Jean-Jacques, he says there is no problem. But maybe it is not as easy as he thinks. The grand-mère – Michelle Frelé – she wished her younger son's family to inherit.' Jeanne hooded her eyes at me, smiled. 'She hated Matthew, you know. Really hated him. And was not fond of the others. She wished Bôtnoir to go to her grandson Todd. Even though he is American, from a somewhat uneducated and simple rural background, and so knows very little about the culture of Guernsey, or even Europe.'

Surely it wasn't up to the grandmother? I'd understood that the island laws of inheritance were the usual ones – the next in the blood line was the next seigneur. And Jean-Jacques's wife, being French, must surely know that. 'I thought Matthew was the present seigneur and, as he has no children, the next one is in his gift?'

'This is, as they say, the nub of the problem. It is not simple.

85

The father of the brothers, Mathieu, was le seigneur. He brought his fiancée to Guernsey against her parents' wishes. She was not eighteen when she left Paris.

'Old Madame Frelé did not wish this marriage to take place. She was against la petite. So the young couple went away in their kayak, and did not return until la petite was pregnant with the twins. The young couple claimed they were already married in a register office.'

Opening up all kinds of possibilities... 'That must have upset the family.'

'It caused some big problems. A church ceremony was arranged, later, because la jeune mère converted and became Catholique.'

I thought back to my Catechism. 'In those days it was quite difficult for a Catholic to get a dispensation to marry someone who wasn't a Catholic. Presumably that was another reason for the civil marriage.'

'Perhaps. Todd, he insisted the first marriage never took place, and therefore he is the legitimate heir. That is why all four brothers are searching so hard for le certificat de célébration civile.'

The marriage certificate for a civil ceremony. Right; that explained why the brothers were tolerating that shifty character Todd.

My mind was working overtime. I didn't believe the cousin could possibly have a case because I couldn't imagine that someone like Mathieu Frelé, who'd charged his son with keeping the fief for his blood line, would have exposed his heirs to such a potential conflict. 'I've always understood that a marriage at any time would legitimise earlier children. What was wrong with the church wedding?'

'It does not count on Guernsey, because by that time all four boys were already born. And, in any case, it was not a marriage. It was the reaffirmation of vows already exchanged, though maybe not in a church. Also, here on Guernsey, it is being married before the date of conception which counts.'

Matthew's father would have known that. There *had* to be some proof of his civil marriage – somewhere. And I was sure Matthew would look until he found it. He'd fight for his seigneurie, and his blood line, against all odds. 'Surely Matthew won't take his cousin's claim lying down.'

'Of course that is very true, but it is still unsettling. All four brothers are working very hard to defeat Todd. Jean-Jacques is sure they can win. Which means Jean-Pierre will be the heir, you know.' The slow faraway smile of maternal pride. 'It is good to have one son. Maybe he will produce many grandsons. My Dominique already has a little boy.'

'You have a daughter called Dominique?' This was the final proof, then. Bôtnoir must be Horseshoe Bay.

A radiant smile. 'My eldest, yes. Lucien is only two months old. That is my big regret. I will not be seeing le petit-fils as often as I would wish.'

I had to find out. 'Did Dominique and her husband visit the island earlier this year? In March?'

She stared at me. 'How you can know that?'

'I think I must have come across them on the beach. There's a little bay which goes with the house, isn't there?'

'You mean you already know Bôtnoir?'

'Not the house and garden. I was exploring one of the green lanes when I first arrived. It took me to a water lane and I stumbled on to a beach. I'm pretty sure it was Bôtnoir Bay, though I'd no idea at the time. Dominique didn't mention a man having a heart attack?'

Jeanne shook her head. 'She delivered le bébé as soon as she came back.'

'She's probably forgotten all about it.' I explained what had happened as quickly as I could.

'What a very strange coincidence.' Jeanne was clearly only half-listening, her mind already back on the enclos. 'But then I am getting used to these oddities. I understood Mattieu promised to sell the place to Jake, but now it seems he will only let us live there. As tenants.'

'So why would you take the trouble to turn the garden round?'

Her full-moon face had a rather waxy quality. It made her look younger than the mid-fifties I judged her to be. She was clever enough to have her hair professionally styled. A dark brown, attractively layered shingle close to the head, almost gamine. How well she'd look if she lost a little weight, though that might age her.

'Naturally because of Jean-Pierre.'

'That makes it worth spending all your time on it?' Hope is not, of course, a theological virtue for mothers. It is built in, born with the child.

'What else can I do? I adore gardening, Ruth. And whoever Bôtnoir goes to finally, my efforts will not be wasted. Which is the main reason why I have come to see you. I love your books, so I had a sort of dream – that you would help me plan a new garden. Professionally, naturellement.'

'You're offering me a job?'

'I hope that is not offensive. It is meant to be an expression of my admiration.'

'I'm flattered,' I said. 'But you do understand: I'm a writer on gardening, not a garden planner.'

'You are a superb plantswoman,' Jeanne broke in, confident, her eyes now grave and shrewd. 'I may not be brilliant at gardening, but I am an expert consumer of gardening products. I always know where to find the best. As far as gardening books go, I say that is you.'

'But...'

'And the gardens you create in your books are brilliant.'

I nodded. An idea for a new book was beginning to take shape.

'This is also quite a good house.' Jeanne moved herself surprisingly quickly across the room to the French windows. I noticed her ankles were swollen, the flesh oozing over her sandal straps. She followed my eyes and laughed. 'Apart from all other matters, I thought if I really try hard with the gardening, I might lose weight. What I am hoping is to become so involved that I forget to eat, and go and dig, or plant, or do whatever else is necessary. You give the orders and I do the spade work.'

She smiled again. This time she did not hide her eyes, but allowed them to express a longing, even a resolve, to make something of the rest of her life.

'My children are grown up. Even Jean-Pierre is leaving home. I will not see the girls now that we shall be living on Guernsey. A weekend sometimes, perhaps. Christmas and Easter if we pay their fares. I have been spoilt for family company, and now it is finished. Restoring Bôtnoir will be a wonderful way to take my mind off the empty nest. So I shall be giving the garden my undivided attention, and Jake will pay whatever is necessary to bring it into shape. Will you take us on?'

'I should say let me think about it,' I motioned her to sit down, 'but I don't think I need to. Somehow I think we'll get on well together. And—'

'And you will see Matthew some of the time,' she put in, the brown eyes glinting intelligence. 'Mark — he mentioned also you were seeing something of his brother.'

Prejudice lurks in the recesses of the mind. I should have known better than to judge Jeanne on the basis of appearance. She was the first person not to warn me against Matthew. More than that — she was practically encouraging me.

'We've met a couple of times. I'm going to arrange an exhibition of his paintings. But, if you want to do me a favour, you could tell him you agree it's a good idea,' I added. 'Back me up.'

'If that is the price,' she giggled, 'I am happy to help.' Her face took on a thoughtful look. 'And from a professional point of view?'

'That's the important part. What I'd like to suggest is that we combine work on the garden with my writing a new book.'

'You mean you would use this new garden to illustrate your book?'

'That wouldn't be enough. We need a theme, something which hasn't been written about before. Then I'd be delighted to work with you.'

Her shoulders drooped. 'That is not sounding very likely. It is just an overgrown old garden.'

I held out a bottle of sherry. 'I think I've got an idea. A glass of something to stimulate the imagination?' Jeanne had given my struggling notion a handle. 'So much has been written about small gardens, town gardens, all kinds of special gardens. But I don't know of anything recent about restoring a neglected old garden. If we divide it into small sections, gardens within gardens if you like, it might work in the market place. I'd have to discuss it with my agent and my editor. Give me some time to think about it. But, whatever happens, why don't we drive over to Bôtnoir and look around?'

She stood, waving the bottle away. 'I am sure you will love it. There are some truly magnificent trees, a few shrubs, even climbers.' She was breathless with excitement. 'Shall we go now, right away?'

'What sort of shrubs?'

'The house is enormous. The north side has several camellias. I do not know which varieties as yet. Many old-fashioned roses, a campsis grandiflora which does not have problems—'

'Of course, no winter frosts.'

She nodded. 'It means we can use semi-tropical plants. The passiflora fruit actually ripens. And I found a solanum, and a magnificent specimen of magnolia grandiflora.' She looked at me expectantly. 'That could be of use?'

'You're kidding?' My heart pumped faster as adrenaline spread through my body. 'I need a better photo of grandiflora for *Old-fashioned Gardening*. I was about to go out and search for one. Just let me collect my photographic gear, and my boots. Then we can go.' I was almost out of the living-room door before I realised I hadn't offered the woman anything to eat, and it was nearly lunch time. 'Can I make you a sandwich before we leave?'

'Do not worry about food for me,' she said. 'The water supply is working at Bôtnoir, and I have given up food.'

CHAPTER ELEVEN

Jeanne's sense of direction wasn't much better than mine. I felt my strength ebbing away by the time I'd turned the heavy Saab three times. The fourth time we headed steeply up a track which could only just accommodate the car's width. If we happened to meet another vehicle its driver would have to back or we'd be stuck there for the duration.

The track had no obvious end, and no light. I switched my headlights on, intending to express my doubts about where we were. The Saab lurched over a large pothole, I revved the engine, and we emerged into daylight. With accompanying noise, and the necessity for windscreen wipers. Last night's rain had loaded low-lying branches with water. I congratulated myself on my decision not to buy the cabriolet.

We'd actually arrived at Bôtnoir. The drive, like Charles Grichard's, was large and circular. A loose use of the term. It had once been circular, but now the circumference was jagged by nettles, briars and hogweed. The small space in the centre had been roughly cleared. The narrow path hewn out to the front door was layered with nettles.

And there the resemblance to Charles Grichard's place ended. The building looked dejected, unloved. Black holes for windows, the glass so dirty it didn't even reflect light. The windows menaced us beneath shaggy protrusions of overgrown climbers. And there were a great many of them.

'I have brought the key, though none of the ground floor windows have locks. We would not have problems to climb through.'

91

The first thing I look at in a garden is its aspect. The sun was high to our left, the house built with the west side facing the sea. The drive faced east.

Jeanne nodded to show she understood what I was doing. 'The ancestor who built the house, also a Mathieu Frelé, I believe considered it a good way to keep the winds at bay.'

'Mathieu. Is that Matthew's actual name?'

'The boys all have Christian names français. They soon found out people on the mainland can't say most French names properly, except Jean-Jacques. So les frères use the English forms. Probably now they will revert.' She walked ahead of me. 'The house is built right on the cliff, but there are no direct sea views from the main reception rooms. One descendant built a veranda having good views, and up at the top you will find the usual Guernsey attic – a captain's cabin.'

'Very interesting.'

'It means the garden is divided into two – pleasure gardens to the south, kitchen garden to the north.'

'Completely split?'

'The west wall merges into the sheer cliff down to the bay, so the building is becoming one, joining into the rock face. That is the reason why the cellars are actually in long tortuous caves below the house.'

All very intriguing. 'So when was it built?'

'I do not know for sure. Some time in the eighteenth century, then perhaps added to in the Victorian era.'

'Added to?'

'Delusions of grandeur, maybe. It is a very large building, as you can see. Eight rooms on the ground floor, six rooms on the second floor, then another eight rooms on the top. Then also the glass attic up in the sky! As well as extensive cellars below.' She wrestled with the enormous key, turned it. I helped her push open the door. 'Not really cellars. A sort of cave complex. You can approach from the garden, or from the shore of Bôtnoir Bay.'

'Matthew said something about the four boys having four identical bedrooms next to each other?'

'Jean-Jacques always talked about it also. Four of our girls must double up in our Chalfont house, and my husband did not like that. Shall we take a tour of the house?'

'I'd love that.' The building wasn't of particular interest to me, but it was important to see the garden from the rooms. And the magnolia might best be photographed from above, using a telephoto lens.

The hall was vast. A spacious graceful staircase wound a wide curve to the first floor.

'All domestic rooms are on the ground floor. Kitchen, scullery, larder, laundry. Staff bedrooms.'

'The living room's on the first floor?' That would make for an unusual view of the gardens.

'Yes. Salon and dining room are on the first floor. The master bedroom is also on this floor, as well as a night nursery, a study and a dressing room plus bathroom. Day nursery and children's bedrooms are on the top floor, also bedrooms for the staff.'

As we walked into the dining room I had the oddest feeling of déjà vu. I couldn't explain it, just an idea that, somehow, I'd been in this room before. I looked around. Two large wall-length windows facing east, a door leading through to a veranda on the left. Good proportions, two fine chandeliers hanging from the ceiling, an imposing Victorian mahogany table which could obviously seat up to twenty people when extended, matching chairs. Nothing that seemed remotely reminiscent of anything I'd seen before. I walked to a door on the left and meandered through. 'The veranda's nice. Almost homey.'

'Such a good idea. Maybe you haven't noticed, high wind is everywhere, the garden is very exposed to the sea. Maybe we turn it into a winter garden?'

'Three outside walls, aren't there?'

'Oui, oui. It would be cold in winter. But old central-heating pipes run along the walls.'

I was still preoccupied by a weird sense of having been here before. And there was something odd about the veranda — a draught on my right as I went in, but no missing glass.

We walked back to the dining room and through to a magnificent living room. Three floor-to-ceiling windows looked east, and south-facing French windows led out to a balcony leading down to the pleasure gardens. 'A beautiful room,' I said, admiring the white marble fireplace, a series of three chandeliers. The parquet flooring was in terrible condition. There was no furniture at all.

'It is regrettable these places were looted during the war and even afterwards. I believe old Madame moved into Lascervelle as soon as she could after the Boches left. She decide to forget Bôtnoir, and now it is become a ruin.'

'Odd that the dining room furniture survived.'

'It was only recently discovered. Jean-Jacques said his parents stored a little in a special hiding place.'

'But not the rest?'

'Most of the furniture is still at Lascervelle.'

'The family were here during the whole of the Occupation?'

Her eyes avoided mine. 'Jean-Jacques does not like to discuss the occupation years very much. I think they had no choice, there was nowhere else for them.'

The amount of restoration needed was awesome. 'You're going to have your hands full bringing the place back to life. You really want to take it on?'

'I will be happy to be busy.' She led the way up another fine staircase to the second floor rooms. A huge day nursery was straight ahead, beyond it a corridor branched left and right. The bedrooms off were, as Matthew had described, all lined up in a neat row of virtually identical cells, with bathrooms at both ends. Jeanne tried to open one door, and found it locked.

'La grand-mère locked the boys in at night. Often they broke the curfew imposed by les Boches, so it was highly dangerous.'

We tried two other doors. The last one gave way. I walked into the room. It had the air of a monastic cell, about twelve foot by ten, with a small high window looking out to sea and a fireplace at the side. I walked up to it, skirting the skeleton of an iron bedstead. Had this been Matthew's room? 'Do you know anything about their parents? What happened to them?'

94

Jeanne walked over to the window, looked out away from me, shrugged. 'I am told the parents tried to escape from below here – from the beach. To leave the island using a kayak. The kayak was found, but not les parents. It was assumed they drowned.'

'Mark said that.' Matthew hadn't exactly disagreed, but I was convinced he hadn't told me all he knew. Had they been got rid of, not necessarily by Germans, and the Occupying forces had colluded with that for some reason? I was clear there was more to the story, and that Jeanne didn't know it. 'Don't you think it strange that they were prepared to abandon their children at such a time?'

'Naturellement I do. But I suggest you say nothing to the brothers. All become very upset if anyone bring it up. All four claim the parents had no choice. La mère was going to be deported. She was une Française, not born on Guernsey.'

'Everyone I've talked to insists the Germans treated the deportees quite well, did not send them to the death camps.' Not that I believed that, but I did wonder whether Jeanne knew anything more.

Jeanne shrugged. 'Maybe the future deportees did not believe it.'

'No doubt. But at least the children would have had their father to bring them up. They must have known their chance of escape was small.' There had to have been another reason. Not guerrilla attacks against the Germans; Matthew would have known about that, mentioned it, been proud of it. Something else.

Jeanne walked away from me. 'Now let us go to the garden. You can see if the magnolia is good for a photo.'

I hadn't noticed the grandiflora from any of the windows. We walked down to the living room and out through the French windows. The balcony was large: the whole width of the south side, serving the master bedroom as well as the living room. Two fine sets of curved steps, obscured by clumps of valerian and tufts of sedum acre, led down into the garden. A pungent lemon scent caught at my olfactory sense.

'Wonderful smell, you agree? Can you see it beyond the sprawling buddleias and the hebes?'

Swarms of butterflies were keeping their balance in the breeze. I borrowed Jeanne's stick and hacked my way round several bushes of buddleia alternifolia. If I could cut some of the rampant growth away, I could get a good close-up shot of Magnolia Grandiflora flowers and leaves.

'You got any secateurs I could borrow?'

She dug a pair out of her bag and handed them to me. 'I will go down and keep the bigger branches out of your way.'

I knew I'd got excellent shots even without viewing the transparencies. A good day's work. I put my gear away and concentrated. The garden was certainly neglected, the lawn had gone back to field. It looked as though it had been given over to grazing by local sheep, which meant the coarser grasses had been kept in check.

There was a garden house which had been used as a piggery. The hedges had straggled into unkempt trees, the fruit trees hadn't been pruned for years. They were leaning away from the wind, their branches covered in lichen and ivy. Canker was rife. Several fine decorative trees were still there. Ivy was doing its best to establish a stranglehold. An outstanding example of arbutus andrachnoides was carrying a crop of pink flowers which would turn into strawberry-like fruit. A splendid liriodendron tulipifera was bursting with tulip flowers. I spied a pterocarya rehderiana, the long catkins just beginning to form. There were signs of smaller trees: a magnolia or two which could, no doubt, be resuscitated, a couple of Japanese maples for their bright autumn foliage, and trachycarpus fortunei palms to give a tropical effect.

'It all looks extremely promising. There are several good trees and shrubs to give the garden structure. The rest will grow quickly enough.'

Jeanne's face was round and smiling like a sun. 'Avec précision. Also now and again you find a special treat. A beautiful myrtle has a place right by the front door, nestling in the shelter.'

We trampled and stomped our way through the side and back to the front. I looked at the formation of the wall beside the front door, and frowned. Surely that didn't quite match what I'd seen inside? The wall there was straight, going directly from the front door to the end of the hall. Here I could see the house jutting out, as though the inside was about four foot wider, making a kind of vestibule adjacent to the hall itself.

'Some of the climbing roses could be cut back, not necessary to uproot them.' Jeanne was sniffing at the heady perfume of Gloire de Dijon.

'I always like to grow climbers on their own roots, you know. It saves all that tiresome trouble with suckers. Most species roses do very well that way. You could take cuttings in September,' I advised her. 'Some of these old varieties are hard to find now.'

'You mean we are not obliged to buy from a nursery, we can just take cuttings?'

'I've done it successfully for years.' I stared again at the jutting wall, and tried to remember the inside. 'Could we just go inside once more? I was trying to remember one thing...'

'You feel maybe we continue planting inside?'

It took me a little while to understand what she was driving at. And then I did. She meant she was willing to let me take over the indoor plantings as well. If the veranda were really to become a sort of winter garden that could be quite exciting.

The hall was as I'd remembered it. The wall was straight, but the outside one jutted nearly four foot beyond the door. Why would that piece of wall be quite so thick? I didn't believe it was.

'Possibly we station some plants here, in the foyer?'

I hadn't given it any thought at all. 'It always makes a pleasant impression,' I waffled vaguely. 'We could stand large tubs by the staircase and several more in the niches going up.' Was there a secret room? Is that where the furniture had been hidden? And what else, besides?

'A wonderful idea, Ruth.' She was puffed from all the exertions, but her eyes glowed. 'I am so happy you will undertake this project. Bôtnoir will regain an outstanding garden.'

I made a mental note to warn my agent that Todd Frelé might take over the fief. If she thought the project had legs she'd have to write the contract very carefully.

97

CHAPTER TWELVE

This morning wasn't the best time to be late, and normally I'm punctual. I was due to pick up Pete Tanner, the producer of a possible TV series involving the Bôtnoir garden, at Guernsey Airport. My agent had been really pleased with herself that she'd got him interested.

The Saab was blocked into the car park by the white Maserati I'd seen once before. Parking spaces were going to be at a premium during the season. The Maserati sat right in front of my bonnet, and I was backed on to a wall. I'd no idea how to get out of that predicament. Contact the police? It seemed unlikely that they'd be able to find the owner any more quickly than I could. Get a cab? I needed my own car. Pete and I were driving to Bôtnoir straight from the airport. The proposed series about restoring a completely neglected old garden had excited him. He wanted to see it.

'I am so sorry, dear lady. I knew I would only be ten minutes.' I froze. Where had I heard that voice before? A charming bow, a smile, while I tried hard to place him. 'I thought that I would be secure from discourtesy.' The easy way he assumed he'd charm himself out of blocking me in told me he was used to getting his own way.

It all came back to me. Resentment turned to anger. This was the man in black – though dressed in a neat grey blazer today – the one I'd come across on Bôtnoir Bay. Obviously Southampton General had brought him round from whatever had been wrong with him.

'The last time we met you had some sort of seizure,' I told him, my voice oozing hostility. 'On the beach.' He'd said he was a friend of the owner, said she was an old lady. He could easily have been talking about the Frelés' grandmother. She'd died in March, but it was April when I came across him. Still, he might well not have heard about her death right away.

He put his glasses on, looked at me carefully. 'I am so sorry. I do not remember it at all. I had a minor heart attack while walking on a beach. They told me a lady came across me, and saved my life. You must forgive me that I did not try to thank you. No one knew who you were.'

'The young couple with the kayak saved your life,' I told him. Did he remember shouting at Dominique, trying to get at her? 'Look, I'm meeting someone off a plane. Perhaps you'd move as quickly as you can.' My tones were icy, but polite. Even my usual curiosity was subdued by my nervousness at being late.

'Some kinda problem, Otto?'

A nasal American intonation. I recognised the man I'd bumped into outside Lascervelle. Matthew's cousin. He walked right up and scowled at me.

'The car is in the lady's way, Todd. If you could move it for me.' He turned to me. 'A thousand apologies, dear lady.'

So I'd chanced across cousin Todd again. Closer to, this time, and as unattractive as his reputation. How come he knew the man in black? It all seemed rather sinister. I turned my back on both of them, got into the Saab and slammed the door. Todd moved the Maserati. As I eased the Saab out of the car park I saw him take my space.

The drive to the airport involved a crawl at twenty-five mph or less. It wasn't far, but I managed to worry every inch of the way. The dashboard clock moved at its allotted pace. I found the time-distance graph highly unsatisfactory.

I hadn't met Pete before, but he was easy to spot. Indefinite age, dark mouse hair, creased clothes, shambling gait. The clincher was the heavy video camera slung across his left shoulder. He was squinting at my plates, identifying me by my car registration.

I wound down my window. 'Sorry I'm late. Hope you haven't been waiting long.'

'We got in early, would you believe. Dinky little airport.'

The patronising tone irritated me. 'It seems to cater to all the island's needs.'

'Dinky aircraft, too. After those jumbo jets.'

'Guernsey is quite small. We haven't the space for long runways...' Why was I talking about 'we'? I'd only been here a short time.

'Dinky cars as well.'

'Many of the lanes are quite narrow. You'll see the Saab's not all that brilliant for getting round.'

'Right you are. We're off to see a dinky garden, then?'

'Bôtnoir's on a surprisingly large scale. Three acres under cultivation. There's further land if it's needed.'

I'd arranged with Jeanne that Pete and I would have the place all to ourselves that day. I didn't want him crowded. His non-stop chatter allowed me to concentrate on the way. I surprised myself by finding Bôtnoir easily. I even recognised the turn-off to the parking spot near which Matthew had been sketching the day he'd first come across me on Guernsey. I decided Charles Grichard had been wrong: Matthew hadn't followed me at all. He'd been there coincidentally, and discreet about the MG. He'd offered to drive because he knew I wasn't used to coping with those tight turns. Now I was. I turned into the drive up to the manor house.

'I see what you mean. Can't afford to put a finger outside the window.'

'You're quite safe. I've done it before.' We lurched our way to the front drive. It had been cleared a little more by the man who lived in the gardener's cottage, Nicol Rochet. He was the son of the Italian nanny Matthew had talked about – Maria, the one they'd been so fond of. Jeanne told me that Nicol had worked on the land at Bôtnoir during the war, then turned to fishing while living in the cottage. He'd retired from being a fisherman a year or two before. When the Jakes arrived to look over the gardens he'd suddenly appeared and offered his services to Jeanne. Something worthwhile to do in his retirement, he'd told her. He said he could remember the grounds exactly as they used to be and would enjoy bringing them back to life. Unfortunately he'd already made a start. He'd need restraining if a TV crew wanted 'before' shots.

'The house looks quite imposing.' Pete stepped out and avoided the puddles in the neglected drive. 'Must have been pretty grand in its day.'

'A small manor house. Appropriate for a small fief.'

'A thief?'

'Robber baron originally, no doubt. It's 'f', not 'th' – fief. Some islanders pronounce it fièf.'

He laughed. 'I prefer thief. What the hell is it?'

'All it means now is a type of land holding. In the eleventh century the fiefs were held by Norman knights – seigneurs. Then, in the thirteenth century, the land passed into the hands of local families.

'All going back a bit, then.'

'Indeed. Guernsey still has feudal elements, and memories tend to be long. In Norman times there were only two fiefs on the island. Since then much of the land has been termed fief du roi – belonging to the Crown...'

'Which crown?'

I held an overhanging branch out of the way. 'The House of Windsor. The French Revolution removed the competition.'

Pete took the branch from me and crept under it. 'So this is royal property. That could stir up a few problems.'

'No, no, not at all. There are quite a few small independent fiefs, including this one. Each has its seigneur, and they still subscribe to one or two feudal customs which won't concern us. Apart from that, everything's perfectly normal.'

'So the man who owns this place is a seigneur?'

'Yes. The first Mathieu Frelé's line has descended to his great-great-grandson, another Mathieu Frelé. He's the present seigneur.'

'You've checked that he's willing to allow us to make these programmes, I take it.'

Not directly with Matthew. Jeanne had assured me that he and Jake had sorted it all out between them, and I'd left everything to my very competent agent. 'Provided the terms of the contract are passed by his lawyers. My agent's seeing to my side of it. Best get the BBC legal department cracking.'

'He wants to make something out of it?'

'No way. I thought you might offer a little for expenses he wouldn't otherwise have had.'

The face which looked up from another jungle of branches scowled. 'If you say so. Tight budget and all that. You know how it is.'

We toured the garden. I showed Pete some of the seigneurie as well. The outside of the house would have to feature as part of the programme, at least to a small extent. He was enthralled. Not just because of the feudal background to the place, the marvellous position on the cliffs, the balmy climate of the Channel Islands. It was primarily because the grounds were so neglected, and yet the bones of a fine garden could be made out even by amateurs. Good visual stuff.

I wanted his opinion on the odd discrepancy between the outside jutting of the east wall and the inside of the hall. I was convinced it was some sort of hiding place. 'What d'you think? Odd, isn't it?'

He had other things on his mind. 'Maybe it's a priest's hole.'

'Did they have those on Guernsey? Anyway, it's not in the right place, there's no access of any kind.'

He humoured me for a few minutes. We tapped around. There didn't seem to be a hollow sound. It was a proper brick wall. Surely not four foot thick? I was convinced there was a walled-up space behind that bland inside wall. It nagged at me, but I'd have to investigate another time.

Pete was back to his filming recce. 'A few essentials, Ruth. No one's to touch the place again before we've done the prelim shoots.'

'I'll curb Nicol Rochet's enthusiasm.'

'D'you think the old lad would agree to be filmed?'

'Today, you mean?'

Pete rested the heavy camera on a terrace step. 'Later. If we do decide to go ahead. He'd know what it was like before, he could point us to the differences between then and now. That would be brill.'

Was this turning into a TV series rather than a book? 'I can ask.'

'Regular updates. Don't know about the format of the programmes yet, but filming every month. Can you do the stills?'

'Thirty-five millimetre trannies?'

'What camera body d'you use? Nikon?'

'I'm used to the Minolta 7000i. Dedicated lens.'

'They're pretty good. Should do. Give it a whirl and let me see the results. I'll be in touch.'

CHAPTER THIRTEEN

I raced back to Bôtnoir after I'd dropped Pete off at the airport. It was my first chance to explore the place on my own.

I parked, stepped out of the car, stopped to look around. Something was making me nervous; I sensed I was being watched, though there was no other car in the drive, and the house was as remote from any other as was possible on Guernsey.

What was I doing here, snooping around? Debs had been scandalised about my taking on the job at all. I'd rung her up last night, pleased at the notion of a TV connection.

'I simply cannot understand why you're even considering it.' Her voice was loud and testy. 'I thought you were a writer. Why are you suddenly turning yourself into a landscape gardener?'

'I've told you. It's much more than that, a series of my own. You should be pleased for me.'

'They've done dozens of programmes like that.'

Why was she so against it? 'Hardly dozens. And not about this type of garden.'

'That's another thing. What's the point? Most people have small gardens.'

'You might just as well say what's the point of illustrating the use of period furniture in large country houses? They can't fit into modern boxes. The attraction is history. People enjoy seeing the past recreated. I want to show what can be done with just a few fine trees to start with.'

The line crackled as she twitched the lead. 'Whatever I say, you're not going to take any notice.'

I had to admit I was fixated on the place, not the programme.

I realised what was drawing me to this new project was the idea of working at Bôtnoir.

An image of the house in its full glory fired my imagination. I heard music, saw the huge windows open on a summer's day, heard snippets of conversation interspersed with the clinking of glasses, the gurgling of liquid, the chinking sound of cutlery on plates. Women dressed as my mother used to dress before the war – long slim line skirts, cloche hats, silk stockings, platform shoes – flittering across a beautifully kept lawn. Men in bow ties, cigarettes in long holders, a croquet game. What had these ghosts to do with me? Well, they were alive at the time of Matthew's childhood. I wanted to immerse myself in that, to ferret out what made him as he now was.

I brought myself back to the present. The feeling of unease persisted. But now I did not sense a bygone age: no chiffon floating in the wind, no twenties' youth clapping hands to the Charleston rhythm. This time the feeling was oppressive. I brushed it aside and began to walk round the garden. A fleeting figure disappearing behind a tangle of overgrown shrubs caught my eye. I knew it was a person, and not an animal, because I heard the tearing of material. But, though I followed the sound, I could not make out anyone at all. All seemed deserted.

The amount of work to be done on the garden was colossal. I discovered a couple more shrubs worth saving, some lovely stones which could be used as the basis for a rockery, a derelict pond, several sculptures.

I must have taken about an hour to take stock. Eventually I decided to go into the house and look out from the rooms which overlooked the garden. It would be important to blend the planting with the wider views. I walked up the balcony steps and slipped the key into the French windows leading to the living room. The door was open. Had I really been careless enough not to lock up properly after I'd shown the place to Pete?

I walked around the room, admiring its proportions, then gazed out of the French windows, trying to imagine the garden as it would be in twenty years, and the way it would look from that particular spot. I made notes, already enthusiastic about the suggestions I would make to Jeanne.

The empty room echoed with my footfalls which seemed to break into my thoughts. As I stood still, annoyed at the interruption, I realised I'd sensed some noises off. I listened, nervous now, then walked out of the double door and on to the landing. The staircase curved gracefully into to the hall. I walked down a little nervously, stood by the front door and listened. Had someone driven up? Jeanne, perhaps? There was no sound of any kind.

Curiosity got the better of me. I put my hand on the straight wall which didn't match the one outside. I knocked on it in several different places. There was nothing to suggest a plastered-over door. Just an ordinary wall.

The sound of something moving upstairs made me catch my breath. Was someone else in the house, or was wind banging a loose window, a shutter, a door? I wouldn't have noticed any of that when I was going round the place earlier, I told myself. And tried not to panic.

The distinct sound of a creak made my heart pound. A burglar? To steal what? I felt my blood draining from my head, pinched myself. All I had to do was to get out and drive away, then come back another time with someone else. But the whole point of coming had been to be on my own. I stared up the stairs and again had that feeling of déjà vu. I focused on what was around me – nothing but the chandelier, the staircase and the pock-marked walls.

A door above me opened. The dining room, judging by the direction of the noise.

'Who's there?' I shouted out, my voice trembling when I'd meant it to sound decisive.

'Sure could ask you that.' Another American accent here on Guernsey? 'Reckon I'm the house guest here.'

I turned and recognised the man I seemed to be fated to come across time and again – cousin Todd. The last person I'd have expected to be staying here. Maybe the German – Otto – drove him over. Whatever the reasons for his presence I realised they had to be significant. 'I thought you were some sort of trespasser.'

'Well, now. I'd say that description fits you some. And I'm the guy on the spot.'

How very odd. Jeanne had told me Jean-Jacques had no time for his cousin, that none of the brothers did. So why was Jake allowing him to stay? A holding action, presumably, while they sorted out who was the legal heir to the fief. Which could only mean they weren't sure of their ground. 'I'm afraid I had no idea.'

'That a fact?' He sauntered down the wide staircase, disbelief in every step. Tight-fitting blue jeans emphasised the bulge of his stomach. He wore trainers and a check shirt with the sleeves rolled up. The bare arms were covered in a black fuzz, the undone buttons of the shirt showing the same on the chest. He looked threatening. 'So what's the deal here?'

'I'm redesigning the garden for Madame Jean-Jacques Frelé.' Why had no one warned me about his staying here? 'Didn't Jeanne mention my meeting with Pete Tanner? A producer from the BBC.'

'Said you'd be checking out the garden, sure. What are you doing in the house, all on your lonesome?'

The look was challenging. And disconcerting. 'It's important to consider the planting in terms of views from the main windows. And we were also going to make a couple of indoor gardens.'

'I guess that would be later.' He'd come right up to me. 'You're looking for something, right?'

This man was distinctly threatening. And unnerving. 'I've no idea what you mean. It's very important to have the house in mind when thinking about the garden.' I could see he didn't believe a word of that.

'Why were you tapping this here wall?'

He must have been spying on me before he came downstairs. 'Jeanne and I thought some plants would soften up the entrance. This wall doesn't tally with the one outside. There's about four foot by twelve unaccounted for. I thought empty space like that might make a nice foyer.'

He stalked past me and went out. I followed, watched him take in what I'd said. 'Sure thing. Guess it slipped my mind.'

He came back inside and tapped the wall. It sounded like a single course, not as thick as the outside wall with twenty-inch window recesses. What was this curious anomaly?

'You know about it?'

He shifted further away. 'Gran'mère talked about it. I guess they stored the valuables here.'

Did he think the missing marriage certificate was hidden in a secret room? If so, I was the idiot who'd made him aware of where it might be. 'Furniture, you mean?'

I thought he was going to ask me what business it was of mine and tell me to leave. 'Antiques maybe. Jewellery, valuable wine, papers, I guess. I'll bet my bottom dollar there's nothing left. There's a houseful of stuff at Lascervelle which don't really fit. Guess maybe it came from here.'

His eyes showed he was going to investigate as soon as I'd gone. I had to stay around and make sure that, whatever he found, he wouldn't destroy it. 'Where's the entrance? Can't see a door.' I walked up and down, knocking the wall at intervals again to see whether a door was hidden behind the plaster.

'If it were that plain it wouldn't be that great a hiding place.' He'd come to within six inches of me. It made me nervous, but I knew I'd have to stand my ground if I wasn't to invite some sort of attack. In spite of this, I found myself drawing back against the wall, using it to steady me.

He put his left arm just above my right ear, leaning towards me. I tried to duck under his elbow, to move away, but he stepped forward, leaned his body into mine. 'What's your hurry, lady?'

I stopped myself from cringing, and tried to think my way out of the situation. A dialogue was still going on. I must try to keep it on that level. I forced myself to smile. 'I rather wanted to—'

Forceful lips covered mine, cut off my breath. I went limp, trying for escape by dropping my body low and squirming away. He was practised. His left arm hooked around my right one, his body pressed against it, while his right hand infiltrated underneath my blouse.

I pulled him further to myself, brought up my knee and aimed at his groin. He wasn't expecting it, so he didn't try to evade the sudden jab. I could see the surprise in his eyes as he felt the pain. He didn't let go. I hadn't found the right place.

He leered at me, interpreting my actions as encouragement. 'Knew all along you were asking for it.'

I ducked my lips away by swivelling my head. 'Why would you think that?' Keep vocalising, I told myself. 'I'm working here, that's all.'

He changed tactics, grabbed my shoulders as he tried to pull me away from the wall. Unsuccessfully. He drank too much, and wasn't as fit as gardening had made me.

My back clung to the wall in imitation of gripping ivy. 'What *is* this? What d'you want?'

His head was moving forward. I snaked sideways, dropped slightly down, grabbed my hands together and pushed my elbow, hard, into his groin. I felt his breath push out, the momentary loosening of his hands. Taking my chance I twisted out of his grip and ran towards the door.

It opened before I'd even reached the handle. I had the presence of mind to push my hair back from my face, to pull my blouse completely out and to brush it straight over my jeans.

Matthew walked in, glancing over me and squinting at his cousin. 'Rather thought we were due to meet outside, Todd.'

'That a fact?'

He turned to me. 'I didn't realise you'd be here, Ruth.'

'I just came to get the proper feel of the place,' I said. Debs's singing teacher taught her the trick of controlling her voice by using her belly muscles to control the air passing over the vocal cords. She'd shown me how to do it and I used it to effect. 'I'm terribly sorry to be in your way. I didn't realise you two had arranged to meet here.'

Sometimes I wonder how, at my age, I can still be such a simpleton. The struggle with Todd Frelé wouldn't have led anywhere because he knew Matthew was coming. He was simply trying to compromise me – and to annoy Matthew, perhaps.

'Jeanne's gardener thinks there's a secret storage chamber

behind this wall,' Todd said, grinning at me.

'Are you referring to Mrs Samuels?' Matthew's monotone voice told me he was really angry. Probably with me as well as Todd. He turned his back on Todd. 'I thought you were helping Jeanne plan a new garden, Ruth. Why does that involve the house?'

'We thought of hanging plants indoors...'

'Not at this stage, presumably.' He turned away, walked past me, swung up the stairs and on into the living room.

Did he know why a wall had been added? And what was behind it? Impossible to say. 'I'm just off, Matthew,' I shouted up the stairs. There was no reply.

I had to find a way to warn him about Todd's plans. Better give Jeanne a ring. She wanted her son to inherit Bôtnoir, so she had a really strong motive to sort it out. I drove myself away.

CHAPTER FOURTEEN

Now that I was linked to the Frelés with a job I felt bold enough to tackle Matthew about his paintings. To my surprise he agreed to let me photograph a number. He even allowed me to take a small canvas to show as a sample of his work.

I decided to approach Andrew Canwaller. The gallery was small, and brilliantly sited within the pedestrian haven of South Molton Street. I'd picked him out because I'd heard he not only had the courage to show unknown artists, he also had a good eye. Diana Wendle, my agent, offered to see if she could get me an appointment. Apparently that wasn't a problem.

'Elizabeth Pilton. I'm a great fan.' Canwaller was thirty-nine, and holding. A short genial man with long dyed curls. The grey roots were beginning to show through, making the dark hair look as though it floated just above his scalp. His smile was warm and assessing.

'You're very kind.'

'Do sit down.' Both manicured hands waved me to a leather armchair opposite his desk. 'So you paint as well? What a plethora of creative gifts.' The warmth had turned to cool enquiry.

Diana's enthusiasms can lead her astray. I hoped she hadn't been rash and given the impression that I was trying to change from writing to painting. The name Elizabeth Pilton, though known in a different field, is better than an unknown name. He consulted a large desk diary, then looked up.

I resisted the momentary temptation. 'I wish painting were a talent.'

The silk-suited shoulders froze.

Perhaps I'd made a mistake, perhaps I'd underestimated his self-confidence. I opened my briefcase to give myself seconds to formulate the right words. 'What I do have is a gift for recognising genius. You'll be able to judge for yourself from these slides.' I flourished out some transparencies. I'd shot about twenty of Matthew's paintings. Not up to Tate Gallery standard, but I'd thought them serviceable enough. Why on earth hadn't I had them professionally done? After all, my photographic repertoire was limited to shots of plants.

'That's quite a claim.' He was already standing.

'And I've brought an original as well.' A small cloudscape, only twelve inches by sixteen. It wasn't really representative of Matthew's larger works, but it was one of my favourites.

He walked round his desk and took the wallet of transparencies from my hand. It might have been more politic to stay seated. Canwaller was a short man, but I don't like being looked down on even from a small height. I unzipped the canvas bag in which I'd brought the painting, walked over to the mantelpiece, cleared a space and leant the picture against the wall.

'Now you can see what I'm talking about. Your dream come true, the discovery of a major talent.' I smiled to show I was being jocular, but still serious.

Silence hung heavy. The fixed polite smile moved to the painting. And stayed on it as he walked up to it, retreated, stepped to one side and then the other. He went back to his desk and took up a magnifying glass. Certain areas of the canvas seemed to interest him more than others. He picked up his phone and rang through to his receptionist. 'No calls.' Then he turned to me. 'There's a light table and a projector next door. Let's go and look at those trannies.'

The magnifying glass was used again. Fifteen transparencies were set aside for viewing through the projector. 'How about mid-August?'

'But that's in only three weeks.' I frowned. 'And everyone's away on holiday.'

'That's the only slot I've got left till next year. I think we'll do well. Tourist trade.'

'I'll discuss it with the artist.'

'The artist has nothing to do with it. You're representing him. Yes or no?'

I'd have agreed to any timing. It would be desperately hard work to get it all together, but I decided that delay wouldn't make it any easier. The sooner the better.

'You're responsible for the framing and the initial choice of paintings. Send me a hundred transparencies and I'll do the final selection from those. You and I hang them. Fifty percent commission.'

'That's pretty steep.'

'This is central London.'

He misinterpreted my hesitation. I was pretty sure Matthew didn't care about the money, but I was bemused by the way things were going.

'All right, then: forty-five. That's my best offer.'

The feeling of elation lasted until I stepped off the plane on Guernsey. My sense of triumph dissipated as I began to appreciate that the achievement wasn't mine. It was all because of Matthew's extraordinary talent. He wouldn't need me any more after the exhibition. Nor would he need his brother's help to restore Bôtnoir. Canwaller had made it clear that each painting would sell for thousands. Matthew Frelé would be rich, famous - and out of my league. Why was I doing this?

CHAPTER FIFTEEN

The canvases I'd chosen, properly framed and displayed, looked even more sensational than I'd dared hope. There was a strength, a drive in each one, which meant the viewer's opinions would go beyond mere liking or disliking. Every single painting on show oozed with vigour, with a force unleashed yet kept within the confines of the canvas.

I was staying with Debs. She'd joined me the day before the opening, when I was busy checking the names of people coming to the private viewing. Canwaller had seen to it that a number of well-known collectors were invited. I also noticed Frank Bowers' name. Matthew had mentioned his work several times. I hadn't realised he actually knew one of the most talented sculptors of the post-war years.

'A pretty impressive guest list,' I pointed out to Debs.

Instead of smiling, she scowled. 'You've really pulled out all the stops.' Though not as possessive as my sons she didn't like my working with Matthew. She said it was because he seemed so — well, secretive.

'Secretive?' I frowned. She'd never met him, and she'd only met Mark in passing. 'I must have given you the wrong impression. Self-contained, perhaps.'

'He's such a...' An animated beginning which stopped.

'What are you going on about? You don't even know him.' A sudden suspicion formed. Had she come across him somewhere, fallen for his undoubted charm? I was being ridiculous. Matthew hadn't left Guernsey since I ran into him. 'Do you?'

'Of course I don't know him. I ran into Mark at our last dress rehearsal. We had a coffee afterwards and he talked about Matthew.'

I'd mentioned Debs's singing to Mark. Several times. I was surprised he'd taken the trouble to go and listen to the choir. 'You mean he went to one of your concerts?'

'He's into choral music,' she brushed that off. 'What really bothers me is why you're changing your job.' Her face had contoured into fury. 'You're an outstanding writer on gardening. What are you spending time on all this for?'

'I'm helping a fellow artist.' Dignity was dripping from every pore – in the form of a cold sweat. 'At least postpone judgement until you see the paintings.'

'He's so damned tricky, Mum.'

What was all this? I hadn't told her that much about him. Had my children engaged a private detective to check Matthew out? 'That's what creative artists are all about.'

'This one certainly gets full marks on that scale.'

Her dislike of someone she didn't even know irritated me. 'What's it matter? The work is there and that's all that counts.'

'No need to be so defensive.' She looked at me, her perceptive eyes examining my get-up.

In spite of the connotations of scarlet woman, I enjoy wearing red. With black accents to tone it down. I shut my lips tight. I'd no intention of giving anything more away.

She walked around, examining the paintings, determined to be critical. She ended up open-mouthed. 'You say he's never shown before?'

'Apparently he'd arranged an exhibition sometime in his early twenties. Something went wrong at the last minute.'

'But that's nearly forty years ago!'

I had to admit that that was peculiar, even allowing for the artistic temperament. 'Some family problem. I've no idea about the details. He never bothered again.'

'You mean the gallery owner reneged on giving him a show?'

'Nothing to do with that, apparently. Matthew refuses to say more. Somehow I formed the impression that a personal crisis was involved.'

I wasn't going to tell Debs I was sure Mark was part of it. The more I thought about his reactions to my mounting an exhibition for Matthew the more irrational they seemed. Had the brothers quarrelled about the girl in the portrait? Was that why Matthew refused to show that painting?

'So I have a notion that what happened had to do with a love affair. I don't know anything at all about it, you understand. Just a hunch I have.'

'The famous intuition.' My daughter grinned. 'You know, I wouldn't mind buying one or two of these.'

'They aren't cheap.' Canwaller and I had agreed that people would either love Matthew's work or hate it, so we'd made the prices fairly steep. The cheapest was going for five thousand pounds.

'You really fancy him, don't you?'

'Him?' The cold sweat turned to an uncomfortable flush. I told myself I wasn't sure. My feelings went from one extreme to the other. One moment I imagined myself his wife, the next I could hardly wait to get as far away from him, and from Guernsey, as soon as possible.

There was something I couldn't understand. Nothing to do with Charles Grichard's hints, or anything Mark had said. It had to do with the way Matthew always held back, always appeared to look at life from the outside, never acted as though he were a part of it. He kept such rigid control that I decided he suppressed all feeling, that the famous heart-breaker did not lead women on, he simply did not respond to them. When we were together, and I thought getting on well, it was as though, catching himself enjoying my company, he'd punish himself by leaving. He'd done this several times, once even during a discussion on which particular pigments he favoured.

All the same, I couldn't complain about his general attitude. He conducted himself well, even charmingly, the perfect gentleman. But when we were on our own I often had the sense of being with an automaton.

In a way it was worse than that. Matthew behaved as though

he had no worth. I recognised the feeling because I used to suffer from that myself. In my youth, in the days before women stood up to be counted, and because I was a Jewish refugee, I'd suffered from just such sentiments. I'd had to unlearn them, to teach myself to respect myself. Was it, perhaps, because he was nervous, felt his paintings weren't good enough? If so, that would soon change.

'Is there something between you?' Debs asked. 'Not that I think there shouldn't be. I just want to know.'

'It's a purely business relationship. I knew the paintings were quite exceptional when I first saw them. They needed to be shown. I offered to organise an exhibition, and Matthew eventually agreed. That's all.' I drew myself up to my full height, but I was still four inches shorter than Debs. 'What's more, I won't lose financially by it.'

'I know that's a big consideration.' Deborah laughed. 'I know you haven't got two pennies to rub together. That's why you're looking at houses worth a million or so. Almost at starvation point.'

The gardening books were selling very well, and that was only the beginning. The BBC had been back to me in record time. They were thrilled to commission a TV series based on restoring the garden at Bôtnoir. Part of the agreement was that they publish the books that went with the series. My agent had been delighted, my publisher enthusiastic. The new programme would boost sales of my previous books as well.

But Debs did have a point. I didn't have time for organising exhibitions. And I hadn't achieved my private aim. The painting I'd been angling for, the portrait of the young woman I'd spied that first time in Brixton, was not forthcoming.

'I need around a hundred paintings,' I'd explained to Matthew when we'd signed the papers his law firm had drawn up. 'As many different types and sizes as possible.'

'I do mostly abstracts.'

'I know, but there are some lovely impressionistic seascapes and skyscapes–'

'Early work, purely imitative. Not really relevant.'

I prided myself on my sideways approach. 'I thought perhaps we could think of this as a retrospective. Give the public a chance to see examples of all your work.'

He stared straight at me. 'My best stuff is with the secret fan I told you about.'

'That still leaves plenty of outstanding work, Matthew. Now, what about a portrait or two? That small painting I saw...'

We were talking in the small studio he'd set up at Charles Grichard's place. He strode away from me, as far as he could get, heightening my curiosity. If I didn't try for it, I'd never see it. '...the one I glimpsed in your attic studio that time...'

'Not for sale.' The reverberating voice was low. His back was turned to me and he was staring out of the window at Charles's garden.

'Not to sell, if you don't wish to. Just to show—'

'Or for show. Or discussion, Ruth.'

In fact he'd refused to show any of the portraits he'd done. There were some outstanding self-portraits, and one or two studies of his brothers which would have sold within minutes of the opening. He refused to discuss the issue. I couldn't even find out whether his brothers knew about their portraits. He'd caught their differences very well. A stranger would have recognised them.

'They're my paintings, my private work. I do not intend to show them, or to sell them.'

I said nothing further. But my instincts were spot on. It was because I eventually guessed who the girl in the portrait was that I solved the riddle of Matthew's phobias. At the time I heard the danger signals and kept quiet. He might decide to cancel the exhibition, or even make a bonfire of the 'private' paintings if really roused. There was historic precedent for that with other artists.

CHAPTER SIXTEEN

'So he has them on show at last, has he?' A husky voice with a guttural accent sounded behind me.

Frizzy grey hair was tied back in a ponytail, balancing a dominating nose. The shrewd face was alive with lines, a mesh creasing the forehead up or in according to his expression. Rough chapped fingers brushed across the surface of a cloudscape. Who had invited this man to the preview? And how had he got beyond the virago Andrew Canwaller had carefully selected to guard the door?

I looked again. A fine grey dust was ingrained in the creases of the man's jeans, and in a T-shirt which hadn't seen a washing machine for at least a week. The V-necked sweater was grubby, frayed at the hem, with jagged holes displaying filthy elbows. There was something familiar – perhaps. 'Quite right, it's the first exhibition of this artist's work. Please don't touch the paintings.'

'So you now are his latest slave, is that it?'

The German accent wasn't strong, but it was there. The fingers drew back, clawed. The broken nails had grey dust flaking around the cuticles. Now that his face was still I could see deep grooves from nose to mouth. The Semitic features gave him a melancholy expression which reminded me of my father, and of the other men I'd known as a child. Then a more personal familiarity got through to me. Did I know this man?

'I believe slavery was abolished over a century and a half ago.' I stared at him, eyes unblinking. He stared right back. 'Even for women.' My lips succeeded in curling into a sneer.

'Don't try to get out of it like that. Matt's always had a gaggle of female slaves around him.' The light-grey eyes narrowed, took in my face, my hair, my figure. 'You are not the usual candidate,' he drawled. 'He used to be a keen cradle-snatcher. Only beauties, of course. Perhaps he's abandoned youth for money now?' He'd stopped looking at me. His attention was focused on an abstract, a mingling of purple and blue relieved by highlights of scarlet. 'This is St Peter Port in the mid '40s. After the war. That is when we first met.'

The painting was named *Study in Red and Purple, Eleven*. Hardly a give-away title. 'You're an old friend of his?'

'Enemy.' He moved on to the painting hanging next to *Eleven*, a study in earthy yellow and a greyish shade of green, the sky reflecting rain. The ticket read *Ochre and Jade, Fourteen*. 'That doesn't mean I can't recognise his genius.'

His eyes swivelled to me as he stared in the way continentals do. It reminded me of something... Maybe I did know him? 'You're a painter?'

'I am a sculptor. Evidently you don't remember me.' His eyes looked sad.

I frowned. Marble, that's what the dust was. Canwaller had invited Frank Bowers. This had to be the famous sculptor. I'd never met him, never even seen a photograph, but I'd always admired his work, particularly his busts of eminent people. A Francis Bacon working in stone. 'I don't believe...'

'Have I really changed so much?' His eyes were delving below my skin, flesh and muscle, down to the bone structure. 'Kennst du mich nicht – Don't you recognise me? I'd have known you anywhere, Ruthi.'

Franz Scheiderbauer. How come I'd never made the connection? Because the last I'd seen of him was in Vienna, when the Gestapo had dragged him and his family out of the apartment across the corridor from us. I was watching from our door. Frozen, furious, unable to do anything.

'It's really you, Franz?' Sensibly anglicised to Frank Bowers. 'How wonderful. I'd no idea you'd survived.'

'That is one way of looking at it,' he said. 'Over others' dead bodies. I hack at marble to avenge the ones I left behind.'

'You're brilliant.' I tried not to stare but couldn't take my eyes off him. 'Your work, I mean. Just in case you get the wrong impression. You were an obnoxious child. You pulled my pigtails.'

'So very pullable. You're looking well, Ruth. Do you think I would really try to prise you away from Matt? I would never attempt anything like that.' The skin on his face had a greyish hue. He pulled out a black cheroot and put it in his mouth.

'No smoking in here, Franz. Sorry.'

'No need to be. My doctor lectures me all the time. I put it in my mouth for the taste. Better than those ghastly pads.' He sucked on the cheroot as he stared at me again. 'A warning from an old friend, Ruth. Stay away from Matthew. For your own good.'

Cautions against Matthew were becoming absurdly repetitive. I decided Franz was either jealous of Matthew's work, or he thought Matthew had poached a girlfriend in the past. 'Your model, was she? You think Matthew stole her?'

'Think? No question about it.' He turned his back, stared at a painting in russet and gold at the far end. 'That is the first study he did of her. How much?'

The painting was exhilarating, but I'd had no idea it was a study for a portrait. There was still much for me to learn. I handed Franz the list. 'They're going fast. We've already sold half the show. If you want it you'd better make your mind up in a hurry.' The price I'd put on that particular canvas was seven thousand five hundred. Canwaller and I had underestimated the demand – badly. We could easily have doubled the prices and still sold.

His eyes grew round. 'You certainly believe in starting him in at the deep end.'

'He's been waiting for a long time.'

An impatient hand grabbed the cigar out of his mouth. 'Waiting, you call it? That was his choice. For years he did not even try to sell.'

Was it possible that Franz knew more about Matthew and his work than he let on? And then I grasped what the connection was. 'You're not the secret fan, are you?' Franz could afford to buy anything he wanted. His success had been phenomenal.

'Secret fan? What do you mean? He knows I value his work.'

'The secret collector...'

'My admiration for his work is not a secret.' A deep gurgling laugh exploded out of the lean taut frame which hunched with a tickling cough. Marble dust might not be much better for his lungs than asbestos. Cheroots on top of that could well be lethal. 'Please do not tell him I am buying without speaking with me first.'

'Of course not.'

He leaned against the wall, his slight frame hugging it. 'I have always known of his talent, understood it. In every direction. Where is he, anyway?'

So the Franz Scheiderbauer I knew as a child had survived the Holocaust. I was sure that was why he'd always admired Matthew's work. I guessed he'd seen the deeper meaning behind it, had wanted the best paintings to survive in a hostile world. I deduced he might well be the secret collector. How extraordinary. 'Flying in from Guernsey.'

'You mean he has gone to live back there again? Has that Tartar of a grandmother died at last? I was beginning to think she was immortal.'

'Early this year.' It would be fascinating to renew acquaintance with this man. And his viewpoint of the family, from a standpoint I could identify with, was likely to be astute. 'You knew her, did you?'

'I met her in the late '40s. Downside offered me a place, after the war, and I spent a few summer vacations on Guernsey. An interesting old lady, very powerful. She was left to look after those boys on her own.' A sharp look. 'I am sure you know they were orphaned at a young age. The grandmother was very able to direct their upbringing. From what I have learned, she was even capable of keeping the Occupying Forces in order.'

'Catholic Downside offered a place to a Jew?'

'Non practising. Their way of showing solidarity against the Nazi doctrine.'

He'd met the grandmother, seen her in action. Maybe he could fill me in about Matthew's background. 'I've heard she entertained high-ranking German officers.'

The lifted eyebrows, the central-European shrug. 'People called her a collaborator. I am not sure. Perhaps she was just being clever. We all have to survive in the best way we can. No one is able do it without scars. Not even you, Ruthi.'

Being uprooted at the age of six, thrust into a different culture and a different language, had seared itself into my psyche. It isn't possible to escape one's destiny. But it's possible to shape it. 'I wouldn't think of denying it.'

The rough skin of his fingers brushed mine. 'You were always spunky. You didn't kow-tow to those ghastly storm troopers.'

He'd have been as interested in the Frelés' attitude to the Occupying Forces as I was. Someone like Matthew, who'd done his best to annoy the Nazis from the moment they arrived, would have been irresistible to Franz. No wonder they'd become friends. I was convinced that some of Matthew's oddities could be put down to traumas which happened during the Nazi Occupation. His parents' deaths, of course. But I sensed an added dimension. And why was he so much more affected than his brothers?

'D'you know much about that time in their lives, Franz?'

'Matt's been evasive, as usual, has he?'

'We only meet occasionally. I have my own work, but naturally we do come across each other on the island.'

'You actually live on Guernsey?' His furrows grew deep. 'Tax exile, are you? I would not have said you were this type.'

'That isn't the reason. My husband died and I wanted a complete break with the past. I'm renting a house to see how I like it there.'

He put a friendly arm around my shoulders. 'So you arrange art exhibitions for a living? I'm surprised. I would have expected you to do something of the creative yourself.'

'Actually I write. On gardening.'

The pale eyes swivelled back at me, as though my face would reveal the sort of books I wrote. 'I also have a place in the country. What I like to do is to arrange the garden round my pieces. A sort of living backdrop.' He laughed, then doubled up coughing. 'Sorry about that.'

'Can I get you a drink?'

'Perrier,' he gasped. 'Or anything non-alcoholic.'

By the time I got back he was already talking to several other people, including Deborah. 'So you are Elizabeth Pilton now. I have dipped into several of your books. Switching Christian names is not above board, you know. At least I stuck to a form of Franz.'

'Christian name is what it's about,' I said. 'I've converted to Catholicism. And there are author photographs on the book jackets. I don't believe you've read anything I've written.'

He bowed. 'The books, a little; the jackets, not very carefully. The only photograph I can remember showed a heavy disguise. A large expanse of hat and only a small amount of author.'

I grinned. It was a very successful photograph, giving my rather undistinguished face a frame. 'It's important to remind gardeners about the effects of too much sun.'

'In England?'

'We live in an age of skin cancer,' I said. 'Gardening is a fair-weather occupation for most people.'

His eyes had sunk even lower down into their sockets. He was terribly thin. 'Your daughter tells me you are also designing the gardens at Bôtnoir. I did not realise you were working in that direction.'

'I don't,' I said. 'I just write. I haven't even got a garden of my own at the moment.'

'So this is a special undertaking, a favour to Matthew?'

'She says she's doing it for one of Matthew's brothers and his family.' Deborah was drinking rather a lot of champagne. It made her giggle at the end of every sentence.

'Is that so?' The light eyes held a sardonic gleam. 'Which one?'

'Jean-Jacques. The most successful one.' Debs seemed to know a great deal of Frelé background. Had I really talked that much about them to her? I certainly didn't remember that.

'Only as the wheel of fortune spins. It might stop somewhere else quite soon,' I said.

But there was no stopping Debs, and Franz had the look of an avid listener. 'Jean-Jacques took silk at only thirty-one, apparently. Head of his chambers, and the best criminal defence lawyer in the country.'

'You mean he will use Bôtnoir as a holiday home?' Franz's ponytail bobbed up and down.

'He's retiring to Guernsey. So are Mark and Luke.' Another giggle as the champagne continued its effects. 'Just like my mum.' She took a couple more swigs from her glass. 'But Jake can't work there. Their laws are different and, well, very insular. He wouldn't be allowed to practise.' This time she burped. 'And criminal activity is on a small scale. It's too hard to get away from those few cramped square miles.' Deborah's eyes became animated. 'Now if he were working in financial fraud on an international scale, that would be different.'

'So he will be twiddling his thumbs on that little island?' Franz cast his eyes around more of the paintings. 'Matthew will stay there permanently, I presume.'

'He's taking over Lascervelle House, his place in St Peter Port. Once everything is sorted out.' I ticked another painting as sold on my list.

Franz nodded sagely at one more canvas. 'I take that one as well.' It was a recent work. Not really a painting – a painted collage in a variety of blue and rust fibres, enlivened by glints of white. The effect was far more subdued than much of the work on display. As though the fire which burned so brightly in some of the earlier work had become a smoulder. No less heat – perhaps more – but not as spectacular.

'I'll tell the dragon, shall I?' Deborah took another flute of champagne, drifted off, her eyes glinting amusement at me as she did.

Franz steered me away from the crowds. 'I should have known he would be rushing back as soon as he could manage. He always was hankering after that place. Maybe he told you his father talked to him before the attempted escape. He made him promise to lay claim to the fief, to fight for it if necessary.'

'You mean he thought there could be a problem?'

Franz shrugged. 'I do not know. Maybe to do with money, or not splitting up a small estate. As far as Matthew was – is – concerned it is simply a question of carrying out his father's wishes.'

It still struck me as peculiar. But it confirmed my conviction that the four sons had not been born – or conceived – out of wedlock. And I was glad that it was a solemn promise to the dead father, not snobbery, which had motivated Matthew to buy his brothers out. 'Which makes it even stranger that he left. Was it really the grandmother who kept him from going back?'

'He absolutely loathed her. Reciprocated, I should tell you.'

'Do you know why?'

'I can only guess. She'd been a great admirer of Germany years before the war. She spent many holidays there, staying with some aristocratic friends in Prussia. Along the lines of Diana Moseley.'

A cold chill ran through me. Did Matthew's grandmother know the man in black – Otto – even before the war?

'That was enough for him. He insisted it meant she had been a Nazi sympathiser, and that she still continued to agree their policies. Therefore he held her as responsible as the Occupation Forces for his parents' deaths.' The grey eyes focused on me. 'Matthieu said she betrayed his parents. He insisted that that was the reason they were not able to escape.'

'You mean he maintained she informed against her own son?' I tried to take it in but, as a mother, found it impossible to believe. 'Did he have proof?'

'Only the fact that they were not able to get away. He said it meant someone must have informed on them. They would never have failed otherwise.'

'But–' If that were true, why weren't they arrested, taken to court? Why were their bodies never found? It didn't add up.

Franz linked his arm in mine. 'Please forget the bloody war. Shall we get out of here? Have a meal somewhere?'

That took me by surprise. It would be fascinating to discuss old times, to find out what had happened to his people, whether they'd survived as well. But not tonight. 'I promised the Frelés I'd go to the...'

126

Matthew chose that moment to make his entrance. I heard the bass rumbling a greeting through the hubbub, heard the squeal of excited females as they mobbed him.

'We could go ahead. Matthew will not mind if I join you.'

I looked at his clothes, his general dust-covered greyness.

He smiled, shrugged his shoulders. 'All right, all right, I will change my clothing. Where is the party?'

'The favourite haunt is the Connaught.'

'It is necessary to wear a suit? Or even white tie get-up?'

'Don't you think–?' Then I saw Matthew looking in our direction. He must have caught sight of Franz – Frank Bowers to him. I could see the dark head above the sea of bobbing platinum blondes and redheads blow-dried into formal negligence advancing through. The teeth remained on show, but the eyes had grown cold.

He was beside us within seconds. He put a casual hand on my arm and smiled at me. 'Hello, Ruth. They tell me you've been brilliant.' It was the first deliberate touch in all the months we'd known each other. I was unprepared for the fire it effected in my veins, and quivered. He took his hand away, turned. 'Frank. How did you know?'

'Not very difficult. I read the arts pages in The Times. And Andy is an old friend.'

'My work was featured?'

'Advertised. You have an excellent PR system.' His eyes swept over me again, he raised what was left of his Perrier and nodded in my direction. 'I see you do not lose any of the old skills.'

The assumption that I was, somehow, in Matthew's thrall infuriated me. But I knew better than to protest too much. I thought maybe that he would do it for me.

'The same could be said of you.' Rather to my surprise Matthew was wearing a formal suit, charcoal with a faint red stripe and a white shirt. Only the brilliant waistcoat gave away the artistic bent. Peacock and gold.

Now was not the time to raise old spectres. But Matthew would have known from the casual way I held my hand out to say goodbye that Franz was not the man I was interested in. He was astute enough not to kiss it continental fashion, though I saw him thinking about it.

'Leaving already?' The surprise was evident in Matthew's eyes. 'I just wanted to let you know I've noticed. Your work is going from strength to strength.'

'It is good to hear you think so. I understand there will be a celebration later on...'

'You'd like to join us?'

'Unless it is just for family.'

'Ruth will be with us,' he said, smiling at me but making the relationship clear. 'And her daughter, the gorgeous Deborah. My niece Sylvia is coming as well, so you won't need to bring a lady. Plenty of time to change. We're meeting at the Connaught, around eight. And now, if you'll excuse me, I'd better circulate.'

And he was gone, leaving Franz and me staring at his retreating back.

It was all so bizarre. I knew Matthew enjoyed my company, I couldn't get that wrong. Yet he'd never made any physical move towards me. The closest he ever came to it was the hand on my arm today, and when he'd held a door open for me to walk through, and brushed against me. Was he really a heartless philanderer, or were all the warnings wrong? Hard to believe that such a large consensus of opinion could be completely mistaken.

My family say I'm stubborn. Franz reminded me that it was more a question of not allowing myself to be shoved around. I preferred to make my own judgements. And I hadn't decided about Matthew – yet.

CHAPTER SEVENTEEN

Franz was sitting at the Connaught bar, abstemiously drinking tomato juice, when Deborah, Matthew and I arrived. The barman had slipped a bottle of vodka towards Franz so that he could mix himself a Bloody Mary, but I could see he'd only helped himself to the cocktail stick. He was moving the ice in his glass around in a desultory fashion.

We collected Franz, and the four of us went through into the dining room. Matthew's three brothers were waiting for us there, together with Jeanne and Caroline, and Mark's daughter Sylvia. Of the younger generation Frelés, she was the only one to have taken the trouble to come to her uncle's exhibition.

It was Matthew's party. He took charge of the seating, placed me next to him. There was a rosa gallica sprig in a cut-glass vase standing beside my champagne flute. I realised he'd remembered it from the cover of my *Roses through the Ages*. A delightful touch. The magnum of Dom Pérignon was already cooling by the table. The waiter poured on a nod from our host.

'To the determined lady who made it all happen.' Matthew stood and raised his glass to me. The rest of the party followed suit.

He sat down, with Sylvia on his other side. He'd placed Franz on my left, then Debs followed by Mark. Franz was becoming animated, showering me with words, chattering about his new exhibition in Vienna, the cost of importing marble from Italy. And Matthew talked as never before in my presence. I heard for the first time that he intended to switch entirely from oils to acrylics, that some of the latest pigments were less likely to fade than the traditional ones, especially when using the acrylic medium. None of the other members of the party said much. Except Debs. She raised plucked eyebrows at me, then talked animatedly to Sylvia across the table from her. They appeared to get on well. No wonder, really. Same generation, and both of them interested in singing.

'Dance?' Matthew asked at last.

It's been years since I've even tried. And then it was with Jonathan. He'd only managed to master a single step: the slow foxtrot. *'You are my sunshine, My only sunshine'* he always hummed when dancing. The rest of the words came back to me, and I swallowed hard as the last line went through my head: *'You were gone and then I cried.'*

I had to accept that he was gone. Gone like the late '40s, the New Look, dancing cheek to cheek. I summoned up the pre-Jonathan past. I'd always had my pick of partners. Quicksteps, jitterbugging, polkas, the Viennese waltz. I'd managed them all. I willed my body back into that past, stood up. Then I remembered the way Matthew had danced with Caroline the first time I'd met him. Twinkle-toed. At least I was wearing red shoes - and I wished magic into them.

'I'm very rusty, I'm afraid.'

'Don't worry.' He held out his hand. 'I'll lead.'

Of course I hadn't doubted it. My shaking knees were mercifully hidden under the deceptive folds of a handkerchief hemline. Such foresight. My outfit was easy to wear, easy to dance in. I'd lost almost a stone in weight in the last few months, my figure was back to a sleek ten. It had been a real temptation to encase myself in the tight-fitting black which seemed to be a uniform for fashionable London women. I knew it wouldn't have worked, Mata Hari just wasn't my style. I was much better off in the black and red layered skirt, red top. Crowned by the triple string of pearls Jonathan had given me.

The floor was good. Slippery, bouncy – and crowded. There was no need to panic. I felt Matthew's arm around my waist, his hand holding mine, in the remembered ballroom-dancing stance. I relaxed, forgot the present, floated into the past where dancing was the testing ground for sexual compatibility. We fitted, my hand in his, my head just under his chin, his knees telling mine how to move.

'All right?' I could feel his breath on my hair, my eyes. The smell of masculinity was overpowering.

'Of course. And you?'

He didn't answer, but then there was no need. The electricity I'd felt crackle before was as nothing compared to the voltage now quickening through me. Concentration on the steps left me as I peeked up at him. He held me closer. My limp hand responded to his grasp, my body adapted to his shape. I saw a slow smile was lifting the corners of his mouth, his eyes were soft. As he unwound, a gentle dreamy look replaced the guarded one he usually wore. The slow waltz helped. I had no trouble at all following the simple steps Matthew chose to use.

We did not speak again. I knew I could not have been the only one to feel the melding I had felt only once before. Was it possible that I could fall in love again? At my age? After thirty-five years with a man I thought could never be replaced? But he was gone, the fifth anniversary of his death already passed. His presence had begun to fade. I'd sensed him leave me.

"Don't feel you can't marry again," he'd told me, holding my hand the day before he died. "I've never wanted anything but your happiness. Don't let our past get in your way. You still have life to live. Enjoy it."

The music stopped, the magic with it. 'I hope that wasn't too demanding,' Matthew purred. 'You dance beautifully. You have a natural sense of rhythm. Thank you.' He led me back to the table.

Franz's eyes glittered as he looked at me and began to talk non-stop again. He seemed to think I was longing to know every detail about how he used his garden as a backdrop for his work. 'What I want is a sort of ha-ha effect. The latest figure is a pretty large piece, you see...'

I tried to listen, but all I could achieve was a mandarin nodding of my head, a widening of my mouth. I wanted to savour the warmth of Matthew's arm around my waist, the feel of his breath on my cheek, that dreamy gentle look...

Matthew asked Deborah to dance. Suddenly I was afraid. She was beautiful, and young enough to bear a child. To bear a whole family of children, in fact.

'Your enthusiasm about my work is devastating, Ruth.' Franz was as sensitive as any other artist. 'They are playing a Viennese waltz. Shall we show these English how to dance?' He pulled me up and on to the dance floor.

The band was playing a Strauss medley: *The Blue Danube* merged into *Wiener Blut* as Franz and I whirled round and round. I remembered the trick: you had to keep your eyes on your partner's face which, relative to you, would appear still. Otherwise dizziness would make you lose your balance. I stared, first at the hollows under Franz's eyes, then at the deep shadows from nose to mouth. I shifted my look to his tie. It was a surprisingly unexciting stripe. I realised it was one of the ties the hotel kept to lend to guests.

His grip tightened. 'I do not understand why you contemplate my navel.'

'Unintentional, I assure you.' I looked up, smiled dutifully into his eyes. 'I'm just concentrating on something which isn't spinning round. The tempo's rather fast. You're wearing a tie pin I can concentrate on.'

'What? Oh, I see. You need glasses. It is only a safety pin. Also I do not think you are the type to be swept off your feet.'

Type, no. The music stopped. I was about to head back to the table when the band went into a polka. I didn't need glasses to recognise that Debs was on the dance-floor with Mark. They fitted well. My wave of enthusiasm was entirely genuine.

'Echte Musik – decent music at last,' Franz roared, and twirled me round. The red shoes worked. The rhythm brought our roots back to us and we pirouetted fast and reasonably expertly. The band slid from *Tritsch Tratsch* into a slow waltz.

We calmed down. I might never get a chance to talk to Franz again. He was so very evidently unwell. 'What happened at Matthew's first attempt at an exhibition?'

'That story. Quite unbelievable. He was living with Mark, they shared a flat. Mark was still a medical student, attached to one of the big London hospitals. They were both pretty hard up because they were still under twenty-one.' He grinned. 'The parents left some money, but Mark's share was not yet available and he lived on the amount his grandmother sent. Matthew did not have anything. He took nothing from the grandmother. Maybe you heard about this?'

'Yes. He used his share of the inheritance to buy his brothers out. In order to keep the fief intact. He told me about that.'

'He would not take a single penny from Madame. Judas money, he called it when the old lady offered it. He actually threw the notes at her.'

Betrayal with a kiss. A love affair with the man in black, or worse? Would Matthew ever tell me?

'The story Matthew told me was that both he and Mark saved one hundred pounds. They put these notes into the drawers of a bureau Matthew insisted to be shipped from Guernsey to London. It was housed in Mark's flat. A very beautiful bureau-bookcase – I think they called it a secrétaire-bibliothèque – which they both used. One side was Matthew's, the other side Mark's.'

'You mean the sort of thing that has a sloping front covering dozens of pigeonholes and little drawers?'

'Exactly. And there was a top with bookshelves covered by panelled doors. The whole thing was made in walnut. An outstanding piece which had been brought into the family from France.'

'The mother?'

He shrugged. 'Possibly. I do not know that.'

'D'you know what her name was?'

'The mother's name?' He screwed up his eyes. 'Yes, well, I did know. A French name, reminded me of some actress—'

'Michelle?'

'That was the grandmother's name. Eventually I will remember,' he said, scowling at me. 'I thought you wanted to know the story about the money?'

'Sorry. I do.'

'As I said, they both saved some cash and both of them put it into one or other of those little drawers. Then Matthew found this dealer, in Albemarle Street, willing to show him. On the usual conditions: Matthew was to frame all the paintings in a particular way, but only if he used the framer the dealer specified.'

'Manipulative stuff.'

'And costly. He took all the canvases to the framer and went back to collect his hundred pounds. Mark was there when Matthew took the bundle out of one of the little drawers. And announced that it was *his* money.'

'Matt thought Mark was making a mistake and started counting the notes. One hundred pounds exactly, all in singles. They were held together with a blue ribbon on top of a rubber band.'

'That was significant?'

'According to Matt. Because Mark swore he'd saved a hundred pounds, and held it together with a blue ribbon covering a rubber band. The coloured ribbon was to make sure they knew which wad belonged to which brother.'

I remembered they were identical twins who were likely to think alike. 'So they looked in all the other drawers?'

'Exactly. They searched each one, and there was no other bundle of one hundred pounds, with or without a blue ribbon – or even a rubber band.' Franz looked at me quizzically. 'The reason I believed Matt was because he said his ribbon was cerulean blue and Mark's an unsubtle shade of royal.'

I had to agree that that sounded conclusive.

'Unfortunately, blue is blue to Mark. Maybe light or dark, but no other special variation.'

'So Mark said he couldn't take the money?'

'It was worse than that. He accused Matt that he had already spent his money, and was pretending that the notes he was holding now were his. In effect that he was stealing them.'

'Wasn't that on the unreasonable side?'

'Not entirely. Matt did spend a lot of money for his circumstances. Not on frivolities. He spent everything on pigments and other painting necessities. I think Mark was already sensitive because he was paying the rent. Matt lived there, painting, without contributing his share. He did a few odd jobs to get cash for his painting expenses. Unfortunately Mark chose that particular time to get at his brother about all that.

'Matt denied that he was stealing. He wanted to compromise rather than to fight. He asked if he could use the money for the time being, explained what he needed it for, suggested they decide on ownership later.

'Mark decided this meant Matt was admitting to taking the money. He refused. Matt snatched the wad of notes and rushed to the framer. After he came back he found the lock changed, his gear in front of the door. Mark refused to let him in.'

'Even though he didn't need the wretched hundred pounds in the same way?' Franz stepped on my toe and I winced. 'Steady on.'

'Matt was beside himself. So he asked me to help him; we were good friends at the time. But I did not have enough cash to buy food for the day. One hundred pounds was out of the question.'

'Your parents…?'

'They died in Dachau. The whole family. I was the only one to come out alive, though it felt more in the nature of a living death. Matthew finally breathed some life back into me.'

I understood what he meant. He was a direct survivor of a concentration camp, I was an indirect one. Hitler had shaped both our destinies, and with them our characters. What made us survivors rather than victims was luck combined with hanging on, and a resolve to defeat the Nazis by showing them that Jews were not Untermenschen. We were determined to show the world, to contribute.

Franz stood still, in spite of the music. 'Matthew insisted he was going to get the money back from the framer, and forget the whole thing. I tried to argue with him. It did no good. He went, got his money back, and returned it to Mark.'

'So that healed the rift, but ruined the exhibition?'

'Only superficially. There was no question of his moving back with Mark, so I invited Matt to share the studio. We lived and worked in this warehouse, we used the same models.'

'How did you manage for cash?'

'I worked as a waiter. Evening work. Matt wanted to earn enough so that he no longer needed to worry the whole time. He took on a job as a lorry driver, can you imagine?'

'At night, so he could paint in the daytime.'

'He has told you that.'

We found ourselves standing in the middle of the floor. The music had stopped, and the other couples had drifted off. I led the way back to the table, infuriated that I'd got myself so absorbed in the subject of the conversation that Matthew would think I was preoccupied with Franz.

'I thought you said you didn't dance?' Mark greeted me as we returned. 'You seemed to have no problems with that Viennese waltz. And the polka was impressive. I suppose it all depends on the partner you're dancing with.'

Somehow I got the feeling that he thought I'd dumped him for Matthew, and that I was now dumping Matthew for Franz. Irritation seethed through me as I toyed with the food remaining on my plate. I pushed it impatiently aside, took a long drink of wine and felt my blood pound through my veins. As I looked up I noticed everyone's eyes riveted on a group of three men in black suits. They were circling one of the tables nearest the entrance to the dining room. Extra waiters? They couldn't be, they were wearing evening dress. I was still trying to work out what was going on when one of them turned to face us. I saw the black mask over his face. Just like the old films – Lesley Howard playing the Scarlet Pimpernel.

The man who'd turned was holding a deep velvet bag. They stood over a woman whose hands were at the back of her neck – unfastening her necklace. Number One took it. Then he scooped flashing objects from her hands and from the table.

It wasn't only the band which was silent, the whole dining room was hushed. The threesome moved on to the next table.

'Take off your jewellery, put it on the table. No one gets hurt if you don't panic,' Number One was instructing the diners two tables away from us. He had a young man's plummy voice. Number

Two was holding a handgun pointed first at one, then at the next occupant of the table in turn. Number Three was holding what looked like an automatic weapon pointed at the head waiter backed by his staff.

'Let's not take all night, ladies,' Number Two called out. Another young educated voice. 'Now for the gentlemen's wallets, please. And those cufflinks will do nicely.'

The only sound was of tinkling rings and necklaces, of gold on damask. The trio moved to the table next to us and the whole routine was repeated. Out of the corner of my eye I saw a woman at the first table keel over, her face hitting the table in front of her with a resounding thud. And a splash.

'Leave her to it,' Number One yelled. He strode back, pulled her head up, removed the soup plate. 'We won't be long.' He waved the bag at the four people sitting at the table next to us. 'Get on with it.'

I stared at my engagement and wedding rings, began to twist them off, then twisted them back on. They were the most poignant reminders of my marriage to Jonathan, apart from our adult children. I thought back to the day he'd proposed to me. Damned if I was going to let those young bastards have them. I looked up, caught Mark's eye across the table. He shook his head, trying to calm me.

The fury of a few minutes ago had raised my metabolism to boiling point. I turned to look at Matthew while slipping the rings into the remnants of a roll on my side plate. He stared back, his eyes glowing intent.

I picked up my wine glass, my hand shaking, the red liquid spilling on to the cloth. 'I need another drink,' I said, my voice echoing in the silence. I held up the glass, and Matthew stood, leaned over to pick the bottle up, and began to pour. Even in the charged atmosphere I noticed he was using his left hand. It struck me as meaningful.

The three young men were now at our table. 'Freeze,' Number One shouted at Matthew.

We were the last table in the row. Number Two, the man with

137

the revolver, pointed it at Caroline and rolled his eyes, nervous. The one with the machine gun uncocked it, then ostentatiously cocked it again.

'C'mon, let's get it over with,' Number One snarled. He grabbed the necklace and earrings Jeanne had taken off, seized her hand and began to twist the rings on her left ring finger. She cried out, evidently they would not come off without a struggle.

Out of the corner of my eye I could see Matthew. The new suit was very good, but it couldn't hide the movement of his shoulders, the tightening of his muscles.

The man with the velvet bag was pulling Jeanne's hand back, and she let out a scream. Something snapped inside me. I threw the full glass of wine into the revolver man's face. It seemed to me that Matthew heaved his chair back in that same instant, crashed it into the arm holding the machine gun, and bashed the revolver man with the bottle he still held in his left hand. The machine gun tipped sideways and a single shot rang out before the gunner reeled back and up, exploding bullets all over the ceiling.

The handgun was smoking. Franz, I saw, had snatched up another bottle and hit the robber with the collection bag over the head, grabbing the booty. Other men joined in to help, the alarm bells were ringing, and several young waiters ran towards us. The man with the machine gun was bunched on the floor, the weapon silent by his side, blood gushing from his arm.

Luke rushed over, bent towards him, felt for his pulse, checked his breath. 'Someone get an ambulance,' he shouted out. He and Mark laid the man on his side and stanched the wound with a napkin.

I was outraged. The police had taken a rather odd view of the incident at the Connaught. They'd insisted on questioning Matthew, though Jean-Jacques made sure that a solicitor was present. He and I were waiting for the interview to end. I didn't understand what was going on.

'The police may charge Matthew with battery,' Jean-Jacques was saying, looking grave.

'Why would any of it be construed as Matthew's fault? I threw the wine into the hand gunman's face. That's what started it.'

'Nonsense, Ruth,' he dismissed that. 'Matthew bashed him with the bottle. That's what made the revolver go off.'

'The robber pulling the trigger made the revolver go off!' I shouted. 'He was the one who released the safety catch and had his finger on it.'

'That was only for show.'

I couldn't believe the man's attitude to his brother. The robber wasn't intending to use a gun he was pointing at people, but Matthew was guilty because he used force to protect us all? 'You're telling me that Matthew will be charged for trying to stop a robbery?' Whose side was Jean-Jacques on, anyway?

'They'll take the line that he was putting everyone in danger. The man with the machine gun might have started spraying bullets all over the place. Bôt's a mature man, not an impetuous child. He should act more responsibly.'

Was the implication that he'd done this sort of thing as a boy? Had he done more than irritate the Germans — had he been a saboteur? 'We were just supposed to sit quiet as dormice and let it happen, I suppose.'

'Nothing will come of it if Bôt admits to battery. He'll get off with a caution. As you say, it was the robber who pulled the trigger.'

'I can't understand why you're taking their side.' Lawyer or not, he did seem oddly resigned to Matthew being at fault.

'I'm playing devil's advocate, my dear. The police are only conducting an interview. Matthew isn't going to be charged with anything. I've already seen to that.'

Always this assumption that Matthew had committed some crime, some misdeed. Was I kidding myself? Surely I couldn't be the only one to see him — not as a victim, exactly, I rejected that — but as a hero rather than a villain.

To me it signalled one thing, and one thing only. Matthew was obsessed by something in his past, something he felt guilty about. His guilt reflected misdoing by those closest to him. It must be because I didn't know his past that I couldn't see it.

All my instincts told me that if I knew more about his relevant past which, I was convinced, was the distant past of the German Occupation, I'd feel compassion rather than revulsion. His family and close friends assumed the worst. I was sure it was because no one knew exactly what had happened that Matthew was always blamed.

I determined to solve the mystery which was so clearly blighting his life.

CHAPTER EIGHTEEN

I recognised Matthew's writing on the envelope. It wasn't too difficult, it went with his character. An enormous capital 'R', plain, no scrolls was followed by 'u' 't' 'h' in small, surprisingly legible, letters. Samuels began with an even larger capital, but the following letters merged into a sort of scrawl. If my name were Sigmunda I'd say the word trailed off into illegibility because it was Jonathan's surname. As my name is Ruth I thought the dragging ink was caused by the effort of writing a longer word. I picked up the envelope. No need to analyse the whole thing to death.

It was thick and heavy, larger than usual, and stiff. Not a letter, then. A card. I turned it over. No return address. Reproduction of one of his paintings already? I flicked it up and down, irritation making me hot. It wasn't Christmas, or any other special day I was aware of. Why had he sent it?

I held it to the light, but the paper was of much too high a quality to be transparent. Impatient, I tossed the rest of my post out of the way and tore the envelope open and pulled out a plain white card with a small amount of text printed in unimaginative italic black Times Roman. The whole thing was so banal I had trouble reading it. I forced myself to concentrate.

'Mathieu Ignat Frelé
At Home, Lascervelle House, September 23rd, 1991
Eight to midnight'

The rest was a big white blank. Oops, not quite. RSVP, and the address, down in the right hand corner, in a very small typeface. How was I supposed to see that without my glasses on? And what was it all about? Had that exhibition turned him into establishment already?

I wasn't being entirely fair. He'd said he was giving a party to celebrate his house-warming. I retrieved that piece of information somewhere out of the recesses of a reluctant memory. He'd mentioned it when I ran into him coming out of Lascervelle a few days ago. My taxi was waiting to take me to the airport, the meter running.

'Hello, Ruth. Off on your travels again?'

'A business meeting in London. You've moved in, then?' He'd been carrying a rolled canvas. On his way to the framer's, I'd assumed.

'Next week. I thought you'd have known from Jeanne by now. The Jakes moved out to Bôtnoir yesterday.'

I'd been told the plan, but not their time-table. As far as the garden was concerned Jeanne lived there already. An army of builders, carpenters, plumbers and electricians had taken up space on the circular drive. It had enlarged beyond its original size in the process. And I had had to learn the art of manoeuvring in a small space. 'You'll be on your own?'

'The Lukes moved out last week.'

No mention of where to. 'And Mark?'

'He's renting some suitable mansion along Glategny Esplanade.'

'What about your cousin?'

'Still at Bôtnoir.' The few seconds' silence told me that Todd Frelé's claim to the fief remained a contender, and a strong one at that. 'Jake thought it expedient to let him house sit while the first part of the renovation was going on. He insisted that that was useful. I'd have booted Todd out. He should have taken himself back to France weeks ago.'

Matthew had never mentioned the dispute. I wouldn't even have known about it if it hadn't been for Jeanne. But Jean-Jacques's caution confirmed my suspicions that refuting Todd's claim was causing substantial problems.

I reread the card and concentrated on the fact that Matthew had moved into his house at last. We were finally neighbours. The invitation was for Saturday fortnight. I checked my diary and found no pressing engagements on that day, except that Debs was coming to stay for a couple of weeks. Presumably I could bring her along. I'd have to give Matthew a ring to check that out. Well – later, maybe.

The little courtyard at the back of the house was glinting early September sunshine, Indian summer warm. I sauntered through, taking my mail and settling on my favourite chair. Matthew's very formal invitation had left me flat and unenthusiastic. Maybe I wouldn't bother to go. He hadn't been in touch since that one dinner he'd taken me out to, after the opening of the exhibition. That had been several days later, when he'd come back to London to inspect the few unsold paintings, and to decide whether to bring more for the gallery to have on permanent display. But I was kidding myself. I knew curiosity would overcome pride. I was already thinking about suitable party gear.

I glanced towards Matthew's upstairs windows overlooking his courtyard. They reflected gold but were firmly closed. I willed him into an upstairs room, opening a window, leaning out. Nothing moved. Disappointed, I put my reading glasses on and sifted through my other mail. Bills, royalty statements, invitations to speak on gardening topics, the usual assortment of catalogues and junk mail. I sorted through, scooped up the empty envelopes, placed the padded ones aside for reuse, discarded the rest. I lingered over the one from Matthew. A pity to throw out such good quality paper. Except, of course, I'd mauled it out of shape, torn over the corner and through the stamp. As I flicked it towards the pile of throwaways my eye was caught by the top left-hand corner. Not the envelope-maker's logo, as I'd assumed, but a tiny drawing set diagonally across. How had I missed it? A spray of rosa gallica, exquisitely detailed in pen and ink. My heart started to fibrillate as I put the envelope on one side and searched the pile of letters for the card. My fingers turned clumsy and it dropped on the flagstones, upside down. I noticed the short hand-written message in Matthew's forward-slanting script:

'Any chance of your playing hostess for me? I'm sure you know I'd like nothing better.'

Signed with a very large B trailing off to a small t. 'Bôt'.

My pulse pounded through my ears. Mind over emotion, I told myself, and slapped my wrists. No appreciable change, but I told myself it was absurd to be so affected. I'd thought that the dinner on our own, when we were both in town and away from prying Guernsey eyes, would be – well, perhaps romantic. But it had been an oddly distant meeting.

Franz's name hadn't come up until Matthew was dropping me in front of Debs's flat. 'I gather you enjoy Frank Bowers' work,' he'd said, each syllable distinct and flat.

'Like you,' I'd been quick to point out. That slow waltz must have done some damage. 'What really draws us together is that we knew each other in Vienna – as children.'

His voice had lightened. 'Really? And you've kept in touch?'

'No. I saw him dragged off by the Gestapo, so I'd always assumed the worst. He recognised me at your exhibition. I've always admired his work, but I had no reason to connect Frank Bowers with the Franz Scheiderbauer I knew as a child.'

He drew in his breath. 'What an extraordinary coincidence. You went to Kindergarten together?'

A rather charming touch. 'Actually we lived in the same apartment house. One of those monolith town houses split into gracious apartments after World War I. We lived on the Prinz Eugen Strasse.'

'I've never been to Vienna,' he'd said. 'I've always wanted to go.' He'd sounded friendlier, there was even a hint we might go together. 'Good-night, Ruth. I'll be in touch as soon as I get back.'

There'd been no direct invitation since then, just a couple of messages on my answer phone. And when I'd returned his calls, ringing Charles Grichard's place, he'd been out. I hadn't pursued it. Charles had made increasingly coy remarks, successfully putting me off.

The exhibition had catapulted Matthew to the top, the latest darling of the Arts Sections. His connection with Guernsey hadn't been detrimental, either. Nor had the heroic account of childhood years spent under the jackboot been a hindrance to publicity. It gave the quixotic story of late success even more poignancy. The inheritance of a feudal fief delighted the more snobbish of the papers, adding an unusual angle to write about. Matthew himself remained enigmatic, refusing to add to the press release put out by Andrew Canwaller. The effect on reporters' imaginations was sensational.

I began to count up reasons why I hadn't seen him since the closing of the London show. There had been valid ones. I'd stayed several days with Debs, working with Pete Tanner, hammering out the format of the TV series. And when I was on Guernsey I'd been out in the garden at Bôtnoir, with Jeanne. So it wasn't surprising that, apart from that one chance meeting, we hadn't come across each other at all.

The last place I'd seen Matthew to speak to was in Balzac's, the restaurant in Wood Lane many of the BBC producers used to dine their guests. Matthew had stopped by my table, where I'd been waiting for Pete Tanner to turn up.

'Hello, Ruth.'

He wouldn't be there by chance. 'You're on a chat show?' I'd asked, intrigued. With a tinge of envy.

'I'm seeing a producer about my paintings...'

'You mean Melvyn Bragg?'

He blinked two or three times, looked directly at me, shrugged. 'He's with the other lot. But we did meet. He's hoping to do a programme sometime—'

'The South Bank Show?'

'Yes, matter of fact.' A sort of musing frown, as though he couldn't quite understand what was happening to him. 'Bit odd, actually. I told him I'd led a rather unconventional life as far as painting was concerned.'

Did he really think the rest of it was completely normal? How many seigneurs drove lorries for a living, I wondered? There was more precedent for the jazz groups. 'That would have encouraged him,' I'd said. 'Gives him a new slant, something to work on. Absolutely marvellous that you haven't been discovered until your sixty-first year. Grandpa Frelé.'

There was no sign he'd caught the jocular tone. 'Hardly that. I have no children, let alone grandchildren.'

So that did worry him. How slow of me not to realise it was more than producing an heir to the fief. 'There's still time.' I'd tried to sound negligent.

'Women of child-bearing age are too young for me,' he said. Sober and matter-of-fact. 'It wouldn't work out. I've given it all very careful thought. As you know, Jean-Pierre will take over Bôtnoir. I don't think we need worry about young Jean-Pierre not marrying.' His nostrils twitched, his lips lifted in a smile. And then it died as his eyes became empty.

Jeanne had already mentioned several times that her son's obsession with the opposite sex had started at an exceptionally early age. His father's expertise had come in handy for extricating him from various unsuitable involvements. For all his family's criticisms of Matthew, it was Jean-Pierre who seemed to me to be the roué. I'd never known, or seen, Matthew acting in anything but a proper way. Almost insultingly so.

'She wouldn't have to be that young.' Annoyance at the idea of the nephew taking over was my biggest irritation, since I don't believe that genetic inheritance is the sum total of a human being. Anyway, Jean-Jacques was very different from this brother. Matthew's son would have turned out to be quite different from the son the Jakes had brought up. And, of course, I was taken enough with Matthew to wish him an heir of his own, as well as lasting success as an artist.

He would soon have that, I'd told myself, with a pang or two about his swift rise. I'd been working hard for years, and no one had taken the interest in me that Matthew had managed with just one show. Even the TV series was more to do with Bôtnoir than with my work. And now Matthew was about to be the subject of one of the most prestigious arts programmes transmitted on TV. Prospective wives would be hurling themselves at him in droves.

I'd decided to clue him up about modern motherhood. 'Special hormonal treatment means that even women in their sixties can bear children. For women under fifty there's no problem at all.'

His head had jerked towards me. 'Really? I've not heard that.

146

Has it actually been done, or is that just theory?'

'I heard that some woman in Italy produced a son at the age of sixty-two. Apparently the only requirement is that the prospective mother should be in excellent physical condition. Then the doctors can, they say, do the rest.'

Was it my imagination, or had I gauged the look correctly? It seemed to me he'd thought I might be a candidate.

And now he was asking me to play hostess at his party. I rushed upstairs to my bedroom, tore off my working gear, examined my body in the full-length mirror. Not bad. The physical demands of my work were keeping me fit, my muscles were in good trim, there was no sagging flesh. The weight I'd lost recently had stayed off. I was back to just over eight stone which, I judged, was the optimum weight for me now. Less, and I'd look scrawny. More, and I'd have to think how I wore my clothes.

I stared at the self-satisfied smirk and examined my face. Not quite as easy to deal with. Nothing wrong with it, exactly. Same eyes and bone-structure I'd seen reflected back for years. But it was the face of a woman in her sixties. The grey in my hair was easy to disguise, highlights ensured that the henna was not too dark, too stark a contrast to the fading skin. No need for change there. But what about make-up? I don't normally bother with it, so I wouldn't be an expert at applying it. Should I have it done professionally?

I put on one of my cocktail dresses, and liked what I saw. To hell with make-up. If Matthew wanted a painted woman he could always find one. Why would I change the way I'd been for the few months I'd known him?

The face in the mirror smiled back at me. Go to the dentist and have your teeth cleaned, go to the hairdresser and have the colour professionally touched-up, the style trimmed. That's all, except to relax.

I kicked the high heels under the nearest chair, slid the dress off my hips and on to the floor, pulled my jeans back on, slipped into a silk shirt, added a waistcoat and my comfortable shoes, rushed out of the house and banged the front door shut. I'd go and see Matthew about the party right away. It would be fun to play hostess for him.

CHAPTER NINETEEN

'We haven't been introduced. Your chance to shine, Grichard.'

Deborah and I were standing in the fine drawing room of Lascervelle, the party in full swing. The thick-set figure of Todd Frelé had just walked in. He made straight for my daughter, his hair glossy with some sort of cream, his eyes avid.

Charles Grichard's greeting was cool as he deliberately turned to me. 'Ruth, this is Todd Frelé, Matthieu's cousin. He's the elder son of Michelle Frelé's younger son.' He nodded from one of us to the other, unsmiling, specifying Todd's father's genesis as precisely as if he were in court. 'Ruth and Deborah Samuels.'

'I already know the mom,' Todd announced, squinting at Debs. 'And you didn't spell it out, Conseiller. I'm the legal heir to the Bôtnoir enclos.' He flared his nostrils at me, then turned to Debs. 'Mathieu imagines he can put a stop to my claim because Jean-Jacques's some kinda legal eagle in London. Wrong. QCs don't count on Guernsey. We have our own system. Grichard can fill you in on that one. He knows the score. And he sure knows I'll hit the home run.'

I didn't see I had anything to lose by being straightforward. 'In that case I'm surprised you haven't taken over yet. Is family sentiment stopping you?'

The lop-sided sneer didn't improve his looks. 'Thought you'd got it figured, right? Reckon you'll marry Mathieu and be the lady of the manor, that the deal?'

Whatever he said next was drowned as the Bluets – the local jazz group Matthew had become friendly with – chose that moment to play again. The saxophone echoed from staid walls, the guests drifted towards the edges of the room. The rhythm quickened and eager young dancers began to disco.

'Dance?' Todd grabbed Debs's arm before she could move away and twirled her on to the floor. I stared nervously after them. If he was looking for a way to annoy – even worry – me he'd found it.

I stopped to chat with Charles for a few minutes. 'What about it?' he surprised me by asking. 'If you absolutely promise not to tread on my toes.'

'Later, perhaps. I've got my job to do.' I was determined to get Debs away from that odious man when I saw she'd already extricated herself. Todd stood in the doorway of the dining room, a plate heaped with lobster in his hand, blocking my path. His heavy jowls were red, brows blackening into annoyance.

He waved his hand over the magnificent buffet. 'Slipped your mind that shellfish ain't kosher, right?'

It startled me. Was he as anti-Semitic as, by all accounts, his grandmother had been? The bulky body blocked me into a corner.

'Think Grichard can save Mathieu's hide? Think again.' His eyes disappeared into folds of flesh which disguised his features. He had the look of a man deeply disappointed with life. 'He's a disreputable old queen. A degenerate.'

'I don't think that came up.' Antagonism to both Charles and Matthew was to be expected, but to imply homosexuality – a possibility which had crossed my mind, but which I'd rejected – and to automatically equate that with degeneracy, infuriated me.

'Any more than they mentioned a whole line of other misdemeanours, I guess.' Fat fingers dug into my arm. 'You've gotta know that Grichard and Mathieu are a couple of fakes.'

'I wonder you came at all,' I said. 'Associating with such despicable characters.'

'You've swallowed everything those guys say. Tough luck. I guess it won't be long before my hold on Bôtnoir will be written up in the local press.'

I snatched a glass of champagne from the tray a waiter was taking round. 'This is hardly the time or place.' I pushed forward, forcing him to move.

'Listen up for just one minute, lady.' The eyes opened, the darkness in them deepened.

'No...'

'Help me out on one thing. You're double digging that old garden—'

'For goodness sake.' I avoided my normal expletive. 'My agent's drawn up a contract...'

'With the wrong man,' he hissed, bending nearer and spluttering into my ear. 'You need to know. Whatever you dig up belongs to the Seigneur. I'll sue you for every penny you've got if you don't hand it over. To me, in case I haven't made it clear.'

I drew away from his hot breath. 'Surely you aren't going to maintain I should act as though Bôtnoir is yours before you've proved your claim?'

'OK, the old guy's in your pocket. He let on where they're hidden yet?'

What old guy? Nicol, presumably. Naturally, I'd already realised Todd was looking for proof of Matthew's claim when he took such an interest in the discrepancy in the Bôtnoir wall. I tried a shot in the dark. 'You mean the boxes?'

The grin was triumphant. 'So you know damn well what I'm talking about.'

That's why he'd spied on me that day in Bôtnoir. He was afraid I might stumble across vital documents which would prove Matthew's legitimacy. 'What makes you think I know?' I moved away as he tried to put his sweaty hand on my elbow.

'I'll only take a coupla minutes to break it down for you. Let's get outa here.'

The small courtyard was empty. Like the one at Riande, it led off the dining room. I walked through the open French windows. For all his bravado, this man was very nervous. He was looking for proof and had this crazy notion that I'd lead him to it.

I noted the envious smile, the stare through the door and across the room at Matthew moving easily, the perfect host, from guest to guest. Todd wolfed a couple of pieces of lobster, put down his plate. Had his grandmother told him about some secret hiding

150

place? And what it contained?

'Sure knew I could count on your snooping.' In the cold darkness I could see his white shirt heave. 'You play along with me and I'll make it worth your while.'

'There you are, Ruth.' Luke Frelé's voice sounded loud as he joined us, easing his body between his cousin and me. 'There's something I meant to talk to you about.' He took my elbow, steered me back into the house, and shut the French windows. 'Not interrupting anything, was I?'

'Glad to see you,' I said.

He nodded. 'I've been wondering how to get hold of you. I have a few of Matthew's early paintings. I stole them, I'm afraid. Not very edifying.'

Another source of paintings Matthew didn't own? Extraordinary. And exciting.

We ambled through into the drawing room now full enough to mean that the dancing was subdued. Matthew was playing the piano. I saw him beckon one of the musicians to take over. Then he moved on to the dance floor, partnering first one female guest, than another. He moved from couple to couple, dancing a few twirls and handing his present partner back. Except for one. He began to dance with Caroline, and he didn't stop the way he had with the others. They moved in unison, twining in and out of each other's steps, expertly shifting their feet in time with the music. The band, sensing a new phase, quickened the rhythm. The floor cleared and Matthew and Caroline gave a display worthy of *Saturday Night Fever*. It was hard to believe that they could dance like that without having practised. Was Luke right to be so tight-lipped about them? Had they had an affair? Was it still going on?

Luke's voice was gruff. 'If I hadn't purloined them, there wouldn't now be anything left from all the really early work, the stuff he did before the '50s. Perhaps you've heard? There was a problem about his very first exhibition.'

I certainly wasn't going to let on that I knew, so I shrugged.

'He was so upset he made a bonfire of whatever he could lay his hands on.'

'Except for one.' The encounter with Todd had left me unnerved enough to be injudicious. I stopped, kicked myself for being so stupid. The painting I'd glimpsed in the Brixton studio must be a portrait of the young Caroline. Classical oval face, luminous eyes, Giaconda smile. I'd only caught the tiniest glimpse, but that would account for Matthew's secretive attitude, for his keeping the painting, for his reputation as a philanderer. And for Luke's ambiguity.

'Really? He actually kept some of them?' Luke sounded astounded.

To tell him about the portrait would be a disaster. 'I could be wrong, of course. I tend to jump to conclusions.' If he didn't know of its existence I could pretend I'd seen something else. 'There was one seascape which must have been painted on Guernsey. So I thought it had to be one of the ones he did when he was still a boy. It was in a quite different style.'

'I didn't see it in the exhibition.'

'He wouldn't show it.'

Luke nodded. 'I'd never have guessed.' He drank deeply from his glass of wine. 'There's talk about a special programme – Melvyn Bragg.'

I was surprised Matthew had mentioned that to his brothers. 'You want to make the paintings you have available for the South Bank Show?'

'Indeed. But it would be fatal to give away the source. That's why I'm telling you, not him.'

'Why? Would it be so terrible if he found out you'd saved his early work? He might be thrilled.'

'He'll destroy them, Ruth. By now you must have some idea what he's like.' He laid a hand on my arm. I withdrew, and he let go. 'But I do, you know. I really do.' He looked at his brother, now dancing with Debs, then back again. 'After all, we were boys together. I was there, I saw him...' He stopped, a piece of black olive hiding part of a front tooth, giving him a sinister look.

I finally grasped he wasn't talking about Caroline. He was talking about their childhood, under the Occupation, about something Matthew had done. My imagination raced through scene after scene, with Matthew successfully blowing up bridges, stealing supplies... 'You mean he was a saboteur?'

'Sorry. I wasn't trying to antagonise you by harking back so many years. You'll find out soon enough.' He sighed. 'You're your own woman, you'll handle it. What I do want is your help to show his early work. He's a great artist, whatever else he is.'

So Luke thought Matthew had done something really reprehensible. I nodded, then realised he wasn't looking at me, he was staring into space. 'All right,' I said. 'I think I can swing that.'

'And the secret collector. That's Frank Bowers.'

So I'd been right about that. 'Is he willing to show some of them, d'you know?'

'So I believe.'

We walked back into the dining room and I left Luke attacking the food, picking up his plate, heaping large amounts of meat on to it.

I moved away, out into the fresh air of the empty courtyard. The laden scent of *lonicera Halliana* wafted towards me as I leaned against the dining room wall. It was a very successful party. I was amazed at the number of Matthew's friends who'd come over from London, the number of locals he still knew. And then I saw that they were not only Matthew's, but his brothers' friends as well. A show of solidarity.

Debs was dancing with Jean-Pierre now. They made a good couple, though he must have been several years younger than my beautiful daughter. Then I saw Mark moving towards them purposefully, cutting in. The music stopped and he led Debs off into the dining room. I could see, even at a distance, that she was not reluctant to go. As they came nearer I saw her gazing at Mark in the way she'd looked when she'd been in love with Mick. And it was only then that I realised why Deborah had chosen to spend two weeks of her annual holiday on Guernsey, staying with her mother. And why Mark had acted so strangely when we'd come across each other at Les Roches. How could I have been so blind?

153

CHAPTER TWENTY

There was no sign of Deborah until well after noon the morning following the party. She'd had a late night, like the rest of us. And perhaps too much to drink.

I'd managed to get myself to 10.30 mass. The triumph of age over youth? I caught my reflection in the hall mirror. One of those old ones which flatter. Ripeness is all I told myself hopefully.

I laid the table, took the roast chicken out of the oven, pounded the gong.

'Hello, Mum.' The fists rubbing the eyes were over busy. 'I thought you'd have gone off to Bôtnoir by now. I didn't ask you to wait for me, did I?'

Because she was the repository of half my genetic heritage I was making excuses for her to myself. But I couldn't stop my mouth tightening into a hard line. There was no way she could miss it.

'I didn't know how to tell you.' The sheepish grin made the dark under her eyes smaller but more intense.

I hadn't noticed what had been obvious because I'd been too preoccupied with my own emotions. Debs had mentioned, in a dismissive way, that she and Mark had run into each other, ostensibly because he'd gone to a couple of her choir's dress rehearsals. I should have worked it out then. Why on earth hadn't she just told me they were seeing each other?

'Mark's a really good baritone, you know, Mum,' is what she'd said. 'He's thinking of joining a choir.' And I hadn't guessed until last night, when I saw her dancing with him: shining eyes, lithe body, nimble feet. That was the simple explanation of why he hadn't been in touch again after those first few abortive calls to

Somerset. So Debs was the "new lady" Matthew had mentioned. Why would any of them imagine I'd object?

'I'm not sure why it's such a big secret,' I said.

'I thought you might be upset.' The eyes had grown wide again and were misting up.

'I can't think why you should.' I suspected that their growing relationship had been as unwitting as Matthew's and mine. But it must have been apparent to everyone last night that they were in love. I looked at my daughter attentively, saw how she'd blossomed, remembered how her eyes melted when she spoke of Mark. That's why she knew so much about the Frelé clan. She'd been afraid of my reactions, unaware that her involvement with Mark might be an unexpected bonus for me.

'No. It's all been completely above board.' She paused, examining my features for a clue. I kept them still. 'You didn't want him anyway, did you? Perhaps you're even relieved?'

'Why should I be either?'

'Well... You met him first.'

'And that gives me the right to sue for breach of promise?'

Her lashes flirted over her eyes. 'Not really.'

'But you think I might be upset, all the same?'

She shrugged. 'In principle, I don't. In practice, I thought you might not be very happy about it all. I'm sorry, Mum. You know the last thing I'd want to do is hurt you.'

'You thought I was interested in him myself?' I frowned. 'I've always made it quite clear, Debs, but I'll repeat myself. I never was, and I'm not now, interested in Mark. I told you that right from the start.'

'People say all kinds of things they don't mean.'

'Why would I have misled you about something like that?'

'He did seem so – appropriate,' she said. 'In spite of Robert being unimpressed.'

So she'd discussed it all with her brother. He must have thought my introducing him to Mark in Boston was significant. 'Well, let me reassure you. I like Mark well enough. He seems a decent man, he has no other attachments that I know of, he's the right background. He's a widower, and I'm a widow. But that's where our mutual interests end. The main point is that I'm not interested in him emotionally.'

'Because of Daddy?'

'He isn't right for me.' I poured myself some water. 'But there are other aspects which are a bit tricky. He's my generation, rather than yours.'

'Why should that matter?'

'I'm not saying it does. But it is something to consider very carefully. I suppose I thought we were friends, and that you'd have discussed the situation with me, Debs.'

She swallowed some coffee, crashed down the cup, stared at me with sudden inspiration. 'There's someone else?'

For the first time that morning Deborah looked at me as though I were another woman rather than her mother.

'I did think you've been looking – different, somehow. Blooming, if you'll excuse the pun.' She put some chicken into her mouth and chewed. She helped herself to more roast potatoes. 'I'm really starving.' She ate some salad, than looked at me again. 'I'd put it down to that TV series. Stupid of me.' She added a grin. 'I did notice that you've stopped behaving as though you're a nun. You looked almost flirtatious a couple of times last night.' She chomped, putting more chicken on her fork. 'Who is he, anyway? Do I know him?' The fork trembled, dropping its load. 'Not Frank Bowers, by any chance?'

I laughed. 'An entertaining idea, but definitely not. Though I do like his work. As you can see, I've bought several pieces.'

She looked at the nude displayed on a pedestal, nostrils twitching distaste. 'You like Matthew's...' She'd put the chicken piece on again, but this time she dropped the fork. 'Not Matthew Frelé, Mum. You told me it was just business. Anyway, Mark says he's the most awful womaniser ever.'

I stared at her in my turn. Mark had discussed Matthew with her? 'If I were interested in anyone, it would be Matthew. But I don't believe in one-way relationships, and so far there's been nothing special between us. We're friends, that's all. And neighbours. And

I think he's a great painter.'

'Along with the rest of the world.'

'His first exhibition was my doing. You can't accuse me of leaping on to the bandwagon.'

'You're terribly touchy, Mum. It's not what I meant to imply. It's just that no one seems to think there's anyone else around. They've all gone potty about him. That's bound to go to his head.'

'No sign of it that I can see.'

'He never went near you last night.'

She was quite wrong. He'd been the perfect host – circulated, played with the band, asked me to dance a couple of times. Then he'd walked me back at around one. Only the stragglers were left by then. He'd told me how well he'd thought the party had gone, that I'd been marvellous. And that he'd be in touch in a couple of days.

'I would say you were pretty well taken up yourself. Too much to know what I was doing, anyway.'

'I was thinking more that, wherever I went, there was Matthew, playing the suave host.'

Why all this resentment aimed at a man she didn't know? 'There's something wrong with that, at his own party?'

'You're always telling me how self-contained he is, how wrapped up in his work. He never goes out, you said. Just plays in a jazz band to earn his crust, and paints in a cold-water flat without any heating.'

'That was last March. His sources of income have increased since his grandmother died and he came to Guernsey.'

'He's come into money?'

'I wouldn't know about that. But he's the heir to Bôtnoir and Lascervelle,' I said, staring at her. 'You already know that.'

Debs's eyes seemed to cloud over. 'You sure? That weirdo last night insisted he's the rightful heir. He said his cousins couldn't prove their legitimacy. Unless they find their parents' marriage certificate he can claim the fief.'

I shrugged. 'I find it hard to believe that the seigneur of Bôtnoir had four sons without getting married first. The only problem seems to be finding the proof.'

'That's that odious Todd's point. There's no record of a civil marriage between the parents, and no certificate. He told me he's already searched records here on Guernsey, as well as the rest of the UK. And France.'

'Has he now. But even if Matthew can't prove he's the rightful heir, you've obviously forgotten that the exhibition was an enormous financial success.'

'That's just a one-off.'

I laughed out loud at that. 'Not with programmes about him on the BBC, and the South Bank Show. And he's been painting prolifically at Charles Grichard's place.'

'Another disreputable character.'

'According to St Mark?'

'Well, he has known him for yonks. You might bear that in mind.'

Was she suggesting that she'd accept whatever Mark said without question? How could a modern woman react like that? I'd been irritated by Mark's macho attitudes right from the start, in spite of his urbane ways. Naturally Debs would not be so sensitive to the undercurrents, if she considered them at all. Her generation assumed equality, mine had to fight for it and is inclined to continue the battle. And she was in love, after all.

She was wolfing down the chicken now. 'So it's OK by you, is it?'

'What is?'

'My seeing Mark.'

'OK as far as my relationship with you both is concerned. But he is rather old for you. Sixty to thirty something. That's quite a gap.'

'I do know that,' she snapped. 'But I don't think it matters. I've had relationships with younger men and, except for one, they don't compare that favourably.' She sat quiet for a moment, and I didn't interrupt. Mick's ghost flittered between us. He'd been her first, her true love. And he was gone just as Jonathan was gone. 'Mark and I really hit it off. For a start, we both love to sing. And we both enjoy going to concerts and the opera.'

So they'd been seeing far more of each other than I'd guessed.

'He's so civilised, Mum. I'd have thought you'd be glad I've been given the chance to marry someone like that.' She pouted at me. 'He's even a Catholic.'

'And marriage is for the procreation of children. He will be nearing eighty before your first offspring has finished school.'

'I know all that. But at least men can father children into old age. And it would be much worse if I chose to be a single mother. I think this is the better option.'

I knew Debs wanted children. I also knew she wasn't prepared to marry just for that. What I didn't realise was that she was prepared to have a child on her own. 'I didn't even know you'd considered that.'

'I've thought about it. Lots of women of my generation do. Anyway, Mark might live to ninety or more. His grandmother lived to ninety-six.'

'And you'd be looking after him.'

'Come on, Mum. Who knows? Anyway, I'm prepared to take the risk.'

'You might have told me why you wanted to come to Guernsey for your holiday.'

'It wasn't the only reason.' She exaggerated the pout. 'You know I enjoy being with you.'

Were they engaged, or still considering it? 'All settled, is it?'

'We're neither of us as foolish as that. I've decided to take a couple of months' sabbatical. We're going to drive through France and Italy together. For a month to start with.'

I couldn't deny that that was sensible. 'Sotheby's will give you the time off?'

'Without pay, yes.'

'And if you do get married, where will you live?' Though I already knew Mark was looking for something 'suitable on Glategny Esplanade'.

The masticated chicken showed as her mouth dropped open. 'Guernsey, of course. Where else?'

My gregarious daughter holed up on a small island? 'You'd buy a house here? What about your career?'

'We've thought it through,' Debs said, her face as eager as a puppy's. I felt a pang at her ingenuousness, her innocence about how tough life could be. 'I'll buy and sell antiques in a small way. After all, I am an expert on porcelain. I'll stick to the small stuff. I can go on buying trips, come back to Guernsey, sell to visitors. And I can keep the business as small, or as large, as I like. The hours will be flexible, so if the children do come there won't be any problems.'

'You've got it all worked out.'

'You don't seem to have grasped what I'm telling you. I thought you'd be really thrilled. We shall be neighbours.'

'You mean you'll be taking over Lascervelle House?'

She laughed. 'I wasn't being as literal as that. Not really. Mark thinks Matthew might want to stick to that. Assuming the Todd issue is resolved.'

Why was she allowing Mark to think for her? 'So what d'you make of it?'

A dismissive shrug. 'I don't care one way or the other about Lascervelle. Anyway, you don't own Riande. What I meant was, we'd both be living on Guernsey. You'll have grandchildren on your doorstep instead of three thousand miles away. Aren't you pleased?'

In a sort of way. Truth to tell, I could see some disadvantages. The Frelés were close knit, and once Deborah was married to Mark she'd be part of all that. I'd be peripheral, and not exactly sought after. I had to admit that the role of being Mark's mother-in-law wasn't altogether appealing.

Another thought occurred to me. What if Matthew and I...? Was it against Guernsey law to marry the brother of your son-in-law? And if it were, would I try to stand in Deborah's way?

Yet another, much more disruptive, idea insinuated itself. 'There's something I think you haven't thought about, Debs. What if you have a son?'

She frowned. 'I hope I do. What would be wrong with that?'

'The fief, Debs. Mark is older than Jean-Jacques, so Jean-Pierre would be disinherited.'

She stared at me, pushing chicken-greasy fingers through her hair. 'You're right, I hadn't thought of that. I don't think Mark has, either.' She began to collect her lunch things together. 'You know, I've always wanted to look at that place of theirs. Why don't I go along with you? I'd really like to see the famous Bôtnoir.'

Was she, by any chance, already thinking she might eventually live there?

CHAPTER TWENTY-ONE

My next meeting with Jeanne had been scheduled for that afternoon. It was an important stage. The autumn filming was to start on Thursday, and I wanted to run through what I was planning.

Apart from Jeanne herself Nicol Rochet, the retired sailor now working as head gardener, had turned out to be a gem. We'd hit it off, right from the start, though Nicol's first allegiance, he always made quite clear, was to 'le Bôt'.

There'd been one disagreement between us. Nicol had grubbed up every single fuchsia in a collection old Mrs Frelé had cherished. And then he'd treble-dug the plot. As though burying all traces of the Occupation. 'Those German plants,' he'd called them. 'Weren't there before the war,' he'd muttered. 'Knew you wouldn't want them.'

He maintained he was prejudiced against the whole genus because it had been introduced by the German Leonhart Fuchs, though there were plenty of other plants with a connection to Germany. Philipp Von Siebold, for example, introduced the flowering crab-apple, forsythia siebaldii, and hydrangea paniculata, all of which were represented in the garden. I was a little resentful. I'd looked forward to taking cuttings of the rarer plants – unusual fuchsias were among my favourites. And they were particularly apt in a climate where most of them managed to last through the winter.

I took it he was in his late sixties. A youth during the war, he'd taken the brunt of German brutality against the young living at Bôtnoir. His body had the lean agile look of a man who used his muscles every day, but his walk was slow and measured, not simply because he was a retired sailor. He husbanded each stride so that no gram of energy was wasted. And his face was deeply lined.

After the initial filming, he'd disposed – as though by magic – of most of the overgrown clumps of bramble and nettle which had filled large areas of the garden. He despised modern equipment. Armed with nothing more formidable than a Stafford billhook and a double-edged slasher he'd turned wilderness back into garden in a remarkably short time. Then he'd double dug the whole place with the spade he kept polished to a mirror shine. 'Gets rid of weeds without harming the plants,' he'd announced. 'Herbicides aren't natural, not fit nor safe for the soil.'

After last night's encounter with Todd a different explanation occurred to me. Had all that digging been because Nicol was searching for buried boxes? Was that why the fuchsias had to go? And, if so, had he found what he was looking for?

The TV crew had filmed him eagerly. The weathered face and tranquil eyes came over brilliantly on camera. It was Nicol who'd become the real star of the television series. He and I, both circumspect, had soon become firm friends. And his knowledge of gardening at Bôtnoir before the war was the sort of luck one needs to make an outstanding and lasting programme.

I drove Debs and myself over to arrive on the dot of our arranged time, two o'clock. I didn't want to trespass on Jeanne's domestic arrangements, but I didn't want to waste any time, either. I parked the Saab in the now huge circle in front of the house, got out and was surprised to see the front door opening. And, instead of Jeanne, Todd Frelé walked out to meet us.

'Oh,' I said, gathering my wits. 'I was due to meet Jeanne at two. Is she at home?'

'Snooping again, are we?' The heavy shoulders moved towards us threateningly. It didn't help that he was dressed in black, and that he was wearing boots, not shoes.

'You know perfectly well that Jeanne and I are restoring the gardens, and that we're filming for the BBC.' The monotone was my attempt to keep calm. 'That's why I'm here today – to make

163

sure everything is ready for the TV crew.'

'And the doll? She's part of that?' He stared at her braless bosom heaving under a thin T-shirt and short skirt. 'Dressed for gardening, sure thing.'

Debs must have made her distaste clear last night.

'Just looking,' I dismissed that. 'It's all coming along so well, Debs was longing to see what we've managed to get done so far.'

'There's still loads of colour.' Debs walked towards the magnificent solanum crispum draped over the front door, its mauve potato-flowers glinting in September sunshine. The second flowering of large, deep violet-purple flowers of clematis The President leant their pointed sepals and cream stamens towards the light. 'It must be wonderful to restore a garden like this.'

'I could care less.' He walked up to the Saab and opened the driver's door. 'This is my place, and you're not welcome. Get lost.'

Deborah stood tall. 'The front of the house looks great, Mum. Now, why don't we drive home and give Jeanne a ring?'

I stood by the driver's door and stared as Todd was turning on his heel to go back into the house. Just then another car, with its unmistakable roar, drove up. Charles Grichard parked next to me and opened his door. I was startled to see him there. If I'd understood his innuendos, Charles was definitely persona non grata with the Jakes.

He turned off the noisy MG engine and levered himself out. 'Hello there, ladies. Todd.' He stared from one of us to the other. 'You all look enthralled to see me.'

Todd stood silent, staring at us, his arms across his chest peasant fashion, his body blocking the front door.

Charles turned to me. 'Bôt said I might f-find you here f-for the afternoon. I'm in the middle of rep-planting my border.' The smile was meant to be winsome, but it was too crooked for that. 'I just wanted to get hold of the name of your f-favourite nurseryman.' He looked over the drive, took in the new shrubs I'd planted around it. 'Bôt keeps on about the wonderful plants you get from some small p-place near Sherborne.' He turned to Todd, smiling. 'He also told me you were house-sitting. I've just come to take a nosy round—'

'Fuck off, Grichard. Along with Mathieu's latest.'

Charles's jaw, literally, dropped open. 'What the hell gives you the impression you can order us off?'

The leer was wide and infuriatingly smug. 'Haven't you heard? I'm claiming my inheritance, served the papers at the Greffe. No need for me to quote the law at you, but I'll help out the trespassers. No one can touch Bôtnoir until it's all settled.' His fingers drummed against his arm. He wasn't too sure of his ground.

'That's absurd, Todd. You know what's going on. Ruth has f-filmed three months of Summer. The whole point of the p-programme is to go through the seasons while restoring an old garden. She'd have to wait until next year to start again.'

I couldn't keep quiet. 'The most relevant bits are the 'before' shots,' I pointed out. 'That's what made Bôtnoir such a find.'

'Tough break. Your contract with Mathieu ain't worth a dime.' He turned, about to walk back into the house. 'That's the way the cookie crumbles.'

Even if I hadn't been astute enough to cover the Todd problem my agent would have done so. The contract was with the legal owner of Bôtnoir, presumed to be Mathieu Frelé. But I preferred not to bring that up at this stage.

'That really is p-prep-posterous. You're telling me she has to have a c-contract with you before you'll behave decently?' Charles's stutter was explosive on repeated consonants.

Todd's widened nostrils concentrated on poor Charles. 'High noon. A professional should have gotten ahead of problems.' The stained-tooth smile was far too complacent. 'Now I gotta straighten you out. Beat it.'

'I told you about our Clameur de Haro, Ruth,' Charles hissed into my ear. 'Use it.'

He was reminding me of a practice still legal on Guernsey. 'I can't remember the details,' I hissed back, using my best histrionic whisper. 'Can you do it for me?'

He grinned, the left side of his face almost reaching his eyes. He hunched a shoulder, closed one eye. The imitation of the hunchback of Notre Dame was striking, if mystifying.

165

'Todd Michel Frelé, I ask you to desist in trying to deny my partner's right to make a television series of gardening programmes restoring the garden at the fiefdom of Bôtnoir belonging to my client, the Seigneur, Mathieu Ignat Frelé,' Charles intoned.

Todd turned sneer to insolence. 'Partner? You and this beat-up broad are partners?'

'Ruth is a director of my winery,' he lied.

'What kinda frame you trying to pull? No way that affects my—'

'Are you going to desist?' Charles interrupted.

'For crying out loud. What half-assed thing you trying on for size? I'll lay my beef with the gendarmerie.'

The man beside me suddenly fell to his knees. For a moment I thought he was having a heart attack, then assumed his melodramatic bent had got the better of him, that he was pleading with Todd. I knew such a thing could do no good whatsoever. And then I remembered snippets of the quaint medieval form of injunction still occasionally used on Guernsey. The complainant falls to his knees and bellows out a phrase in front of two witnesses. Then he recites the Lord's prayer in French.

'Haro! Haro! Haro! À l'aide mon Prince, on me fait tort!' Charles shouted out, no hesitation in the consonants, his sense of drama evidently enormous.

As Deborah and I watched and listened, transfixed, he began to recite the Our Father in French. I rather wished the cameras had been there to record it.

To my surprise Todd did nothing to stop him. He merely backed into the house and banged the front door shut.

'Splendid stuff, Charles. This going to work?' I asked. 'And what is all that rigmarole about my being your partner?'

'P-pipe down, Ruth. I just thought it might come in handy. We'll have to sort it out. But the main point is that Bôtnoir isn't Todd's p-place – yet. He may think he's got proof, but he has to get it through the courts.'

'How did he manage to get rid of Jean-Jacques? Surely a top barrister doesn't think Todd has a case?'

'I t-tried to ring you earlier on to warn you, don't you know.

The Jakes have rushed back to England for the time being. To support their daughter, Dominique. She's been involved in a c-car crash. Jeanne's gone to look after the grandson, and Jean-Jacques is sorting out the legal stuff.'

'Is she OK?' Had the man in black gone after Dominique? I was becoming ridiculously melodramatic.

'She's shaken up. A child on a b-bicycle ran into her. He broke his arm. It wasn't her f-fault, but of course she's nervous.'

'So cousin Todd is taking advantage. I see. The thing is, I can't make a programme with that madman trying to wreck everything. What on earth am I to say to the film crew?'

'You c-can't just give up, Ruth. Meet me at Old Government House and we'll sort something out,' Charles suggested, climbing into his MG. 'I can ferret around the law library about the Clameur de Haro after we've had a drink.'

'It's Sunday, Charles.'

'As it happens I still have the key to my office. Anyway, we can discuss things.' He leant his head down. 'I must say, Ruth, you've l-livened things up a bit since you arrived on Guernsey.'

It was kind of Charles to try to help. But this was something I had to discuss with Matthew first.

He noticed my reluctance. 'You d-don't understand, Ruth. I still occasionally represent Bôt. Besides, my old f-firm acts for him. I do s-strongly urge you to discuss things informally with me before you approach him.'

The smile had gone. This time I saw what I'd not seen before: Charles really was Matthew's friend. And lawyer. I nodded, slid the gear lever into drive, took off the hand brake. 'Old Government House,' I said. 'Race you there.'

CHAPTER TWENTY-TWO

The lanes were far too narrow and winding for the MG to pass the Saab, so Debs and I won the race to the car park by default. The real race was the walk to the hotel. We installed ourselves in the courtyard of Old Government House and waited a good ten minutes for Charles to catch us up. His mincing gait, I took it.

It was one of those balmy sunny autumn days which made sitting outside not only possible but desirable. The sheltered quadrangle, its tables set invitingly around the central pool, were laid for tea.

Charles scrunched unhappily towards us over the pebbles, picking his way. He sat down heavily, wiping his face with his handkerchief. 'S-something to eat?'

'Just a drink for me.' I was feeling a little sick after Todd Frelé's performance.

'What about you, Deborah?'

'A glass of white wine will be fine.'

'From what I g-gathered at Bôt's p-party, you and Mark have got to know each other pretty well,' Charles started off, smiling at Debs. 'Should we assume it could well be your son who inherits Bôtnoir?'

She shrugged, staring at me to signify I wasn't to talk out of school. 'It's early days.'

'What I'm g-getting at is that you might f-find a short rundown on our curious island laws, particularly the way they affect the Frelés, reasonably interesting.'

'I'd certainly like to see that creepy man seen off the island.'

Charles laughed. 'I'm not sure we can arrange that, whatever happens about Bôtnoir. Let me s-start by explaining that I'm the senior douzenier for the parish both Bôt and I live in: Bôtgriche.'

'Douzenier? That's a Guernsey word?' Debs helped herself to the roasted peanuts which had been put out.

'The douzaine is the governing body of each p-parish. Bit reminiscent of the jury system, in that it consists of twelve men.' He stared from me to Debs. 'Well, we include women as well as men nowadays. Things have changed a l-little. Up to 1844 douzeniers were elected for life but, to be eligible for office, they had to own real estate of significant value. And, once appointed, s-service was compulsory.'

'What does significant imply?' Debs asked.

Charles was signalling for a waiter. 'Technically, ten quarters of wheat rente in the c-country parishes, more in St Peter Port. Let's just say it was s-substantial by island standards at the time. Now anyone on the electoral roll of the p-parish, not just a property owner, is eligible. That's exactly like the jury system in England. But we're a t-traditional lot here on Guernsey. In the past, sons usually followed fathers into the office. My own f-family has always had a serving douzenier. And the longest serving one in a particular parish is the doyen. No prizes for guessing who that is in the Parish of Bôtgriche.'

I could see Debs listening hard. She really was serious about Mark. 'And this office of yours isn't just a feudal practice to entertain tourists?'

'Still very relevant. We're responsible for seeing that p-property is preserved in good order and, more importantly, that the land is k-kept in good heart. We make it our duty to see to it that hedges are t-trimmed, walls and banks kept in working order – that sort of thing. So, in effect, I'm r-responsible for seeing that the Bôtnoir état is kept up to scratch.'

So why had he allowed it to get into such a state, I wondered? 'But it was terribly run down for years, Charles.'

'Quite correct. I didn't feel I could approach the old lady about it. But I have now made it a p-priority to see it is brought back to its former glory. It would not have been right to bother the old lady, and Bôt didn't have the cash. But I take the line it's his responsibility now, and he's in a position to do something about it.'

'So that's why you were there today, to check on how things were going? You could have rung me about the plants any time.'

'I did want to see what you'd put in, how the p-plantings looked. But you're right, it wasn't the main reason.' He leaned down and undid his shoelaces. 'You don't mind, do you? My feet swell.' He loosened the shoes and sighed. 'What I actually c-came for was to see if that rat Todd was still about.'

'But you weren't expecting quite what you found.' Debs grinned at him.

Charles gave a great sigh of relief as his feet eased out of his shoes. 'I knew Jake was p-pandering to him by allowing him to squat there. I told him he was making a mistake, but he p-pointed out that the alternative was to wait until the dispute about the succession was resolved. He wanted to get on with the restoration. Even if he were to win, Todd will have to p-pay back the costs incurred.' Charles leaned down to rub his feet. 'I've always been a little n-nervous of that c-claim. Fact is – we haven't f-found Mathieu Frelé's marriage certificate, or any other proof of marriage before the ceremony in 1935.'

I gaped at Charles. 'You're saying that that horror Todd will win and there's nothing anyone can do to stop that?'

'It's not impossible. The old lady left him everything she had.' Charles beckoned impatiently to the waiter. 'He's got enough to live on as well as c-cause trouble. As long as the Jakes kept him sweet it worked. Now that they're temporarily out of the picture Bôt wanted me to f-find a way to get rid of Todd. Legally, I mean. He wanted to boot him out. Bad idea.'

I'd never forgiven Charles for warning me against Matthew that first day at his house. It had clearly blinded me to his virtues. 'You help Matthew with family problems?'

'He listens to my advice, Ruth. As it happens I drew up the draft c-contract for the TV series. I went through the final version your agent sent Bôt. I saw to it that you have n-nothing to worry about. I'm also responsible for administering the laws of Préciput.

170

It was I who alerted Bôt to press for that, otherwise he might well have let it lapse.' He sighed. 'Unfortunately that now c-counts against us. As I said, if we can't find proof of Mathieu senior's marriage it all goes to Todd.'

'What's a Préciput?' Debs looked round. 'I'm getting hungry.'

'A s-snack, then.' Charles picked up a menu and handed it to her. 'Unless you want tea?'

'A baguette would be good.'

'The boys' father was legally declared dead in 1945, after the war. Normally, when someone goes missing, the police will try to establish whether they have died by checking bank accounts, brokers' accounts. If they think there should be an inquest to help the family receive a death certificate and reach closure, they'll file a report. That was done.

'I don't think we'll have any problems re-establishing Bôt's parents are dead. Eight years after his parents' disappearance – in 1952, when he was twenty-one – Bôt claimed le droit de Préciput. That meant he c-claimed the house and land to stay in one p-parcel.'

Matthew had been accurate about that. 'In effect he disinherited his brothers?'

'Not exactly. He was required to p-pay them monetary compensation for their share.'

'How could he, if he had no money?'

'The boys' mother had some m-money in her own right. Bôt's brothers agreed to let him have the enclos for his share of that money. Anyway, that particular law was repealed in 1954. I saw that c-coming, which is why he applied in time.

'You advised him to claim earlier rather than later?' The whole Frelé affair had taken a quite unexpected turn. I could hear a fascinating story behind the dry words. But would Charles tell it?

'Exactly. There is another legal s-safeguard against splitting up small estates. It's called retraite, or sometimes retrait lignager. If someone s-sells a place, and near relatives want to have it, they have a year and a day in which they can reclaim it from the buyer.'

'So if Todd wins, and wants to sell Bôtnoir, any of the brothers could bid for it?' I made a note that I'd have to watch out for such a clause if I bought on Guernsey.

'For a purchased property, anyone can do it. For an inherited property, it has to be a male relative of the original owner. Which is why Jean-Jacques thinks Bôtnoir can be retained even if Todd wins.'

'Typical feudal stuff.' Debs sounded irritable. I wondered how long she'd last on the island.

'Guernsey does still have feudal elements,' Charles said, benign. He turned to me. 'Did Bôt t-talk to you about all that?'

'Some of it.' I could see Debs listening intently. I also realised that Charles was trying to help me for Matthew's sake. 'Have you always championed Matthew?'

'I certainly have. Waiter!' He waved his hand at a young man near the dining room French windows. There were no other guests in the courtyard. 'Bôt's the most l-loyal friend I have. I like t-to think I reciprocate that.'

It was the first time anyone had praised Matthew rather than carped about him. 'But you warned me against him, just like far too many others. As though I were incapable of judging for myself.'

'I said he was a l-lady's man, Ruth. Though that wasn't quite true, I'm afraid.'

So Matthew was a homosexual after all? I felt a pang, a devastating sense of loss.

'He's quite a heart-throb, but he can hardly be b-blamed for that. As far as I know he never encourages any of these ladies. He's a loner. What I should have said is that Bôt finds it impossible to form new relationships. The friends he has date from his early childhood.'

'What about Frank Bowers? He didn't meet him till after the war.'

'All right, childhood. Anyway, they aren't friends any l-longer. But I suppose they were. They did see a lot of each other at Downside.'

'Really?'

'Absolutely. It was Frank who encouraged Bôt to become a full-time painter. He convinced him that anything else would be

172

neither here nor there.'

I thought back to something Jeanne had mentioned. 'That's why he refused to try for a scholarship to university? And did it really make sense to turn down his grandmother's offer to pay for art school?'

'He said she was t-trying to buy him off. He wasn't having any.'

'A very emotional response, wasn't it?' Debs asked.

'He got away from her as s-soon as he could. He's l-loathed her guts from a long way back.'

'To the war,' I said, without really knowing why.

'Before that, matter of fact. He couldn't abide her attitude to his mother.'

'I see.' A Wagnerian figure rose up in my mind. Had old Mrs Frelé been more than an onlooker, but actually an exponent of the Master Race? Nazism wasn't, after all, confined to Germany. But, surely, her grandsons were beyond reproach? The Frelés had been on the island for generations. 'What did Matthew say she'd done to his mother?'

He steepled his hands. 'Belittled her. Held on to the role of seigneur's widow when her son's marriage meant his bride was the 'grande dame'. But primarily Bôt was convinced it was because of old Madame that his parents died.'

'You mean she actually told the Germans about the planned escape?' I stared at Charles, and shivered. 'Because she didn't like her daughter-in-law?' Could she really have done that?

He looked uncomfortable. 'Not necessarily deliberately. As f-far as I can make out Bôt thought she was too damned friendly with the Boches. She may have indulged in c-careless talk when she was squiffy. She invited the German elite to the house, played up to them. T-treason, in Bôt's book. He reckoned the only way they c-could have worked out what was going on was because they were lying in wait. That's why he held her responsible.'

'And did she talk?'

'There wasn't any p-proof, if that's what you mean. Anyhow, he never forgave her, never c-could stand being anywhere near her.' Charles glared at the waiter who'd finally arrived. 'Didn't you see us out here?' He turned to us. 'Pouilly Fumée all right?'Debs and I nodded our agreement. 'And a ham baguette.'

'Two bottles of Pouilly Fumée, three ham baguettes.' Charles sat back in his chair, his face composed. 'Bôt was quite a little s-saboteur at the time. He s-saved my life, you know.'

It was fascinating to see that Charles's mouth had straightened out. His eyes, usually roaming and disdainful, were grave now. He was back in his boyhood. 'Do tell us about it,' I said, my mouth dry.

'You're really interested?'

Interested in Matthew's antics as a boy under the Nazis? I could hardly contain my excitement. 'I'm longing to know.'

He sat back, closed his eyes, breathed slowly, nodded, then waited for the wine to arrive. Then he drank almost a whole glass before speaking. 'The Occupying Forces insisted on a c-curfew. We all had to be in by seven in the evening. There weren't that many children on the island – the Frelé boys and I were the only ones in our parish. You can imagine what happened. We egged each other on. The b-bloody Boches wasn't going to tell us what to do.'

I knew exactly what he meant. I remembered myself as a six-year-old girl on her way to school, resenting the men in black uniform, unable to do anything but hate them in silence.

'Bôt and I were to meet on the shore, below Bôtnoir,' Charles began. 'As you know, our houses are quite c-close together as the crow flies. We liked to m-meet on Bôtnoir beach after curfew. Reasonably safe because no one else was there.

'We had it all worked out, or so we thought. Bôt abseiled down from his bedroom window, I scrambled down the water lanes. One night there was a reception c-committee waiting for me.' He shuddered. 'Three soldiers. They were expecting saboteurs. Five t-trucks had been t-tampered with during the past two weeks. Everyone knew about it, no one knew who was responsible. The Germans were at boiling point.'

'How old were you?'

'Tail end of 1942, so I was thirteen. Bit older than the Frelé

174

twins.'

The waiter arrived to uncork a second bottle of wine, refilled Charles' glass. He gulped it down, saw the waiter look at him, simply held out his glass for more.

'What happened?' Debs was as curious as I was.

'They grabbed me.' He stopped, stared at the waiter pouring more wine, waited for the man to leave.

'And?'

'Bôt must have t-twigged what was going on and decided to help.'

'He could have left you to it, you mean.'

'Indeed. Not that he would have. He wasn't – isn't – that s-sort. Plays the knight errant.'

'What could he possibly expect to do?'

'I'm coming to that. He was to the right of us, and I heard a racket c-coming from the left – a series of what sounded like small explosions. He always had some tins rigged up, and fired his c-catapult to imitate gun shots. Fooled any Boche around even during the day. I s-suppose it made them think they'd caught the saboteurs in the act. One s-stayed with me.' He took another gulp of wine. 'He grabbed my shoulders so I couldn't run, set me to face him, then s-stamped on my right foot, then my left, with his boots. Broke several of the small bones.'

'That must have been agony.'

His eyes gazed vacantly into the glass. 'To t-teach me not to g-go where I wasn't supposed to, he yelled at me. Something – a stone, I suppose – hit the man in the back. He swore, swung round.'

'And?' Debs was on the edge of her chair.

'Bôt was c-crouching a few yards from us. There was a moon with cloud cover. The clouds broke slightly and I c-could see his eyes gleaming, and a long dart-like glitter catching the light. It lunged towards the soldier. He doubled up and lay still.'

'Dead?' Debs breathed.

'No such luck. But he was wounded. The t-tide was coming in and that beach is very dangerous. The other two carried him off.'

'How did you get away?'

'Bôt gripped my arm and p-pulled me towards a cave we always played around in. The incoming t-tide would fill it with water. I didn't dare speak, but I thought we'd drown. I couldn't walk. He made me c-crawl into the sea.'

'And then?'

'He told me to take a deep breath, to hang on to his shoulders while he swam. We ended up right in the cave, at the far side. There was a very narrow ledge. Someone had put an iron bar there years ago. We c-clung to it until the tide went out again. They'd scoured the area by boat by then. Bôt's determination was just incredible. He wouldn't let us leave. And remember, he was only eleven.

'We stayed till daylight, till after c-curfew. Bôt went to fetch Nicol, and they brought the wheelbarrow. They p-put me in it and wheeled me to the house. Maria helped me take a b-bath, gave me c-clean clothes - and we managed to convince Madame Frelé that I'd played a prank on my mother and slipped into Bôtnoir the night before. She probably didn't swallow it, because of the state I was in, but she pretended to.' He took another long drink of wine. 'Reports the next day said there'd been a marine commando raid from Britain. The Germans insisted on it. The two unwounded soldiers swore they'd seen a destroyer off shore.' He grinned. 'I've checked it out time and again. There were no c-commando raids on Guernsey in 1942. Anyway, those that did take p-place were pretty much bungled.'

'So what about your feet?'

'They never healed p-properly. My fault, in a way. I never dared tell anyone the extent of what happened. Not even my mother.'

'And Matthew's parents?'

Charles poured more wine into his glass and drank. 'This all took p-place after they'd disappeared.' He stared at his feet. 'He was one hell of a rapscallion to bring up once his p-parents had gone. He managed to do a great deal of damage.'

'What an extraordinary story.'

'He's an extraordinary chap.'

'I always thought so,' I said. I couldn't help feeling smug. When

176

I looked at Charles Grichard again I could see he was in love with Matthew, clearly unrequited. That's why he'd warned me, been jealous of me. 'So, where does that leave us as far as the garden at Bôtnoir is concerned?'

'What? Of course.' He began to munch his baguette. 'It's an interesting situation. What we have to do now is lodge your p-protest, in writing, at the Greffe. And this has to be done before the bailiff, the lieutenant-bailiff, or at least t-two jurats.'

'You're suggesting I become your client?'

He shook his head. 'It would make it easier. But I can introduce you to s-someone else, if you p-prefer.'

'Can you represent me in this, and also act for Matthew as far as the contract is concerned?'

'I see no particular c-conflict. Your quarrel isn't with Bôt.' He smiled. 'In any case, should the case come to court, the p-prosecution is carried on by the Crown, which represents the prince who has been invoked. At present that's Elizabeth II.'

I felt the need of alcohol myself. 'What happens if I lose?'

'Apart from problems with your programme? You may be given a heavy fine. Raising the Clameur without due reason is regarded as the c-commission of a tort.' His hand was gripping the glass hard enough to crush it. 'But I don't think we have to worry about that. You're definitely entitled to use the garden to make your p-programme, and I strongly s-suspect the island would be all in favour of the publicity. Why, it might even become a garden open to the public. There's only Sausmarez doing that, at the moment. And that's only open for short times.' He filled his glass yet again. 'Don't worry, Ruth. The worst that can happen is that you have to go through the Clameur p-procedure yourself. I'll c-coach you, if you can't remember it exactly. The rest is a foregone conclusion. The contract was drawn up here, and is subject to Guernsey law. By the terms of Elizabeth I's Charter of 1560, any attempt by an outside Court to supersede the Guernsey Court's jurisdiction over islanders – and I think we can certainly argue that Mathieu Frelé is an islander, and it is his status which is relevant here – constitutes an action in derogation of the Bailiwick's legal autonomy. Todd

Frelé has to challenge you here.'

The three of us walked over to Riande House. It didn't take long to put the matter in writing on my computer. Not unnaturally, neither the bailiff nor the lieutenant-bailiff was available on a Sunday. The consensus of opinion was that I should invoke the Clameur myself, by returning to Bôtnoir and asserting my right to film there.

'I'll have to think it through, Charles. It's one thing for you to have done this on Matthew's behalf. It's quite another for me to do it. I would prefer to discuss it with him first.'

Charles assessed me carefully. 'So – d'you want to g-go and see him on your own, or shall I come?'

'On my own.'

'I think Mark's there this afternoon,' Debs put in. 'I promised to go round and value that desk they're both so fond of. They had it shipped back from London. Apparently it was their mother's.'

'Desk? What desk?'

'A sécretaire-bookcase, the one in the far right-hand corner of the living room.'

'At Lascervelle, you mean?' I hadn't noticed it. Antiques are not my thing. As far as I'm concerned the pieces may be works of art – I don't doubt they are – but I prefer furniture built for the age I live in.

'Bôt was c-crazy about his mother,' Charles told us. 'I'd say he'd go to any lengths to acquire that p-piece. She brought very little with her from France, you see. The sécretaire, some other pieces of furniture, a little fine lace, jewellery. The only other thing of value she possessed was the Frelé jewellery her husband gave her.'

'Matthew has it?'

'All except the wedding and engagement rings. No doubt she was wearing them when she disappeared. The jewels formed p-part of the estate, so Bôt does have them. When they were going over the grandmother's effects he walked up to the jewel c-case and removed it. He wasn't interested in anything else. No one raised any objections.'

'So why don't you and I go over, Mum? I'll look at the piece, and then I'll take Mark off somewhere.'

I sat in silence, thinking it through.

'Hello? Are you receiving me?'

'What? All right,' I said. It was as though I could read Matthew's mind. He'd taken the jewellery, and he was going to look for a bride. Because, after all these years, he'd decided that it was going to be *his* heir who'd take over Bôtnoir.

CHAPTER TWENTY-THREE

If Matthew was surprised to find both Debs and me on his doorstep he didn't show it.

'Mark's here already,' he said, opening the door and waving us through. 'I've got some coffee on. I'll bring it through.'

Mark was standing, proprietarily, by his mother's desk. He ran his fingers down the fine walnut, opened a drawer or two, and smiled at Debs. 'Like it?'

'Ah, yes. A sécretaire-bibliothèque.' She walked up to it, took out a drawer, turned it upside down. 'Excellent condition.'

'I've looked after it very carefully.'

'A seventeenth century piece, I'd say. First made by the Dutch, then copied in France. A lovely example.' She smiled at him in her turn. 'I can see why you'd like to keep it.'

Matthew came in bearing a tray with a cafetière, four porcelain cups, the saucers remarkably deep, a silver sugar and creamer. There was also an odd-shaped ornate piece on the tray with the other things.

Debs took one look and rushed over. 'You're not going to use those, are you?' she sounded quite out of breath.

Matthew squinted at her. 'Why not? They're cups, aren't they?'

'They're Sèvres.' Her voice held the reproach of a teacher for a misguided student. 'Not Vincennes, but still far too valuable for ordinary use. Didn't you know?'

His face was expressionless. 'You like the vaisseau à mât?'

'Duplessis design, isn't it?'

His look was direct this time. 'I see you know your stuff.'

'Originally painted by Jean-Pierre Ledoux. I've seen it in the Wallace Collection. This, I would guess, is a nineteenth century copy made in the Herend factory. Hungarian.'

''Fraid I can't vouch for that. But it was a favourite of my mother's.'

'She had good taste.' Debs picked up one of the cups, turned it over. 'The marks suggest it's Sèvres 1758. They could be forgeries, of course. There are so many about. But it feels right.' She was lifting the cup up and down, then placed it carefully in its saucer. 'Would you mind very much if we drank out of something else?'

Mark patted her shoulder. 'He was having you on, Debs. Of course he wasn't going to use any of it. Just testing.'

Matthew left the room and reappeared almost at once with another tray containing less valuable demitasses of Royal Worcester. He poured the coffee into those. 'So. Tell us about the bureau,' he said, looking towards the sécretaire.

'Another fine piece. Your mother obviously knew how to buy antiques.'

'She didn't buy them. Her personal things were sent over from France.'

'Her family were well off?' Debs was more interested in the porcelain than in the answer. I remembered it was the mother's money which had helped Matthew buy his brothers out. An heiress of some sort?

Matthew turned away from Debs, but I could see the pain in his eyes. 'We don't know much about them. I think my parents hid some important papers which might well tell us more. I've looked, but I haven't found them yet.'

Those could well be in the boxes Todd had angled for – buried in the garden, if I'd grasped what he was hinting at. He, I took it, had been coached by his late grandmother.

'They had to be quite rich, or an old family which knew how to look after exquisite heirlooms.' Debs turned a drawer upside down.

'I'm not interested in what the piece is worth. That's more for Mark's benefit. I just want it because it belonged to my mother. Can you value it for us? We spun a coin. He's agreed I can buy his share of it at a fair price.'

Debs was taking out more drawers, examining them, putting them back. She flipped the lid down, displaying pigeonholes. 'One point of interest about many of these old bureaux,' she said, sliding her fingers up and down the beading between the pigeonholes, 'they often have a secret drawer, occasionally two.' She laughed. 'Perhaps those papers you're looking for are hidden here?'

Both men came over now, and watched. I looked at Matthew. He was focusing his whole attention on Debs's fingers. Why was he so interested in the memory of his mother? Why not his father? A Mummy's boy? Did that explain why he'd never married?

'Wait a minute. Yes, I think I've got it.' Debs pushed what looked like a small joinery pin, fingered an ornamental panel, and drew out another drawer. 'Brilliant, don't you think?'

At first there didn't seem to be anything there. Then Debs put her hand inside, right towards the back, and pulled something forward. 'There's something there.'

She pulled out what looked like a wad of old bank notes. Old pound notes, I recognised. They were in a neat bundle surrounded by blue ribbon. Something – some story someone had told me – triggered vaguely in my mind. And then I looked at the two men.

'Wha…at?' A sort of croak from Mark. 'What's that?'

'Looks like your money, Mark,' Matthew said. He picked up the bundle by the ribbon. A determined middle finger pressed to his thumb-pad held the ribbon tight, dangled the parcel. 'Royal blue.' His voice was so low I had trouble distinguishing what he said. 'I told you mine was cerulean.' He swung it towards his brother. 'There you are. All yours.'

Mark didn't take the package. Instead, grey-faced, he lunged towards a chair and sank into it.

Deborah stared at him. 'Is something wrong? Aren't you feeling well?'

The story Franz told me came back to me. Debs had found the money Mark had accused Matthew of stealing. So that was it. Matthew had told the truth, all those years ago.

'Let's go now, Debs,' I said, my voice clear and loud.

'What?' She stared at me, then at Mark. 'What's wrong with everybody?'

'Now, Debs. We're going home.' I used the tone I'd used when she was a child. It worked. She followed me meekly.

CHAPTER TWENTY-FOUR

I was certain that Charles would try to be in touch with Matthew that evening. I rang Grichard House as soon as we were back in Riande to explain that it would be wiser for him to leave things for the moment.

'Why? What's the b-big mystery?' He sounded deprived. I guessed he'd been looking forward to telling Matthew about the afternoon's theatricals.

I didn't want to sound coy or mysterious, but I couldn't think of a plausible excuse. 'You'll have to wait, Charles. I can't tell you at the moment.'

The explosion at the other end of the line was dramatic, but futile. 'And y-you expect m-me not to get in t-touch with my best friend – and my c-client – s-simply because you say so?'

'The problem with filming at Bôtnoir doesn't affect your client. It affects me.'

More exasperated noises off. 'Rubbish. The s-status of the f-fief is affected. It's up to my c-client to decide whether he c-cares or not.'

It hadn't occurred to me that Matthew might think along those lines. I was about to say so when his expression, whenever there was talk of Bôtnoir, swam in front of me. He cared about it. And the fact that he cared enough to have had a contract drawn up with me and also, as it turned out, a careful rental agreement with Jean-Jacques, suggested that he hadn't altogether given up the idea of living in the manor of his fief himself.

'Wait till to-morrow morning,' I said. 'Please. It really is important.'

'I thought you wanted to f-film on Wednesday, that that's what led to the Todd débâcle in the f-first place.'

'I want to drive the producer over and look around. That would still give me the rest of Tuesday for last minute adjustments, just in case there's a problem I need to work out. Everything's ship-shape as far as I know.'

'You're not being realistic, Ruth. Rat Todd c-could have turned the place upside down by then.'

'I know.' It was certainly a gamble. The timetable for filming was a tight one. A little leeway for the weather – a couple of days at most. Three days were to be spent at Bôtnoir, filming the early autumn season. I needed to revise my notes, to make sure everything I wanted to discuss was covered. The real question, I realised, was which alternative I cared about more: the programme, or Matthew. 'I'll have to risk it,' I told Charles firmly. And knew then that I cared more about Matthew than I wanted to admit.

'You've got till t-ten to-morrow morning.' The phone clicked off.

Debs's reaction to the story about the missing money was incredulity. 'You mean Mark actually threw Matthew out of his flat because he thought he'd purloined the money?'

'Apparently. At any rate that's what Frank Bowers maintained.'

'Where did Matthew go?'

'To stay with Franz – Frank. He was living in a cold-water studio in Bermondsey. The two of them shared a sort of revamped warehouse – and a model. She was Frank's girlfriend, then promptly fell for Matthew. So that arrangement fell through.'

'Dear Matthew certainly has a gift for trouble.' She looked at me with those penetrating eyes. 'I'd watch it if I were you, Mum.'

'I keep telling you, I'm not emotionally involved with him.' I swept my arm in a dismissive curve which couldn't have fooled either of us.

'So he moved in with the girlfriend, did he?'

There was always a point in these stories where Matthew was exonerated. 'I said she fell for him, not that it was reciprocated. He found himself the proverbial garret and lived on his own.'

184

'And lost touch with Mark?'

That was perceptive of her. 'No. The other two brothers made sure the four of them met regularly.' I was tired of protesting too much. 'I've got to get to work,' I said, wearied beyond all discussion. 'If I'm to be ready for the filming, I have to work tonight.'

I worked till midnight, then tried to get some sleep. Impossible. The Frelé brothers intruded into my dreams. I saw them, as boys, charging across the gardens at Bôtnoir. Cowboys and Indians, Chicago gangsters – preparation, I guessed, for baiting the Occupation Forces during the war.

I thought back to the four youths in Brixton, remembered Matthew's swift dispatch of them. There'd not been any hesitation, he knew he'd rout them. Because he'd practised on Germans?

The scene at the celebration dinner was another pointer. Matthew's suppressed rage as he assessed the robbers, the instant understanding as I took off my rings, asked for more wine. This man was used to using violence – and winning. "You don't know very much about him. But I do, Ruth. I really do," Luke had said. What could he have meant? I was positive Matthew wasn't involved in anything ... what? ... deviant, unacceptable ... I shuddered in the cold of night and solitude – criminal? But what about the past?

I tossed and turned, but the thoughts would not go. I knew Matthew now regularly played the blues with a group based in a small club in Torteval. He usually returned home around two in the morning. One-thirty. I slipped into some clothes, found a chair to sit by the window in the front room nearest to Lascervelle House, and waited.

It was a vigil, and the feeling was all too familiar. This was how it had been with Jonathan when we first met. I'd read his novels in manuscript, thought them wonderful, pushed them at publishers because Jon couldn't be bothered. At parties we'd gone to, I'd noticed only him. Journeys I'd taken to meet him had passed with my staring at his photograph. The cheap friendship ring he'd given me after we'd known each other a year, and which was all he could then afford, had meant more to me than the expensive dress ring he eventually gave me. I sighed. Was I really falling for

Matthew? After all the warnings I'd had?

The town was quiet. No traffic, no pedestrians along Candie Road. My head began to nod, and I dropped into a doze. I startled up. My clock said half past two. Had Matthew come back? Dare I go and call on him? I wondered whether Mark would still be there.

An overpowering desire to see Matthew, to hear his voice, overcame all inhibition. I stumbled towards the hall, the phone. Nervous, I tapped in the wrong number and got the unobtainable tone. I tried again. He answered on the second ring.

'Ruth! What on earth are you doing up?'

Was it my imagination, or did I hear delight in his voice? 'Are you on your own?' My tone was meant to be nonchalant, but it sounded conspiratorial.

There was a pause. 'Well, yes.'

'There's something I need to discuss with you.'

'Now?'

'Before ten o'clock this morning. We're both awake, so I thought—'

There was a pause as he worked his way through that one. 'How did you know I was awake?'

'I heard a car door slamming shut.'

Another pause. 'I never slam it. Listening out?'

'I wanted to, then I dozed off. But it's so quiet, something woke me.'

'The drummer drops me off. You must have heard his engine rev. You want me to come to you?'

'Debs might wake up. I want to talk to you on your own.'

'I'll come and fetch you. St Peter Port may be quiet, but it's not villain proof.'

And he was there within minutes, standing outside my door, a smile on his face. I could not stop the thrill of sensual excitement coursing through me as he put a hand on my arm and squeezed it.

I ached for him to put his arms around me, to hold me tight, to whisper in my ear. What was happening to me? Had I allowed it all to go too far? He'd been proved innocent of theft. I was sure he wasn't a cad or a philanderer any more than he was a thief. I could no longer hold my feelings in check. "He's quite a heart-throb," Charles had said. It was too late to heed that warning now.

I brushed past Matthew, intent on cold autumn air. I felt the heady scent of his body, his warmth. I gulped the cool of night and walked the few yards along the road, and through his front door.

'Let's go into the kitchen. The Aga keeps it warm.'

I didn't need outside heat. My churning hormones fired my blood.

An old-fashioned wooden table stood in the centre of a vast room, four wooden chairs around it. The place hadn't been renovated. It must be as the grandmother had left it. Clean, but worn. It can't have been touched for more than forty years.

'Are you OK? Would you like something hot to drink?' There was a saucepan simmering on one of the rings. 'I was just about to make some milk and honey. Join me?'

I nodded. As Matthew busied himself preparing the drinks I looked around. He was used to living on his own but, unlike most men, he'd worked out how to do it. He was comfortable here, in his old-fashioned kitchen. Preparing food was something he enjoyed. And he had the easy grace of the practised host.

'So what's it all about?'

'I wouldn't have brought it up, but Charles will if I don't.'

'Charles Grichard?' He frowned. 'He's been bothering you?'

'He says he represents you.'

A frown, a stare. 'Legally, you mean?' The milk saver began to chatter. He took the saucepan off the stove. 'And you're doing something which affects my legal rights?'

'It's about Bôtnoir. Well, the garden.'

'The programme, I take it.' He looked over at me. 'You're not able to finish the series after all? Cuts at the BBC?' He smiled. 'Or have you found somewhere more suitable?' He looked carefully at me. 'I don't think my contract with you stipulates that you have to use Bôtnoir. Just that you may.'

'That's precisely where the problem comes in.' As I described what happened it sounded not merely weird, but surreal. The filming at Bôtnoir couldn't have been the issue – whoever owned the place would have to restore both the garden and the house, as Charles had explained. It seemed unlikely that my work was unsatisfactory from that point of view. Todd Frelé's aggression – antagonism – had been directed at Debs and me personally. Distressing even in retrospect.

'I see.' No expletives, no sign of anger except a stillness which made me shiver. He ladled teaspoons of local honey into two mugs, lifted the saucepan high, poured the milk over it to froth, and stirred. He passed a rose-patterned mug to me, sat down opposite, began to sip. 'And filming the September scenes can't be postponed. You always film at roughly the same time each month. I quite see that.'

'The schedule's very tight. The crew is allocated to that particular programme on those days.'

He nodded, then drank. I watched his Adam's apple move and felt protective – he seemed suddenly vulnerable. I put my fingers round the scalding milk and returned to sanity.

'The producer comes to check out what they need. He rings it through. Then the cameraman and soundman come over the next day and we start filming.' I smiled. 'The weekend is there in case the weekday weather is impossible.'

'Did cousin Todd give a reason?' He looked at me keenly. 'Or is there a personal antipathy between you two?'

'You probably remember we stumbled across each other at Bôtnoir some time ago. But we didn't meet socially until last night. I can't pretend I take to him. I may have been a little sharp.'

The smile wasn't altogether flattering. 'He made a pass at you that first time. Did he try it on again?'

'No.' I tried to focus, but I was groggy with lack of sleep. 'He boasted about being the real heir to the état. I probably made it very clear I wasn't impressed.'

'And at Bôtnoir yesterday – you tried to reason with him?'

'Yes.' I looked into my mug. 'I just couldn't believe it. He was dressed in black from head to toe. He stood back against the door, like a giant tarantula, oozing menace. When I tried to talk to him he became abusive.' To my embarrassment there were tears forming

188

in my eyes. It had been a degrading humiliating experience. A feeling I remembered from Vienna...

Matthew went on sipping, apparently unperturbed. Didn't he care? 'How did Charles get involved?'

I could feel, rather than see, his eyes probing me. I told him about the chance visit, the scene involving the Clameur. He began to laugh. 'That's rich,' he said, then another bout of laughter racked him. 'That's really funny.'

'You aren't upset?'

'I've no idea what the hell Todd is playing at, but I can see your problem. Sorry, Ruth. You must think we're all completely mad.'

'More Byzantine than most families, I suppose. I feel terrible. The last thing I want to do is stir up hostilities.'

'Todd's already arranged that for himself. Actually, my late grandmother engineered it. He's merely carrying out her last wishes.'

I'd almost expected him to tell me to get lost. Todd was his cousin, I was a mere outsider. I remembered how he'd reacted in Brixton, when all that had happened was that we'd spent a little innocent time in each other's company. He'd changed since then. No longer quite so self-effacing, so apt to take the blame. Where he'd submitted – no, deferred – to his family before, he now sounded more confident, more suited to the role of head of the clan that he'd obviously played in the past. But that clan did include his cousin Todd.

So what had happened? The sensational find of the missing hundred pounds, perhaps. But why, since he knew he was innocent, had he allowed Mark's accusation to affect him all these years? It had to be some sort of guilt. But for what? A yen for Caroline, even if true, would hardly involve Mark. Whatever it was had to do with his childhood, and unexpiated guilt. I was convinced of that.

I pulled myself back to the present. 'Charles insists you, or I, have to do this unbelievable Clameur bit again. And that it has to be done today.'

'So that the filming can go ahead?'

'Because he's going to the Greffe first thing in the morning.'

The mug hid his mouth so I couldn't tell whether he was laughing at me. 'Ah. Right you are. You seem to have made quite an impression there.' He drained the mug. 'No need for all that melodrama. I'll go and sort out dear cousin Todd.' He must have noticed my crestfallen look. 'Don't worry about it, Ruth. The filming can go ahead. I'll vouch for it.'

He sounded calm and resolute. His head leaned towards me across the table, dark eyes clear, smiling at me. I felt the reverberations all through my body, tingling, melting.

'You can get some sleep now,' he purred, putting his hands across the table, taking mine in his. 'I'll take you back right away.' He saw that I was hesitating. 'Something more?'

'I've got to go round the garden before the producer turns up,' I said. 'That's why I arranged the Sunday meeting with Jeanne. I have to check which plants are right, precisely what I want filmed. I might need the Tuesday to do some last minute gardening.' I smiled uneasily. 'I can't predict exactly how things will look.'

'Of course,' he said. 'I'll go over at the crack of dawn. Why not join me after lunch – at two, say. I'd rather like to see what you've been up to myself.'

His civilised urbane attitude both delighted and unnerved me. Because deep down I knew that there were undercurrents of something buried about to erupt. Charles had sensed it too, though he assumed he was dealing with inheritance complications. Matthew's uneasy relationships with Frank Bowers and Mark could be accounted for. But not his ambivalent relationship with himself – perhaps a split persona? There was something deadlocked – perhaps unacknowledged – between the Matthew of the present and the young Matthew of the distant past. And I knew very well that there could be no relationship between Matthew and me until that was resolved.

CHAPTER TWENTY-FIVE

When I arrived at Bôtnoir, grinding gears because I was so nervous, Matthew was standing by the mysteriously jutting-out wall, sniffing the climbers and talking to Nicol Rochet. He greeted me noncommittally and pronounced himself eager to see what we'd accomplished. There was no sign of Todd. I hadn't the nerve – or the opportunity – to ask any questions. All three of us toured the garden and Matthew left without explanations. I could hardly discuss it with Nicol, so I assumed everything was back to square one.

The filming session began as scheduled, but spread over the weekend because of persistent drenching rain. It refused to stop both Thursday and Friday during daylight hours. Pete and I, as well as the rest of the crew, were invited to take shelter in Nicol's cottage so that we could be on hand for the occasional forays out.

Nicol disappeared whenever he wasn't needed, reappearing magically when he was. I wondered how he did it. Somehow he knew whatever was going on.

We had to return to work on Saturday, when the weather decided to be glorious. By the time the footage we needed was safely in the can I was utterly exhausted, my energies at an all-time low.

Perhaps TV wasn't my forte. I normally lead a cloistered working life. The contrast with the last three days had not been favourable. Pete's non-stop chatter, the camera man's need for nicotine, the sound man's ignorance of the laws of hygiene, all made me long to work by myself again.

Debs had taken herself off to devote herself to Mark. 'He needs me, Mum. That business with Matthew has really shaken him.'

I was keen to know how Mark felt. 'Business?'

'About the money, Mum. He's devastated.' A perfunctory look in my direction. 'You don't mind my spending most of the day with him, do you?' A matter of form. She was tapping her watch, checking the time on my clock.

'I do understand.' One woman to another. And they were due to leave on their European tour the next day.

The crew took a late afternoon flight on the Saturday. The light had gone by then. Stills would have to fill in if we hadn't shot enough film. I fled back to my solitary life, locked the front door and breathed an enormous sigh of relief. How could I ever have allowed the idea of a permanent relationship – living with someone else on a daily basis – to cross my mind? I'd become used to the hermit state, and even my immense admiration for Matthew would not necessarily allow me to abandon it. At that moment his strong attraction paled beside the need for privacy.

Todd's furious face came back to me. I was used to rushing away from people, hiding behind my work. But this time I'd been attacked for no reason that I could think of, and it had upset me. I'd tried hard to turn the garden at Bôtnoir into something which would delight whoever lived there. Why had this man reacted so appallingly to me? What had I done to him? Now that I'd had the time to think again I'd found the whole incident remarkably distressing. Matthew evidently had, as he'd promised, sorted it out. But I hadn't seen him since that Monday, and I had no idea what had passed between the two cousins.

'Don't hesitate to use your key to the French windows if you need to shelter in the house,' Matthew had said, handing it to me. 'The Jakes won't be back for several weeks.' Had he really managed to get rid of Todd? He certainly didn't seem to be around, but I didn't want a repeat of our encounter in the Bôtnoir hall. I kept away from the house.

The filming had worked out well in spite of the rain. I was about to sink, thankfully, on to the lounger I'd dragged into the little courtyard at the back of Riande to enjoy what might be the last of the Indian summer sun. I pulled the chair, piled high with reading matter, towards the sunniest corner. Tendrils of honeysuckle clung to me, but I ignored the need to trim them. I smiled ironically to myself. How strange to think that I actually enjoyed the fact that this house didn't have a garden.

The telephone began to trill. I toyed with allowing the answering machine to take the message. I'd come out to unwind after all the hard work. At the third ring I decided the BBC had scrapped the whole series, and to face bad news rather than to run away. I rushed to answer it just as the answering machine was taking over. 'Ruth Samuels speaking.'

'Matthew here, Ruth. I hope I'm not interrupting the creative flow.' The rumbling bass flowed through the receiver, into my ear, on to my brain. An almost hypnotic murmur filled the roused nerve-ends of my mind, stroking them into expectant attention.

'Hello, Matthew. No, not at all. I'm taking a few days off, lazing in this unexpected sunshine.'

'Quite right. You must be exhausted.'

'It's been a strenuous time.'

'You know I'm playing with the Bluets on a regular basis now.'

He'd joined the jazz sextet to fill in for the pianist – and to sing. They played every night except Mondays and Tuesdays, trying to recreate the atmosphere of the Cotton Club in New York's Harlem in the '20s.

'You are? I thought you were standing in for someone who was having a by-pass operation.'

'He's not coming back.'

Was Matthew putting music before his painting? Was he really masochistic enough to throw away his recent success? 'You mean you're a permanent member of the band?'

I could sense his irritation, though his voice had hardly changed. 'I haven't given up painting, if that's what's worrying you. I'm used to doing both.'

'What energy.'

The tinge of exasperation was carefully controlled. 'I don't need much sleep. Playing the blues relaxes me. And forces me to mix with people. In case you haven't notice: I'm inclined to the reclusive.'

This took me by surprise. From what I'd seen of Matthew – and it wasn't that much, I realised with a pang – he seemed easy in company, positively gregarious. But I empathised with what he was saying well enough.

'Just wondered whether you'd like to join us for the end-of-season gig. Apparently we semi-hibernate through the winter. We only play week-ends.'

'No tourists.'

He laughed. 'Exactly. No money, no blues. The wrong way round, somehow.' There was a slight pause. 'So, can I interest you in a jam session?'

'I'd love it,' I said. 'Anyone else coming?'

'The Jakes and the Lukes are over in England. And Mark and Deborah are touring Italy, as you know.'

'Indeed.' Debs and Mark had left to explore their relationship in San Felice Circeo, a small town set between Rome and Naples. They'd found themselves a tiny flat in the old town. The weather there was said to be so balmy all winter there was no need for heating of any kind. One up on Guernsey.

'But Charles is coming. So you won't be sitting around on your own while I'm working.'

'That sounds wonderful,' I said.

Instead of leaving it at that, he cleared his throat. 'You seem to hit it off with Charles.' He sounded hesitant. 'He's not exactly known for making new friends, especially ladies.'

Was he asking me whether I was interested in Charles Grichard? Had Todd's repulsive insinuations about homosexuality been maliciously slanderous? 'I'm flattered,' I said, sounding as offhand as I could, 'though I expect it's the gardening aspect which interests him.'

The silence was as noisy as if he'd yelled at me.

'I certainly liked the way he stood your ground,' I explained. 'All that drama about the Clameur. He's obviously a true friend.'

'That's settled, then.' He sounded relieved, and much more friendly. As if some sort of stumbling block had been removed. 'I'll pick you up just before eight on Saturday.'

CHAPTER TWENTY-SIX

Matthew arrived at half past seven.

'Charles will drive us over in his MG,' he greeted me. 'Miles Johnson, the drummer, usually gives me a lift. But I thought...'

'The MG? Can all three of us fit into that?'

'You'd rather take the Saab?'

I was wearing a dress. Nothing too ritzy, but not exactly suited to climbing into the back of an MG. It would have to be me – Matthew wouldn't be able to fit his long legs in.

'Either that, or I could change into jeans,' I said, looking at Matthew's. I was obviously overdressed.

He looked at my body openly for the first time. 'They'll show off your figure. And there's a bit of a walk from the car park down to the restaurant.'

What was I letting myself in for?

'Don't look so worried. Charles can manage it.' His tone sounded jocular but reassuring.

He'd come early to make sure I'd be wearing appropriate gear. I changed into stretch-fit jeans, a silk shirt and waistcoat, and settled for low heels with light soles. In case there was dancing. I'd no idea what to expect.

Charles hooted his arrival the moment I was ready. Matthew climbed into the back while I was locking my door, hugging his knees to fit into the space.

The Bluets, they told me on the way, played at Tielle Bleue, a clubhouse which had become the favourite haunt of jazz lovers on the islands. It was popular enough for people to plane hop from Jersey just for the evening.

Perhaps the dedication needed to get to the clubhouse was an attraction. The place was perched on a small promontory beside one of the wildest coves on Guernsey, the Baie de la Forge, in Torteval. Parking was on Les Tielles cliffs. A meandering rocky path, with a few steps cemented into the rock at the steepest parts, lead down to two small stone-built buildings. These had the look of old fishermen's cottages. A tall solitary lamp lighted some of the way. I wondered how customers who drank too much got back to their cars. Perhaps they simply slept on the restaurant floor until the following morning.

'I'll leave you two to choose your meal,' Matthew announced as soon as we'd arrived. 'I need to check the programme.'

Charles and I walked into the building on the right. A huge marble slab had fish and shellfish laid out for our inspection.

'You choose what you'd like to eat from today's catch,' Charles explained, 'and they cook it any way you'd like it. Grilled, deep fried, pan fried. Nothing remotely fancy, but the result's out of this world.'

High praise indeed. There was bass, moules, lobster, crab, squid – a wonderful assortment, all gleaming fresh. I chose a mixed sea-food salad, marinated in the chef's special sauce, for my first course. Squid, skewered and grilled like a kebab, looked a succulent and delicious main dish.

'Sounds good to me, too,' Charles said. 'Bôt wants us to choose for him. I'm sure he'll be delighted with your choice.'

'He's going to join us for the meal?'

'The band eats around ten. Then they play again till midnight, sometimes later. I would guess more like two in the morning tonight. It's a special occasion, don't you know.'

'You a jazz lover?'

'Matter of fact.' He ordered the meal, then led me across the alleyway into the restaurant.

Fishnets covered the ceiling. There was no glass in the spaces used for ventilation. Instead, wooden shutters, all except one closed against the sea, made it impossible to see outside. The tables were placed short side underneath the shutters, jutting out into the circular room. The centre was cleared for dancing, and the band itself was to the side, at the far end.

'Gets pretty hot in here later, I'm afraid, so they open some of the shutters. Let me show you. You get a wonderful view on a night like this, with a full moon.' Charles opened the shutter above our table, and a huge blast of air came in. He laughed, seeing me snatch up my anorak. 'I'll shut it again in just a moment. Look, you can see Pleinmont Point to the left and Fort Grey, with Rocquaine Bay behind it, to the right.'

It was spectacular. The moon reflected off the water, pouring ethereal light across the waves frothing towards us. 'Sensational,' I agreed. We were in the path of the wind coming off the sea. 'But maybe we can shut it now. It's blowing a gale.'

The sextet had assembled on the small platform opposite us. They began to tune their instruments, to sway into *I'm gonna sit right down and write myself a letter.* The piano glittered in and out of the tune, the saxophone sang. I could tell it was going to be a wonderful evening.

'You seem to have all these connections with the States,' I heard Charles murmur. 'Been to Chicago?'

I nodded. 'Muddy Waters, Willie Dixon and so on. Early '50s.'

'New Orleans?'

'On a short visit. We didn't make it to a jam session. The temperature was in the nineties. Too high for Jonathan – my late husband.'

Charles beckoned to the waiter for more wine. 'Jolly bad luck.'

We drank a little, listened to the music. The players were good. After the first few tunes they began to improvise. That made them better. The piano wheedled in and out of the tunes, high and low to the saxophone, adding, strengthening, enchanting. Someone began to sing:

Ashes to ashes, dust to dust,
If the women don't get you, the liquor must.

The bass sounded so real, so much a mixture of Louis Armstrong and Paul Robeson, that when I looked up I was surprised to see Matthew, singing as his fingers stubbed the piano keys.

'Bôt s-sorted out the ghastly Todd, I gather.' Charles's eyes met mine. 'Little Clameur of their own. Took that f-foul-mouthed impostor by the scruff of the neck and slung him out.'

'Physically? And that worked?'

'Daresay you know: bullies are usually cowards. He hasn't b-bothered you since, I take it?'

'Haven't come across him again. But I made sure I was always with Nicol.'

'Very wise.'

'He's an extraordinary chap,' I said, taking a few more sips. 'Said he'd been with the family before and during the war. Too young for the services, I suppose.'

'Exactly. And the apple of his mother's eye. She wouldn't allow him to be evacuated to England.'

'His father was dead?'

Charles downed another glass of wine. 'No one talked about his f-father. Nicol was Maria's son, and therefore part of the household. Bôt must have said how d-devoted they all were to her.'

The woman who'd spiked the Germans' drinks. 'Ah, yes. A cross between a nanny and a maid.'

'There you are, then. She refused to t-tell the authorities who Nicol's father was. That made her fair game.'

'Matthew said she was born in Italy, that the Germans were going to deport her, and she killed herself at the prospect.'

'He's jolly well played it down. One of the German NCOs who regularly came to Bôtnoir – batman to the colonel – got more drunk than usual one night. He started mauling Maria. She ran out into the garden, then tried to hide in the caves. He followed her. Blighter ruined his uniform in the puddles there.'

'You mean he lost face and blamed it all on her.'

'Exactly. The swine held M-maria responsible, insisted she'd lured him out. Then the officers got hold of her and held a k-kangaroo court. Annie, Nicol and Henri were forced to witness it. Maria became completely hysterical.' He waved at the waiter for another bottle. 'Then they arrested her, put her in s-solitary. She was f-found hanged in her cell.'

I shuddered in the heat of the room. Maybe not even suicide. 'And Nicol vowed eternal vengeance.'

Charles's eyes were as bleak as the cliffs surrounding us. 'Actually, he c-claimed he took it – said he was responsible for the deaths of two of the Germans who hounded her.'

'Really? How?'

'Water under the bridge, my dear.'

I could see he didn't want to go on, but I was gripped by the story. 'You can't leave it there.'

'The bare bones, then. He said he p-provoked one of them to chase him out into the garden, then veered aside at the last minute and the man tumbled over the cliff.'

'He was responsible for that German's death, d'you mean?' I felt a shudder going through me. Thou Shalt not Kill. Strictly, Thou Shalt not Murder. Killing is justified in certain circumstances – like war.

'Absolutely.' Charles blinked, emptied his wine glass. 'That first death was officially noted as an accident. They built a fence to stop it happening again.' He stared into his drained glass. 'Dare say you've seen it, rotting away.'

I pulled myself back to what Charles was telling me. Surprising Nicol hadn't mentioned the fence. 'Terrible state, yes. I've been wanting to replace it with a hedge. What about the second German?'

He looked at me, his eyes searching mine. 'D'you really want to d-drag up all that m-murky past?'

'I work with Nicol every day.'

'One of their chaps died in a jeep crash. They said the brakes had been t-tampered with. This time they didn't let it go. They accused Henri of s-sabotage, though Nicol swore he did it and that he confessed. They took no notice, s-sentenced Henri to death.'

'They had the death penalty on Guernsey?'

'Didn't carry it out. Thing was, no sentence over six months was carried out on the island, so they sent Henri off to Germany, to a camp there. He's never been heard of since.'

'All this happened after Matthew's parents disappeared, I take it?'

'Just after, matter of fact. The Germans still visited, as before. The attraction had always been Michelle Frelé – the grandmother. Those officers t-treated her as though she were some patrician lady in their own country.'

'D'you think she was a collaborator?'

He shrugged. 'Not entirely sure. You could take the view that she had no choice. A single woman, young for her age, living in a gracious house. It was very t-tempting for lonely officers whose wives were f-far away in Germany. Her social position appealed to the Kommandantur. Let's say she was p-popular, and she didn't discourage them. There was a good deal of partying.'

'You were there?'

He poured from the new bottle. 'Before the incident with my feet, then that was the end of it.' The crooked smile appeared. 'She definitely had f-four regular admirers.'

'The ones who, in effect, killed Maria?'

Charles shrugged. 'Quite probably. The same four always went out there. And three of them met with a sticky end. All in damned peculiar circumstances.'

'Three? And Nicol only claimed to have killed two?'

He grinned. 'Must have been a p-profound disappointment to him. The third was said to have died of n-natural c-causes.' He smiled that crooked devious smile of his. I could see it wasn't the pipe stem he'd held in his mouth for years which was responsible for that. It was the way he was. 'And the fourth one disappeared. We were all damned sure he ran for his life.'

'D'you believe Nicol really was involved in some way?' I thought back to my dealings with the man. *Yon Cassius has a lean and hungry look.* I listened to the lashing of the Channel outside the shutters. The sea round Guernsey could be as wild as anywhere. It almost screamed.

Screamed like the man in black. "I spent one of the war years here. I wish I could have stayed for all of it," he'd said. "I was transferred to the Eastern front in 1941." Could he be the fourth

German – the fourth man?

'Don't d-doubt for a moment he helped them towards their deaths. Let's not dwell on all that. Bôt's the one to talk to. He and Nicol are great pals, don't you know. C-comrades.' He poured more wine. I judged he'd got through a bottle and a half by now. 'Well now: what's happening about that gardening programme of yours?'

'The next filming?' I smiled uncertainly. 'I haven't heard from Jeanne. I'm not quite sure where I stand.'

The mouth shot upwards and sideways. 'You haven't heard? The Jakes are moving out altogether.'

'Of Bôtnoir, you mean?' I gasped, I couldn't help myself. 'Todd's won his case?'

Charles beckoned for another bottle, poured himself a glass. 'I've made sure the p-preliminary hearing won't come up till next year. T-to give us time to p-prepare a cast-iron defence.' He picked up several coasters, built them into a pile, knocked them down. 'I do hope I'm not talking out of turn. Bôt's intending to live there himself. I've arranged that he can, until after the hearing.' He downed some more wine. 'Bôt dealt with Todd himself. Successfully, it would seem.'

Was it Todd's claim which had catapulted Matthew into asserting his rights? 'But the Jakes have had the whole place done up. That must have cost a fortune.'

The coasters were built up again, and Charles added more from a nearby table. 'Bôt's picking up the tab.'

True he could easily afford it. The paintings were selling for very large sums indeed. Matthew had agreed to be filmed for the South Bank Show, and another exhibition was planned. No doubt Andrew Canwaller had already arranged for copies and postcards to be made of the most popular work. Any new paintings would now sell for quite colossal sums.

How could Matthew be so sure Todd wouldn't take over? Was he prepared to gamble, or did he know how to stop him?

'So, be p-prepared,' I faintly heard Charles's voice. 'You'll be dealing with the Seigneur himself from now on. The way the garden goes will depend on him. As, of course, it should.' He grinned. 'Not that that will pose a problem. He's only too keen to recreate precisely the state the place was in before the war. Well, the way his m-mother arranged it before the war. I can only hope you and she share the same tastes. Otherwise, I can p-promise you, there'll be real trouble.'

We'd been so engrossed in our conversation that we hadn't even noticed that the music had stopped. Matthew came up to our table, drew out a chair, sat down.

'So what have you ordered?' He signalled to the waitress to bring another glass. 'I'm famished.'

I found it hard to gear my mind back to food. And I was acutely aware that I'd paid virtually no attention to the music, that I had no idea of how he'd played apart from the first two numbers. And singing that one song.

Pulling myself together I dutifully recited the menu. I could have saved myself the trouble for the first course. It arrived promptly, together with the extra glass.

'We'll need another bottle of wine. More of the same?'

We both nodded, watching as Matthew began to eat. Neither of us seemed able to do more than dabble with food.

He stared from one to the other. 'Is something wrong?'

'I'm sorry, Matthew. You invited me to hear the music, and all I heard were the first few numbers. I did enjoy the way you improvised on the piano. And I thought your voice was a cross between Paul Robeson and Satchmo. Quite a shock when I looked up and saw it was you. You're a really good blues musician.'

He started to eat again. 'Listening isn't obligatory.' It reminded me of what he'd said about the paintings. 'I take it the conversation was more interesting.'

'Charles was telling me stories about the Occupation.'

He pushed the rest of his seafood salad away. 'A great raconteur, Charles, when he feels like it.' His nostrils flared at me. 'And in my experience you make an avid listener.'

'He filled me in on events at Bôtnoir at that time.' I swallowed food I hoped wouldn't choke me. 'About the way the Germans behaved.'

'Ahh.' He drank some wine slowly, carefully. 'Such unforgettable memories.'

'Our generation was certainly exposed to an unusual early education,' I agreed. He knew that I, and above all Frank Bowers, had at least equal claim to Nazi exposure. And, in spite of the horrors of Dachau, Franz had managed the transition from concentration camp to freedom remarkably well. By no means a negligible achievement.

I could have sworn Matthew ground his teeth. 'Lessons so well learnt from outstanding teachers.' Learnt, not taught, I noted. 'And only available to the specially chosen.'

The specially chosen. Something clicked in my mind, but I couldn't quite catch it. It was so fleeting I had to let it go. 'Charles told me that you were taking over Bôtnoir yourself.'

'Really, douzenier. You're supposed to be my legal adviser. What's all this talking out of court?' He made it clear he was teasing, but I could see Charles redden.

'H-hardly a s-secret, Bôt. The whole of St P-peter Port – the whole of Guernsey – knows about the C-clameur. And that you threw Todd out. There could be only one reason for that.'

'It would have been nice to tell Ruth myself.' He turned to me. 'You don't mind, do you? I won't stand in your way about the garden, you know. You can do anything you like with it.'

'It's your garden,' I said. 'You're entitled to make exactly what you want of it.'

'Believe it or not, what I want is what you want.' The dark eyes had grown softer. He smiled slightly, raised his glass. 'Here's to Bôtnoir,' he said. 'Let's make sure it stays in the Mathieu Frelé line, and that we'll bring it back to its former glory.'

CHAPTER TWENTY-SEVEN

At first I didn't answer the phone. I don't always put on the answering machine, so I couldn't screen the caller. It went on ringing. Curiosity got the better of me.

'Hello.' I tried to make my voice less brusque-sounding.

'Melvyn Bragg tells me you know who the anonymous patron is.' The bald statement without preamble, followed by a pause, sounded peremptory. And when I didn't answer immediately Matthew's voice took on that Downside element of stiff politeness. 'That true?' The rumble coming down the line might have been intimidating if it hadn't been for the excited tremor in the deep voice.

'I have been approached.' I was a refugee, so caution is second nature to me. Lying is not.

'You mean you know where the paintings are?' He didn't even bother to cover his surprise. 'How come?' The tone could not be mistaken for being friendly.

'Not exactly. The collector your late agent sold to introduced... themselves.' My talents for dissembling have been well honed. Franz had maintained his collection of Frelé paintings wasn't a secret, and I was tired of playing games. But that didn't absolve me from getting in touch with him before I gave his identity away to Matthew.

'So who is it?' The voice was steely as last week's trombone.

'I can't tell you that.' Irritatingly provocative, but I couldn't think of a way to avoid that. Even my throat let me down. I spluttered for several seconds. 'I'm sorry, Matthew. I gave my word before we really got to know each other.'

'What's that supposed to mean? We got to know each other

because of my paintings.'

Hardly accurate. But presumably he meant that everything that had happened since that first chance meeting at St Olaf's had been because I'd shown an interest in his art. Nothing remotely personal. Charles, Mark, Franz – I realised all of them were right to warn me against him. His feelings weren't in the least involved. My own fault for thinking I knew better.

The cloudscape I'd bought at the exhibition glinted at me, smirked. 'You said you weren't prepared to sell,' I reminded him. 'Even to me.'

I heard the clatter of a falling chair. 'But I agreed to the show–'

'You let me organise it, yes. I couldn't make any other assumptions. So when the collector offered to allow Bragg to film some of those special paintings, I didn't think it right to turn him down. They'll only be shown with your approval.'

The pause was tangible, hard and cold. 'How far back do they go?'

I couldn't honourably tell him that, either. Then I realised Matthew must already know when the agent had first approached him. He was simply hoping for a lead. 'You know I can't answer that.' As for Luke's little hoard – I hadn't yet worked out how to handle that.

More crackling down the phone, a thump. I sensed him venting fury on inanimate objects. 'Name your price.'

I gulped. 'I told you. I promised not to say.' Silence, but no click. 'Hello?'

'Not just a good businesswoman – an iron lady.' The voice had lightened, there was even an undertone of jocularity. I couldn't decide whether it was phoney or genuine. 'Right. Maybe they should be shown, at least some of them. Are you willing to act as go-between?'

'Of course.' The confused signals reinforced the ambivalence I found so unnerving. 'I told you right from the start. The public should have the chance to see as many of your paintings as feasible, to judge for themselves.' Even the truth can sound banal.

'What about commission?'

Another trick question. 'That's very kind, but no.'

'Why not?' The cool professional tone sounded more like an insult than expletives would have done. 'That would be perfectly proper.'

Whatever my motives were, money had no part in them. 'No, thank you. Really.'

'Perhaps you'll allow me to mention what you've done when I do the programme.' This time the voice was gentler, almost normal. It startled me. And turned me back to jelly.

'I'll give it some thought.'

'Let's say till Sunday. That gives you two whole days. What about meeting at Bôtnoir? We could discuss your future garden plans. I'd really like to be included in those.'

'You're moving out there already? Charles said—'

'Charles doesn't know everything about me. I'm considering living out there. I haven't decided yet.' I could hear a window opening or shutting. 'Just one thing. I'd like to take some part – take Jeanne's place, so to speak – in restoring the grounds. If that's acceptable.'

'That was the basis of my agreement before. Perhaps we should draw up a new one, make it all above board.'

'That's up to you.' A short pause. 'Are you free Sunday morning?'

A tingle I could not control swept through my limbs. 'After 10.30 mass?'

'Perfect. Madeleine will be at Bôtnoir, cooking a massive lunch. Nicol will be there as well. You'll join us?'

The tingling feeling vanished, leaving a trace of bitterness. I grimaced into the mirror above the phone but couldn't eliminate the lines of age even when I forced my features into a smile. 'Madeleine?'

'She's with him at the cottage.'

Was Nicol married? Or did he have a girlfriend? Somehow, I'd not expected that. I'd never come across any indication of a wife or partner. The invitation to lunch was – unexpected – but I was happy enough to accept. Nicol and I agreed on plants, and garden design. The tapestry of life.

'Lovely.' I tried to put some enthusiasm into feelings steeped in frustration. 'I look forward to it.'

CHAPTER TWENTY-EIGHT

Matthew sat next to me at mass, and we drove out to Bôtnoir together afterwards. An ethereal young girl greeted us as soon as I'd parked the Saab. I tossed aside the wife theory. To my relief she dimpled as much at me as she did at Matthew, massed dark hair frizzing out around her head, soft brown eyes huge. Something about her reminded me of someone. I searched my mind. And then it clicked – something about the eyes. Nicol's eyes... A relative?

'Madeleine's from Rouen; like Jeanne. She's visiting Nicol for a couple of weeks. She's training under Paul Craddoux.'

'You're today's guinea pigs.' Her English was not tinged with French, but it did have a Guernsey twang. 'I do hope you're hungry.'

'That smell of roast lamb is irresistible.' Matthew steered me in the direction of the kitchen.

'She'll have them queuing up in no time.' Nicol was already installed. A bright airy room which was now transformed into a modern kitchen. He pushed a hand ingrained with soil at saucepans swinging artistically above a central unit. 'If she gets a place equipped with proper tools. Not bloody toys.' He banged at inoffensive stainless steel with a wooden spoon which promptly split.

'You're so old-fashioned, Pépère. The kitchen's beautiful.'

It wasn't so much the physical resemblance to Nicol I'd noticed. Madeleine didn't look much like her grandfather. Something else...

Her face was flushed as she opened the oven door and basted the roast smelling of rosemary. 'Did you have a designer in, Monsieur Mathieu?'

'My sister-in-law did the kitchen.' Matthew pulled out a chair from the round table placed by the window overlooking the garden. 'A kitchen-diner is a definite improvement on lugging the food all the way upstairs to the dining room.'

'It could be made workable.' Madeleine's hands were busy with cloves of garlic and a press. 'A little time and motion study is all it would take. And some decent worktops.' The smell of garlic now began to overpower the other aromas as Madeleine stirred what looked like the white flesh of scallops among a mixture of sliced mushrooms and pressed cloves sizzling in a frying pan. A second pan contained bread crumbs turning gold. She placed some coral with the scallops, deftly turned the mixture, spread out four plates and began to dish up. 'Coquilles St Jacques are much better if the bread crumbs are fried separately.' A huge knife moving up and down at speed expertly chopped a large bunch of parsley. She flung some over each dish. 'Pépère said they were a special favourite of yours.'

'Nicol's got a long memory.' The two men's eyes met, parted, stayed apart.

'Remarkable likeness.' Nicol was not looking at anyone in particular as he pulled out the chair opposite Matthew's. 'Same colour hair.' He stared at the round table top.

I followed his eyes. He was looking at the knotted pine surface. It was a deep chestnut colour. More the russet of winter beech, actually. He couldn't have been referring to Madeleine's raven tangle when he talked of a likeness, and clearly wasn't.

I looked up, saw Matthew's eyes flash, then veil. He tasted a scallop, savoured it. 'Outstanding.' He smiled at the budding chef. 'You planning to open a restaurant here on Guernsey?'

The translucent skin turned pink as Madeleine understood the compliment. 'Eventually, maybe. I've got a few years' training to get through yet.' The pink turned redder and I could see Nicol's granddaughter was one of Matthew's devotees. I pin-pointed what was familiar about Madeleine at last – she looked at Matthew in the way Nicol did. Devotedly.

'There's better places than Guernsey for the young.' Nicol's fork stabbed at the scallop pieces, splashing bread crumbs across the table. 'You could do worse than France.'

'Monsieur Mathieu's come back to Guernsey. I expect I will, too. They say no islander is ever really happy anywhere else.'

'Don't know what he's come back for.' Nicol looked slowly around the kitchen, fastened on the larder door leading off.

'It's time to lay the ghosts, Nicol,' Matthew said. His voice sounded gentle.

A dark shape, with a hood covering the head but showing an area of light inside, appeared at the window and looked in. A frisson made me shiver. Was the place actually haunted?

Matthew had his back to the window. Madeleine saw my expression. 'You'll frighten your guest, Monsieur Mathieu. I'm sure she doesn't know about...' Her voice tailed off as Nicol shook his head.

Apparently he'd also seen the figure outside the window. 'Never told mon Seigneur you were back, Bôt. Didn't think it useful.' He went on staring at the hooded shape without expression. 'Thought he might work it out, though. Don't know how he knew you'd be here at all, let alone today.'

Matthew turned right round, then back to Nicol. 'I've been looking all over the island for him. Surely he can't be living in the caves?' He paused as the figure behind him moved slowly across the second window. 'That isn't right. He must be well over eighty. I'll see he's properly housed.'

'No point.' Nicol shrugged. 'It's the way he wants it. And what he wants he gets.'

The figure moved out of sight. I could hear the back door creak, my heart thump. Were they saying this was not a ghoul, but a real person? Mon Seigneur – a neighbouring seigneur, an eccentric who lived in nearby caves? Anything seemed possible on this island.

A man covered from head to toe in brown sacking walked in. Not a seigneur – a monk. And a high-ranking priest – a monsignor, presumably called monseigneur on the island.

'I knew you'd come back, Mathieu. There is unfinished business.' A fluting voice, cracked with disuse. Although I'd accepted that he wasn't a ghost the impersonation was excellent. Gaunt, almost transparent, with a floating upright blanched face. The opaque veil covering his irises must mean cataracts. No shoes, feet caked in earth, white toenails. That's what had given the impression of drifting rather than walking.

Matthew stood. We all stood. 'The Abbé Saint Jude,' he explained him to me. 'I dare say you remember Madeleine as a little girl, Monseigneur.'

It came back to me that Matthew had mentioned him before. The Abbé Saint Jude was the man who'd taught Matthew and his brothers the Catechism. During the time of the Occupation, presumably. When he was a lowly curé.

'It's lovely to see you again, Monseigneur. Has Pépère told you? Monsieur Mathieu is coming back to Bôtnoir,' Madeleine bubbled, her young face creased into a smile.

That will leave lines, I wanted to warn her. Keep your face straight.

'He's restoring it.'

There was still no sign of interest from the monk. He just stood there, his face serene. I had the feeling he was already in the next world, merely marking time in this one. But the blind eyes were turned to me. 'And this lady?' Had he heard me breathe?

'Ruth Samuels, Monseigneur. She's an outstanding writer on gardening, and a first-rate photographer. She's here to return the Bôtnoir grounds to their pre-war state.'

'How do you do,' I said faintly. How did one greet a Franciscan? Particularly one who'd chosen to live a hermit's life.

His eyes, sunk back into dark holes, suddenly burned with life. 'Ruth among the alien corn?' he asked me. Blind people's hearing becomes acute. He'd spotted my slight accent.

'It no longer seems alien to me,' I said. 'I left Vienna in 1938. I've always felt grateful to the British for giving me asylum. Now I feel at home.'

To my surprise he held out his hand. I gave him mine and felt his fingertips brush the skin. 'Honest toil with your hands, my daughter. The garden will be blessed.'

'Will you join us? I'm sure Madeleine can manage...' Matthew's voice was low enough to be hard to distinguish.

'Thank you. I'm not used to rich food. Nicol leaves some bread and milk every day. And vegetables from the garden.' He must be almost blind not only from the cataracts, but because the caves had very little light. 'The agreement with your grandmother was that I could live in the large chamber in the cave. Will you object to that?' Though he could not have seen much more than blurs, he turned towards Matthew. 'You remember the cave, Mathieu?'

'I remember everything.'

'I'm sorry to hear that. But God is merciful. Some day it will seem like a bad dream, nothing more. I came to assure you of that.' He bumped into a gleaming cupboard. Because he didn't recognise the new kitchen layout, I took it. 'Peace be with you, my son.' He spread his arms out to give the pastoral blessing.

'And also with you, Monseigneur,' I heard Matthew say. A reflex? Or because it applied both ways? This priest, rather like Matthew, appeared to think he should punish himself.

Nicol Rochet crossed the room and, very gently, guided the Abbé Saint Jude's elbow. 'I'll see you back.'

'See me out. I find my own way.'

It was not fair on Madeleine's marvellous cooking. Hard though we tried, none of us could find real appetite for the roast lamb.

CHAPTER TWENTY-NINE

We stalked the garden, Matthew and I, pretending to be thinking about which bulbs to plant for spring. My mind ached at the thought of the new season: young lovers meeting in new-leaf bowers...

'Drifts of single snowdrops under the beech?' I suggested.

Matthew's shoulders were tense with his black mood. 'There used to be plenty.'

'If you can remember where, we could split the clumps.' I tried to sound jolly against the gloom. 'If they've survived. Nicol's dug the whole garden at least one spit.'

He kicked at a molehill near a clump of rust-coloured leaves. 'I'm afraid I can't. You'll have to wait and see.'

'What about crocus species? D'you remember those?'

Something – some pleasant memory perhaps – stirred the deep eyes to life. 'I do remember patches of lilac early on, yes. And very bright yellow, with loads of flowers opening like miniature suns.'

'Ancyrensis.'

The memory appeared to fade. He looked as dour as before. 'If you say so.'

'There are some sativus and speciosus over there.'

He looked across the grass, listless, then frowned. 'Good grief. I thought crocuses flowered in spring.'

At last a semblance of real interest. 'There are also several autumn-flowering varieties.'

'Are there now.'

Autumn has always been my favourite season. I like the softening colours after summer brashness, the rusty russets, the bronzes and golds which blend with purple hues reflecting colder temperatures. Was I also yearning for autumn-flowering love? 'Something's worrying you. Why don't you tell me about it?'

He scuffed at some moss. I'd made a note to get rid of it from the path, but to leave it as a ground cover for bulbs. Pretty, and very little upkeep. 'What makes you think there's something to tell?'

'The Abbé Saint Jude was a small pointer. He was the one who taught you the Catechism, wasn't he?' And made a thorough job of it, I guessed.

It isn't true that only fear has an odour. Guilt does, too. I could smell its acrid and withering pungency. He turned his back on me. 'It's nothing to do with the here and now. It was all so long ago.'

He must have known that I couldn't let that pass, that I'd realise he was trying to put me off. 'We are the past, Matthew. You know that as well as I do. And we can't escape it. I can't hear the tramp of boots without breaking into a sweat because I remember the cobbled streets of Vienna. And a wailing siren brings back the drone of Dorniers loaded with bombs.'

He kicked at the dislodged moss, bringing up earth.

'I take it the sounds you hear are worse.'

The pain which crossed his features aged them. He looked defenceless, exposed. 'Much worse.'

A gull circled overhead, screeched at another. Like a Messerschmitt screaming its whine of attack. It took me back to the distorted features of the veteran in black. He fitted into Matthew's past – somewhere. 'Screaming?' I asked Matthew. 'A human voice?'

'That. And cursing.'

He withdrew into himself as though he were a snail. The eyes sank back, the hair seemed to lose its bounce, his rigidified body shrank into something smaller in front of me. He had to be thinking of some horror which happened during the Occupation, a trauma not yet resolved.

I looked over the cliff and noticed several figures below us on the beach. My imagination recreated the scene Charles Grichard had told me about. 'Charles told me how you saved his life.'

The first distinct signs of grey were toning down the black of Matthew's hair. He was squinting at the children scurrying about. 'That man always did talk too much.'

'He said you rescued him from three Germans.'

He pulled a pair of binoculars out of his pocket and trained it on the beach. 'Bôtnoir is a private beach. They're trespassing.'

Invading his personal space. He turned the binoculars on me, focusing them. Every wrinkle, every nuance of expression would show. 'How can they know? They're just attracted by the beauty, Matthew.'

'It's up to them to find out. And flood tide can be very dangerous.'

This was my chance to get beyond his defences. 'Charles told me you risked your life to save his.'

He brushed that aside impatiently. 'He'd have done the same for me.' But he seemed to have come back to life. He gently took my elbow and steered me into the entrance to the cave which did duty as a garden shed.

This time we didn't stop there. Matthew walked up to what looked like a boulder, heaved it open, and pointed beyond it. 'That leads down to the secret stores, to the other caves, and eventually to the sea.'

I glimpsed a series of intercommunicating chambers leading off. 'Is this where they used to pull the boat up?'

'That's further on. Several paths meander down to the beach. It's covered at flood tide, but adequate for loading and unloading at ebb tide. It isn't difficult or anything.'

'You want to go down now?'

'I thought you might like to see the catacombs.'

Did he mean his forebears were buried there?

He waited for me to walk through, then pulled the boulder back into place. The actions had the ease of old habit. Indelible memories, written into the very fabric of his body. I followed as he went first, holding my hand, winding through a labyrinth of sloping pathways, sure of his destination. We ended up inside a cavernous vaulting cave.

'We can walk out on to the beach now, but when the tide's in there's only a small ledge.'

Charles Grichard's story came back to me again. 'Charles told me you dragged him through the water. Is this how you got away?'

'The tide was coming in. We waited here until the ebb. There, on that ledge, holding on to the rail. Quite uncomfortable.' The hand holding mine had begun to grip. I could feel it clammy with a cold sweat. 'The bastards broke several of the bones in his feet. He was in agony.'

'He told me one of the soldiers stamped on them.'

'Deliberately, as a sort of torture, with a pebble underneath his arches. That's why he's ended up with such small feet. He's always in pain, rather like those Chinese women whose feet were bound.'

Apparently Charles had underplayed that part of the story. And what I'd thought of as a mincing gait was the reality of stepping gingerly to avoid too much discomfort.

'Charles is OK, even if he is a bit of an old woman.'

Charles was in his sixties, I reflected. A contemporary of Matthew's – almost of mine.

He laughed as he realised what he'd implied. 'Well, that's a stupid thing to say. I've known some pretty courageous old women.'

'He said you had to half-carry him back.'

'Not far.' He shrugged, dismissive. 'I whistled for Nicol and we took the wheelbarrow. That's how we got him back. Let's forget that now.' He put his arm around my shoulders and I turned to face him. It was a quite natural reaction. I hadn't planned it. I didn't yet understand my feelings for this man. Had I been able to think, rather than to allow my body's instincts to get the better of me, I would have drawn back. I didn't want to become emotionally embroiled until I'd understood Matthew's past, grasped what had made him the man he now was.

But I did not draw back. We embraced, found each other's mouths. The hunger of more than five long years consumed me, fired blood into veins grown slack with disuse, brought tears into my eyes.

It was he who broke away. 'It isn't right, Ruth. I can't do this.'

'Can't? You have been doing it.'

'You misunderstand. Not that I wouldn't wish to. I do. I knew you were the woman I'd been looking for all my life the moment I met you.' He pushed me, gently but steadily, away from him.

'You're married already?'

'No.'

Perhaps I'd been right that first day at Grichard's. 'You're gay,' I said. 'You and Charles are more than friends.'

He laughed. An abandoned chuckling laugh which echoed around the cave and convinced me as no words could have done. 'Well, that's a new one from a woman, I must admit.'

He kissed me again, but this time I didn't respond. Spleen had got the better of me.

'That feel as though I'm not interested in women?'

It didn't feel at all. Feeling depends on mood, and mine was no longer amorous. My mind clicked back into searching the clues. What could make him react the way he had, unless he simply didn't want to know about a relationship with me? Then why insist he did? 'HIV positive?' I came up with.

'Worse, in its way.'

I drew my coat around me. I was beginning to feel cold.

'I'd better spell it out. Impotent, Ruth. I've never been able to have intercourse.' We both stood there, looking out at the sea as though the waves could wash away those last few words.

I resisted it. No one could look, or act, the way Matthew did and not be male – all male. 'I find it hard to believe...'

'It's true.'

'Everyone says–'

'You mean my brothers, Charles, the sisters-in-law...'

'And Franz.'

'Not forgetting friend Bowers.' His eyes were bleak, looking in rather than out. 'Simpletons. They think because so many women fall for my looks, and because I've tried so often – hoping somehow it would work itself out if the right one came along – I'm the archetypal Casanova. The irony is, that's not my nature. I'm strictly a one-woman man.'

One woman. And quite suddenly I knew who she was. It was as though I was struck by the proverbial thunderbolt. I saw the two people in the kayak the German veteran saw. Matthew's parents, as they were trying to escape. "It isn't possible, it can't be true," I heard the man in black shout. "Where have you come from, you repulsive horror, you damned bloody bitch?"

He could be the fourth German, mistaking Dominique for her grandmother just as I'd mistaken the girl in the portrait for Caroline. Both of us quite wrong. 'Your mother,' I said, my voice hollow. 'She's the girl in the painting.'

There was no answer at all. When I looked towards the place where he'd been standing there was no one. I stared around me – no sign of him. Had that been an inexcusable thing to say?

'Matthew?' I called.

There was nothing but the pounding of the waves. They were coming closer, the tide was coming in fast. I walked towards the back of the cave, called several times. No movement, no sound other than the swelling sea.

I called out again and again, at first not able to believe that he'd simply gone. Charles tried to warn me about Matthew's obsession with his mother. And I'd been stupid enough to mention her, mention the portrait he obviously cared deeply about. I tried to empathise with what he must feel and called again.

No answer. Nothing.

I could hear the waves coming in, remembered the stories of how dangerous the place was at flood tide. How could he simply have left me to fend for myself? Empathy turned to anger. The lair of the Minotaur, and I had no string to guide me out of the labyrinth. All I had was a rotten sense of direction, and wits sharpened by fury. I walked out towards the water, the light. What had Charles Grichard said? When the tide was out you could walk to the bay.

The beach of Bôtnoir Bay was not yet cut off, but the other visitors had gone. If I walked briskly I should be able to get to the cliff path and back to my car. I was determined never to go near Matthew Frelé again.

I started out, unsure how quickly the waves would come towards me. There didn't seem to be a choice. The noise of the incoming tide was loud. I didn't hear footsteps behind me, didn't see Matthew until he'd caught up with me.

'What on earth are you doing?' he shouted at me.

I stopped and faced him. 'You'd gone. I couldn't find my way in that dark maze of paths, so this seemed the best way. Charles told me it's possible to walk to the beach when the tide is out.'

'It's too late!' He put his right arm through my left one. 'I'm sorry, Ruth. Of course I wasn't abandoning you. What do you take me for? I just needed a moment or two on my own.'

I tore away from him. 'You could have said something, made some sort of noise to show you were still there,' I yelled.

'How was I to know you had ambitions to play Canute?'

'It seemed the safer option.'

He was staring at me, eyes pinpoints of antagonism. Then he grabbed my arm and yanked me back to the cave. 'What made you jump to the subject of that portrait you only glimpsed?'

'Nicol Rochet.'

'Nicol?' His eyes practically bulged out of their sockets. 'Nicol's talked to you about my mother?'

'We never discuss anything directly. He makes monosyllabic remarks about the garden. I've learned to interpret them.'

He swallowed hard. 'What exactly did he say?'

'You were there. He said it was a remarkable likeness, and his eyes flicked over the pine tabletop. I took it he meant the colour of the wood. Everyone tells me you're a terrible womaniser, yet you've never shown any such signs with me. I concluded I remind you of your mother in some way. And what he was looking at was the colour of my hair. And hers, I presume. Certainly that of the girl in the portrait,' I gambled. Though I hadn't had time to take it in.

'The russet hair, yes.'

Which Dominique had inherited, and which glinted fiery in the sun that day. 'I'm afraid mine's not entirely natural.'

'I can work that out, Ruth.' The grooves of memory do not

respond to reason. 'Anyway, it isn't just that. Somehow, the set of the eyes, the line of the jaw, the nose...'

Something began to prick at me, something I was aware of but couldn't bring into consciousness. I tried to catch it, but it fluttered away.

'I don't know why, but your presence stirs up the past. I wouldn't mind dispersing the shadows.'

'You think of your mother as a shadow?'

'Shadows of evil pursued her, overpowered her, did for her in the end.'

'You mean the waves...?'

'It was nothing to do with the sea. My mother died because of the Boches. I've already told you that.'

Because there were no bodies he had to wait until after the war before he could officially pronounce his parents dead. 'You told me she'd vanished at sea. How could you know for sure that she was dead?'

He turned from me, stared at the waves coming into the cave, then pulled me back the way we'd come. 'Time to go. I told you, the sea covers the whole of this part of the cave.'

I couldn't leave it at that. It wasn't the way I wanted it, I'd have been happy to stay ignorant. But Pandora's box had been opened, even if Matthew was doing his best to put the lid back on. I had to know more about his mother. 'Tell me about her, Matthew. The whole story, not just part of it.'

He took my arm again and pulled me towards the top of the cave. 'Perhaps one day.'

The waves were crashing in, filling the bottom with a moving mass of black. When we reached the top we looked down at the churning water, daylight chasing white foam across its surface, throwing grey shadows on the walls. Silhouettes which writhed and billowed in and out of twisting curves as though in agony.

'It doesn't matter, you know,' I said as I put my hand in his and tried to distract him from painful memories.

'What happened to my mother, you mean?'

'Of course that matters. I meant what happened to you.

It wouldn't worry me. I like being celibate. I've never really understood why everyone harps on about the physical act. There are other ways of loving.'

'You would resent it, eventually. It's only natural.'

'I don't know why you assume that, Matthew. My husband died more than five years ago, of cancer of the prostate. Use your imagination. He was ill a long time before it was diagnosed. Not making physical love to the man you love wasn't a problem for me then. It wouldn't be one now.'

'It's not that simple.' His eyes searched the dark waters below us, and out to the sea beyond.

Did he see a kayak floating there? A double-seater, a man and woman trying to flee the power of the Third Reich?

'I made a pact with the devil. If he helped me avenge her death, I'd give up my manhood.'

'You mean you've taken a vow of chastity?'

'I mean I'm impotent.'

CHAPTER THIRTY

Matthew might have asked Nicol Rochet to be particularly helpful to me. I couldn't tell. Nicol might have decided that for himself. I knew he enjoyed working with me. Jeanne would apologise, say she had no idea where he'd got to, he should have been around to help her. Then, as soon as I walked into the garden, he'd be there, spade in hand, grinning at me.

'Anything special?' he'd ask. I could never be sure whether he winked or not. His eyes were permanently slit, set to focus on the horizon. The seaman's hat was pulled well over them.

I'd felt for Jeanne, understanding what she was about. She tried the usual stratagems – perfectly proper ones – which women learn to use on fathers, brothers, husbands, sons. She offered coffee, tea, even sandwiches. His answer was always the same.

'No, Madame.' The stare out to sea. Thanks blown away on the wind.

He and I shared a silent language. I'd size up one of the old shrubs and he'd be able to tell whether I thought it needed grubbing out or pruning, without a word from me. And then he'd do it perfectly. The only time we clashed had been about those fuchsias. I still felt deprived.

'Le Bôt said you wanted snowdrop bulbs. He said to split the clumps before spring. The Abbé let on where I can find some.'

The blind monk remembered the site of snowdrops? I shrugged it off. No odder than anything else that happened at Bôtnoir. It seemed churlish not to accept, though Nicol must have known that planting bulbs in the green was always better. Safer, too. The reason I'd talked about bulbs last Sunday hadn't been about the garden. Surely Matthew knew that? 'Only the interesting species.'

The grin was broad and conspiratorial. 'Knew you wouldn't be bothered with rubbish.' He was carrying a spade. His usual large stainless steel blade more suited to digging spits of soil than raising bulbs. A fork would have been the sensible choice.

He beckoned with his head, the peak of his cap pointed towards the walled-in kitchen garden. The tight set of the jaw showed suppressed excitement. He strode ahead towards the gate, holding the rusted wrought-iron open for me. I went through meekly, waited for him to close it, followed him. He set the spade on soil at the far end, near the wall beside the compost heap. He leaned on the spade, screwed his eyes up to virtual closing, stared at the sun, then the soil. Round puckered lips drew back into a snarl. Long in the tooth I told myself. But I wasn't convinced.

'Heap's moved every few years. Leaves a fertile patch.'

'I like mulch gardening myself,' I began. Nervousness made me talkative. 'I like to do it by spreading greenery between plants without bothering about a heap. Untidy, of course...'

His look of quiet indifference shut me up. He began to dig. Not fast, but deliberately, methodically, as though he knew exactly what he was doing. And that it would take time. It bore no resemblance at all to looking for snowdrop bulbs.

'You've decided to prepare a special bed, have you?' Nervousness had turned to apprehension. I could feel my armpits moisten with cold sweat. There was no new movement, no sound except the spade slicing into bare earth. 'To increase the bulbs for replanting?'

He took off one spit of soil in an area roughly six foot by two. Like a grave. Then he stepped down and prepared to dig another one.

'Snowdrops are quite shallow in the ground,' I pointed out. I sounded breathy with unease. Nicol had killed two Germans – the plot he was digging looked like a grave...

'Roots go deep, here at Bôtnoir. It's what Monseigneur always says.'

No arguing with that. I sauntered away from Nicol, lessening the feeling of paranoia by inspecting the vegetable garden. I squatted down to enjoy the purple sprouting broccoli at eye-level. He'd put in some white sprouting as well. People think it's cauliflower, but it's nothing of the kind. It tastes delicious. The mild winters meant that fresh vegetables could be harvested every day. I'd introduced the non-blanching variety of chicory. It was coming along well, together with the lamb's lettuce and the American cress. We'd have no need for insipid greenhouse lettuce.

The sound of metal on something solid made me straighten up and Nicol pause. I walked over and watched his next move.

'Has to be around here.' He took more care now, shifting the soil delicately away from something dense, substantial. Then, with one heave of the spade, he brought it up. Some sort of crumbling cloth – oil cloth? – enveloping a tin: a square metal tin. Quite large, quite solid-looking.

'Been there a while,' he said. 'Reckon the contents are all right. Covered in oil cloth and the lid's on tight.' Callused hands unwrapped yards of rotting cloth, then prised off the rusted lid.

I'm not sure what I was expecting, but it wasn't what Nicol levered out of the earth. Because when he'd taken off the lid he held the tin out towards me, and all I could see was some sort of brown mess.

"He let on where they're hidden yet?" Todd Frelé had quizzed me. Now I understood that the 'he' wasn't Nicol. He'd been talking about the Abbé Saint Jude. Who'd chosen me – via Nicol – to find whatever Todd so desperately wanted to get his hands on.

Nicol looked triumphant. 'Thought he was past it. Told me to dig. In the walled garden where the wall casts the deepest shade at noon. Deep down, at least three spits. "You will glean the harvest that is Mathieu's, the seeds that I planted long ago," is how he put it.'

So the old man knew where something important was hidden. Seeds in the plural – several things. Were the missing documents buried here?

'Said to dig in the most fertile soil. "Find them and give them to Ruth. To her, you understand, Nicol. Only to her."'

He wiped his forehead. I'd never seen him sweat before. 'Best if you slip the cake out indoors,' he muttered. 'Their wedding cake. Top layer.'

So they'd buried the top layer of their official Guernsey wedding cake here, on Guernsey. And they hadn't unearthed it on the first anniversary of their sacramental marriage. Why? Because there'd already been a wedding before? Was Nicol unearthing proof of the date of the first wedding? And why for me, and not Matthew or Charles Grichard?

Small bits of silver glinted round the object in the tin. Cake decorations perhaps. I was about to leave with the booty when he unearthed a second object and unwrapped a second tin exactly like the first. He took the lid off, showing rotted tissue paper over what looked like glass. Then he clamped it down again.

He shovelled earth back carefully, like a good gardener. Lower spits first, then the topsoil. 'Takes care of that little lot,' he said, wiping the spade on nearby grass and walking towards the cave. 'Likely to be fragile. Been in the ground for more'n fifty years. Time to give them an airing.'

'You didn't know where they were?'

'Monseigneur's the only one alive knows that. Sat with his crucifix in his hands and spouted at me: "Ruth is to keep the name of the dead man in his inheritances, so that Mathieu's name may not die out among his brothers, and at the gate of his enclos." Don't ask me what it means.'

CHAPTER THIRTY-ONE

All thoughts about the garden fled. I picked up the two tins, undeterred by the mud they left on my anorak, clasped both of them against my body and hurried to the car. Strange how quite ordinary actions take on a tedious slowness at times of stress. It can't have taken more than a few minutes to get there, but it felt like an hour.

I placed the tins on the floor in front of the Saab's back seats, careless of the mess the earth around them made. I steered the car down the steep drive leading to the road to Forest. Impatient to find what was in my hoard I accelerated, then pumped the brake when I grasped just how steep the incline was. I felt the tyres skid over the gravel and applied more force, blessing the ABS. The second German had crashed here. Now I realised why. I slowed to my usual crawl.

It was hard to hold back my excitement. Back in St Peter Port at last I lugged the two tins from the car park to Riande House. Candie Road was crowded in the late afternoon. My eyes flitted anxiously around. The last person I wanted to bump into was Matthew. I prayed he wouldn't choose this particular time to leave or come back to Lascervelle.

The phone rang as soon as I opened my front door. So Matthew had spotted me. I'd have to talk to him. I put my load down and interrupted the machine.

'Hello?'

'Ruth. I thought I saw you come back. What were you carrying?'

'Just some stuff from the garden.' The Abbé meant me to look at what was inside the tins without Matthew. Until I knew why I

225

was honour bound to keep their existence to myself.

'I told Nicol to dig up whatever you wanted.' He sounded puzzled.

'Very good of you. He found just what I was looking for.' Not a direct lie, nor even a lie of omission. A lie of diversion, so to speak. A falsehood but not, I felt, a sin.

'The Melvyn Bragg interview's tomorrow. The producer rang. He thought it would be a good idea if you came along as well.'

'Me? Whatever for?' And giving me such a lot of notice, too.

'One artist finding another, that sort of angle. They want us to do part of the recording together.' He laughed. 'Apparently that would make the interview less static. He'd like to film us in the Brixton loft.'

Mathieu Frelé was a great painter. I'd made it possible for the rest of the world to see his work, done my bit. But I wasn't going to work in someone else's shadow, however much I admired him. What I wanted now was to solve the riddle of his past – and I was convinced the tins held several clues. The idea of Matthew being safely off the island for a few days was a bonus. And I saw an opportunity to add a new dimension to the interview by bringing up Luke's treasure trove of early paintings. 'Did he give you a number?'

'Matter of fact.'

'I've come across someone who has some of your very early work.'

'What on earth d'you mean?'

I wasn't going to spell it out. 'A few pieces you did at Downside,' I prevaricated. Because I felt I had to. I was beginning to tire of all these secrets. I was relying on the tins to solve the mysteries of the past, then I was going to go back to telling the truth. 'I'll see he gets those as well as the collector's. That'll liven it all up a bit. All right?'

'You mean you don't want to be part of it.'

So he was more interested in my appearing with him than in finding out about the early paintings. Very gratifying, but it didn't change my mind. So I said nothing.

'Still upset about last Sunday, I suppose.'

'No. Affected, perhaps. I can't see how a double interview would add anything to your art. You don't need it, and I don't want to play second fiddle. Let's leave it at that.'

'Meaning?'

'I like to think I've contributed to British gardening. My view is that it's worth a show of its own. Failing that, I'll do without.'

I could hear the telltale tapping of his finger against the table. 'A professional decision? The other day you seemed quite keen.'

'I don't want to be rude, Matthew. I do have a lot to do.'

'You wouldn't like to join me for dinner?'

'Not tonight.'

'See you when I get back.' He put the receiver down. I saw the light go out next door.

Stripping outer gear off as I went, I rushed the boxes to my writing room, turned on the five hundred watt halogen lamp and searched for my reading glasses. I looked out the magnifying glass as well. I spread the Sunday papers, still unread, over my working table, then put the two tins down.

I'd left my boots on. What's a little mud? First I opened the tin with the wedding cake. The top tier, with the remains of icing and decoration all over it. Several loose ceramic wedding ornaments: bells, a bride and groom, all stained but showing glimpses of original silver. The icing had gone brittle, powdered into fragments. Pink mixed with white and gold. The sort of old-fashioned wedding cake I'd had myself. I jolted back to my own wedding in 1950, tears forming in my eyes. I could just make out the numerals crumbling into decay: one, nine, three. The last number was hard to decipher. At first it seemed to be a five, but when I looked again it seemed more like a zero. My heart beat rapidly. The twins were born in 1931. An indication of a 1930 marriage? Though naturally that still wouldn't prove that Matthew had been conceived before the wedding.

I got a cushion, turned the tin upside down, revealed fruitcake at least over fifty years old, possibly over sixty. There didn't seem to be anything it could tell me. Unless you count the fact that it had survived.

I clumped down to the kitchen. It wouldn't be right to let this cake, buried so long, deteriorate now. It was my duty to treat it as carefully as an Egyptian mummy. I'd cover it in tin foil, wrap it in plastic, then stow it in my fridge. Could it still be edible? That would certainly be a true test of an unknown baker's skill.

I went back and concentrated on the second tin. Nicol had closed it tight again. I was sure I'd glimpsed glass. I'd have to be very careful how I opened it.

Patience is an acquired skill, essential for photography. Slowly, painfully I prised the lid off. I folded back the tattered tissue paper and brought out two small glasses. They were fine lead crystal, with names engraved in Gothic script on both, together with a date. The script was encrusted with crystals, and hard to read. I made out the dates: March 13th, 1930 on both of them. Was that the day they'd married? The glasses were only engraved with the names and the date. No indication of the occasion.

I stared, trying to decipher the entwined script. A large M followed by smaller letters. Six or seven, I judged. I deciphered Mathieu. The second goblet was even more encrusted. I made out a capital R, followed by several small letters – less than seven. Ra, I was pretty sure. How many girls' names started that way: Raphaela, Rachel, Ramona, Raissa... I plumped for six small letters, ending in el. The two middle letters baffled me. Two distinct letters, neither of them 'c' or 'h'.

I thumped the table in triumph: Raquel, the French for Rachel. Raquel Welch – that's what Franz had remembered when he'd said the mother had some actress's name. Raquel – charming and fragile. Just like the woman I'd glimpsed in the portrait. She wasn't like Caroline at all. I imagined her as a beautiful Dresden china creature who'd captured the hearts of all who'd known her.

I was about to put the lid back on the tin, then clean the glasses. But what I'd taken to be soft bedding to cushion the glass was another object, under more tissue paper. Dark, spongy, crumbling.

The paper came out in handfuls. The surface underneath was flat and streaked with mildew. A book? Too thick, even for that time. My heart beat turned erratic, making me breathless.

I put the same cushion over the opening, turned the tin upside down and allowed the contents to slide out, slowly, on to the newspaper. The mildewed leather crumbled dark brown. But it had kept the paper inside reasonably safe. Leaves of expensive mounting paper, the white turned to streaky beige as though it had been dipped in water. A wedding album.

My fingers fumbled as I opened it. The photographs were stuck in with those little triangular corner stickers that used to be in vogue, protected with sheets of onion skin paper. The colour prints hadn't faded that much because light had been kept away from them. I trembled as I saw the image of the girl Raquel had been. A glorious mane of russet hair, doe eyes, an hourglass figure – but womanly, not waiflike.

I stared at the wedding pictures. Four were colour prints, no doubt very expensive at the time, the rest in black and white. The photographer's stamp on the back of each print said Thomas Senvelle, St Peter Port. No date, unfortunately. But if the secret marriage had taken place on Guernsey, why was it hard to prove the date?

I was being stupid. This was a society wedding, not a secret one. These were the photographs of the church marriage, after Raquel had converted to Catholicism. Why on earth did the Abbé want me to see them? Or was it just the crystal he wanted me to find?

Whatever he intended I concentrated on the images, studied each photograph using the magnifying glass, moving slowly from one to the other. Elizabeth Taylor, Titian hair instead of black. When I'd seen the actress for the first time I'd thought she was the most beautiful girl in the whole world. And I'd been wrong. Raquel Frelé, around twenty years her senior, had been competition she hadn't even known about.

One picture showed Raquel wearing the veil with its blusher down, another showed it pushed back over her hair. Such regular features, a pert nose – not quite as young as I'd expected. One was in profile. I looked again. Something familiar, and yet I couldn't place it. Where had she come from, this fairytale girl? Why was it such a mystery, why wouldn't anyone talk about her?

The other faces took on more form. The bridegroom stood tall, virile, Gallic. I took it that the best man was standing beside him. His brother, Michel Frelé, I guessed. And then the woman who had to be their mother, the redoubtable Michelle - Gran'mère. Poised, surprisingly young, tall. The large hat she wore hid her eyes and cast a deep shadow over her young daughter-in-law. And then I noticed another man, standing behind Michelle Frelé. Blond and Nordic, a very handsome man, in an Aryan sort of way. Where had I seen that face? Was I going New Age, with all this déjà vu?

The pictures weren't complete. No sign of the bride's parents or siblings. Why? Was she really an orphan, someone who'd had no family? The Frelé brothers had mentioned their paternal grandmother, their uncle in the States, their cousins. They never referred to any other relatives, anyone from their mother's side. All they seemed to know was that she came from France – Paris. 'I never knew my maternal grandmother,' Matthew had said. Nothing more.

I searched the photos of the larger groups, the ones showing the assembled wedding guests. Not a hole-in-the-corner affair. They proved it had definitely been a seigneur's wedding. The people I saw in those meant nothing to me. The magnifying glass moved from one face to another. No one I recognised. What was I looking for?

Then I saw who it was. The reason I'd passed him over before was that he was standing right at the back, hidden by the people in front of him. That wasn't a jacket he was wearing, it was the top part of a cassock. The young Abbé Saint Jude, no doubt a lowly curate at the time. A priest, not a monk. It was, of course, possible to be both. The man Matthew and Nicol called Monseigneur. So he'd been the one to marry the young people. Why hadn't he come forward and called Todd Frelé's bluff? Why this elaborate charade?

Because this wedding didn't count, Jeanne had said. So why did the Abbé want me to look at these bits and pieces? Had he gone senile, or were they significant?

The background turned to foreground for me. The liriodendron tulipifera, the pterocarya rehderiana... the wedding party had been photographed in the grounds of Bôtnoir! The garden as it used to be. That couldn't be the reason the Abbé had wanted me to see the pictures. Just to recreate a garden? Absurd.

I decided to make a copy of the photos, to blow them up to show more detail. The garden would be an extra dividend. I'd see exactly what I'd tried to glean through Nicol's eyes all these months.

My next stop had to be the dark-room. I set up my stand, put copying film into the camera, photographed the black-and-whites, bracketing five exposures for each. Eventually I'd get round to making blow-ups of the negatives that interested me. The colour prints looked at me when I'd finished. This was no time for laziness. I'd use transparency film for them. Then I'd be able to project the slides and isolate important sections. I photographed each colour print, bracketing seven exposures for good measure. Satisfied at last, I took the album back to my writing room.

I closed the album, patted the leather cover down, shifted the tin to place it in. I felt a small bump, felt something I'd overlooked. Using a cushion again to allow the contents a soft landing, I turned the tin upside down. A tube-like, blue velvet bag was stark against the light cushion.

It must have been wedged beside the album. Something borrowed, something blue... I undid the bow, loosened the fastening, opened it and, putting my little finger inside, felt several rings. I slipped them on and pulled them out.

Two matching wedding bands, one very small, the other large – and another ring. An engagement ring: a deep amethyst set between two large diamonds, the gold matching that of the wedding rings. I stared at the gold bands. The diamonds in the engagement ring were at least half a carat each.

I pulled the tube back over itself. There was nothing more, not even dust. Had the Frelés hidden their precious rings, and their lovely goblets, from the Germans? Was this all Raquel Frelé possessed? Not really. She also owned a sécretaire. An unusual expensive piece of furniture with a secret drawer.

The rings were here, on their own. I knew I should be able to deduce something from them. But what?

My absent-minded fingering of my own wedding ring told me the answer. What were these rings doing in the tins? Was it likely that a devoted pair like Mathieu and Raquel Frelé would set out to leave Guernsey without their wedding rings? Impossible. That could mean only one thing – the couple's bodies *had* been found, and the wedding rings taken off the corpses' fingers. The Abbé was making sure I knew the story I'd been told was false.

I wrapped up the album and the goblets carefully. Wrapped in extra wadding they were too bulky to put back into one tin. I put the album back where I'd found it and used the cake tin for the goblets. Then I sealed them both with sellotape. I had no idea why the Abbé wanted me to see these things. They belonged to Matthew, and I would take them to him.

I realised I'd forgotten to replace the little velvet bag with the jewellery. I'd been told there isn't much crime on the island. I decided to hide them all the same, together with my own jewellery. The safe was built into the base of my halogen lamp. It was right next to me, by the table. I put the rings inside.

By now it was late afternoon. I felt exhausted, wallowed in a bath. Matthew would be in London tomorrow. I'd go and beard the Abbé in his lair.

CHAPTER THIRTY-TWO

The sea fog which has a tiresome habit of settling over the Channel Islands during the autumn and winter months hung heavy in the air. No planes would be able to leave that morning, and probably not that day. It looked too dense even for boats. Matthew would be forced to cancel the appointment with Melvyn Bragg. Would he come looking for me?

I'd lain awake all night. Had I read the tins' contents right, or missed vital clues? I got up before dawn to develop the films, intending to drive out to Bôtnoir as soon as possible. The Abbé wanted 'peace' for Matthew. He'd involved me, nudged me into his past. Why? Because I was a woman? A gardener? A photographer? Surely all that was irrelevant.

The Abbé was a monk, a priest. Bound by the seal of the confessional. I was a refugee from Hitler's country of birth. Perhaps he thought I'd understand the Occupation Forces better than the islanders. Perhaps he hoped I'd work out the things he was forbidden to explain? Because he thought that would help Matthew keep his inheritance as well as find peace? I sensed the two were bound together.

I had a personal stake as well. There could be no future for Matthew and me unless we understood, and empathised, with each other's pasts. Mine was relatively simple – his was a maze I was still lost in. I knew I had to decipher the Abbé's message.

I walked up Candie Road, the gardens looming out on my right. Matthew wouldn't be able to see me leave. The car park was full, no one else foolish enough to drive. This was no time for worrying about the elements. I used to drive on the Somerset Levels. The willow outlines dimmed with mists often obscured the ditches lining the narrow roads. I was used to negotiating those. It had made me confident I'd be able to drive in poor visibility.

The Saab was parked right by the entrance, facing forward, shown up by that white Maserati cabriolet. Good news. I could be fairly sure that neither Todd – nor the man in black – was at Bôtnoir. The pale colour reflected what light there was and I nosed my car out. I inched along the roads. I had them to myself. My trip meter would tell me when I'd arrived at the house. As soon as it showed I was within five hundred yards of Bôtnoir I slowed down even more.

The turn to Bôtnoir was shrouded in billowing mists, but the archway of straggling beech turned a reflective rusty-red oriented me. The drive up the steep approach had to be negotiated virtually blind. Not only mist, but the darkness of overhanging trees festooned with ivy blotted out what light there was. I couldn't have been doing more than two miles per hour. I bumped and heaved my way, sensing the banks, skirting the brushwood. Would I recognise the drive in front of the house, or would I crash into plantings, or the front door? I pulled myself together. Of course I'd know when I'd reached flat ground.

The car levelled out and I centimetred to what I judged to be the middle of the drive. My bumper nudged into something. The shape looming up ahead was no higher than my car, and solid. Another vehicle. Another crazy visitor? I refused to back and park properly. Whoever it was could work his own way out if he wanted to leave.

I turned off my engine, waited. Sound was muffled as though covered by a thick blanket – no whistling breeze, no birdcalls, even the waves were inaudible. I could hear fog horns out at sea. I pulled back the door lever, edged out and stood. No sign of anyone else. It's possible to shut a car door without noise. I stood and waited in the unbroken silence. The other car in the drive was an MG. Charles Grichard's.

At first the front door didn't give way. I turned the handle and used force to lever the door upwards at the same time. I shut it again – silently.

The hall was dark, but I could see a light on upstairs. Voices; men's voices, arguing. The kitchen was across the hall to my right. I padded towards it, by-passed the central unit, felt my way towards the scullery door beyond. I turned the handle and pushed. Solid wood refused to budge. The kitchen renovators had not touched the old-fashioned lock with its enormous key. I turned it, cringed at the click, opened the door and slunk out into the old scullery, now turned into a laundry. The machines were new, but the ledge by the window to the outside door had been left undisturbed. I remembered that Matthew had taken a torch from there. I felt for it, found it.

The expanse of kitchen garden could be overlooked from the veranda above, but I felt safe keeping to the side of the walls, creeping towards the pruned-back shrubs and the best of the fruit trees which had been allowed to stay.

My ears were intent, but not for the soft pad of the inflated tyre of the wheelbarrow across the grass. It loomed out at me and I leaped aside.

That could only be Nicol Rochet. He must have heard the scrunch of tilled earth under me. I heard him pass the currant shrub I'd landed in, kept still as I watched him go, then I slid towards the shed door in the cave. And beyond that, the boulder.

It moved more easily than I'd expected. I pulled it back behind me, shone the torch round. The path Matthew and I had taken was straight ahead, but I remembered another to the left. Not bad for someone with such a rotten sense of direction, I patted myself on the back. It's a trick I use when my body would rather not take risks, and my mind is searching for answers.

This time I'd brought a coil of old telephone wire. Because it was insulated with a green plastic, and very strong, it made an ideal and cheap binding material for staking plants. The rock wall beside me was rough and free of the artefacts of man. Matthew had mentioned some mechanism for hauling small boats up from the shore below. It must be near by. I kept close to the rock face on my left and slithered on. The reward was less darkness coming from my right, and the soft sound of a calm sea. The torch made out a railing, the pulley mechanism and sheer drop towards the light. I twisted my wire to the rail and felt much more secure.

The torch beam showed the path leading on. What small amount of light there was dwindled away as I sidled further along. The whisper of the sea grew less until there was only a murmur. Pools of water had gathered in potholes, but the path was still there. Paths lead somewhere, I told myself, my pulse racing as I recovered from a slip.

The light ahead strengthened and began to move. Like the light of a candle, flickering back and forth, licking the dark away. I turned off my torch, allowed the wire to uncoil on my left.

A muffled sound I tried to interpret. An animal? Bats live in caves. Would one swoop out at me? I strained my ears: swish, swish. Like the froufrou of a skirt, of someone pacing back and forth in bare feet, the mumble of a human voice. At last I could connect it with something I understood. The Abbé Saint Jude reciting the prayers from his breviary. Did he know them by heart, or were they available in braille? Priests are not required to celebrate mass every day, but when they do, they need at least one in the congregation. Who came to the Abbé's masses? Nicol, when he brought the bread and milk?

The human eye is a wonderful instrument. Allow it time, and it will adjust to fog-shrouded air, to almost dark. A sort of calm overwhelmed me. The impetuous rush of yesterday had been replaced by the certainty that I would solve the mystery. In good time.

Second by second the shadows became less dark, the light in front of me took on a luminance which seemed to spread across the cave. I could distinguish different strata of rock, runnels of water seeping down, an opening the size of an upright coffin in the wall leading to the cave the priest was pacing in.

I cleared my throat.

The rustle of the monk's habit stopped, and so did the mumble. 'Come in when you're ready.' The voice was thin, but steady.

I laughed inwardly at my naïveté. He'd planned this, he was

expecting me, his sharpened hearing would have announced my presence minutes ago. He might be over eighty, and virtually blind, but he'd known that I'd visit him. He'd lit the candle for my benefit – and perhaps for a prayer.

'You are alone. I hope you were not frightened by the lack of light?' He'd come to the opening, carrying the candlestick in one hand. The light seemed positively brilliant.

'Ruth Samuels, Monseigneur...'

'I remember.' He spoke softly, almost enticingly. 'A fine Old Testament name meaning friendship.

Wherever you go, there will I go,
Wherever you live, there will I live.
Your people shall become my people,
And your God, my God."

The *Book of Ruth*. He'd interpreted passages for Nicol before, he was quoting one to me now. He seemed to be obsessed by it. My legs felt weak. Why was I intruding on a holy man? 'I don't mean to impose...'

'Come in. I've been expecting you.'

It was difficult for me to lay aside all suspicion. I am a descendant of a long line of Central European Jews. Generations of pogroms ensure that the survivors are the most alert. The mantle of priesthood was just another fact I took into account. I knew it wasn't an automatic guarantee of holiness or asylum. I continued to unroll my wire, and walked through the opening to his cell. His eyes couldn't have seen it, but his ears heard the faint rustle on the floor.

'You are familiar with the Greek myths. You have brought Ariadne's ball of thread.'

'I have a very poor sense of direction.'

'Only physically, I think.' He motioned me to a stone slab which I took to be his bed. I'd noticed the small flashes reflecting from the metal crucifix he wore suspended from the girdle around his waist. It had disappeared. He'd sat down, the metal's weight

237

falling between the folds of the rough brown cloth of his habit and making a hollow in his lap.

'You know you are not to glean in any other field, not to leave here, but to stay with my servants.' The white face and hair loomed out of the dark at me, a little below me, the hood now thrown back from his head. I was reminded of Raquel's veil without the blusher.

Was he quoting from the *Book of Ruth* again? I was too nervous to respond, to be polite. I needed answers. 'Did you marry Matthew's parents?'

Silence does not perturb the solitary. The question ricocheted back to me, and there was no reply. I waited. I heard a drop of water splash on stone. And then another.

'The sacramental form of marriage in the Church, yes.' The voice sounded quavery. Was the strain of my visit already beginning to tire him?

'When was that?' I had to know whether I'd read the icing numerals correctly.

'Let me see, yes.'

The voice faded out. Is dissembling a lie?

'The autumn of 1935,' the voice came back, strong and sure. 'I was curate to the parish priest at the time. He was old-fashioned. It was considered a grave sin to live together before the sacrament of matrimony had been conferred.' I must have started up, I was so overcome. 'You are uncomfortable?'

'A little surprised.' The icing on the cake had crumbled badly, but that was no excuse. The last figure wasn't a zero, it was a five. That cake definitely wasn't the original wedding cake, it was baked for the Guernsey marriage. So the Abbé had no proof of an earlier wedding. What use was he, what could he tell me? Todd Frelé had a case, damn him.

I'd used my magnifying glass to examine the image of the young woman in the photographs. She looked in her early twenties. 'I've looked at the wedding pictures. The bride was quite young.'

'Twenty-three. A civil marriage had taken place five years earlier, when she was only eighteen.'

I gasped. So he was prepared to acknowledge an earlier, legally valid, marriage. Which meant the Frelé sons were legitimate. 'You mean the couple eloped? Had the bride's parents refused their consent?'

'Indeed.' A curiously emphatic agreement.

It rang a bell. 'Because they didn't want her to marry a Catholic?' Surely he'd have seen the original marriage certificate? Even if it had been lost why wasn't his word, now, good enough?

'I have been told all you have done for Mathieu since his grandmother's death. How you left your home to come among a people you knew nothing about before you came here. Ruth among the alien corn.'

'I didn't come here because of Matthew, Monseigneur.'

'God has made you the woman who is to enter his house. Like Rachel.'

He was very old, probably senile. I would have to work out any connections for myself. The paternal side of Matthew's family was Catholic. So his mother must have been a Protestant. How was that important, and why didn't the Abbé just say so? 'So she wasn't a Catholic?' I asked.

I counted fifteen drips before he answered. 'She converted to the Faith.'

'But she hadn't been received into the Church at the time of the civil ceremony.'

He didn't agree, or nod assent. I could see the white head, motionless. He cleared his throat. 'If you consult the Parish Register at St Yves you will discover that it states I assisted at a reaffirmation of the couple's vows, on October 15th, 1935. That was possible because both were now communicants.' He said it slowly, emphatically. It was what he wanted me to know. 'The shadows of evil were already towering over us.'

What could he mean? The ravings of an old hermit, or something vital I had to know?

He was a priest, bound by the seal of the confessional. He was protecting someone. Matthew, his parents, his grandmother? Another Greek myth came to mind: Oedipus. The Abbé Saint Jude was drawing my attention to Matthew's mother. I have read Freud.

In the original. I deduced that Matthew was impotent because of a sense of guilt about his mother. The mystery was why. I needed to find out more about her. 'Which part of France did she come from?'

I could see the glint of light as the Abbé took up the cross and pressed his fingertips over it, obscuring parts of it. 'From Paris.' A whisper.

A Parisienne, young but confident. No wonder she looked like a film star. 'Which part of Paris?'

He hesitated again. I was sure it was not because of a faulty memory. 'Rue Boissy-d'Anglas.'

'A suburb?'

The pause was long enough for me to wonder whether he would answer at all. 'Quite central, I believe. Her parents were well off.'

The sécretaire. The only link so far. That certainly pointed to such a past.

'A fine eighteenth century house. Her father expected to get his own way.'

'I saw a Christian name engraved on a crystal goblet, together with a date: March 13th, 1930. I think it spelt Raquel.'

'Another fine Old Testament name.' The symbol of Calvary glinted as he moved it, I thought, in the motion of the sign of the cross. 'The St Yves records show a small error. They give her maiden name as Raquel Fleur Vallon.'

'That wasn't her name?'

Another pause. The voice, when it came, was low. 'A slip in the handwriting. Her family name was Fleurvallon.'

'That explains it!' My voice sounded far too loud, amplified by the surrounding rocks. I lowered the key. 'I mean, I recognise the name.' Surely his handwriting, his slip? Was it deliberate?

'It was well known.'

Now I took in how Raquel had come to wear what looked like genuine antique Belgian lace in the wedding picture. 'Indeed it was. The famous Parisian auction house, destroyed during the war. Did that belong to her father?'

'To her family, yes.'

'And Mathieu Frelé wasn't good enough for them? I thought he'd inherited a fief, that he was a seigneur?'

'The problem was religious differences. The Fleurvallons were appalled when they found out Mathieu was a practising Catholic.'

'So she wasn't given a dowry.'

I saw the white head move up, as though in surprise. 'They sent whatever was hers after her,' he said softly. 'Jewellery, personal knick-knacks, the furniture from her bedroom, money left in trust for her. They wanted to be shot of anything to do with her. As far as they were concerned she no longer existed.'

Why had they been so drastic? Poor young thing. And then to die at sea, escaping from the Germans. Perhaps her family had been collaborators... Something kept flashing through my mind, but I couldn't grasp it. I'd have to think about it later, away from here. 'And after the war. Did none of the brothers ever try to contact their maternal grandparents?'

I saw the white blur of face shake from side to side. 'There was no trace left. The house they'd lived in had been destroyed. Not a single member of the family survived.' It was clear he was describing something he'd gone to investigate for himself.

I thought again about the wedding rings. Matthew's parents hadn't been lost at sea. This man knew what had happened, though not necessarily how, or why. For some reason he wanted me to find out what he knew without telling me directly.

The image of Michelle Frelé in one of the wedding pictures came into my mind. She stood there, towering above her young daughter-in-law, the deep shadow of her hat falling on the young woman's face. Had she betrayed her? Told the Germans that she'd been born off the island, in France? Matthew had detested his grandmother. Perhaps he had had good reason. What had he done to revenge himself on her?

And the man with me now knew what that was – perhaps because Matthew had confessed it to him. He wanted to make me aware of it. Why was he risking his immortal soul, breaking the seal of the confessional? Because, however much he made me figure it out for myself, he was the one leading me towards what he was meant to keep secret.

There could be only one answer: to save one of his flock. To save Matthew's soul. "I made a pact with the devil," Matthew had told me. "If he helped me revenge her death, I'd give up my manhood."

'You are returning Bôtnoir from death to life, Ruth Samuels. I hope you will rejoice in the return of the prodigal son with a celebratory slice of cake.'

What a strange way of putting it. With a start I realised the Abbé Saint Jude had snuffed the candle out. Deep black impenetrable darkness surrounded me.

'God be with you, my daughter,' the disembodied voice said. I heard his habit rustle as he stood. It jerked me into action.

Somewhere there must be papers belonging to Raquel Frelé. A birth certificate, a passport, her marriage certificate. No death certificate – of that I could be sure. The papers weren't in the box with the wedding album. Had the Abbé thought they might be? Was that why he'd asked Nicol to unearth the tins?

I felt my way out of his cell like a blind woman, recoiling my wire. Once I was outside the opening I turned my torch on again. It flickered on, then off. The battery had run out. Ariadne's thread led me to the pulley, and I found my way from there to the outside world.

CHAPTER THIRTY-THREE

The mist was lifting. The sudden shifts in island weather always startled me.

'Madame!' A hissing from behind the big Bramley Seedling on my left. 'Garden gate's unlocked for you.' Nicol put a finger to his lips and beckoned me through the heavy wrought-iron gate which led to the drive, and the cliff path beyond. I handed him the torch.

The MG hadn't moved. I slung the coil of telephone wire on the Saab's floor, popped into the driving seat, turned on the motor, backed. Within moments the front door had opened. There was no time to lose. I put the car into forward drive and parked, neatly, rapidly, beside the MG. The achievements of adrenaline.

'Ruth. I'd no idea you were working here today. Bit of a gamble, driving in this. The mist's only just clearing.'

Matthew was standing by the front door, peering at me. I had to get to him before he came over, put his hand on the bonnet and realised that the car was cold. I slipped out, sprinted towards him, smiling my cover. 'There was no sign of life at Lascervelle. I thought you'd gone in spite of the fog.'

'Well, no. I wasn't there. Charles and I spent the night here – some papers I was trying to find. The interview's been postponed.'

'There are a few things I wanted to check on.'

'You're very wet.' Charles was standing behind Matthew. 'And what's all that muck on your coat sleeves? You been scrambling around the cliffs?'

'You know, Ruth, you're not at all sensible. You take no heed of tides, and you go cliff climbing in the mist. You'll have a serious accident.'

243

'I'm fine. What have you two been up to?'

'We could use your powers of detection,' Charles said. 'We've been trying to locate some family documents.'

'You know my cousin's lodged a formal suit against me. We need documentary proof to counter his claim to the fief.' Matthew shut the front door behind us, motioned us upstairs. 'It must be around somewhere.'

'You think he really has a case?'

'He's maintaining that my parents were never legally married. He claims no one ever saw a marriage certificate, that he doesn't believe one exists. All we can find is an entry in the St Yves register. That's for a ceremony which took place in 1935. Obviously too late to make any of us legitimate under Guernsey law. Unless we can find an earlier marriage certificate, Todd's the legal heir to Bôtnoir.'

I was sure the civil ceremony – the one which would have been registered wherever they'd been married – had taken place before the twins' birth. Raquel married without her parents' consent, so she'd have had to be eighteen. The Abbé said she was twenty-three in the spring of 1935, so she was eighteen in 1930. March 13th, 1930 I guessed – the date on the crystal glasses was both her wedding day and her birth date.

A marriage before April in that year would make the twins legitimate. As I knew from that first birthday party at the Connaught, they were born on February 20th, 1931, and therefore conceived after March 13th, 1930. I already knew the Guernsey ceremony was irrelevant. That's one of the things the Abbé had been telling me.

'You didn't look into this before?'

'None of us had any idea he was hatching this. He's only made noises since Gran'mère died, The formal claim was lodged two days ago. Apparently he's done some research. He looked for my parents' marriage details in the Paris equivalent of the General Register Office.' Matthew's eyes roamed around the living room. 'He didn't find them, and he's brought a microfiche of the register from 1930 to 1935 to prove his point. He says it's conclusive evidence they never married.'

'So he assumed they were married in France?' I tried to sound as nonchalant as I could. 'Just because your mother came from there doesn't mean she married there, does it?'

Charles shrugged. 'We've thought of that, Ruth.' He looked round the room as though it would yield a clue. 'They could have been married at a register office here, instead. Or anywhere else in the British Isles.'

'Todd's had the records at St Catherine's House searched, as well as the Registrar General's Office here on Guernsey, and the appropriate equivalents in the rest of the UK. Charles double-checked. That leaves us with the records at St Yves,' Matthew said slowly. 'That Parish Register must have some value.'

Charles snorted. 'We've been over that, Bôt. You know that's no use.'

'But it was a society affair. Everyone there would vouch it was a wedding.'

'You're forgetting the point. You need proof of a marriage before around April 1930. Before your conception, Bôt.'

'My parents wouldn't just have lived together. Perhaps we're missing something in those details, some clue.' He flung the fire irons into the room and put his hand up the chimney, dislodging soot.

I could see Charles flinch. 'You know I looked into all that right from the start. And you've had the chimney swept.'

The Abbé had told me the St Yves register gave Raquel's maiden name as Vallon, when it was actually Fleurvallon. Didn't any of the younger generation Frelés realise that? Why hadn't the Abbé told Matthew? Should I tell them that Charles's research was based on the wrong name?

I knew as soon as I thought of it that it wouldn't matter, because if the records showed a Mathieu Frelé marrying a Raquel Fleurvallon Charles would undoubtedly have picked that up. I didn't want to raise false hopes. And I sensed I was still missing the whole point of the Abbé's story. I wanted to give myself a chance to work it out.

245

Matthew and Charles had to be right. The marriage licence must have been hidden so that the Germans wouldn't find out Raquel had been born outside Guernsey. That's why it had never come to light. So why wasn't it buried in those tins? Why else would the Abbé have had them dug up?

'Have you looked in the secret room?' I asked. Even if Todd didn't, Matthew would know how to get into that.

'The storeroom, you mean? You spotted it's there?'

'Because of the discrepancy between the inside and outside walls.'

'Good for you. We've been through the whole thing.'

'How d'you get into it?' I'd worked out there was a room, but I'd never figured out how to get into it.

Matthew laughed. 'Not particularly difficult once you know. You get to it from the veranda.'

'So that's what the plants have been telling me.'

'You talk to plants?' Matthew was watching me intently, a small smile round his lips.

'They can't stand a draught. See? This South African violet is positively cringing. So the entrance must be underneath this shelf, on the left.'

Matthew nodded. He came over and pulled the door of the cupboard underneath open, clicked a switch, and pulled it forward. A trap door opened onto a flight of steps leading down.

'Practically empty,' he said. 'Just some exquisite porcelain, a couple of outstanding pieces of Louis Quinze furniture, a mirror, a carpet. All of French origin.'

'Your mother's things.'

'Presumably. A precautionary measure when they guessed the Germans might be coming.'

'But no documents.'

They took me down to show me. The Tilley lantern shone on an enchanting bonheur du jour with Sèvres panels.

'We even found another secret drawer.' He shrugged. 'There was a little jewellery. Appealing, but beside the point.'

Matthew had to be right. His parents must have been legally

married. They'd been young in the early part of the century. Matthew Frelé, Seigneur of Bôtnoir, a man who cared about his blood line, would not have allowed his children to be born illegitimate. All we had to do was find out which country they'd been married in.

'If I were you,' I said, 'I'd check the registers in all the countries they might have taken their kayak to. Apart from the British Isles, I mean. Spain and Italy as well as France. Even other places in the Mediterranean, I suppose.'

Matthew nodded. 'Mark's been looking into the continental ones. Charles has checked every relevant register in Europe. He's started looking into the other Mediterranean ports.'

CHAPTER THIRTY-FOUR

Debs and Mark came back from their trip radiantly in love. My daughter had been transformed into someone I barely recognised. After the months of grief over Mick's death, and the years without meeting a soul mate, Debs was the daughter I thought I'd lost.

This hadn't been her first visit to Italy, but it was the first one in which she hadn't gorged herself on museums. Heads of department at Sotheby's do not scorn the chance to enjoy the glories of the past, even when it isn't part of their speciality. But Deborah confided that she had a more pressing career now.

'Career? You've decided to go in for singing?' She had a wonderful contralto voice, a beautiful instrument which she had put to use singing with a Bach Choir, and for the greater glory of God. So far she'd chosen not to sing professionally. Thirty-two was too late to start.

'Singing?' The look she gave me was almost contemptuous. 'You know that isn't an issue. Mark and I are getting married.'

Upsetting my daughter isn't one of my amusements. Pointing out the dangers of a potentially unwise course of action is a mother's duty, even with adult children. Marriage isn't the end of a fairy-tale, it's the beginning. 'You don't mean that as a career, I take it. I thought you'd toyed with opening an antique shop in St Peter Port?'

A small pause before she blotted out the past. 'Some time later, maybe. I'm going to concentrate on making a home for Mark. We both want a large country house, with a big garden. It's going to take all my time.' She watched my face closely. I tried to expunge all reactions. 'And we expect to start a family right away.'

The maternal instinct, once roused, is very strong. Not even the early appointment at Sotheby's had given such a glow to my daughter's eyes. The miracles of modern medicine ensure that women can safely bear their first child in their thirties and forties. 'D'you think that you'll be able to cope without your job? You've always loved it so.'

'You really are extraordinary, Mum. I thought you'd be thrilled.'

No need to remind her that her children might not have a father for long. She's always been good at mental arithmetic. 'I'm delighted for you, Debs. Where are you getting married?'

'Mark says his parents married at St Yves, in Forest. Well, reaffirmed their marriage vows in the Church. After his mother converted.' She twisted at an earring I hadn't seen before. 'We could have the reception at Bôtnoir. I thought that would be marvellous. D'you think Bôt would mind?'

An oddly proprietorial way of putting it. There was no valid reason for my dislike of her calling Matthew Bôt. He was going to be her brother-in-law. The Abbé had reaffirmed the parents' vows in that little church, and their reception had been at Bôtnoir. So it was actually a rather charming touch.

'I've no idea, Debs. Why not ask him?'

'Mark thought dinner tonight, just the four of us. Better at Lascervelle than in some noisy restaurant.'

Debs hardly ever ate at home. She didn't know the business end of a wooden spoon from the handle. 'Who's going to do the cooking?'

'Mark says Bôt loves to cook.'

Presumably they weren't thinking of employing Matthew in that capacity. One of them might have noticed that he was no longer in need of a job. Why was I being so catty? I pulled myself together. 'I meant, when you set up house, not tonight.'

'What an old fusspot you're turning into, Mum. Mark says any intelligent person can learn to cook. You can always lend me a hand.'

'My expertise is writing on gardening, not cookery.' I restrained myself from adding that I wasn't looking for a job either.

'You're a very good cook, Mum. Even at your age.'

'I wasn't thinking of living with you.' I smiled, disarmingly I hoped. 'Mark will be on hand. Maybe he has hidden talents.'

'You sound just like a mother hen.'

Why was she so determined on underlining my motherhood, and my age? Which was, after all, three years younger than her future husband's.

'Mark says I'm perfectly capable of coping with such a simple skill. If I want to. We can always eat out.' She pulled her ear lobe right down, making me blink. 'Mark says it would be best if I stayed with you until the wedding. St Peter Port is very old-fashioned.' She paused, looked at me. 'You won't worry if I'm not around every single morning, will you?'

It would have been pleasant to have been consulted about whether staying with me was convenient just then. 'I know you'll be in good hands,' I said. I realised I was annoyed. "Mark says" had begun to grate on me.

I was sipping some of Charles's Pommegriche while waiting for the happy pair to make an appearance. Dinner had been set at seven-thirty for eight and they were already late. 'Debs is never late. I wouldn't have thought Mark was, either. They must have lost all sense of time.' My daughter really was in love again. I felt elated, thrilled. Mick's untimely death was behind her at last.

Matthew had bought himself new clothes. So he meant to socialise, live in style. He looked far too handsome. I turned my eyes elsewhere.

'Are you hot? Shall I open the window?'

'Thanks.' His walk across the large room was springy, eager to fill the waiting with something practical, maybe something he could do for me. He opened the French window overlooking his courtyard.

Released from his close physical presence I found myself empathising with him. I knew he'd always been attractive, but after the South Bank Show the number of women who tried to get in touch was awe-inspiring. Yesterday he'd been accosted twenty times in the middle of St Peter Port High Street. He'd sworn never to appear on the box again. The good news was that the programme had already multiplied the price of his paintings by a factor of two, ten for the more representational ones. People were queuing up for Matifs, the name he'd chosen to sign them.

'Better?'

I nodded and moved out of range. 'I'm sure Mark's told you they're officially engaged. They're planning to start a family right away.' I thought it judicious to mention it, just in case Mark hadn't got round to it.

'Marriage is for the procreation of children,' he agreed, a glint in his expressive eyes. 'You're thinking that Jean-Pierre will find that trying.'

The silence hung between us. I sipped at the cider brandy and tried to disown the noise of my stomach rumbling round the large room. I'd forgotten about lunch. 'I think they're going to ask you if they can live at Bôtnoir,' I finally said.

He blinked, tossed back a glass of dry sherry, poured more. 'I was thinking of moving out there myself. Sooner rather than later.'

I was careful not to look at him. Would he allow his brother's wishes to override his own? He'd done that with Lascervelle – to start with.

He stared at the glass in his fingers as though it were a crystal ball. I could see our reflections in it. Separate. 'It's a big place for one person.'

Would our conversations ever be straightforward, or were we doomed to vague allusions and double meanings? I decided to ignore the subtext – if there was one. 'I don't think you'd find that a problem. I lived in our family house for years after my husband died. Not as grand as Bôtnoir by any means, but it was quite a bit larger than average. Its size was never a problem.'

He stood and held the decanter out, looking questioning. I shook my head. 'I was thinking about you. You're designing the garden, it's a major part of your life for the next year or so. Would you find it easier to be on the spot?'

The guessing game had to stop some time. 'How d'you mean?'

'Your lease on Riande runs out in March, doesn't it? We could

251

divide Bôtnoir into two separate apartments. It could all be ready by the time you want to move in.' This time he ate some peanuts. He was out of practice. One slipped down the wrong way and made him choke.

I poured some water, handed him the glass. 'That is a little unexpected.'

'You must know how much I think of you.'

Was the circumlocution purposeful, or habit? 'As in quantity, or quality?'

His hand stretched towards my shoulder. 'Both, naturally. I mean I hope you know how fond I am of you.'

'Last time we were on our own you made it clear that you weren't in a position to have a relationship. Well, that you didn't think I could manage one in your – circumstances.'

He stood again, and moved towards the open window. 'Not a physical one, no. That's why I can't ask you to marry me.'

'But I told you that that isn't a problem as far as I'm concerned.' I realized it wouldn't be easy, but of course I also knew it could be done.

'Marriage has to be consummated before the sacrament of matrimony is complete,' Matthew said, his voice very low.

He really had thought about it. I felt on firmer ground. 'True. But there's no time limit on that as far as the Church is concerned. It wouldn't be against doctrinal teachings to live together as brother and sister until the problem sorted itself out.'

'Indeed. But I couldn't make the vows knowing I could never fulfil them.' He sighed. 'I thought you'd understand that, you're so perceptive. I would love to offer marriage, Ruth. I've wanted that from the moment I met you. But it wouldn't be ethical to marry in the Church. And if we had a civil marriage you couldn't go to the Sacraments.'

'Why not?' Was he just making excuses? 'A register office marriage between Catholics doesn't count as a Christian marriage. It's simply a legally binding contract, like buying a house.' I knew my Catechism reasonably well. 'Which means we could live as brother and sister, so there'd be no problem about the sacraments.'

252

He'd turned round to look at me, but I couldn't see his expression against the light. He just stood, rigid and silent.

It catapulted me into going on. 'You see what I mean?'

The glower turned his handsome features to a disturbing gargoyle of pain. 'Impotence doesn't affect intelligence.'

But it must influence the way he thought. I was more concerned with emotional responses. Consequences. And those were undeniably affected – and affecting, I guessed. 'If you really want to live with me, Matthew, you're going to have to say so. Unequivocally.'

'I really want to live with you.' Hostility had changed to eagerness. 'Will you come to Bôtnoir?'

'Without a civil marriage?'

He frowned. 'You're worried about what people might say?'

Was he so used to running away from women that evading the real issue was a reflex, or was he not prepared to commit himself? Whatever his feelings I could not go on in this half-life of a relationship which only surfaced occasionally. I preferred to do without entirely.

'Not in the least, Matthew. But if we were to decide to live together it would have to be on a permanent basis. Don't misunderstand me. I would in any case be happy to go on with the garden, and to see you as often as we both wish. But I have no intentions of living as a tenant at Bôtnoir.'

The doorbell bleeped three times in rapid succession. Mark used his key to open the front door and come in. Matthew walked up to me, briefly put his arm around my shoulders, brushed a kiss over my hair. Then he went to meet his guests.

CHAPTER THIRTY-FIVE

Debs and Mark came in holding hands, plonked themselves down on Matthew's sofa and continued to hold hands. But it wasn't until Debs leant over and started kissing Mark, and he made no attempt to stop her, that I began to feel uncomfortable.

'I understood you'd come to talk to us?' Matthew's rough voice had the desired effect. Mark jumped back into the sofa, his face reddening.

'Sorry. We tend to forget everyone else.' He smiled at me as though we were collaborators.

I blinked.

'We have no plans to intrude on your private life.' Matthew stood, holding the bottle of Pommegriche. 'Perhaps you would prefer another time? A day or two's notice would be appreciated.'

Deborah pouted. I've been told this can be attractive, but I could see Matthew wasn't impressed.

'We know you rustled up dinner at short notice, Bôt. We're not being ungrateful.' Mark stood, looked round the room, found an easy chair too far away for holding hands with someone sitting on the sofa, and sat down on it.

'Pommegriche? Sherry? Gin and tonic?' Matthew sounded almost his normal self.

'I didn't think you'd be so old-fashioned.' The tone Debs always used when she sulked. I knew it was a mistake with Matthew in his present mood, and probably at any other time.

'You're entirely welcome to express your love for each other in any way you wish, it's just that I don't think this is the right time or place.' He poured himself another dry sherry and gulped it down.

No equivocation there. I could tell that the major point of the evening was already lost.

'We came to ask you something,' Mark started out. I had a pang of empathy for him, so obviously trying hard to please his young fiancée.

Matthew walked over and handed his brother a glass of Pommegriche. Mark took it, frowning at it. 'Ruth told me. You'd like to hold the reception at Bôtnoir. Of course, delighted. A perfect spot.' But his eyes weren't smiling.

'Very good of you.' Mark took a sip of the Pommegriche and grimaced.

'What we meant–' Debs began, smiling at Mark. His flat stare stopped her going on and she raised her eyebrows at him. Meaningfully.

'Are you intending to live at Bôtnoir yourself now, or would you consider letting us have it?' Mark's question was a mere formality. Since I knew what Matthew felt, his twin brother could hardly be in any doubt.

'You know I've already turned down Jean-Jacques. I've decided to live there myself.'

'But you're not married,' Deborah began, ignoring Mark's desperate looks across the room. 'And we're likely to produce the heir.'

'This may come as a great disappointment to you, Deborah. Actually, I'm also thinking about marrying. If I can persuade the lady.'

'You are?' Debs's surprise made us all restive. 'I thought you were a confirmed old bachelor?'

Matthew was always at his best when openly challenged. 'Only ten minutes older than a confirmed old widower I know of.'

There really wasn't anything to say to that.

Mark looked at his brother and smiled. 'So who is she? Some girl young enough to be your daughter? Madeleine Rochet, perhaps?'

Matthew was still standing. The nibbles he picked up could have been bullets. 'Don't you mean granddaughter? My daughter would be a contemporary of Sylvia's, I think. Practically middle-aged.' He walked right up to Debs, looked down at her, concentrating on the odd strands of grey among the blonde. 'As it happens I prefer my own generation.'

She stared from him to me and back again. 'You can't mean Mum? She's too old to have children.'

'I don't believe I've mentioned who the lady is. And I'm not contemplating a brood mare.'

'Debs isn't thinking, Bôt—'

He waved Mark silent. 'In any case, don't rule out miracles.' He stared at Debs with those deep dark eyes. 'Remember Elizabeth? A namesake of your mother's in the Bible.' The slight lifting of the corners of his mouth told me that he'd finally thought it through. 'You've just been to Italy. A wonderful country for marvels of all kinds.'

Deborah's mouth dropped open. She turned to me. 'You're talking about Mum having fertilised ova implanted? It's unnatural. You wouldn't do anything like that, would you, Mum?'

'Jumping the gun, I think,' was all I could come up with under such pressure. A sort of joy ran through me as I grasped that Matthew really did want to marry me, and was considering our having a child using donor ova. And, almost immediately, it came to me that Debs would not only make a wonderful donor, the child would be blessed with family genes.

'I'm sure you can understand that, in the circumstances, Bôtnoir won't be available.' Matthew's deep voice had taken on a commanding tone. 'So, where will you look for a house?'

'Actually it may not be available to you, either.' Debs's voice echoed round the beautiful room. 'We checked the national birth register records in both Madrid and Rome. Your parents weren't married in Spain or Italy. Mark rang up Berlin. Nothing there.'

'I've already told him, Debs.' Mark walked over to the sécretaire. 'It's possible that Todd's case may stand up in court. There's just one more hiding place which might help us.' Mark walked over to the sécretaire, ran his fingers along the top, pulled open the flap, and began to pull out all the drawers. He managed to unlock the secret drawer again – empty this time. He turned to Debs. 'Didn't you say there were sometimes two secret drawers? Could you look for the second one?'

'I suppose I could try.'

'I'd really appreciate that, Debs.' Matthew's eyes positively glowed with hope. 'How about a painting for giving it a go?'

'Will you do a portrait of her?' Mark had gone over and put his arm around my daughter's shoulders. 'I'm sure she'd sit for you whenever you said.'

'If Debs will risk that, I'd be delighted. Pax?' An old Downside expression Matthew occasionally still used. He was smiling at Debs.

I could see that made her nervous.

'He'll make me look ugly.'

'You're a handsome woman, Deborah. I paint what I see, and the character I see is up to you. You can have a studio photograph done any time.'

Mark had gone to join Matthew by the desk. 'Come on, Debs. See if you can find another secret drawer.'

She went over to the little piece, pushed the drawers back again, then ran trained fingers around the wood of each partition. We watched as she took her time. She was shaking her head, then pulled all the drawers out again, pressing home on the housing of the one second from the right. 'I think I've got it.' She put her hand inside, wiggled it back and forth, and finally drew out another drawer. 'Open Sesame.'

'Brilliant!' Mark applauded. 'Isn't she a clever girl?'

'Fantastic!' Matthew agreed.

The drawer was shallow, and deep. I could see the yellowed fragments of old papers – documents. Debs was about to pull them out when Matthew put his hand over the drawer. 'Mine, I think.'

She let it go. He took a silver letter tray from a side table and eased the papers on to it. 'They may be in a delicate state. They must have been hidden for at least forty years, probably fifty.'

'How d'you work that out?'

'I had the desk shipped over to London in the early '50s. But if Gran'mère had known that documents were hidden inside she'd have taken them out herself. My guess is they've been there since before the Occupation.'

These had to be the papers the Abbé had tried to steer me to, though I couldn't see how I was supposed to guess the hiding place. How ironic that Debs should have been the one to find them. Because if they proved that Mathieu and Raquel's civil marriage took place before the conception of any of their sons, the fief was secure. And, assuming we weren't into Elizabethan miracles, perhaps for Debs's first-born son as well.

'Here goes, then.' Matthew tossed aside the envelope, opened the flap of the desk, and slowly, carefully, laid four pieces of folded paper on to it.

He carefully opened up four similar sheets. 'Our birth certificates,' he breathed, his face a deep frown. 'Why on earth did they hide these? Gran'mère had copies.' He suddenly smiled. 'But those are the short forms. Perhaps these long ones give the marriage date.'

Each one of us read carefully through each certificate. Mathieu Ignat, born February 20th, 1931, at 10.21 pm; Marc Maximilian, born February 20th, 1931, at 10.31 pm; Luc Eugène, born January 15th, 1933; and finally Jean-Jacques Dominic, born March 1st, 1934. And, in the appropriate space for each one, their birth place was given as Guernsey, their father's name Mathieu Maximilian Frelé, his religion as Roman Catholic. The slot for their mother's religion had been left blank, but her name was given as Raquel Esther Frelé, née Fleurvallon.

Matthew and Mark stared at each other. 'Our mother's name was Raquel Fleur Vallon,' Mark said, rereading his birth certificate. 'That's what is says on the short form certificates. These don't make sense.'

The Abbé had made very sure I should know he'd falsified Raquel's surname in the church register, after the blessing. 'Your parents did everything they could to hide that your mother was born in France, didn't they?' I said softly. 'I think this is her actual name.'

'But Gran'mère gave us our birth certificates. We each have a copy. They say Raquel Fleur Vallon!' Mark insisted. The brothers read and reread the pieces of paper in their hands.

'Forgeries, I suspect,' I said. 'In case the Germans checked. Vallon is a common enough name on the island not to cause problems.' Spot on, but I still missed the real reason for the change of name.

Matthew fluttered his certificate in the air. 'That's why we haven't found an entry for their marriage! We were looking for the wrong name...'

Mark put his hand round his brother's shoulder. 'Sorry, Bôt, but I don't think that would make any difference. Charles would have searched for a Mathieu Maximilian Frelé marrying. The name of the bride would have been secondary.'

'Don't be absurd.' Matthew took the paper from Mark's hand.

'No need to get so worked up. He'd have cottoned on if there'd been a marriage to a Raquel Esther Fleurvallon. He isn't stupid.'

Exactly my reasoning. So where was that missing marriage certificate, and why had Raquel changed her name? The Abbé knew, but he had no intentions of divulging anything further. Which meant that every word he said to me was significant. And he'd said the parents had eloped.

'Do you know when your mother was born, Matthew?'

Both men stared at me. 'March 13th, 1912, actually,' Matthew said. 'How is that relevant?'

'So March 13th, 1930 was her eighteenth birthday.' The date on the goblets – both of them. That had to be the marriage date.

'So?' Debs said, sounding irritable. 'I don't get your point.'

I wasn't going to tell anyone but Matthew about the Abbé's contribution. 'You have to be eighteen to marry without parental consent. I think the young couple eloped, and married on your mother's eighteenth birthday.'

'Right,' Matthew said. 'We know that they did run off in early 1930, so they could have married then. How does that help us? They'd still have been given a marriage licence. Not the sort of document you throw away.'

'I've had an idea.' Debs knocked into the sécretaire in her

excitement. 'At that time, late '20s, early '30s, people eloped to Scottish border towns. Gretna Green, for example. The people who conducted the marriage didn't always keep registers. That would explain why your lawyer drew a blank.'

'Really, Debs? You think that's possible?'

'There's a sporting chance.' Debs rushed over to the telephone. 'One of my colleagues at Sotheby's is a 1930s specialist. I'll give her a ring.'

While Debs was on the phone I thought I'd clear up one other point. 'Why have you been using the anglicised forms of your names?'

Mark was riffling through the birth certificates. 'It made life easier at Downside, that's all. It made it easier in England altogether. Dealing with Frelé is bad enough.'

'Thanks, Hilary,' Debs said, putting down the receiver with a self-satisfied air. 'I think I know where we should look. Eloping was the fashionable thing to do in those days. Not just to Gretna Green. Coldstream was another popular one. Many other Scottish towns performed the same service – lucrative, no doubt. All that was legally required was the couple's consent to the marriage given before witnesses and followed by cohabitation. No clergyman was necessary. Such a marriage might be very difficult to prove without the original certificate. The people who performed them often kept the registers themselves, then went out of business at a later date.'

'So the proof may no longer exist?' Matthew's features seemed to crumble. For the first time I'd known him he looked his age.

'I'll have another look, just in case.'

But, however hard Debs searched, there was nothing more. The piece of paper we'd all hoped to find, the marriage certificate, simply wasn't there.

CHAPTER THIRTY-SIX

'These the snowdrop bulbs you wanted, are they?' Nicol's faraway seaman's look gave nothing away.

'So you did know where they were?' Autumn was with us; many of the leaves had dropped. My purpose here today was to assess the winter garden. Creating beauty in winter is not the challenge one might suppose. Once the deciduous trees are bare their form becomes important, the colour of their bark significant. Add to that the surprisingly large number of winter flowers, and the cold season can provide as much colour as the summer months, though more subdued. The mild Guernsey climate, the virtual lack of frost, had tempted me to put in a number of semi-tropical plants. I was enjoying the groupings of eucalyptus gunnii as well as the coccifera, both grown from special seed taken from the mountains of Tasmania. They stood a good chance of surviving even a hard island winter. Clumps of five of each variety had been pruned back to stop too much lanky growth. My reluctance for company must have been obvious, but Nicol stood and waited.

'Did the Abbé bury the tins himself? Know what was in them?'

'Might have been someone else entirely.'

And clearly not someone whose identity he was about to divulge. Perhaps keeping secrets was an island pastime, with special prizes for the best kept given out each half century.

My boots felt sticky. That was due to the large clumps of earth around the sprouting bulbs Nicol had dumped on the soil below the trees.

I moved on a few feet. The plum-coloured bloom on the new growth of my favourite willow, salix daphnoides, gleamed against the grey background of the sea. Though the little group had been planted only a few months before some shoots carried a sprinkling of the fat buds which would turn into silky silver catkins in January. They would provide another yearly thrill, turning golden with pollen in February and making them one of the earliest of the flowering trees. Drifts of snowdrops below would add to the delights.

Nicol had shuffled after me, carting a clump of earth-bound bulbs. I could see tiny shoots among the mud. 'How tall d'you reckon they'll get?' His eyes darted from tree to tree.

'Normally eighteen feet. The sea breezes'll keep them down to fifteen or less, but I like them pruned. You get that glorious purple growth from last season's shoots. Look at them glow. You can't beat that for colour in winter sun.'

He heaved several clods sprouting with snowdrops into his barrow and wheeled it over, determined we should plant bulbs. I gave in.

'Can't promise that they're the best ones.'

I was uneasy, feeling watched. I turned round quickly but saw nothing except the movement of a shrub in still air. A bird alighting, perhaps.

'We can always move them if they're not.' Nicol handed me a bulb planter.

I'd brought my fork. I don't believe in spades unless the soil is very sandy. My method of planting small bulbs to show as drifts is to stick a garden fork into turf, as deeply as possible. By twisting the handle back and forth four deep holes appear. Drop a bulb into each hole and tread the turf back, then make the next quartet by setting the fork at a different angle. Continue haphazardly. There's no need to plan too much, the system produces a natural scattering effect.

'Where d'you learn that? Horticultural college?'

'My little trick.' Jonathan was the one who'd fired my enthusiasm for gardening. We were walking round our first garden, admiring a particularly fine carnation.

'Wouldn't it be lovely to have a couple more of those?' I'd said, drinking in the perfume. 'I wonder what they're called.'

'Doesn't matter. All you have to do is take some cuttings.' And he'd taken his secateurs, cut off a couple of shoots, and stuck them in the ground. Four weeks later they'd rooted. That was the miracle which got me hooked.

'You seem to be good at those.' Nicol's eyes vanished under squinting lids.

Another veiled meaning. What did he want from me?

His fork was larger than mine, the spacing wider. We mingled our plantings. 'Uncanny, the likeness. Or can't you tell, seeing as one of them is you?'

I was squatting on my heels. Odd how even the Abbé had commented on a likeness, presumably to Raquel Frelé. Though how he'd been able to tell through thick cataracts was a another riddle.

I looked up. 'The mirror isn't that good a guide. But I did my research. I compared a couple of my wedding pictures with Matthew's mother's. Your powers of observation are enviable. You can see beyond the years.'

Nicol nodded. 'He needs you.'

The 'he' could only be Matthew. 'Special friends, were you?' It was time to straighten up, to stand to what height I could muster.

'Comrades. A small guerrilla war of our own.'

'Against the Germans?'

'Only one war here in my lifetime.' He began to stab the fork into the soil again, shaking it back and forth, making spaces into which the bulbs would sink too deep. 'I'll make the holes. You bury 'em.' He looked up momentarily. 'Got two of the bastards.' His face was a torment of anger.

I retreated away from him. My boots were in danger of being split.

'Always after the women, the first one. Pig-head, pea-brain.' The fork was jabbing in and out of soil at a furious rate. 'Damn him! Thought my mother was an easy touch after that first Boche got his comeuppance. Scared the bloody life out of her. And she was the gentlest creature.'

'Your father: that was Henri?' The most likely candidate for burying the tins.

He didn't disagree, he just went on attacking the earth. 'Stood where you were standing just now.' His eyes gleamed with hatred. 'Just bare cliff dropping down.'

'Time we planted a low hedge. Something like golden elder, or tamarisk. Choisya ternata would be good. That'll stop people going too close to the edge.'

'Stood there, as though he owned the place. Bloody jackboots, feet wide apart.'

Like the man in black, that day on the beach. I shuddered.

'Something wrong?'

'It feels a bit cold,' I said. The past was spreading its tentacles over the present. Shadows of evil, the Abbé had called them. I felt them now and was glad to warm myself with physical work. We'd almost finished the planting. I placed the remaining bulbs carefully. 'That's the lot, I think.'

His eyes stared, but not at me. 'It only took one little push. Smug bastard. Didn't think boys our age counted. Didn't think anyone mattered except him and his fellow shits. Bôt was the decoy, the one who took him to the edge. I shoved him over.'

Where do you draw the line? Had that been murder, or a guerrilla attack? And what about Matthew, what had his role been? Did playing decoy count as being an accomplice?

'How old were you?' My voice was shaking

'Not what counts. But you can work it out: middle teens.'

Matthew had been ten. 'So they didn't deport you, because you were too young?'

He laughed. 'Never knew, never even guessed. We all swore the snotty Boche was drunk.' He crashed his fork into the barrow. 'True enough, but not the truth. Couldn't have been outside, could we? Curfew made sure of that. Dozens of Boche measuring up.' He grinned as his fork jabbed into the soil, again and again. 'Came up with he'd lost his bearings in the dark, fallen over by mistake. Part of their old fence still in the ground.' He kicked at rotting posts. 'You give the word, I'll have it out today.'

'I give the word,' I said. The more of the past we could dispense with the better.

CHAPTER THIRTY-SEVEN

Matthew and I were in the huge master bedroom overlooking the gardens. Beyond them the sea was brilliant with late October sunshine. There were two full-length windows on the garden side, echoed by the windows in the living and the dining rooms. A glass door led to the balcony.

Matthew took my hand and walked me over to the windows. 'Like the view?'

'No need to sell me on it. I love the view, the house, the garden.'

'What about the man?'

'I knew the moment I saw you, Matthew. In spite of another man who looks so like you, and whom I met first.'

'You're going to go on using that formal name?'

'Everyone else calls you Bôt. If you'll give it a chance, I'll think of something just for you and me.'

'My mother called me Matif.' He put his arm around my shoulders, I put mine around his waist. We stood, our bodies blending into each other, leaning our heads towards each other, fusing our lips.

Suddenly Matthew drew away. 'Probably just maternal pride. She was convinced I'd be another Matisse. My early work was a little derivative.'

'She found a way of joining your initials, you mean? Mathieu Ignat Frelé becomes Matif. That's why you sign your paintings with that name?'

'It's a tribute to her.' The voice rumbled, I had to strain to hear. 'I paint them for her.'

It explained why he didn't care whether they sold or not. 'You were going to tell me about her – Matif,' I tried out. It takes time to get one's tongue round a new name. It sounded stiff, but I knew it would mellow with use. And it would change, I knew that too. 'Tell me what happened.'

'It wasn't true, what I told you.'

'That they'd disappeared? I guessed that. Were they deported?'

'It wasn't true that I never saw them again. Unfortunately for me, I did.'

The bedroom was still bare, just the two chandeliers and the carpet which, though recently taken from Lascervelle and cleaned, was threadbare with the traffic of generations of Frelé feet.

'Let's sit on the window seat.' We leaned against each other in the subdued autumn sun. The golden softening beams which lead towards inevitable winter. But they are still a season. 'What did you see?'

'Too much, Ruthi. Far too much,' he whispered, his lips touching my ear. The pounding of blood made it hard to hear. He drew back slightly, kissed my hands and held them in his own. 'It was a full moon night in May. The swell was there, but not very strong. Maman had spent a long time saying goodnight to us. She came round every night, you know, to each of us in turn. Told us a story, or read to us.'

'She sounds a wonderful mother.'

'I can't imagine a better one. She always came last to me. That night we talked for a long time. She sat on my bed and leaned against me, because by then she found it hard to sit up straight.'

The image of Dominique on the beach of Bôtnoir, laughing with pleasure, big with child, came back to me. 'Your mother was having another baby?'

He gasped. 'How can you know that? I'm not sure that I realised it then, but yes, she was.' He looked at me, and smiled sadly as he remembered her. 'She told me how important it was for me to paint, how I should never let anything stand in the way of that.'

'You were ten?'

'Old enough. Most children are human beings with a small experience of life. Mine was too grow all too quickly that night.

Something was going on. She looked strained, I thought she might be ill. I asked if she was going away, to hospital or something. She didn't answer that, but she told me never to forget how much she loved me, how I was the son she'd always dreamed of.'

His voice had become higher, as though he were physically going back in time.

'And then?'

'We gazed at each other, for what seemed like a very long time.'

'That's what you painted.'

'I painted what I saw then. My father came into the room and pulled her up. His eyes were moist. He embraced me, told me I was the heir to Bôtnoir and to keep it safe for my heirs. And then they left.

'I couldn't sleep. I had some pencils and paper in my room, and I began to sketch her. At last I was exhausted and lay down. And within minutes, or so it seemed to me, I heard her cry.'

'You heard her? From their bedroom?'

'From outside. Not with my ears. I just knew she was in danger, in serious trouble. I grabbed a chair and climbed up to the window. I looked down to the bay and saw four men in German officer uniforms. A cloud covered the moon, but then it went and I saw the kayak, and they were dragging two people from it. I knew right away that it had to be my parents. One held my mother as she struggled, the other two held my father, bound his feet, his hands behind his back. The fourth one was tearing the clothes from my mother's body.'

'My God! You saw all that?'

'Made out enough to tell me what was going on.' His voice was harsh, he was pacing up and down.

'What did you do?' What could he have done, a young child of ten?

He stopped and looked out into the garden. 'It was weird. I became very calm. I put my catapult into my left pocket, some spent bullet cases in my right. And I put an ice-pick Maria had taken from the kitchen for me in my teeth. Then I let myself down from the window.'

My heart beat faster at the thought of his bravery. A mere boy, swinging against the rock, determined against the might of the Third Reich. A fury yet unstilled.

'You don't need me to spell out what I heard and saw.'

'No, please don't.'

'They were too busy to notice me. I got to the beach, stopped about six feet away from them, the ice-pick ready to undo the binding round my father's hands.' He swallowed. 'Too late. His head was lolling and they were already cutting her. Criss-crossing her face with knives, yelling obscenities.'

'Tell me,' I whispered.

'They slit her belly open.' He was staring out of the French windows, up at the sky. 'The screams...'

"You can't still be alive!" I heard again the harsh gutterals of the man in black screaming as Dominique turned towards us. 'Are you saying she was late on in her pregnancy?'

'I don't think I'd registered that before. But when they slit her open I grasped they were pulling a baby out, and that it moved. They trampled it underfoot, shouting again. I looked at my father, and his dead eyes spoke to me. There was no way I wasn't going to avenge her. Them.' He swallowed hard, and I could see the Adam's apple struggling.

'There was a single rifle shot which stopped the Germans in their tracks. They looked around, presumably assumed a commando attack had started, and took off at speed. Then I saw Henri and Nicol tearing towards us from the cave. No stealth, they ran as fast as they could, Henri charging with my grandfather's ancient rifle, bayonet fixed, Nicol brandishing garden tools – a pickaxe and a slasher.' He shrugged. 'Pathetic, really.'

'But they got them?'

'No. Nicol had seen one German jump over my dead father as he and Henri charged. The bloody cowards took off fast, up the cliff path. They probably got straight into their jeep and drove away.' He pushed his hands through his hair. 'Strange, but it was almost like an understanding. Henri let them go. There was no chance they'd report what they'd done. The Kommandantur wouldn't have tolerated that sort of insubordination. Everything had to be done by the book. All four would have been court marshalled.

'Then Henri turned back to see if my mother was still alive, if we could save her.'

His voice broke, stopped. There was nothing but the sound of his heaving breath as he tried to gain control.

I waited for a long time. Finally I broke it. 'And you couldn't.' I whispered it.

Tears were pouring down his face. 'I had to give you an idea. Otherwise it would always have been between us.'

Could such scars be healed? Half a century on, and they had not.

'The three of us made a pact there and then to kill all four of them. Whatever it took, we were going to get those bloody Boches. But we would have to plan it.'

'Nicol told me about the one he pushed over the cliff.'

'Ahh.' He searched my face. 'That one was easy.' He cupped my chin in his hand. I opened my lips expectantly, but he was looking deep into my eyes. That's when I knew Nicol had lied for Matthew's sake. 'It wasn't Nicol, Ruth. I pushed that German. Deliberately, because of what he'd done to my mother. I murdered him.'

'It was an act of sabotage...'

'No, Ruth. It was murder. Calculated premeditated murder. And I still can't say that I regret it.'

No repentance, no absolution. That's what the Abbé would have spelt out. 'That's why you don't go to Communion.' For a moment I just sat there. I don't think what Matthew had told me had really sunk in yet. 'You mean you killed three of them?' I remembered Charles had told me that three Germans had died in suspicious circumstances. 'How could you? You were just a boy.'

'You have to understand, Ruth. I didn't kill them – I murdered them. Henri, Nicol and I between us saw to it that they died, though it was I who did the actual killing in at least two of the cases.' He'd released me, stared down at his hands. Did he wash them often? Did he feel he could not get them clean?

'I still don't see...'

'Surprise is everything, not strength. The first one was almost too easy. Nicol lured him out on the cliff, right by an outcrop. I was hiding behind it, jumped out, a small push.'

So part of Nicol's story had been accurate, he'd just reversed the roles. 'And the second one?'

'Henri rigged the brakes on their vehicle. It was parked in the drive. I threw stones at the living room window. The curfew was in force, you see. One of them rushed out after me. I was ready. I biked ahead of him, he jumped into his jeep, blared the horn, clamped his foot on the accelerator and careered down that steep slope. I jumped off, on to an overhanging branch. The windscreen hit my legs, but I clung on to the branch. The jeep went out of control and crashed.'

'He was killed?'

'He died of his injuries.'

'And you?'

'They rushed after the jeep. I crawled into the undergrowth till morning, then back into the kitchen. I thought my legs were broken. I was lucky, just very bruised. I wore long trousers so no one would notice.'

'An act of war,' I tried out.

'Henri was acting as saboteur, not me. I was acting as executioner. The Abbé refused absolution.'

'Because you didn't repent?'

He stood apart from me. 'I was – am – sorry to have offended God. But I wasn't willing to make a firm purpose of amendment. I intended to go on. And did.'

'But how? Surely the Germans must have had some idea by then?'

'I was a boy of ten, as you pointed out. Nicol was a bit older. There were no men about, apart from Henri. For some reason they thought the jeep crash proved the first incident was accidental. They found out about the brakes, and said it was an act of sabotage. Committed by Henri.'

'Charles told me he was tried and sentenced to death.'

'They deported him, yes. We never saw him again.'

'And the third and fourth Germans?'

'Old Annie, our cook, was pretty good at herbs. She fed the next candidate valerian root.'

It's my job to know about plants. 'But that's not poisonous, just a strong sedative.'

'Exactly.' There was a chilling silence. 'I knew where he was living,' he said at last.

'Lascervelle,' I said.

'Full marks. I stole the key from Gran'mère, crept into the house, hid in his wardrobe. When I thought he was fast asleep I held a pillow over his head. I noticed when I started that he didn't seem to be breathing. The inquest said it was a heart attack. Valerian can be dangerous.'

'So old Annie killed that one.' Even so, the story of the deliberate plan to suffocate a sleeping man by a boy of that age did shock me.

'The intention was there.'

'You took some chances. You were very brave.'

'No. I couldn't have cared less.' He looked at me, his eyes fierce. 'You could say I enjoyed it, in a ghoulish sort of way.'

Things were beginning to fall into place. 'So what about the last one?'

'He caught on.'

'He'd seen you?'

'Not exactly. Guilt, I think. We put on some theatricals. Used the old Hamlet trick. I dressed up like a woman, wore my mother's clothes. He was a highly educated man, he'd have got the drift.'

'He didn't try to pin the deaths on you?'

'No. He kept away from Bôtnoir after what happened at Lascervelle House. Then he got himself posted back to North Germany. He was from there originally.'

'From Prussia?' I asked. That explained the man in black's – Otto's – reactions. I was now convinced he was the fourth German. Did Matthew know he was on the island, that he knew Todd?

"It isn't possible, it can't be happening!" I remembered him

271

howling, his voice pitched high above the sound of the waves. "Where have you come from, you ghastly fiend, you bloody bitch?" he'd shouted, a despairing wail in his voice.

It all fitted. Dominique was in a kayak that day on the beach, with a young man. She also had red hair, and she was pregnant. And she was Raquel's granddaughter, must have had a look of her. No wonder he'd backed off, screamed "Keep away!" at her

Matthew shrugged. 'I found out eventually that he was from Berlin. I think that used to be the capital of Prussia.'

'So he eluded you?'

'For many years. I tracked him down relatively recently. Gran'mère knew where he came from. I think she knew him before the war.'

I thought back to the figure behind Michelle Frelé in the photograph. The upright man behind her could easily be the same man – Otto when he was young. He must have decided to come back to Guernsey after he'd heard the old lady had died. To keep a promise? Something to do with Todd Frelé?

He'd gone back to the scene of his crime. He must have thought Dominique a reincarnation of the woman he'd treated in a way which I could not even allow myself to think about. No wonder guilt had made him confuse her with Raquel, made him think she'd come back to avenge herself.

'Your grandmother told you about him?' I asked at last.

'She certainly did not. I went through her papers after she died. I found one letter from him to her, one she didn't destroy. A love letter dated the time he left, in 1941. It gave me the clue to finding out who he was, where he came from.'

So that was why I hadn't come across Matthew when I first moved to Guernsey. Not because he was staying with Charles Grichard, but because he was in Germany, hunting down the fourth German. How had he escaped Matthew's revenge?

'He'd settled in Lüneburg, though he came from Berlin. Nice old town, proud of its war heroes. He made up an elaborate false past. They told me about his Maserati. White cabriolet, white leather seats, the works. He never lets anyone else drive it.'

Same car. Which he allowed Todd to drive. That must be proof he was the fourth German. I was sure Matthew had no idea of the connection with Todd.

He looked me in the eyes. 'A perfect opportunity. I always was good at chemistry.'

'You mean you made a bomb and the authorities blamed the IRA?' Had Matthew really blown the fourth man up? In the last few days, on Guernsey, without my hearing about it? Out of the question.

'Quite a gift for jumping to conclusions, haven't you? The IRA aren't an active force in Germany. But driving such a distinctive car does make one a target.'

There was no triumph in that shrug, that stance. I didn't believe he'd even tried to do it. 'But you didn't do it.'

'Not yet.' He put his arms around me. 'It's weird. Somehow I no longer see it as a pressing need.' He let me go, stood away from me. 'Well, Ruth? What d'you think? Would you be able to marry a murderer?'

My mouth opened and closed as though I was a fish out of water. Which was, perhaps, an accurate description of my feelings. I'd thought of marrying Matthew, hoped for it, longed for it. And now that he was proposing I was as reluctant as I'd been with Mark. Had I been fooling myself that I wanted a permanent relationship?

The sin is as much in the intention as in the carrying out. What was I doing, philosophising when the man I'd told myself I was in love with was proposing? 'You had the opportunity to kill that fourth German?'

'I did.' I could see him watching my body language, sensing my drawing back. 'I don't really know why I didn't take it. Somehow it seems to be connected with my meeting you.'

I breathed out the tension, felt my limbs lighten, felt the heaviness leave. He'd chosen not to kill the fourth man. I made another leap into the unknown and assumed he never would. Matthew may have murdered as a child – that was between him and God. But he wasn't doing it now. I was sure it meant that the time for revenge had finally passed.

273

'I can't quite accept your version, Matif. You were killing in wartime – not on the battlefield, but as a guerrilla.'

'My enemies were personal and so beyond the justification of war. You were the one who said it: we are the past. And we can't hide from it.'

He was right, devastatingly honest. I owed it to both of us to be the same. 'I'm sorry, Matthew. It really would be wrong to answer right away. I need a little time to think about it all.'

But he hadn't killed that German. Which meant he could make a firm purpose of amendment, and get absolution.

CHAPTER THIRTY-EIGHT

The cliff path down to the sea glistened yell grey in dank autumn air and drew me down to the beach. The tide was out, the moving mass of turbulence safely away. That's how it must have been on that May night half a century ago. A semi-darkness intermittently brightened by churning white sea-horses, the moonlight reflected to double its intensity. I walked around the little bay, inviting old ghosts to speak to me. What had really happened here? Matthew's story was incomplete. He'd stopped at the point when Henri and Nicol had come into the picture.

Did the Abbé know more? Had Matthew confessed to him what he'd kept from me? I stared out to sea, unblinking, waiting for my eyes to tire, waiting for my unconscious mind to see instead.

My eyes dutifully blurred, ran over with tears. It was as though the sea stood still. The cry of a gull pierced into me, shrill and stark. Like the sound of a new-born infant.

A baby had been brutalised into the world. An innocent baby, not even ready to be born. And four adult men had stomped out what little life there was, had treated this human being like vermin. Simply because the parents were running away? It was beyond understanding. Dormant fury made me gag.

Jesus bade his followers to turn the other cheek, or so the Gospels tell us. He also spoke of righteous anger, and putting a millstone round the neck of someone who harmed a child. Not quite so meek and mild. Had Matthew merely followed that commandment when he saw the infant ripped from its mother's womb? It wasn't up to me to cast the first, or any, stone.

The void in the story loomed up with the spearhead of the

275

returning tide. What had happened to the three bodies? The official whitewash of the parents lost at sea did not explain it. Had the Occupation Forces really swallowed that? It had perhaps been convenient for them to do so. It wouldn't do for me.

I used my boots to shuffle away the pebbles overlying the sand, to dig holes in the soft mass. I used my hands to fashion a structure. Shells to make windows, stones for the doors. I bruised my fingers to scoop deep, to hollow out caves... Where were they buried?

Buried. You bury the dead. Matthew had told me that his father had been shot at close range, was dead when he came up to him. The baby had been trampled under foot. And Raquel? Was Raquel dead by the time the Germans ran?

Dying, not necessarily dead. Had she talked to Matthew? What had Henri, and Nicol, and Matthew, done to help her? Had Matthew been forced to watch her die?

The clouds gathered darkness above me, the sea washed at my castle, threatened my boots. Rain dripped large drops on my head. Somewhere in the labyrinth of the caves there was a grave which held three bodies. And the bodies had been stripped of rings, of every identifying artefact. In case they were unearthed.

'Really, Ruth.' The rough loud voice penetrated the swell of sea now turned into a roar. 'It isn't safe to leave you on your own. I thought I'd spelled it out – it's dangerous when the tide comes in. It comes in very fast. Let's get out of here.' He grabbed my arm, held tight.

I dug in. 'How did you know where I was?'

'Later! No time to hang about.' He'd grasped my other arm and frog-marched me towards the path steeping up to the drive of his house. 'If a large breaker catches us we'll be tossed out to sea. The current's very strong.'

As I twisted my head round to protest I saw the huge wave about to engulf us. My eyes must have told Matthew. He lifted me up, literally hurled me a yard or so up the path and, somehow, vaulted against the rock.

'Grab hold of something!'

The prickly spikes of tamarisk digging into my fingertips felt good. The wave deluged, tried to submerge us, poured water on our clinging forms, retreated empty. Matthew clambered up the cliff beside the path, passed me, turned round and pulled me up. 'Move it, Ruth,' he bellowed at me.

I did, we scrambled up. I'd underestimated the timing, the force of the tide, the way it would flood in. It looked so innocuous when I'd watched it from the veranda and the attic windows.

With the sea safely below us, plodding towards the drive, my anger returned. 'How did you know where I was?' I shouted at his rear.

He stopped, turned. 'Your car...'

'I mean: how did you know I was down here?' But I already knew. 'Nicol? He's been spying on me?'

The path had broadened out, was wide enough for two. Matthew waited for me. 'He was worried about you. In fact he was about to come and get you himself.'

That made me even angrier. 'That still means he was watching me.'

'Old habits, Ruth. He used to look out for me.'

The gardener I'd admired so much when I first came to Bôtnoir took on a different aspect. 'I'm not some appendage of yours.'

'That's not at all the right interpretation.' He was walking beside me, firmly keeping hold of my arm. 'He'd seen someone lurking about. But he wasn't able to get a good look at him. My cousin Todd again, I expect. That's why Nicol's keeping an eye out.'

That struck a chord. I'd sensed someone watching me several times, but I'd assumed it was Nicol being proprietorial. A general air of claustrophobia made me shake off Matthew's arm. 'How did you get here?'

'A taxi.'

'Because Nicol rang you?'

'Yes.'

'I won't have it, Matthew. It's up to me...'

'Whether you kill yourself or not? Certainly, if that is your intention. But I don't believe it was.' He chivvied me along. 'You don't understand about tides, Ruth. And, take it from me, you haven't a clue about the dangers of Bôtnoir Bay. Nicol rang because you'd obviously lost track of time.' He suddenly stopped and hugged me. 'I don't want to lose you. So let's not hang about. We're both sopping wet, and it's pretty cold. Hot bath, I think.'

I veered towards my car.

'Where are you off to now? Jake's had this magnificent Jacuzzi built into the bathroom next to the master bedroom. Let's sample that.'

CHAPTER THIRTY-NINE

To my surprise there were towels, dozens of them. Absorbent bath sheets of the most luxurious kind, stacked in a spacious cupboard in the dressing room outside the bathroom. I picked out dusky pink. And there was Badedas, in the original horse chestnut scent. I added it liberally to the water. Why not indulge the body when you can?

My naked figure was still one of my better points. Not waif-like, as it had been in my twenties, even after childbirth. But it was without excessive fat. Narrow waist, wide hips, strong thighs, C cup bust – the figure of a woman, not a girl. Gravity had affected the slack tissue of my breasts, but not my muscles.

Looking at Matthew's body was the pleasure I'd always known it would be. Feeling it was an ecstasy I could not have imagined. Its exploration took time, a lot of time. Wide shoulders narrowing to lean hips, the muscles strong, not bulging. After my fingers had finished, my eyes feasted on it. The hot water surrounding us took on a coolness. I began to shiver.

He heaved himself out of the water. Staying in the nude while he covered himself did not appeal to me. I followed suit, he held the rose bath sheet out for me.

'I've put the clothes in the washer/dryer. We can have a hot drink in the kitchen while we wait.'

When I'd dried, using the rose towel, I rather regretted not keeping that one for the sarong I fashioned out of a dry yellow one. Not quite so flattering. I turbaned my hair in rose.

'What about Irish coffee?'

'Don't you need cream for that?'

'Madeleine stocked the fridge for me. And the larder. There's a free range duck, and all the trimmings. We could drive into town later and pick up some clothes.' He put the kettle on, filled a cafetière with coffee beans he'd ground in a small hand machine.

This time I chose to have my back against the window, though the light from the kitchen was now facing me. I drew the curtains across. Visits from Nicol were not what I had in mind.

The kettle was put on again. I watched as he took the body of a duck out of the fridge, prepared a large bowl, poured boiling water into it, levered in the duck.

'You're going to boil it?'

'I'm just opening the pores. That takes about five minutes. The next step's a bit unconventional. There used to be a fan heater in the old kitchen, just for that purpose. It's long gone. I'll try the fan in the oven. What I'm trying to do is keep the pores open so that, when the bird is roasting, the fat runs out and the skin turns crisp.'

'Chinese?'

'In memory of Maria Rochet. Italian.'

'Charles said she was a kind of second mother to you all.'

He looked up at me. 'For as long as she was around. She was so afraid of being deported.' Had he not known about the way they questioned her, terrified her?

The aroma of rosemary and sage began to fill the room. Matthew chopped expertly, mixing the two herbs, adding salt, pepper, a twist of lemon zest. The duck was laid to drain, all moisture blotted off, blow dried in the oven turned to full force, then taken out and rubbed with the herbs.

The coffee was now ready. Matthew heated two Pyrex cups in the oven, poured in a dram of whisky, and added the coffee. Then he trickled some cream on to the top over a silver spoon.

'D'you take sugar?'

'I learned to do without during the war. I never wanted to go back to it.'

'Same here.' He came to sit beside me. We kissed. The coffee became tepid, the kitchen hot from the oven he'd put on.

'I'll just chop the liver and add it to the herbs and put it all inside the bird. Then it can start roasting.'

This time he sat opposite me, the table between us. The roast in the oven began to sizzle. An intimate domestic scene.

'Smells wonderful,' I said. I slipped out from under the table, pulled him over to the dryer, fished out the clothes. 'They're wearable.'

He pulled my towel off, began to kiss my eyes, my neck, my breasts. It must have been an hour later that we finally dressed. And demolished the duck.

'If we're to start a new life together, let's make it warts and all,' I said, mouth full and juicy.

His eyes were soft. 'Can't see any.'

'Emotional ones. I have to understand them, otherwise you and I can't form a lasting relationship. Jonathan's death taught me to live in the present. We're too old to rely on the future, Matif. The past has formed us. Like it or not, that's what we are. I have to be able to live with yours.'

He nodded. 'I take your point. But that does go both ways.'

'Quite right. It's time you met my sons. I'll ring them when I get back to Riande.'

He didn't even ask whether he should drive. Could I live with such a macho attitude? Maybe I even liked it.

'Mark told me he and Deborah are planning a spring wedding. And they're going to take me up on using Bôtnoir for the reception.' He was looking straight ahead.

'How nice.' Debs hadn't bothered to speak to her own mother about her wedding date. She and Mark were so absorbed in each other she hardly spoke to me at all.

'How about a double wedding?' He stared out of the windscreen, the fingers on the driving wheel tense, the knuckles white.

I put my arm through his, leaned against him, enjoying the warmth. 'That does have its appeal. And if there should be any problems about marrying a brother's mother-in-law, or sister-in-law, they can be outmanoeuvred.'

'So that's a yes?'

'I think there's one more thing you have to tell me, Matif. And then the frog will turn into a prince.' I put my hand on his groin. Did impotence mean no erection, or just not being able to hold it at the crucial moment? But I already knew.

'And what might that be?'

'Your parents. Where are they buried?'

He clearly grasped right away why I was asking this. 'Later,' he said. 'Tomorrow maybe. When we go back to Bôtnoir.'

We parked the car and walked down towards our houses. As soon as we passed the window of the ground-floor study fronting Candie Road I knew there'd been some change to Riande House. But what? The doors and windows looked closed, secure.

Matthew took my key, opened the front door. 'Try not to get into trouble for the next little while, Ruth. See you in half an hour, say?'

'Make it an hour. I'd like to change.'

I was too distracted to pin down what was worrying me. Once on my own, walking into the empty house, the dark, I knew: the curtains had been drawn back in a different way from the way I'd left them. Was there someone here, waiting to pounce? Was that why Nicol was keeping an eye on me?

Who was it, and what did he want? And how had he got in? I felt for the pruning knife in my pocket, pulled it out, stood rooted to the spot holding my breath.

The house was silent. No creak of floorboards, not even the rattling of a window pane. I jumped as a rumble reverberated through – the boiler firing.

My ears strained through the accustomed noises, detected nothing further. I inched my way upstairs, using the lights from the street lamps outside, unwilling to make myself a target.

The door to my writing-room stood open. I always kept it closed. Had someone tried to steal my work?

Even without going into the writing-room I could see my work table upended, papers everywhere. My reading lamp lay on the floor, together with crystal shards and a rusty tin. The tin holding the wedding album had gone. But the safe under my reading lamp was intact.

CHAPTER FORTY

'Someone's broken into Riande, Matif.' My voice was low on the phone. I tried hard not to sound too little-womanish.

'Is he still there? Hold tight, I'll be right over.'

'No rush. He's gone, took what he wanted.'

'Your jewellery?' There was a pause. 'Or were they after your work? That isn't any use to anybody else, is it?'

'He was after something Nicol dug up for me.' The thief had found what he'd come for. An empty tin gaped at me. The wedding album was gone, the glasses shattered. Fortunately he didn't know me, or the way I worked. I'd rushed downstairs to check my darkroom. No one had been there. The developed negatives and transparency films, still hanging up to dry, were safe.

'Rare plants?' Matthew paused. 'That's what you were bringing back the other day? I'd no idea we had any.'

I hesitated. I had no choice but to tell him. 'It's nothing to do with gardening. You saw me carrying two tins Nicol had unearthed. A small cache belonging to your parents – the only valuables they took with them for their escape.'

'Personal belongings?' He sounded baffled. That would soon turn to annoyance once the implications sank in. 'You mean the wedding cake?'

My turn to be surprised. 'You knew there was a buried one? You didn't think it important to look for it?'

'Old Annie always insisted Henri had buried it somewhere in the garden. Are you telling me Nicol knew where it was all along?' He sounded incredulous. 'He told me he didn't.'

'That was true. He was told recently. And the cake was only

283

one part of it. There were two tins, Matif.'

'I see.' He sounded frosty. 'And Nicol decided to give them both to you?'

It wasn't going to be easy to calm him down. 'It wasn't his decision. Part of his brief, I'm pretty sure. The thief got away with some of the contents. Come over and I'll show you the rest.' I clicked off the receiver before he could say more.

I hadn't checked my bedroom yet, I was so convinced it wasn't an ordinary break-in. No one had been there. I pulled on a clean pair of jeans and a T-shirt, and went down again. So far the burglary made no sense. Why would anyone break into my house and steal an old wedding album? Nothing unusual about it. Just ordinary, fairly uninspired, wedding photographs. I took it they included clues to information the thief wanted to keep to himself. Or didn't want anyone else to have. Which could only point to Todd Frelé.

The kitchen was the place to wait. I congratulated myself on the foresight – the luck! – of wrapping the cake up and putting it in the fridge. I'd be able to show Matthew that, together with the rings.

He was at the door within minutes. 'How did he get in?'

'No broken window glass. He jemmied the French windows to the courtyard.'

'So he climbed over the courtyard wall. My French windows were wide open. At first I thought it was because I'd been careless.' He looked around the room as though that might provide the answer, then put his arm around me. 'There's only one person it could have been. Todd still has a key to Lascervelle. What, exactly, was he after?'

Nicol had been right to be suspicious, and I hadn't imagined being watched. Todd Frelé must have seen Nicol digging up the tins and handing them to me.

The story of where the two tins had been buried, and their contents, produced bewilderment, then sadness, on Matthew's face. 'Why on earth didn't Nicol tell me?'

'I told you. I'm pretty sure he had no idea until the other day.' I remembered that he'd dug the whole garden by hand. He didn't know where the tins were, but he might have known they existed. And he'd been looking for them.

'You're letting your imagination run away with you, Ruth. Who else could know, and persuade him to give them to you rather than to me?'

'Only one person. The Abbé Saint Jude.' I decided it was time I told Matthew about my meeting with the old priest. That I was sure he'd been trying to steer me into a direction which would tell me something he was forbidden to and which, for some reason, he thought I'd work out.

'Why would he keep a secret for years, then suddenly arrange something like this? He's an old man, it could have died with him long ago.'

'Because it wouldn't have mattered, except for the business with Todd, I'd guess. Which didn't come up until your grandmother was dying. Presumably the Abbé was taken to Lascervelle to hear her last confession, was bound to silence by the laws of the sacrament. But he also knew he had the key to the threat to your fief.' I explained how I'd found the album, the glasses and the rings. And what had been etched into the crystal. 'Now that you know it's still around, don't you want to see that cake?'

'Cake? I want to see the rings.'

We hurried up to my writing-room. I showed him the shattered pieces of glass and turned on the lamp to illuminate the fragments which still showed sections of letters etched into them. Quite illegible by now.

'You reckon he smashed them deliberately?'

'Out of pique because he didn't find the thing he came for. More likely because the date suggested the original wedding date.' I unlocked the lamp safe, pulled out the velvet bag and gave it to Matthew. He turned it upside down. 'Clever of you to think of hiding them.' The rings rolled out.

I explained how they'd ended up there by pure luck. He laughed, held them under the bright halogen light. 'I can't quite make it out, but I think there's an inscription on the inside of the large wedding ring.'

285

My magnifying glass hadn't been broken. I handed it to him.

'It says "R to M, 13/3/30" inside.'

'So we don't need a magnifying glass to tell us it says "M to R, 13/3/30" inside the smaller one.'

'There's only the hallmark inside the engagement ring.' He held that to the light again, allowing it to shine through the deep purple of the stone. 'Unusual to choose an amethyst to go with those incredible diamonds.'

'Your mother's birthstone. I think that's what the goblets and the rings are telling us. Your parents married on her eighteenth birthday. The earliest date they could.'

'Except we can't prove it.' His eyes were soft again as he looked at me. 'You know I'd like nothing better than to offer this ring to you.' He put a finger on my lips. 'I know you won't take it yet. So: what else d'you want to know?'

I decided to take the chance. 'What happened to the bodies?'

He looked at me for a long time. 'You really want to drag all that up? After all these years? It's hardly pleasant.'

His story had been incomplete. I needed to know. 'I think it will give me a better idea of how you must have felt.'

'And how I reacted,' he said, laconic. 'It was pretty grim. Here goes, then. After the Germans ran off Henri attached a loop of rope around my parents' ankles, tied them together. He told Nicol and me to squeeze into the back seat of the kayak.'

I jumped up, sat down again. The wedding album must have been in the kayak with them. As well as the goblets.

'You all right?' I nodded. 'The tide was beginning to return. Henri slid the bodies into the water. Then he told us to hold the rope while he paddled to the cave.'

'You dragged the bodies there?'

'Pulled them behind us, yes.'

'And the infant?'

'He'd put it on the kayak floor, under his seat.' Matthew twisted the engagement ring around, shone the light through the diamonds. They dazzled. 'When he'd paddled us into the cave he tipped the baby into the small blowhole cave at the side. Then he dragged both bodies up to the metal bar there, made Nicol and me hang on, tied the bodies and the kayak to the side. Now comes the grisly bit. He stripped the bodies bare, waited for the tide to lift them as high as possible, then shoved them after the baby.'

'That was their grave?'

'Yes. The tide wouldn't be able to float them out. They'd decompose in time. Meanwhile, Nicol and I put everything Henri had given us and dropped it all into the kayak. He must have taken off the rings and put them on his fingers. Then he bundled everything up. When the tide went out again we made our way back through the caves.'

'And dragged the kayak up.' Some time soon I'd tell him about my first day on Bôtnoir Bay. How I'd met that fourth German on the beach of Bôtnoir, how that was my introduction to the island.

'No. Henri left it to drift, for the Germans to find.'

'Really? Why?'

'You may have been in Vienna when the Germans came, Ruth, but you don't know how ghastly being occupied was. If we'd allowed the Occupation Forces – apart from the four murderers, that is – to assume that my parents had fled successfully they'd have made life here on Guernsey even more miserable.'

'Stupid of me. What did Henri do?'

'He told us that he was going to destroy everything he'd taken off the bodies or from the boat so that the Germans couldn't find any traces of my parents.' I saw the resignation on his face.

'That was the last you saw of them?'

'Saw, yes. The Abbé went down there and said a Requiem Mass. Annie, Henri, Maria, Nicol and I were the congregation.'

So it was almost certainly the Abbé's idea to bury the rings, the wedding album and the goblets. It was probably Henri who carried it out. The cake could have been buried before. In the way people do.

Now there was a new threat to Matthew. That's why the Abbé had told Nicol where to find the tins. They would provide valuable clues to the past, to what had really happened. Why wasn't the marriage certificate with them?

Matthew was still fingering the engagement ring. 'I would have liked to see the wedding pictures.'

I hadn't even told him I'd copied the prints. And I hadn't thought it through. Presumably he'd have seen them as a child. It was interesting that he and his brothers weren't in any of them. 'You can,' I said triumphantly.

He put his arms on my shoulders, turned me to face him. 'Really? You hid some of those as well? Why didn't you say so?'

'Not exactly. They're what he came to steal, Matif. That's what he took, and why he didn't bother to look for more.' I hugged him. 'But you can still see them. He couldn't know how obsessive I am. I copied every single one of them. The coloured ones are on transparencies. I can project those for you in my dark-room. Right away!'

We rushed down and I set up my equipment. Matthew was thinking aloud while I worked. 'I suppose Henri couldn't bring himself to chuck the rings and the goblets out to sea.' He squinted at some of the black-and-white negatives. 'You think Todd actually saw Nicol giving you the tins?'

'I'm positive. I've had this feeling of being watched... and once he'd seen me driving off with them, he must have known he could get hold of them.'

'I did think of changing the lock. I dismissed it as an over-the-top reaction. After all, he's been in and out of Lascervelle for months.'

'Why would he want those photos? Hardly sentimental reasons.'

He shrugged. 'Perhaps he thought that the marriage certificate would be hidden inside the album somewhere. He'd want to destroy that. You're absolutely sure it wasn't?'

'Positive. I double checked each page, under each photograph.'

'What I can't understand is why he waited till now to act.'

'That's easy. Because your grandmother is dead.'

'That can't be it, Ruth. She'd have encouraged Todd. You know she hated me. She didn't have much time for the others, either.'

'Then I can only assume,' I said, thinking on my feet, 'that she didn't want the passing on of the fief to come up until she was dead.' Now I knew the reason why the man in black had come back after the funeral. To help Todd carry out an old sweetheart's last wish. It didn't explain why, but everything pointed to some connection with the marriage – with Raquel.

'That doesn't make any sense.'

"A fine Old Testament name," the Abbé had said when I told him who I was. An idea began to take shape. It was so obvious I couldn't believe I hadn't thought of it before. "Ruth among the alien corn," he'd said of me. And "another fine Old Testament name" he'd pronounced on Raquel.

The young couple had eloped because of religious differences, and Raquel's family had disowned her. How could I have been so slow? Surely I should have known right away what that implied?

'I'm sorry, Matif. My paranoia is taking over, but that doesn't mean it's mistaken. I think it all happened because of your mother.' Not all that paranoid a reaction, more a realistic one. Matthew had told me his grandmother had spent time in Germany, that she'd admired, and visited, Hitler. Like Diana Moseley, Franz had mentioned to me.

'Are you saying she hated my mother so much she couldn't stand the idea of a son of hers taking over the fief?'

'I don't think personal feelings were what it was about. I think she thought along Nazi lines.'

His jaw had dropped down as he stared at me. 'I realise she was in love with that fourth German. You're saying she knew he was a committed Nazi, not just an also-ran? And that she agreed with his views?'

'Exactly.' I remembered the way Otto had looked at my profile, his clear distaste when he took in the shape of it.

'But so what? My mother came from France, I know, but the Nazis weren't particularly anti-French, were they?'

Should I tell Matthew what I was now sure of, but for which I had no proof? Raquel wasn't a Protestant, as I'd assumed. What the grandmother had objected to was that Raquel's family were Jews, perhaps even Orthodox. That's what Michelle Frelé knew. She was determined that the fief should not go to one of Raquel's children – because, according to the Nuremberg Laws, they too, were Jews. That was, after all, Nazi doctrine.

'I do believe the answer might be in the cake,' I squeaked. Because at that moment I remembered the Abbé's last words to me, the ones I'd thought so odd: "I hope you will rejoice in the return of the prodigal son with a celebratory slice of cake."

I rushed upstairs, flung open my fridge door, hauled out the plastic-wrapped parcel. The buried cake wasn't the top tier of their original wedding cake – they probably hadn't bothered with a cake for their elopement. This cake must have been specially baked for the festivities which took place in October 1935. And for a very special reason.

'Now what are you up to, Ruth?' Matthew had followed me, stood staring at me.

'Your parents' wedding cake, Matif. I think we should sample it.'

CHAPTER FORTY-ONE

A slim package, carefully wrapped in wads of oilcloth, had been baked inside the cake. I handed it to Matthew. He unwrapped two sheets; two legal documents.

The creases in the first one were sepia sharp, the paper thick with spiky borders. A birth certificate. In French, dated March 13th, 1912. The recorded birth of Raquel Esther Fleurvallon, of the district of Faubourg Saint-Honoré. Father: Solomon David Fleurvallon, auctioneer. Mother: Sarah Hannah Fleurvallon, née Rosenbach.

Rosenbach. My guess had been right. The Abbé had chosen me – the alien – to put the jigsaw together because he knew I'd understand the shapes, and how they fitted. I looked to see whether the name Rosenbach signalled anything to Matthew.

'I know when she was born,' he said. 'And I know when she died. This isn't really what I care about. Let's see what else there is.' He put it aside.

I decided not to spell it out just then. Better to try and lead him to it slowly.

He unfolded the second piece of paper. It was the missing certificate, recording the marriage between Mathieu Maximilian Frelé, Seigneur of Bôtnoir, Guernsey, Roman Catholic, and Raquel Esther Fleurvallon, of Paris. The slot for religion had been left blank, as with their sons' birth certificates. Documents were not as detailed in those days as they are now, but it did give the date, and the place: Springfield, March 13th, 1930.

His whole face lit up, his mouth widened as he husked: 'Any idea where Springfield is?'

'Not a clue.'

'I suppose Debs's friend was right. It could be a place like Gretna Green. One of those Scottish border villages runaway couples used.'

The young couple had almost certainly canoed to the Scottish shores in their kayak, and gone inland from there. As I'd guessed, the wedding date was also Raquel's eighteenth birthday. To me it proved that Matthew and his brothers were legitimate. Charles Grichard could confirm it, but I reckoned that civil marriages solemnised between people of eighteen or over, anywhere in the British Isles, were considered legal marriages on Guernsey. 'So they were definitely married before you were born.'

'The relevant date is before we were conceived,' Matthew said softly. 'That seems to work out as well. February 20th is almost a year after March 13th.'

'Pregnancies are of variable length, but I think your cousin will have a problem disproving that you were conceived after the marriage.'

His eyes glowed warm. 'How d'you fancy being the wife of a seigneur?'

'I fancy being your wife.' I sighed. I was part of this man, no longer free. And it felt wonderful.

He led me to the living room sofa, the documents left unfolded on the kitchen table. We held each other close. The stubble on his cheek was beginning to grow – I could feel it with sensitised lips. My nipples were hardening, my breasts fighting to burst out of restraint.

'I do so love you.'

'And I love you.'

It was some time later that we returned to the papers. Matthew had picked up his mother's birth certificate again, was examining it. 'Faubourg Saint-Honoré. Quite classy, really.'

Solid relationships are based on truth. I had to tell him. 'Your grandfather's name was Fleurvallon. You may have heard that was one of the most prestigious auction houses in France.'

'Was it? You know because of Deborah, I take it.'

That wasn't the reason, but it could wait. 'It explains the French furnishings.'

'I suppose it does.' He frowned as he reread the document. 'It looks as though my maternal grandmother was originally German. Why didn't they use that fact, instead of...'

I couldn't keep it from him any longer. 'Not German, Matif. The name Rosenbach was one of the reasons why the papers had to be hidden.' I now understood only too well why the young couple had had to risk the kayak, to leave their sons behind. The Occupation Forces would not have deported Raquel to France, they would have sent her to the gas chambers. And they would have sent her four sons with her. Because Nazi laws classed Raquel's sons as Jews – because they had a Jewish mother.

Matthew's eyes were clouded. Had he guessed? Did he know of his heritage? Now I knew why I'd been so drawn to the Frelés in the first place. It was the attraction of like for like.

'Not German?' He frowned. 'What, then?'

I was afraid to tell him. Had I myself been so brainwashed by the Nazis that I found it shaming to admit to Jewish extraction? I took a deep breath, angry at the very thought. 'I think she was Jewish, Matif.'

'Jewish?' He stared at me, innocent, unaware. 'What on earth makes you think that?'

'Your paternal grandmother's maiden name was Rosenbach. Your grandfather was a world-renowned fine arts auctioneer who ran the firm of Fleurvallon – valley of the flowers. Originally that may have been the French for Blumenthal, but anyway it was a well-known Jewish name. I think your mother's family was Jewish, and the reason the Abbé wrote Fleur Vallon in the parish register was as a cover, so no one would connect her with that.'

'You think she was ashamed of being Jewish and he played along?' He was frowning, trying to follow what I was working out.

'He'd hardly write a lie in a church register for reasons of vanity. Just like your forged birth certificates, I think it was done to protect her – and you. Her family weren't victims of bombs on Paris.' His breathing began to labour. 'The tentacles of the Holocaust caught them, Matif. And spread wide to include every one of them. That's why not a single relative of your mother's survived the war.'

'You think they were practising Jews?'

'As a matter of fact I do. Orthodox Jews don't marry out. That's why she ran away from home.'

'So Gran'mère didn't want my father to marry her because she thought his children would be brought up as Jews?'

'We're talking about the Nazi time. The issue was race, not religion. It wasn't a question of which faith, as under the Spanish Inquisition. Giving up her religion wouldn't have helped your mother. She would have been categorised Jewish by the Nuremberg laws—'

'I've heard of them, of course. But I thought they only concerned Germans?'

'They were a set of laws the Nazis passed to define who was Jewish - and who was not. Nothing to do with their nationality. As early as September 1935. Catholic convert or not, French rather than German, your mother would have been classed as Jewish.'

He just sat there for several minutes. It takes time to absorb a shock like that. I'd have to give him a chance to assimilate these inferences.

'That's why they fled?' he asked. A sort of whisper. 'That's why they hid the documents?'

'And falsified her name. I guarantee it,' I said.

He looked completely drained, white, about to keel over.

'You'd better sit down.'

He sat, elbows on his knees, his face buried in his hands. 'She must have felt like a trapped animal, with those ghouls waiting to pounce.' He was the picture of dejection.

It was now obvious why Raquel's parents had objected to Mathieu Frelé. In their eyes Raquel would be marrying a gentile – a goy. She would have been thrown out, never allowed to return. And all her belongings sent with her. The haunting little face in the portrait came back to me. Those soft gentle eyes, the Mona Lisa smile. Her features were beautiful – a beautiful Semite.

It was very unlikely that anyone outside the family would

have given any thought to Raquel's background when the couple returned to Guernsey for their twins' birth. Even when the Germans came there was no overt persecution of Jews on the island, the way there'd been in the other occupied countries. What few Jews there were had been dispatched discreetly.

I breathed in hard. Had Raquel's mother-in-law told the Occupying Forces that Raquel was of Jewish descent? I saw the overshadowing hat dwarfing the petite figure of the bride in the photograph, the ramrod Aryan behind her. Had Michelle Frelé been so sympathetic to the Nazi cause she'd betrayed her own flesh and blood?

She couldn't have done. Because if she had, her grandsons would not have stayed unmolested. Michelle Frelé knew they had a Jewish mother, and the consequences of that. She had not told the authorities because, if she had, they would have reacted badly to her waiting so long. She would have been in danger herself.

I sat down next to Matthew and tried to comfort him. He drew away from me. Sharing problems is an acquired art. Both Matthew and I had become used to self-reliance. Even great love for another is unlikely to persuade one to give it up immediately.

'You'd better leave me to it, Ruth. One day I may tell you the whole story about my mother, the part only I know. But not now. I'll see you later.'

CHAPTER FORTY-TWO

He came back that evening. 'I still haven't understood how the Abbé was involved. Did my mother practise Judaism? Was that why my parents couldn't marry in the Church until she'd converted to Catholicism?' He frowned.

That was true, but I could tell he already knew that it wasn't the point.

The Abbé must have known the danger Raquel was in as soon as Mathieu brought her back as his bride. Michelle Frelé was a rabid Nazi, and she had connections with Hitler. The priest had been – he still was – a true man of God. It was almost certainly he who had led Raquel to the Roman Catholic faith, he who had made her wait until she was sure.

'Did he falsify her name so that, if the time came, the Germans couldn't trace her?' He frowned. 'Surely that's a bit far-fetched.'

'The time had already come, as far as your family was concerned. Your grandmother was a Nazi.' I thought back to what the old man had said. 'The Abbé told me there'd been a slip in the handwriting, and that's why your mother's name was incorrectly entered. I'm sure he deliberately falsified the Church records because Fleurvallon was a well-known Jewish name – a dead give-away. He did it to keep her safe.'

Was that a sacrilege, the unforgivable sin? If so, could it ever be justified? I was sure that the Christian reward for such a deed would be Heaven rather than Hell. Especially as the sinner chose to live his life in Purgatory. And it did suggest why the old man wouldn't tell Matthew himself. I imagined he couldn't face voicing such a sacrilegious act.

'Safe from what, Ruth? The Germans weren't here in 1935.'

'Not the Occupying Forces, no. But your parents didn't just hide the marriage certificate. They hid your original birth certificates and forged new ones. They must have had their reasons.'

'Gran'mère?'

'Among others, perhaps. I'm sure you know that anti-Semitism was rife long before 1935, even long before Hitler came to power in 1933. Many Jews changed their names and had themselves christened as early as the '20s.

'Your parents had a convinced Nazi right on their doorstep. Their Guernsey marriage was two years after Hitler came to power. They'd probably already heard of the sort of brutalities committed in Germany – well before the horrors of Kristallnacht. Well-known Jewish businesses were attacked quite early on. Membership of the SA was over two million – around ten per cent of German males. They hounded and brutalised thousands of Jews. I think your parents and the Abbé thought ahead – just in case.'

Matthew nodded. The full understanding of what the old priest had done, his courage and true Christianity, were getting through to him.

'You reckon Gran'mère decided to recruit Todd to make sure that Jewish blood wouldn't contaminate the fief?'

'Hard to believe, I know. But that's exactly what I think.'

He walked away from me. 'And that she betrayed her own son to the Germans?'

'I don't think we'll ever know. She kept your mother's secret to start with. Otherwise the whole family – you, your brothers, even your father for staying married to a Jew – would have been rounded up and deported. Those four German officers must have found out about the planned escape, somehow. Perhaps they set out to kill your mother behind your grandmother's back. I very much doubt that your father's death was planned.'

A terrible thought occurred to me. So terrible I didn't think I could even voice it. Was it because Raquel was pregnant – was carrying a child whose legitimacy no one could question – that she was killed? Was that why Michelle Frelé finally signed her daughter-in-law's death warrant?

And now I knew why the Abbé had not spoken to Matthew, had wanted me to see the contents of the tins. Not because he was afraid for Matthew's soul – I guessed he already knew that that was no longer in danger. It was because Michelle Frelé had sent for him, had confessed her terrible sin to the Abbé, had turned back to God before she died. And he was bound by the seal of the confessional even after she was dead.

Perhaps she tried to ensure her son's life, and failed. Perhaps she felt she had to sacrifice him to the cause. But she had saved her grandsons' lives.

Suddenly I knew why the boys had been spared. Neither the German authorities, nor the islanders, would have swallowed wholesale murder. Michelle and her Nazi lover worked out a less murderous final solution for the boys, while being lost at sea was the perfect cover for the parents' murder.

'That doesn't account for Todd waiting until Gran'mère was dead before he showed his hand.'

Matthew still wasn't convinced about what had really happened, but to me it was the final proof. 'I take it she waited for Todd to visit her after the war, then told him she'd written a letter to be opened after her death, a letter which would prove that he had the legal claim to the fief.'

'But...'

'She couldn't take his part against you publicly.'

'Why not?'

'I gather that suspicions about her collaboration were already high. Abetting Todd in trying to disinherit you would have proved her guilt. That wouldn't have helped his cause, either.'

'And the Abbé? Why didn't he just tell me where the certificate was instead of all this cloak and dagger stuff?'

It came to me that the Abbé's main reason might have been because I would filter the past, would divert Matthew's rage against his grandmother, and against his cousin Todd, into more productive feelings. 'He's an old man, Matif. I'd guess he wanted you to know about your Jewish background, not just to find the marriage certificate. Perhaps he also thought I'd be the right person to help you understand the implications.'

He didn't respond. No doubt he'd weigh it all up for himself, perhaps even reach my conclusions. Silence was the most likely path to charity for the dead.

'I suppose I always knew she entertained the Germans because she was in love with Nazism.'

'That may well have been part of it. But she was also in love with a man who was a Nazi. Let's go and look at those trannies now.'

CHAPTER FORTY-THREE

I'd cut the transparencies into sections and was putting the first one into a mount.

Matthew was squinting at the negatives. 'What an unsavoury past. I'd think you and your daughter would want no part of it.'

'Oh, I don't know,' I said. I could feel the grin of satisfaction spreading all over my face. 'It might occur to us that Nazism has been defeated by poetic justice here. In spite of all the pogroms, all the extermination camps, all the might the Third Reich had at its disposal, the fief of Bôtnoir passes on to someone whose mother was a Jewess. And then the Seigneur marries another Jewess, and so does his brother. And if there's an heir from either of these brothers, he or she would be three quarters Jewish.'

'Does that mean you're saying you'll marry me?'

I took a deep breath. 'You chose not to kill that fourth German, didn't you?'

'How can you be completely sure?' His eyes glowed in the dark. 'You only have the word of a murderer.'

'I've come across a white Maserati in the car park.'

He dropped the magnifying glass he'd brought down in surprise. 'You mean he's here?'

'I'm pretty sure he was. Unless there are two German veterans, both touring Europe in a white Maserati cabriolet.'

'Why would he have come back to Guernsey?'

It was then that I told Matthew about my encounter with the man in black on Bôtnoir Bay. Told him that a native German speaker was visiting an old friend – a female one. And that I'd seen the same man with Todd. 'He'd have come back after your grandmother's death because of Todd, presumably. To carry out her last wishes.'

'Why would he care that much?'

'Because he's still a Nazi. But I think there's a more personal reason as well. I spotted a mystery wedding guest on one of the colour prints. A tall Nordic type behind the family group. I'm almost certain that was the same man, and that your grandmother knew him before the war.'

'He's in the photographs?' I could hear the drawn-in hiss.

'I rather think so. I'll show you. See if you recognise him.' I switched on the projector to show the first slide.

'Is that what made you copy the photographs?'

'Not really. It's habit because of my work. I view details by cropping to the right area of the slide, then magnifying them. That's as important as taking the picture in the first place. Take a seat.'

He watched as I focused the lens. It reminded me of the time Matthew had first shown me his paintings. 'This is your mother on her own. A beautiful veil.' The exquisite lace hung down her back and, in this picture, over her face. The Old Testament story of Jacob trying to win Rachel came back to me. I stared at the photograph, fascinated.

'Very romantic, but we can't see her face.'

I moved on to the next photograph, the blusher thrown back. The happy couple, radiant in their love. Her hair, long, curly, auburn, hung round her like a living veil. The delicate features, huge eyes, stared at us in sweet intensity. The essence of her looks had been precisely captured in Matthew's portrait of her.

'Her name was Raquel – Rachel. That's symbolic of the sorrow and tragedy suffered by the Israelites.' I glanced at him, at the intent face. 'Do you remember her, Matif?'

'I shall never forget her.' He blinked tears away.

'I don't actually look like her. It seems odd that people say I do.' But as I said it I could see the similarity. The shape of the skull, the eye sockets, the nose. And then I realised how I'd originally guessed that the girl in the portrait was Matthew's mother. She'd fleetingly reminded me of Matthew's Semitic features. And I'd only recognised them much later on.

'The likeness is more in the spirit than in the flesh.' That's what he was good at. That's why his portrait worked better than any of the photographs.

The next picture was the one where Michelle Frelé's hat overshadowed the bride. And, standing behind her, the man I thought I'd identified as Otto. Would Matthew confirm he was the fourth man?

'Zoom in on him.' He walked right up to the screen and stared at the blurred face of the young man. 'He's certainly Nordic.' His painter's eyes would be able to cut through the years. 'That's him,' he said at last. 'No mistaking it. And damned good-looking at the time.'

'In an Aryan sort of way,' I said. 'If you like the type. All that pale steeliness.' He was definitely the man on the beach at Bôtnoir. 'You didn't recognise him when he was here, in 1940?'

'Don't think we came across him in 1935. Gran'mère lived at Lascervelle, you know. And we were kept away from the wedding party.'

'Really? Why?'

'Well, we were very young – Mark and I were only four. And things were quite different in those days. It wouldn't have been considered suitable.'

I took it that was because the parents had, more or less, admitted to living in sin for years. From an ultra-conservative Catholic point of view.

Matthew stared at the photographs again. 'So that's why Todd stole the prints. To protect him.'

He was quite right. I hadn't even thought that they would incriminate the German. 'So she knew him well before the war. Why d'you think she didn't marry him?'

'He could have been married already. Eldest son of a good family, perhaps. Divorce wasn't the done thing then.' He stared at the picture as though it could speak to him. 'You know, I think the real reason was that he was far too young. He's only in his seventies now. The man I've been checking on is seventy-six. That would make him twenty in 1935.'

'And she was already a grandmother. That's brilliant. They'd both have had to give up everything to be together. And she couldn't have trusted it to last on his part.' I saw Matthew look sidelong at me. 'He probably went home and married, then wangled a transfer to Guernsey during the war. You wrecked their little love nest for them. No wonder she had it in for you.'

'That really does explain why she constantly entertained the Germans. And why we had so much more food than anybody else.'

'You're right about the real motive for the theft, Matif. This print proves the connection between your grandmother and this German.'

'The investigators in Lüneburg think he's a war criminal, but they can't prove it.'

'I think that sprightly Prussian must have built up an elaborate false past. If it came out that he'd known your grandmother, and suspicions were roused that he and his cronies murdered your parents, his cover would be blown. Now we have proof.' I took one set of slides to put into my safe, and gave another to Matthew.

He fingered the slides.

I put my arm through his. 'You aren't even tempted to kill him now, are you?'

'I think not.' He took a deep breath in. 'And it looks as though there's a much better way to win.' He put the slides away, then placed Raquel's engagement ring on my finger. 'Amethyst is your birthstone, too.'

The ring was a perfect fit.

The double engagement party was set for Christmas Eve. Matif had moved out to Bôtnoir. He'd suggested to Mark and Debs that we should celebrate this new milestone in Frelé history there, all four of us together.

He'd grown to value the virtues of his sister-in-law to be. 'I know you want a garden, Debs,' he'd smiled at my daughter. 'But perhaps you'd like to ease yourself into that. How about you and Mark taking over Lascervelle?'

She'd looked round the fine rooms, the moulded ceilings, the original fireplaces, the woodwork still intact. A Regency house, and her favourite period.

'May I restore it?'

'Carte blanche. I know you'll do a marvellous job. It'll give you the leisure to look for that country house you're after.'

There wouldn't really be any need. Debs would be the one to take over Bôtnoir, and the garden would have excelled its original glory by then. She'd still be there when Mark, and Matif, and I, a generation older than she, had gone.

Perhaps, before that time, we'd exchange houses, Matif and I spending our old age in Lascervelle, Debs, Mark and their children taking over the country place. And, if Matthew and I couldn't manage a child, there would be an heir to the fief of Bôtnoir among Mark and Debs's children, as long as they had a son. Mark's genes – identical to Matthew's – mingled with some of mine.

For me there was a yearning intertwined with sadness. Jonathan, too, would be part of Bôtnoir. I'd always known he was rooting for me, for all of us. Was this what he'd planned?

The whole of Matthew and Mark's family was coming to spend Christmas at Bôtnoir. It was high time that my sons met the two men who would marry their mother and sister. And it would be the first Christmas I'd spend with my Bostonian grandsons. I couldn't remember when I'd been so thrilled about planning the Yuletide festivities.

Sylvia and Debs had found each other like sisters. They'd got along from the day they'd met, that time we'd all had dinner at the Connaught, after Matif's first exhibition.

'Can't exactly think of you as a step-mother,' Sylvia had said to Debs. 'I'll think of you as the sister my father never bothered to provide me with.'

And the earliest of Matthew's paintings, the ones his brother Luke was giving him as a wedding present, were no longer hidden in an attic. They were hung in the master bedroom at Bôtnoir. Where they belonged.

CHAPTER FORTY-FOUR

Bôtnoir had come alive again. No need to imagine ghostly forms flitting around ghostly lawns, with ghostly music playing in the background. It was all real.

Tief – that became my own special name for Matthew, perhaps because it is the German word for deep. He and I had worked hard to have a deep relationship. And we'd achieved it.

We'd changed Bôtnoir to suit us. Tief turned the Captain's Cabin into his studio. We arranged Raquel's pieces in the master-bedroom, the refuge she'd spent her married life in, the place where she had borne her sons, where she had mothered them.

The study next to it became my writing-room, the night nursery beyond it turned into a dark-room en suite. It was unlikely to be used for its original purpose by the present seigneur and his bride – though we did not exclude the possibility.

The double wedding was set for March 13th, 1992, just over a year after I'd first met Matthew. It was also the day of his mother's birthday, and the day of the Anschluss. A private victory.

Debs glowed in her new-found role. She and Mark had already taken over Lascervelle, turned it into a treasure trove of antiques. My daughter was marrying the man she loved, and she was likely to produce the next heir to Bôtnoir. To live happily ever after.

And yet there was still one obstacle for Tief and me. However much we tried to forget about it, we were upset that we were not able to achieve full love-making. The process proved frustrating to us both. Signs of irritability were creeping in. I knew there was one last piece of the jigsaw Matthew had held back, one last obsession he had to let go. Only then would we be free of the tentacles of the past, the shadows of evil which were still pursuing us.

'There's one thing you haven't told me,' I said. 'Though you promised you would.' A bleak January wind howled at fierce waves. It was ebb tide, safe to go to the bay. 'Let's walk on the beach.'

'All right.'

I had begun to love the cliff walks, the wild lashing of the waves around Bôtnoir Bay. The path had become wider, easier with use.

We walked out to the edge of the water, wind blowing in our hair, our voices hardly audible. We found our favourite rock, sat in its shelter. The waves stopped pounding, calmed.

I saw her again. Fragile dainty Raquel, bleeding on the beach. Matthew had been right – he hadn't told me everything. One last small detail was missing. And it was vital.

'When the Germans fled because of Henri, and the tide was coming in...' I began.

'It's not what I want to talk about,' he shouted at me. 'Can't you just let her rest in peace?'

'It isn't me, Tief. Or your mother. It's you.'

He picked a pebble up and threw it at the sea. It skimmed the water like the bouncing bomb. Four times. I tried – the pebble sank.

I tried again. 'The few moments before Henri and Nicol arrived...'

A bigger pebble, five skips this time.

'...was your mother still alive?'

Alive – alive – alive the wind sang back at me.

The next pebble sank. Matthew turned to me, put his hands on my shoulders. 'Why do you ask? What's what happened then to you now?'

'Whatever it was, Tief, you couldn't have saved her. Your father couldn't! You were only a boy.'

The pebble whistled as it rocketed, straight, out to sea. It skimmed the surface and disappeared.

I imagined I saw her raise a hand. They'd trampled her baby to death, shot her husband. They'd slit her belly, her face was a mass of blood criss-crossed by slashes.

'What happened when you got to her?'

He stared at the sand the sea had shed so many tears over. 'She was still alive.'

My stomach churned. 'What did she say?'

'D'you really want to know this, Ruth?'

'No, not want. I need to know it, and you need to tell me.'

'She asked me to kill her.'

He was quite right. I didn't want to hear that he'd killed her. Had he? Would he tell me, or would I have to ask? I had to know.

He looked into my eyes, and I looked back. They were not the eyes of a boy who had committed matricide. 'I couldn't do it.'

'She died anyway?'

'I didn't stop him, Ruth. I *let* her die.'

'Him?'

'Henri. He took a pruning knife and cut her carotid artery. I didn't stop him!'

So that was it. He felt responsible for her death. No words of mine would be able to take that terrible conviction away from him.

He began to sob, gently at first, then uncontrollably. I tried to comfort him. He broke away, began to walk towards the sea, to wade into it.

I ran after him. 'She was almost dead, Tief. It was a blessed relief.'

'You don't understand, Ruth. I did nothing to save her. I let him kill her. I worshipped her, thought her the most wonderful thing in all the world. But I let him kill her.'

'You couldn't have stopped him...'

'I didn't try. There was a sense in which I allowed him to kill her – because she'd asked to die. I should have stopped him. It was as though I did it myself.'

'No, Tief. You couldn't save her. And she didn't want you to.'

'That's completely beside the point. You know that as well as I do. I should have tried...'

'If she had survived she would have been transported to a concentration camp...'

'That wasn't something I could do anything about!'

Tell him, the wind whistled at me. Tell him why. 'The reason, Tief. The real reason she asked you to hasten her death. Do you know what it was?'

'Her husband was dead, her baby gone, she was in pain...'

Rachel, weeping for her children. 'She had to die, Tief. Don't you understand? Don't you know what she was trying to do? She had to die to save her children – your brothers and you. You had a Jewish mother. That destined you for the death camps!'

'I wouldn't have wanted to be saved at such a price.'

'There were even more powerful motives involved. I think she wanted to save her sons – and, through them, her people. She wanted to save them for the future. *That's* what she asked you to do.'

He stopped, the waves ebbing away. 'I had no idea.' He stared out to sea. 'I always wondered.'

'It wasn't you, or Henri, who wanted to exterminate her and hers. That was the Nazis. You couldn't have stopped them. She found the only way.'

'We could have hidden her...'

'The Abbé had trouble hiding the tins.'

'...she could have lived for a short time, at least.'

'Without her beloved husband? When she'd just lost the baby she was carrying? Knowing what was in store for you, your brothers, the rest of her family, her people? There are worse things than death, Tief. I think your mother is at peace because you did as she asked. I think she wishes you to be at peace as well.'

'The Abbé said he could not absolve me because I planned to kill the fourth man.'

'You're talking about years ago. The Abbé was the one who made it possible to piece together what really happened. He'll be the one to give you absolution. In Christ's name, and as a friend.'

'You think so? I wanted to ask him to marry us, to celebrate a Nuptial Mass.'

'He will, I know he will. You didn't kill that German, Tief. You told me how easily you could have set about it. You allowed him to stay alive, you won't think of killing him again. That's a firm purpose of amendment. Now forgive yourself for those earlier deaths, give yourself a chance to be happy. That's what your life is for. And, if you feel you need penance, no one can doubt you've had your share of it.'

We clung to each other until the waves began to start their return, and it was time to climb up the steep stone path, and go into our house.

And then peace came to Tief, and to me. And, with the dawning of the new day, love came as well.

And it was good.

THE THORN PRESS

BOOKS IN PRINT

The Dohlen Inheritance Trilogy: Tessa Lorant Warburg
http://www.tessalorantwarburg.com/

The Dohlen Inheritance
Paperback: ISBN 978-0-906374-06-1
Hardback: ISBN 978-0-906374-03-0
Hobgoblin Gold
Paperback: ISBN978-0-906374-08-4
Ladybird Fly
Paperback: ISBN 978-0-906374-09-2

A Woman's World, 138-9 Chri Plus, Hilary Jerome
Paperback: ISBN 978-0-906374-00-9
e-book

Snack Yourself Slim, Richard Warburg & Tessa Lorant
http://buypatential.com
Paperback: ISBN 978-0-906374-05-4
e-book

The Girl from the Land of Smiles, Tessa Lorant Warburg
Paperback: ISBN 978-0-906374-30-6
e-book

The Master's Tale, A Titanic Ghost Story, Ann Victoria Roberts
http://www.annvictoriaroberts.co.uk
Paperback: ISBN 978-0-906374-21-4
e-book

Inktastic, Andrew P Jones
Paperback: ISBN 978-0-906374-04-7

Wordfall, The 2010 Anthology from Southampton Writing Buddies, Editor Penny Legg
http://pennylegg.com
Paperback: ISBN 978-0-906374-26-9

Knitted Quilts & Flounces, Tessa Lorant
Paperback: ISBN 978-0-906374-29-0

Spellbinder, Tessa Lorant Warburg
Paperback: ISBN 798-0=906374-35-1 due March 2013
e-book

The Girl from the Land of Smiles, Tessa Lorant Warburg
Paperback: ISBN 978-0-906374-30-6
e-book

Thou Shalt Not Kill, Tessa Lorant Warburg
e-book

All books are available from Amazon worldwide, and from good book shops
http://www.thethornpress.com

www.ingramcontent.com/pod-product-compliance
Lightning Source LLC
Chambersburg PA
CBHW030932260626
47169CB00002B/453